Praise for *Zion's Fiction: A Treasury of Israeli Speculative Fiction*

"The Israeli *Dangerous Visions*."
— Harlan Ellison biographer, Nat Segaloff

"Remarkably vigorous, inventive and lucid."
— Barry N. Malzberg

"This notable anthology is appropriate for all sf fans and a valuable resource for any library."
— Michael A. Burstein

"What we come away with, finally, is a sense that Israeli fantasy and SF is as lively and rewarding as any body of SF, and just as diverse – both in terms of the topics and themes and in terms of modes of writing, which range from the seriously literary and almost post-modern to playful celebrations of older SF traditions."
— Gary K. Wolfe, *Locus Magazine*

"*Zion's Fiction* is not only an excellent collection of speculative fiction from Israel but also a book that makes us think anew about the real challenges the world must face in the future… *Zion's Fiction* opens our eyes to the creativity and literary invention happening beyond our borders and makes us long for more."
— Rachel S. Cordasco, *World Literature Today*

"From beginning to end, the collection delights, informs and educates – for readers seeking something different, this one's a real gem."
— *Foundation: The International Review of Science Fiction*

"A coming of age of Israeli speculative fiction, and yes it is throughly mimetic science fiction, and more than that, on the cutting edge of speculative fiction period."
— Norman Spinrad, *Asimov's Science Fiction*

"The high quality of work makes this anthology enjoyable and accessible for any fan of speculative fiction."
— *Publishers Weekly*

"The stories, of course, are the real attraction, and 'treasury' is exactly the right word to describe what we find in the collection. Buried in these fascinating exercises in imaginative fiction are glimpses of the anxieties and aspirations of the real Israel."
— *The Jewish Journal*

The complex and challenging stories collected in *Zion's Fiction* are a welcome addition to the world of speculative literature.
— *Jewish Book Council*

"This is a compilation of good writing, pure and simple."
— *Amazing Stories*

"Beyond being good reading, perhaps the greatest appeal of this collection is the insight its stories give into the mind and attitudes of a place that is, in many ways, similar to the USA (a democracy, modern, and industrial) and yet very different, as a nation under virtual siege for two generations."
— *Galaxy's Edge*

MORE ZION'S FICTION

Wondrous Tales from the Israeli ImagiNation

Edited by
**Emanuel Lottem &
Sheldon Teitelbaum**

Illustrated by
Avi Katz

Foreword by
David Brin

Afterword by
Marleen S. Barr

Cover illustration by Avi Katz.
Book formatting by Creative Publishing Book Design

Printed in the United States of America

ISBN Paperback: 9780578969442
ISBN eBook: 9780578969459

Dedicated to my late parents, Zippora and Binyamin
Lubetkin ז"ל.

EL

Dedicated to Ephraim and Yocheved Howard ז"ל
and to Zvi Elpeleg ז"ל.

ST

Contents

Foreword
By David Brin

THE SON OF HERB BRIN (1915-2003), a Los Angeles-based journalist, editor, poet and campaigner for liberal and Jewish causes, David Brin is an American engineer and physicist. As a science fiction writer, he is best known for his "Uplift" series of novels, beginning with *Sundiver* (1980), the Hugo and Nebula Award-winning *Startide Rising* (1983), *The Uplift War* (1987), also a Hugo Award winner, *Brightness Reef* (1995), *Infinity's Shore* (1996) and *Heaven's Reach* (1998).

According to the online edition of the *Science Fiction Encyclopedia*, these novels put him second only to Greg Bear as the most acclaimed purveyor of hard science fiction during the 1980s and '90s. "Despite his professional competence as a physicist – a level of qualification not shared by Bear" – denotes Brin's entry, "he writes tales in which the physical constraints governing the knowable Universe are flouted with high-handed panache, with the effect that – for instance – the Uplift books are as compulsive reading as anything ever published in the genre."

Brin is also the recipient of a stand-alone Hugo for "The Chrystal Spheres" (January 1984, *Analog*). His novel *The Postman*, parts of which ran in *Asimov's* from 1982 to 1984, and which featured a Jewish protagonist in a ruined Earth setting, was adapted for film in a vehicle starring Kevin Costner, in 1997. His 1990 novel *Earth* postulated a global information system much akin to the World Wide Web.

In these stories we see a maturation of storytelling and fresh voices from a realm where humanity's most vivid legends first took root and flourished, in works that that would last millennia.

Oh, there have been anthology collections of science fiction by or about Jews or Jewish themes, including Jack Dann's *Wandering Stars I & II*, followed by Rachel Swirsky and Sean Wallace's *People of the Book: A Decade of Jewish Fantasy and Science Fiction,* through Sheldon Teitelbaum and Emanuel Lottem's first volume of *Zion's Fiction: A Treasury of Israeli Speculative Literature.* Such tales ranged from Avram Davidson's great classics (Davidson fought as a medic in Israel's War of Independence and remained in Beersheva for a few years afterward, earning him honorary, if not official Israeli status) to *Heart of the Comet,* wherein I sent the central character Saul Lintz – possibly the last Sabra – off to Halley's Comet.

But Israelis themselves always seemed too busy forging a boldly improbable near future with their own hands. Earlier collections of fantastic writings seemed tentative, uncertain how to take on the fundamental premise of science fiction – the trait that makes it distinct from the mother-genre, fantasy.

What premise? That things might – through a passage of time or space, or disruption, or perception – turn out to be very different than they are now. In *fantasy* tales going back to Gilgamesh, a king may fall, but there is no end to kings. In *sci-fi,* on the other hand, any and all assumptions may be fair game for what Einstein called a *gedankenexperiment,* or thought-experiment, including the very social order that the author and reader grew up taking for granted.

Even if – across the chapters and pages – a status quo is re-established, at least we've seen that it *might* change. Science fiction is the literature *of* change.

And so, we see socio-political assumptions rocked in Guy Hasson's skillful "The Assassination," using and refreshing a recording-from-the-past motif similar to Bob Shaw's legendary "Slow Glass," in which a hero of Israel's founding generation must question the assumptions that he lived by. "The Word Farmers" by Lili Daie suggests that humanity and our civilization may be among the *less* important traits making Earth valuable and unique.

Oh, purely fantastic and fantasy tales are welcome, so long as they sing! As do "The Thirteenth Fairy," by Nadav Almog, Rotem Baruchin's novella "Latte, To Go."

Reality-bending is a common theme, as in "Life in a Movie" by Yivsam Azgad and Rami Shalheveth's "Dragon Control." Then there is the nervous fatalism of "Dress."

Post-apocalypse shows up in "Grandma and I Go Shopping," by Hamutal Levin.

Where would such a collection be without at least one tale of comeuppance/justice/revenge for the Holocaust, as in the unsettling "Sea of Salt," by Elana Gomel? And the just beautifully empathic and moving "Askuni-Askuni" by Dafna Feldman?

All told, this volume is a kind of coming-of-age story in its own right, joining what has become a worldwide renaissance of internationally mature science fiction. May it bode well for a people – and world – who seem increasingly ready to forge forth across space and time.

Introduction

By Emanuel Lottem
and Sheldon Teitelbaum

*Of course everything one writes about comes from experience.
Where else could it come from? But the imagination recombines,
remakes… makes a new world, makes the world new.*
— Ursula K. Le Guin[1]

WHAT IS ISRAELI ABOUT Israeli speculative fiction? Do Israeli writers of science fiction, fantasy, and related genres have anything in common other than the trivial fact of residing in the same country? In other words, are there any common characteristics to Israeli science fiction and fantasy (SF/F) storytellers that seem to unite them in some way, while at the same time appear to set them apart from their counterparts elsewhere?

Needless to say, there is the common denominator of writing speculative rather than "realistic" fiction, difficult as it may sometimes be to tell the difference between them. There may also be the background – Israeli placenames, Hebrew personal names, etc. But these, too, are almost

---

[1] Ursula K. Le Guin, "Answers to a Questionnaire," appended to *The Birthday of the World*, HarperCollins e-books 2002, loc. 5144.

always trivial. In many cases, they can be substituted by, say, American names – without making any significant difference to whatever the story is about. And indeed, in Israel as elsewhere, SF/F stories are being written that could have been written anywhere. There are even Israeli stories whose authors make them look as if they were written in the USA, intended to be read by an American audience.

Before attempting to give any broad answer to the question of whether or not Israeli SF/F can be readily recognized as having been written in this country and nowhere else, we must hasten to insert the usual qualification that applies to any and all generalization – the rule that says that every rule has exceptions to the rule, except for rules that have no exception to the rule, which makes them exceptional rules. Henceforth, what we are going to say about Israeli SF/F applies to most, but definitely not all, writers and their stories.

Authors in general, including those who write SF/F, are individualistic, not to say idiosyncratic people. They write whatever they feel they should or would care to write. They do not march to any one drummer, and they do not take orders or work to dictates from above. With respect to Israeli literature, this has not always been the case, as we noted in our introduction to the previous *Zion's Fiction* volume[2]; but it is now.

Our position on the question posed above is that the majority of Israeli SF/F stories – and we are speaking of short stories and novellas, because genre novels are still few and far between in this country – are indeed localized in several significant ways. The first, and by far the most important among them, is that they reflect the contemporary mood of the nation, the *zeitgeist*.

As we explained in our introduction to the previous volume of *Zion's Fiction*, during the 1980s – at about the same time, coincidentally or

---

[2] Sheldon Teitelbaum and Emanuel Lottem, *Zion's Fiction: A Treasury of Israeli Speculative Fiction*. Simsbury, Ct: Mandel-Vilar, 2018.

not, that original SF/F began to be written in Hebrew – a sea-change took place in Israeli society. Once an exceptionally equitable one (at least among the Western nations), with strong socialist tendencies, it turned almost overnight into a fiercely individualistic one, with a capitalistic, consumer-oriented economy and ever-widening socioeconomic disparities. Politics became highly divisive, as the right-wing pitted itself against the left, with nationalistic messianism making fast inroads into the body politic, and ultra-Orthodox political parties gaining intoxicating levels of power and influence they had never attained before. These trends are still ongoing, splitting Israeli society right through the middle. At the time of writing, Israel has gone through its fourth general elections in two years that ended in a parliamentary near-deadlock, and many – not only dyed-in-the-wool cynics – regard this as a mere prelude to a fifth round, with a new coalition government that has the narrowest of margins.

The one thing that has remained constant is Israel's geopolitical situation, referred to locally as The Situation, or more specifically, The Conflict. True, the danger of war with neighboring countries has diminished due to peace agreements with Egypt and then Jordan, and more recently, thanks to normalization agreements with the United Arab Emirates, Sudan, Morocco, and Bahrain. But Iran has emerged meanwhile as a new existential threat, what with its nuclear weapons and long-range missile development programs, and its support for international terrorism.

Palestinian territories, moreover, remain under occupation or siege. There is constant friction between their Arab inhabitants and Jewish settlers. Missiles periodically fly from the Gaza Strip into Israeli towns and villages. Suicide bombers and other terrorists are an ever-present danger. Worst of all, The Conflict between Israel and the Palestinians seems irresoluble. And even inside Israel, Muslim and Arab-Christian citizens remain marginalized, and occasionally resort to riots. To mention only some of the more salient aspects of The Situation.

ALL THESE NECESSARILY IMPACT what Israeli authors write about, and more importantly, how they go about it. This is true not only of those with speculative proclivities. Noa Menhaim, the original fiction editor at a major publishing house and one of the SF/F-savvy literati with whom we consulted during the preparation of this introduction, emailed us that

> [B]roadly speaking, there is a sense of listlessness that arises from the hyperactivity of news cycles in Israeli reality. The invasive presence of the political Situation in individuals' lives and personal experiences in this land deters Israeli writers from dealing with it. … It may be an oversimplification, but if we want horror, we watch the evening news.

And this, she explains, applies to mainstream literature as it does to speculative fiction.

There seems to be a general reluctance among Israeli SF/F writers, unlike their mainstream counterparts, to deal with any of The Situation's multiple facets. They tend to fixate on other issues, that is to say, on their personal concerns. As put to us by Rami Shalheveth, who has been running the *Bli Panika* (*Don't Panic!*) online SF/F magazine for more than two decades now and is one of the authors included in this volume:

> Genre writing in this country… [is] highly non-political, which is true not only with regard to The Conflict and the settlements but also for social critique, the Rabin assassination, poverty, violence, parliamentary politics, corruption… even ordinary crime is beyond the pale. There is much engagement with local culture, LGTB rights (the nearest to politics original genre literature ever gets), and day-to-day experiences like school, childbirth, etc. It seems that our [i.e., the Israeli SF/F community's] writers shy away, generally speaking, from controversial issues.

There is a sense of over-saturation, Shalheveth wrote elsewhere:[3]

In face-to-face conversations, writers told me that they felt besieged by politics – The Conflict is ever-present in our lives through news broadcasts, social media discussions, memes, and so on. We live in an unceasing buzz of current affairs. "How can I have anything new to say on this subject?" a well-known writer complained to me. "Everything has already been said, again and again and again."

Instead, they are accused by some – unfairly, we believe – of contemplating their respective navels. It is no coincidence that quite a few stories in this volume, as in its predecessor, are told in the first person. Of course, first-person narrators are not at all rare in literature at large, far from it. As David Brin, who so graciously wrote the foreword for this book, pointed out (in an email to the editors), the first person-singular offers prospective writers the greatest degree of control over their characters. But subjectively, this preference seems to us more prevalent in Israel's SF/F than in the wider world's.

And even third-person stories written here tend to deal with private lives. There are hardly any Israeli space operas. You will be hard put to find Israeli science-fictional spies (in marked contrast with the worldwide reputation of real-life ones) who resourcefully infiltrate the headquarters of imagined evil-mongers. Nor are there ordinary individuals who accidentally find themselves in circumstances that require them to save

---

[3] Rami Shalheveth, "Why Do We Need Politics Now?" [Hebrew], *Bli Panika*, September 1st, 2020. The author told the editors of this volume that he was moved to write this essay by our solicitation of his views on this subject.

the Galaxy, or at least a princess charming, which they providentially manage to do against all odds.[4]

No. The protagonists of Israeli SF/F, by and large, are ordinary people who lead ordinary lives, albeit twisted by the props and memes of science fiction or fantasy. And even in the few stories that provide the inevitable exception to this rule, the protagonists' most outstanding quality is their run-of-the-mill ordinariness.

Israeli SF writers, as a rule, do not sustain themselves by their literary output. Still, some pine for commercial breakout (consider Yoav Blum, whose best-selling *The Coincidence Makers* has been optioned for film adaptation abroad, or Sayed Kashua's 'Let There Be Morning,' which was adapted for film in 2021 and caused some controversy at its Cannes Film Festival debut when its Arab cast refused to appear on stage with the Israeli director because the movie, directed by an Israeli, was presented as such. It is true that the current crop of print and online newspaper and magazine critics of SF/F works grew up within this milieu, if only in terms of popular culture. But there is still a reluctance, even among writers, to engage unabashedly in what back in the (American) day used to be dismissed as "that Buck Rogers stuff."

This arguably adds another layer to the general absence of hard science fiction motifs in the writings Israeli SF/F authors tend to produce. When it comes to the home-grown stuff, the Hebrew book-buying public has expressed a lingering distaste for material reminiscent of what Lavie Tidhar, in his *Central Station* stories, calls the great interplanetary "Up and Out," that is to say, ultra-hard science fiction. After all, what good is the Up-and-Out when you can't get a handle on the ever-stifling here-and-now?

This aversion was made abundantly clear not only by the limited imaginary horizons imposed on so much storytelling but also by

---

[4] À la the *nebbish* Jewish tailor Joseph Schwartz in Isaac Asimov's first novel, *Pebble in the Sky* (1950).

marketing via book covers. Next time you visit Israel, stop by your nearest book emporium and check out their SF/F inventories. Half of it you'll find on shelves labeled as SF/F (a cause of so much anti-ghettoization consternation abroad[5]). But the other half will bear no genre markings at all and will be interspersed among the mainstream titles. And for a good reason. When not told they are reading SF/F, Israeli readers may proceed without protest, rarely grokking that they have, like Wile E. Coyote, stepped off the proverbial cliff into fabulist realms. But if the publishers saw fit to mention science fiction on the cover, the book gets ghettoized not only on the shelves but also in the eyes of potential buyers. As a case in point, Gail Hareven's first SF/F collection, *The Road to Eden*, bore a nondescript and unlabeled cover, which suited her purpose – she is a widely celebrated Israeli author with a vast mainstream fan base, and her book received stellar reviews. One is left wondering whether, had this book been labeled as the authentic science fiction it is, the reviews would have been equally complimentary.

What we have, then, is a body of work that is by and large contemplative, brooding, and self-centered. Furthermore, it is all too often obsessed with death. It may be uniquely Israeli in the limited sense of the names given to places and persons, or it may be more firmly rooted in this soil. But that, as we said, is trivial. The common denominator seems to be the darkness and alienation that creep into an individual's life. Noa Menhaim explains:

> Israeli creators who've grown up within the genre, and more than that, within fandom… already feel – as a broad generalization – as aliens, not part of the Israeli experience, and therefore are not interested in trying to understand it, interpret it, or respond to it with genre tools.

---

[5] See Ursula Le Guin, "On Despising Genres," *ibid.*, loc. 5073.

What they are interested in, we feel, is how they feel. They deal, using SF/F tools, with personalities and interactions between individuals, with emotional conflicts that are often irresolvable. Ehud Maimon, the editor of the annual Hebrew-language series of Israeli SF/F anthologies, *Once Upon a Future*, wrote to us:

> The younger [generation's] writing has become more personal and less national. It deals with the individual as an individual, not as a representative of a generation or society at large. The focus is on quotidian rather than national issues.

This may be true of much new SF/F writing the world over, but what we have noticed about the writers in this tiny patch of land is that, on the whole, their writing tends to be darker than most. How dark? Not only does it deal all too often with death in general, but further than that, it seems to be overly concerned with suicide in particular, in one way or another – either actually taking one's life, or attempting to do so, or contemplating it as the best solution to the emotional situation (note the lowercase) the protagonist is facing.

True, suicide is no longer the taboo issue in world SF/F that it used to be. You could not imagine a Heinlein protagonist considering it as an option, nor would you find an Asimov robot contemplating, never mind attempting to violate the Third Law.[6] On the other hand, in modern Israeli literature – and not just its SF/F stepchild – quite the opposite is true. As a matter of fact, argues Maia Amitai in her study on this subject, "some [scholars] make a case for a higher frequency of

---

[6] "A robot must protect its own existence as long as such protection does not conflict with the First or Second Law." Isaac Asimov, *I, Robot* (New York: Del Rey Books), 1950.

this phenomenon [suicide] in modern Hebrew literature, compared with Western literature."[7]

On the face of it, this seems to run against 3,000 years of religion and tradition. But in fact, suicide is quite common there, as a form of martyrdom or escape from a fate worse than death. Read your Bible: Samson brings down the house (Judges 16), and King Saul falls on his sword (1 Samuel 31). Then there was the mass suicide of the last defenders of the Masada fortress at the end of the rebellion against Rome in 72 ce (as recorded by historian Josephus Flavius), to mention a few prime examples.

In modern times, Israeli culture used to make a great deal of similar self-sacrifice for the sake of the nation, lionizing soldiers who gave up their lives (sometimes in acts of actual suicide) for their country. But much room was also left for anomic or egoistic suicide, to use Émile Durkheim's categories. And indeed, suicide as a motif occurs in the work of many well-known Israeli authors – distinguished poets such as Haim Guri, Amir Gilboa, Yehuda Amichai, and Natan Zach, and prose writers such as Amos Oz, A.B. Yehoshua, Yehoshua Kenaz, and Etgar Keret.[8]

We find this exceedingly strange. Israel has one of the lowest rates of suicide in the Western world (less than 7 per 100,000 for the whole population in 2018[9]), and ranks 14th among the world's happiest nations.[10] Still, this act keeps reappearing in Israel's literary corpus.

---

[7] Maia Amitai, *Between 'the Inner Soul' and 'It Is Good to Die for Our Country': Representations of Suicide in Modern Hebrew Literature*. Doctoral dissertation presented to Tel Aviv University, 2014, p. 24.

[8] See Rachel S. Harris, *An Ideological Death: Suicide in Israeli Literature* (Evanston, IL: Northwestern University Press), 2014.

[9] N. Goldberger et al., *Suicide in Israel*, Israel Ministry of Health website, https://www.health.gov.il/PublicationsFiles/loss_2021.pdf (2020), p. 13.

[10] UN, *World Happiness Report*, 2021.

Several scholars have offered their learned opinions about the origins and causes of this abundance of literary suicide cases. Of these, we find the explanation posited by William Gutiérrez-Jones most convincing.[11] He suggests that SF writers from H.G. Wells through William Gibson have subjected their protagonists to self-induced destruction as a bid to remain relevant in the midst of transformative scientific and technological change. Suicide may be terminal, or the characters may trade in their corporeal existence for uploads into other planes of existence. Trite as may be, one way or another, the strategy is presented as transcendental.

ON THE FLIP SIDE (and perhaps surprisingly, given the Jewish penchant for the comic), there is very little humor in Israeli SF/F. That is not to say that there is much of it in world SF/F, *pace* the late Douglas Adams and Terry Pratchett. But some American reviewers of our previous anthology did express surprise about the absence of any humor in it, seeing as America has a long tradition of Jewish humor, from the Marx Brothers to Woody Allen to Jerry Seinfeld. They appear to have expected a Borscht Belt tradition expressed in the writings that emerged from the Jewish State. Yet in recent decades there have not been many laughs in Israeli literature in general and in Israeli SF/F in particular. Satire is well-founded, but chuckles for their own sake? Hardly.

Well, maybe a few. Rami Shalheveth's "Dragon Control," featured herein, is an exception to two rules at once, being both funny and relating to a particular aspect of The Situation. Galit Dahan Carlibach's "Composting," told from the worm-eaten point of view of a sentient, nicotine-starved cadaver, adds mordant yucks to visceral ughs. And Avram Davidson's "Help! I am Dr. Morris Goldpepper" is, characteristically, drop-dead hilarious.

---

[11] William Gutiérrez-Jones, *Suicide in Contemporary Science Fiction* (Cambridge University Press), 2015.

The overall tendency, let us repeat, is a studious avoidance of any writing that could be interpreted as a reflection of The Situation, even indirectly, even in metaphorical or allegorical ways. Elana Gomel, Associate Professor at the Department of English and American Studies at Tel-Aviv University and another one of our authors herein, uses a term she has coined with colleague Vered Shemtov – "limbotopia": the sense of being stuck in an eternal present. In an email to the editors, she explains:

> SF/F is all about difference: whether utopian or dystopian, its worlds are an alternative to what *is*. I think The Situation has created such a paralysis of the historical imagination that we can no longer think of any such alternative. Maybe fantasy or horror offers a possibility to representing the Conflict in a mediated, allegorical way. But I don't see how Israeli SF can do it directly.

This view is shared by nearly every one of the knowledgeable persons whose opinions we've solicited. Aharon Hauptman, the founding editor of the seminal magazine *Fantasia 2000* (1978-1984), wrote to us:

> Perhaps [SF/F] writers in this land fear being "infected" by politics, accused of being either left-wingers or right-wingers, perish the thought. Write about a future in which there is a Palestinian state beside Israel? That's political. Instead of Israel? Even worse. Unending occupation and apartheid? Again, politics. Perhaps they are just afraid to deal with this.

With the exception of the inordinately prolific Israeli SF/F luminary Lavie Tidhar, a one-person Alternate History (AH) generator who not incidentally grew up abroad in a variety of countries and now lives in the UK, this may explain the relative rarity of AH in Israeli SF/F, compared with some other subgenres. SF/F's mechanisms of escapism tend, in Israel, not to a description of a brighter history than the one we have, starting with a twist in some key point in the past, but rather to desperation.

Author Yitzhak Ben-Ner provides an illuminating example. In 1988 – 40 years after the establishment of the State of Israel – a glossy monthly magazine called *Politika* (now defunct) asked a number of local thinkers to portray Israel 40 years hence. Almost all of them wrote didactic essays describing how the nation *should* look like by then, according to their various scholarly, philosophical, or political views. Only one, Ben-Ner, wrote what would have been regarded at the time as a science fiction story – "Fucking City," a first-person account of a day in the life of an Israeli infantryman tasked with patrolling a Palestinian town under Israeli occupation.[12] The idea that the IDF might still be playing the same old cat-and-mouse games with stone-throwing kids in the West Bank decades hence seemed to the magazine's editors and readers alike to be, per a term Israelis are overly fond of, inconceivable. The author must have regarded his work as an AH story – the occupation of the West Bank would still go on in 2028…? No way.

We had considered including Ben-Ner's story in this anthology, but then we realized that this was no AH at all – today, it reads like journalism pure and simple. What he described more than 30 years ago was precisely what is going on today. This is the stuff the evening news is made of. You could read about it in the newspapers, watch it in TV documentaries, follow it through social media. So we decided to nix the story. The hackneyed cliché, "this is not science fiction, this is fact," has never been more appropriate.

Eventually, we did find one *bona fide* example of Israeli AH – a 2018 dystopian TV series (the country's first) called *Autonomies*. The six-part show, which takes place in the present, envisioned a civil war in 1989 between secular Israel and ultra-Orthodox Jerusalem, splitting the country into semi-independent statelets. Most saw the series in strictly dystopian terms. Yet one reviewer wrote in the left-wing

---

12 Yitzhak Ben-Ner, "Fucking City" [Hebrew], *Politika* 20 (1988): 52–55.

Haaretz, "I do not claim that Israel's cantonization would solve all of the country's problems. But *Autonomies* shows that it could lead to the point where Israel's various cultures would begin to appreciate each other's beauty, rather than feel mutually threatened."[13]

THIS BRINGS US TO a problem we have mulled at great length between us and with our correspondents, so much so that we've begun to use a shortcut for it – *the elephant in the airlock*, namely, the almost complete absence of Arabs – Palestinians and others – or, more broadly, The Situation at large, from Israeli SF/F stories. "Stories" is the operative word, because there have been several speculative novels on the subject by mainstream writers, dating back to Israel's War of Independence. But our concern here is with recent genre writing which, as we said, consists almost exclusively of short stories and novellas.

For instance, in the previous volume we had just one story in which there was an Israeli Arab in a minor role.[14] But on the whole, this absence is a glaring one. In vain, we scoured hundreds of stories that have appeared on paper and online since the inauguration of *Fantasia 2000* in 1978. Ehud Maimon and Rami Shalheveth, the two editors who between them account for the publication of nearly all original SF/F stories nowadays, confirmed this to us. No Arabs, no Conflict, no Situation are to be found, as a theme or even as a background, in this body of literature.

Again, in the light of fortuitous exceptions, we were able to find a single story on an Arab motif – Dafna Feldman's "Askuni-Askuni," about the Bedouin tradition of feud, which we present here.[15] And yes, though she handles the exigencies of Bedouin culture sensitively and

---

[13] Carlo Stenger, "The TV Series That Offers a Possible Solution to Israel's Problems," *Haaretz*, 25 October, 2018.

[14] Nitai Peretz, "My Crappy Autumn," in *Zion's Fiction: A Treasury of Israeli Speculative Literature* (2018): 249–280.

[15] We are grateful to Nadav Almog for bringing this story to our attention.

empathically, Feldman is, when all is said and done, an Israeli Jew. But based on the quality of the story, we decided to embrace it.

The general reluctance to regard Arabs as part of Israeli society, or to deal with them as part of The Situation, seems to us quite puzzling, to put it mildly. All the more so for overseas readership, who seem to have a knee-jerk association between the name "Israel" and The Conflict. Truth to tell, it is the same with Israelis. The Situation dominates their life, yet their speculative storytellers fail to tell about it. It is next to impossible to find science fiction or fantasy stories that offer a resolution – a future (or alternative) history of either peaceful coexistence or Armageddon, futuristic warfare between Jews and Arabs using robots and cyborgs, whatever. There simply is nothing of the kind.

We set out to try to understand why this is so. Racism? Nationalism? Myopia? Are we witnessing here an imagination utterly depleted by generations of struggle? Fears and terrors so near to the surface that they threaten to erupt into chaos if not assiduously sidestepped? Or perhaps worst of all, is Israeli SF/F simply as escapist as its myriad critics charge, its practitioners lamentably isolated in self-imposed literary bubbles?

Science fiction, we have been told time and again, offers up a mirror to realities too glaring, discomfiting, or painful to face directly. By rights, then, Israeli SF/F writers should have been leaping ahead of their mainstream counterparts, some of whom did place The Conflict and its constituent players front and center in their narratives.

This is not to suggest that Israeli SF/F writers suffer any obligation to reflect directly on the Rabin assassination, the Iranian nuclear threat, the recurrent Lebanese and Gaza imbroglios, the *Intifadas*, or any other inflection point experienced by or facing the Jewish State. As we described in our introduction to the previous volume, before statehood and during its early years, writers were indeed frequently told what to write about. Those days, mercifully, are long gone. Still, if we didn't know better, we'd conclude that today's crop of genre writers has placed themselves in revolt not only against their forbearers' prostration before the gods of Russian social realism but against any kind of reality that exists beyond the quotidian concerns of their respective personal lives.

Nevertheless, this is curious. One cannot but think of American science fiction of the late 1940s through the mid-1960s, the height of the Cold War, when people were living under a constant threat of nuclear warfare. So many stories were written on this theme then and there, from Merrill's "That Only a Mother" (1948) to Miller's *A Canticle for Leibowitz* (1959), not to mention Heinlein's execrably racist *Farnham's Freehold* (1964).

Our point is this: during these past ten years, at least, Israel has been living under a similar shadow emerging from Iran, yet Israeli SF/F writers do not find this a compelling, or worthy, or interesting, or appropriate – choose your adjective – subject-matter. One Canadian did: the sea-warfare-savvy Noah Beck engaged these dangers in a novel that featured the Israeli submarine force, Flotilla 7.[16] Over the years, several Israelis also wrote full-length novels depicting Israel's demise at its enemies' hands.[17] But try as we might, we could find not a single Israeli short story that has this threat as its subject or even as a part of its subtext.

To BEGIN UNDERSTANDING WHAT is going on, we must place our SF/F writers in their particular literary and generational context. Rachel S. Harris identifies these millennials as part of "a new generation of Israeli writers, born since the 1970s, who began publishing in the 2000s, and whose writing, though diverse in subject and form, reveals distinct characteristics that suggest cohesion."[18]

---

[16] Noah Beck, *The Last Israelis* (Self-published), 2013.

[17] E.g., Zev Ben-Yosef, *Peace Upon Israel* [Hebrew] (Shed, 1995); David Ohana, *The Last Israelis* [Hebrew] (Kibbutz Hame'uhad, 1995).

[18] Rachel S. Harris, "Israeli Literature in the 21st Century – The Transcultural Generation: An Introduction," *Shofar* 33(4) (2015): 1–14.

Paramount among these, she writes, is a shift away from a single national ethos anchored in Jewish religion and history, the Hebrew language, and the Zionist culture, that had characterized Israeli literature from the founding of the State, toward more variegated yet often overlapping affiliations.

To this, Elana Gomel added, in another message to the editors:

Israeli SF/F is actually not that different from the SF/F of many non-Anglocentric literatures that have to define themselves both in opposition to the consensus reality of their own countries and to the Anglo-American hegemony. ... As the global consensus reality crumbles, it is harder and harder to decide what is, in fact, "fantastic" as opposed to "realistic." So, SF/F becomes a set of conventions disseminated by the powerful English market throughout the world, and Israeli SF/F necessarily has to position itself in relation to these conventions, much like any other national literature. ...

I'd say that what really distinguishes Israeli SF/F is a particular relation to space and time. Space: the Promised Land/the occupied territories; and time: Israeli/Jewish history, continuity or rupture. This is very different from the unlimited space and linear time of American SF/F. The chronotope (to use Bakhtin's term) of Israeli culture is multilayered, paradoxical, and self-enclosed.

Are these factors responsible for the elephant in the airlock? Perhaps. But there are other undercurrents as well.

The Hebrew University's Yuval Benziman believes that the reluctance among Israeli writers who now avoid depicting relations with the Palestinians should not be traced to denial or deflection, to cowardliness or callousness, or even to obliviousness. The problem for those so inclined – and certainly within the Israeli mainstream, there have been many – lies in the problematics of "writing a story of not being able to tell a story."[19] Benziman contends that the Arabs and Jews who do inhabit Israeli literature, however multi-dimensional in presentation, cannot successfully forge any kind of consensual reality, even an imagined one. And if so, why bother trying?

Interestingly, Benziman offers up a set of speculative novels of the 1980s to illustrate just how difficult it was for Israeli writers to do so. David Grossman's *The Smile of the Lamb* (1983), an early and accomplished example of Israeli magical realism, requires four distinct narrators, none of whom can ultimately devise a shared perspective on even the most basic facets of The Conflict. Amos Kenan's *The Road to Ein Harod* (1984), a publicistic thriller about a near-future military takeover of the Jewish state, offers up perspectives on The Conflict that frequently depend on whether the protagonists and antagonists momentarily inhabit the surface (Israel) or the (archaeological and political) underground. Arab-Christian author Emile Habibi's *The Secret Life of Saeed: The Pessoptimist* (1974) begins with the titular fool accounting for the absurdities of life in Israel through letters to visiting aliens.

In each narrative, says Benziman, "the narrators can tell the story [only] by adopting a distant perspective and deluding themselves that the story they tell is not their true reality, but rather a fairy tale. They tell it as a fantasy, which supposedly has a happy ending, yet the ending is unhappy, and the world they describe is revealed to be concrete." Their attempts almost inevitably fall short, with the efforts to "present the [C]onflict comprehensively through one stable prism… [are] dealt with by presenting the interaction between Israelis and Palestinian-Arabs as a dialog between deaf people."[20]

---

[19] Yuval Benziman, "More Real Than Reality: Israeli Cultural Texts of the 1980s and the Israeli-Arab Conflict," *Israel Studies Review* 26(1) (2011): 95.

[20] Ibid., 96–97.

Maybe Israel's speculative cohort has simply been exposed to enough stories about time loops – "periods of time [that] are repeated and re-experienced by a character's consciousness"[21] – to believe that they may be literally living in one. And as we all know, when you're in a time loop, the House is stacked against you, no matter how much you fiddle with the fundamentals. Because *plus ça change…*

CONTRAST THIS WITH ANOTHER issue that seems to some, at least, as much of a threat to Israel's future as The Conflict, albeit in a different way. The abovementioned rise of religious messianism and the expansion of ultra-Orthodoxy (Jewish and Muslim alike) in Israel are issues that this country's civic society grapples with on multiple fronts. It impacts the lives of secular and moderately religious Israelis (and all SF/F authors that we know of in this country belong to one of these categories or the other). And it colors their views of the future of the nation as well as their personal fortunes.

But these issues, in sharp contrast with The Situation, are not absent from Israel's SF/F scene. They are tackled by no few writers in any number of ways, as they depict a takeover of the state by religious fanatics, or civil warfare, or ghettoization, or disappearance of religion, and so on. The authors of such stories, like Benjamin Tammuz in his *Jeremiah's Inn* (1984) or Ben-Ner in his *The Angels are Coming* (1985), do not shy away from these issues, we believe, because this conflict, unlike The Situation, *can* have some resolution – maybe a grim one, but at least it is there. With regard to the religious-secular strife, there can be a future, and therefore stories can be told about it. In contrast, The Situation can only be written about in present tense, as a vicious circle that just keeps going around.

---

[21] "Time Loop" in *SFE: The Encyclopedia of Science Fiction*, http://www.sf-ency-clopedia.com/entry/time_loop.

Most Israelis, including those among them who write SF/F, seem to think there is no possible way to end The Conflict. Ortzion Bartana, a professor at the Ariel University's Israel Heritage Department, wrote to us that:

> Israeli literature has never been able to shake itself free of its inability to look forward. Perhaps it does not look forward because, once it became secular, it started looking from past times into the present, but not beyond… Perhaps the future was left, without admitting this, to the religious culture, and people [became] afraid of any abstract futuristic thinking or any serious thought about our future. …
>
> Let me put it this way – in Israeli society there is an antagonistic duality: either institutionalized religious thinking, and then there is no place for science fiction because it might challenge the traditional metaphysical pattern, or secular thinking, and then there is no place for science fiction because secularism, when it runs against the grain of institutionalized religious thinking, "pours the baby with the bathwater."

As per convention, a good story should lead to some kind of resolution to whatever conflict it describes. Absent any way to settle your central issue, you wouldn't write the story in the first place. Editor Noa Menhaim wrote to us that Israeli SF/F's failure to deal with The Conflict, and more specifically, with the Palestinian point, is

> … particularly painful to me, drawing as it does from generations of education that turns its back to the [Middle Eastern] region, and tendentious media that obfuscates and obliterates the Other. Since science fiction has been dealing with otherness and alienness in profound ways for a long time, it could have been a fertile ground for dealing with the subject. But to represent the

Others, in any manner whatsoever, to be curious about them and give them a place in your work [of literature], you have to see them first. And this, regrettably, is something we simply refuse to do, in each and every level of our existence here.

Rotem Baruchin, the gifted writer whose novella "Latte, to Go" concludes this volume, views things quite differently:

I think SF/F has moved during these past decades away from focusing on the national and political side to concentrate on social issues. In this context, you compare our Situation today to the Cold War – but as I see it, it is very far from it. The Iranian nuclear menace, for instance, does not frighten me at all. I see it as an empty threat that the Prime Minister [Netanyahu] brandishes to scare us, as hate and incitement to violence in this country (which do worry me a great deal) are only getting worse. ...

In my life as an LGTB, incitement against me and people like me is growing from year to year, and this is the social politics I write about... In short, I do write about political and social issues, but they are not the issues that you asked about – and I think any writer in this country will tell you similar things: we write about our own difficulties.

Rami Shalheveth brings together these two seemingly contradictory points of view:

True, many of our writers are not afraid of going into dangerous places. They cope with death and social tensions, challenge fundamental assumptions of Israeli society and culture, and disagree with universal conceptions. But looking at this literature more closely, one finds that it has invisible boundaries. There are topics that are rarely discussed.

Interestingly, Prof. Gomel finds a similar disinclination among "my Arab students, some of them interested in writing SF/F in English: they don't see themselves as Israelis but more as members of an international community of writers who would like to make it elsewhere. I think many of them are just sick and tired of the Situation and have nothing to say about it." This brings to mind Ludwig Wittgenstein's 7th proposition: "Whereof one cannot speak, thereof one must be silent."

However, to these explanations we add another one, namely, the power and influence of the market. As noted above, Israel is politically split right through the middle. This means, in practical terms, that appearing to take any position on the elephant in the airlock issue will immediately alienate one half of one's potential readership, which is scant enough to begin with. Hence, most Israeli SF/F writers avoid any hint of any kind of public controversy.

ARE WE ABLE, THEN, to decipher the elephant in the airlock conundrum? Of course not. It is rooted too deeply in the realities of The Situation and its political, social, and cultural ramifications to have one comprehensive answer. Any attempt to figure out why The Conflict is absent from modern Israeli SF/F stories encounters resistance by the most profound aspects of the Israeli psyche. Yet, at these deep levels, we believe that The Situation is not really absent; it is present in all too many of these writings, but in subtle, almost invisible ways.

It is present in the dark doom-and-gloom ambiance, the overweening sense of desperation, and the death wishes that show up so frequently in the stories we have read, some of which have been included in this anthology as in its predecessor. The insolubility of The Conflict inevitably generates an inability to imagine any possible future that contains some glimmer of hope. If there is light at the end of the tunnel, it is only the headlight of the oncoming train. Barring some totally artificial ending, of the kind eschewed by all readers, The Situation is hopeless, and this hopelessness finds its way into many Israeli SF/F stories, even when they are saying nothing whatever about The Conflict, not even hinting at it.

So many protagonists choosing to die or wishing they were dead. So many of them finding their lives empty, purposeless, leading nowhere. The sense of hopeless desperation that so many stories evoke is, we believe, an indelible mark imprinted by The Situation. And so, we believe, while The Conflict itself is absent from modern Israeli SF/F stories, its shadow looms over many of them.

And yet. Repeatedly, we've emphasized the ostensible exceptions that make the rule and the rules that defy the exceptions. If you're holding this book in your hand, you'll find that despite a few notable exceptions, it isn't at all as dark and dreary as we may have intimated in our overall assessment of the field. After all, this book is not intended to offer a picture of Israeli SF/F in its aggregate so much as to feature a collection of stories we found to our liking.

We think that overall, you'll find that *More Zion's Fiction* lives up to its name as a collection of "Wondrous Tales." The book offers new insights into the national psyche, to be sure. But with its mix of science fiction, fantasy, and yes, unbridled horror too, it amounts to a fun ride through the vagaries of the Israeli ImagiNation. Almost all of these stories were written in the 21st century, most of them in its second decade. Hop aboard, grab onto your lap bars, and as you're barreling through the curves, we dare you to let go and enjoy the rush.

What, do you want to live forever?

The Sea of Salt
By Elana Gomel

ELANA GOMEL WAS BORN IN Kiev, Ukraine. She emigrated to Israel with her mother, noted writer and essayist Maya Kaganskaya. She is an academic with a long list of publications, specializing in science fiction, Victorian literature, and serial killers. In 2006, Gomel published a book in Hebrew called *Us and Them*, about the experience of Russian emigrants in Israel — one of the first comprehensive treatments of the subject. It was subsequently published in the U.S. as *The Pilgrim Soul: Being Russian in Israel* (Cambria Press, 2009).

Gomel has been active in the science-fiction community in Israel, participating in the development of annual science-fiction conventions ICon, Utopia, and Olamot. Together with her graduate students, she organized an international science-fiction symposium at Tel Aviv University. She has also striven to bring Israeli science fiction and fantasy on the world stage by writing and lecturing about it and co-editing the groundbreaking collection of essays *With Both Feet on the Clouds: Fantasy in Israeli Literature* (Academic Studies Press, 2013).

She is also a fiction writer who has published more than eighty short stories, several novellas, and three novels: *A Tale of*

Three Cities (2013), *The Hungry Ones* (2018), and *The Cryptids* (2019). Her story "Where the Streets Have No Name" was the winner of the 2020 Gravity Award, and her story "Mine Seven" is included in *The Best Horror of the Year 13,* edited by Ellen Datlow. She speaks three languages, has two children, and is currently dividing her time between California and Tel Aviv.

She is a member of Horror Writers of America. Find her at https://www.citiesoflightanddarkness.com/

KIRSTEN IS DEAD. Or perhaps she had never been born.

I met her when I came to campus for preliminary registration, still feeling awkward in civilian clothes. I literally bumped into her as I was backing out of the registration office, leafing through the hefty package of meaningless forms. She made a polite sound of protest: a sure indication that she was foreign. She looked foreign too, which accounted for my attraction. She was not pretty. Her peaky face was dominated by bulging eyes. Her large mouth looked squished rather than sensuous. Her only truly attractive feature – or truly abhorrent, depending on your taste – was her milky-white skin, so uncompromisingly Aryan that the Mediterranean sunlight seemed to slide off her in defeat.

We sat on the grass while long-legged ibises stepped gingerly around us, and went through the booklet of instructions together. I wish I could say that by this point we were at ease with each other but it would be a lie. We were never at ease with each other.

But we did have coffee together and eventually I got invited into her room in the dorms. She worked so hard at being uninhibited that I felt more like a medical specimen than a lover. She told me she was going to study the history of the Jewish people. I felt I was demeaning myself in her eyes when I confessed my goal was business administration.

When we went out she would wear tight-fitting black dresses and a golden six-pointed star around her neck. She insisted I call her Avital and told me she wanted to convert. I laughed the first time I heard it. But she was impervious to hints or veiled insults. She took everything at face value. The stare of those pale eyes froze absurdities into horrible truths. Later my grandmother taught me the expression *tierischer Ernst:* bestial seriousness of the Germans.

After a while, we moved in together. She paid the rent with her family money.

It was at this time that she started telling me about her grandfather. She told me his name on one of the few occasions our sex was truly passionate, whispered it like a love confession. It meant nothing to me. All I had gotten from the history lessons in school were cartoon images of waving flags and goose-stepping soldiers. And my grandparents never talked.

Now, of course, I know a lot about him, having read all I could lay my hands on. Some of those stories are stuck in my memory like bits of gristle between the teeth. He distributed sweets to the Gypsy children and they called him "Uncle." He would take his favorites for a ride in his car and sometimes drop them by the gas chamber. Once he gave his prisoner assistant — he called them "colleagues" and was invariably polite to them, especially to women – a box to prepare for delivery. She opened it: it was filled with human eyes.

The first semester was ending and we were making plans for the winter break. I wanted to go to Germany with her but she was reluctant. We quarreled and I even accused her of being ashamed of me. I expected vehement denials but she was silent. I stormed out; she called me ten minutes later and offered, as a gesture of reconciliation, to finance a long weekend at the Dead Sea.

James Joyce called the Dead Sea "the cunt of the world." Set inside the ring of ancient crumbling rocks, so old they have become soft and wistful, edging into mineral senility, the heavy-water lake called the Sea of Salt in Hebrew defies time. It is alive with a frightening concentrated vitality like the flow of a woman's juices: a doorway into the womb of the past.

We went spiraling down the new highway into the oldest place on the planet. The scanty vegetation was disappearing to reveal the baroquely shaped bones of the earth: pink, and scarlet, and dull bronze; elaborately folded and pleated; surrounded by aprons of scree. I felt loose as if the cord that bound me to everyday life was unraveling. I glanced at Kirsten; she looked inscrutable, gilded by the sunset.

On the shore the viscous water glistened beyond the wide stretch of salt flats. Ragged birds swooped over our heads. I still remember the tranquility of that moment.

We checked into the Nirvana hotel. Kirsten went straight to the spa. I walked down to the pebbly beach and touched the oily swell. Under the surface I could see white convoluted shapes like corals. They were salt crystals, growing in the sterile water in a perfect imitation of life. I heard the crunch of footsteps and turned around. Kirsten stood behind me, her white top luminescent in the dusk.

"I thought you were at the spa," I said.

"I like it better here."

We stood together in companionable silence.

"Is this where Lot's wife…?" she asked.

"Somewhere around," I shrugged. "A guided tour would show you the exact pillar of salt supposed to be her. Each tour has a different one."

We went back to the hotel, had a lavish dinner, and made love on the king-size bed. When I woke up in the middle of the night and found myself alone I thought she had simply moved over to the other side. Kirsten was never one for cuddling. But a quick glance told me she was not in bed. A longer investigation assured me she was not in the suite.

I was annoyed rather than concerned. Unable to fall asleep, I turned on the TV and watched a soft-porn film on the hotel's channel. Just as the moans of assorted male and female actors rose to a crescendo (they appeared to speak Turkish on the rare occasions they spoke at all), the door creaked and she walked in.

She was stark naked. In the ghostly TV light her skinny body glistened from head to toe, her hair lanky and wet. I stared. Did she go swimming in the Dead Sea in the middle of the night?

"Turn this filth off!" she yelled. And then she started sobbing.

She was covered in dirt mixed with oily water into a sort of paste. I took her to the bathroom and turned on the shower. The water swirling down the drain had a reddish tint.

Wrapped up in one of the hotel's huge towels, she swallowed a drink I thrust into her hand, pulling a bottle at random from the mini-bar. I was seized by panic, wondering whether she had gone off her head. Kirsten had always appeared to me insufferably self-possessed and such people have the capacity for sudden and spectacular breakdowns. Finally, she started talking.

"It wasn't like that at all," she said. "It was not supposed to be that way."

"What wasn't?" I asked.

"The place. I thought it would be cold. But it was hot, stifling. Summer, I thought. But there was no vegetation, nothing, just a field of ashes. Like the volcanic ash but heavier. Wasn't it supposed to be among the fields? I read about neighboring villages gathering their harvest just a couple of kilometers away. But there wasn't a spot of green I could see."

"There is no green here," I said stupidly.

"And the smell," she went on. "I knew there would be a smell but not like this. I thought it would smell like…like roast, like a joint in the oven."

Kirsten was a strict vegetarian; the cause of many a squabble when we ate out.

"But it wasn't. It was bitter, chemical, like toilet cleaner, only stronger. Disinfectant. What do they do with the bodies to make them smell like this?"

This was getting to be too much for a holiday weekend.

"What the fuck are you talking about?" I yelled. "Where have you been? What happened?"

I think my presence was fully registered only then. She looked at me and smiled, almost tenderly.

"Poor Gilad," she said. "*Mein Süße.*"

I felt like slapping her face but then I saw something that made me gulp in horror. There was a dark spreading patch on the white terry cloth around her chest.

"You're bleeding," I said.

She looked down and lifted the towel. There was no wound. The blood was oozing from her nipples, pooling in the crease of her stomach. She made a face and swabbed it with the stained towel.

"I thought these puddles were sewage," she said.

I rushed into the bathroom and threw up. When I came back, Kirsten was in bed, asleep.

I HAD DOZED OFF ON THE COUCH and woke up, groggy, with the sound of the shower. When Kirsten came out, she seemed her usual self. I postponed serious talk until after breakfast. Then, fortified with black coffee, I told her we should go back immediately to seek medical help (I was careful not to say "psychiatric"). She smiled and shook her head. Despite the dark circles of fatigue under her eyes, she seemed elated.

"No," she said. "You go back if you want. I'm staying here. Perhaps I'll look for cheaper accommodations. I don't know how long it'll take."

"How long will what take?" I shouted.

"I'm going to find him," she said.

The Dead Sea and its environs are crawling with Mediterranean history. There are Sodom and Masada; there are remnants of Roman fortifications; there are abandoned bunkers of the Jordanian army. If the past were to invade the present here, why should it be that alien European past, the graveyard stench of Poland, the war madness of Germany?

But she did go somewhere. I saw it myself. I saw her walk into the heavy water that parted before her like some colossal ameba, the smooth flanks of the sea drawing in upon themselves as she stood on the oily shingles. It was as if she covered an immense distance with each step, visibly shrinking, becoming the size of a child, a toddler, a doll. There was a silver flash as she vanished into somewhere else and the roiling water resumed its normal appearance.

She swore to me there was no magic formula. All she had to do was to visualize the tunnel of light. At the time I did not know what she was talking about. Since then, I have read books on out-of-the-body experiences: people who float up a heavenly rabbit hole to meet their dear departed or have a chat with Jesus. It's easy if you know how.

But wherever she went, it was not to heaven. She was convinced – at least, at the beginning – she had found a door to the past. I quickly realized it was not. But I did not know what brave new world she discovered in the depth of her guilt. That world reached out and devoured her; that much was certain. But was it merely her own nightmare? Was I just a bystander, innocently caught in the turbulence of her family history? I pretended to believe it then; I don't pretend now.

Perhaps the pretense was thin even then for the fact is, I did not run away. We moved into a bungalow in a holiday village: cheaper and more private. We developed a daily routine that was almost cozy in its insanity. The horror only came back occasionally. One morning, looking down into the pink *wadi*, I saw a herd of gazelles pass by so close I could touch them. They walked in a single file and as they passed the fenced overhang where I stood, each of them stopped and looked at me.

After breakfast we would drive down to the sea, seeking a secluded place. It was not easy because the shore is as flat as a pancake. There are no bays or coves. But we counted on indifference. If a passing driver got a glimpse of Kirsten's white buttocks, so what? There is no law saying you cannot go skinny-dipping in the Dead Sea. She insisted on going in naked because this is how it worked for her the first time. But since the time of the day was not affected by her passage, she did not want to go at night. She needed daylight: to see, to observe, to witness.

But witnessing was tricky because it changed every time she went there. The basic outline was the same: a field of ashes; a sullen sky that ran the gamut from fire-gray to crimson; and the watchtowers on the horizon. Those spidery black silhouettes, she was convinced, marked the camp where he was waiting for her. On the first visits she did not manage to come close enough to make out the gates because assorted obstacles barred her way. It was the variety of these obstacles that made me realize she could not simply journey into the past. Sometimes the wasteland would be cut by trenches, filled with skeletons in tattered uniforms like World War I soldiers felled by a cloud of gas. Sometimes she encountered a maze of ravines threaded with foul-smelling streams that built up dams of human excrement. And once the plain was alive with tiny lemming-like rodents that scrambled and fought, rising tiny plumes of ash.

The length of her visits also varied; occasionally she would come out in twenty minutes, faint with hunger, and claim to have spent a whole day there. Other times I had to wait until the moonrise to hear the crunch of her footsteps on salt crystals. I fed her and tried to do something about the stigmata of her journey, mostly with no success. And then I would debrief her. This is how I called it to myself as if I was still in Lebanon. I tried to record her but she refused. So I bought a notepad in the holiday village's souvenir shop and wrote it all down in longhand.

On her fourth journey, she said, she saw a line of prisoners weaving among the hillocks of cinders and stretches of black porous stone that comprised the landscape around the camp. She hid behind the rusty ruin of some agricultural machinery; or perhaps it was a military truck. She was vague about such details. She was very precise about the prisoners and their guards, however.

The prisoners, she said, were both men and women. There were no children. They were horribly emaciated, the striped rags of their uniforms barely covering the skeletal bodies but even this scanty covering was almost too much for the stifling heat of that place, the boiling air reeking with sulfur and acid fumes. Some of them, even women, pulled off the shirts, baring the torso in a vain attempt to escape the heat. The guards did not interfere because the most important part of the outfit was impossible to remove. The yellow patches stuck to the prisoners' bare skin; mostly on the chest but sometimes on the forearm, the upper thigh, the shaven head or even covering most of the face. The patches stood out in relief, as thick as a man's hand: not merely a swatch of cloth but a plump padded thing. The patches seemed to her to twitch and change shape. She wanted to come closer but was afraid of the guards.

"They were not human," she said.

"Sure," I said sarcastically, "make them into monsters so we don't have to accept that we are all capable of cruelty."

"I don't mean metaphorically," she said impatiently. "I mean they were something else."

They wore immaculate black uniforms. But unlike the prison guards in the familiar war movies, they also had shiny black helmets that covered the entire face.

"Like medieval knights?" I asked dubiously.

"Yeah, only medieval helmets are very elaborate, with moving parts. These were completely featureless, a sort of hemisphere with a thick curving edge that sat on the shoulders."

"How did they breathe?"

"I don't know."

But what made her believe the guards were not quite human was the way they moved, slinking with a boneless grace around the stumbling column of prisoners. And then there was the way they killed.

"She stumbled and fell, this woman. I think she was a young girl but ages were difficult to tell. She tried to get up but a guard approached, flipped her over with the tip of his boot, and ground his foot into her chest. She wailed and thrashed but he kept on and his foot actually sunk into her body as if it were made of rotting cheese. Blood jetted out but I think – I could not be sure – that it slid off his uniform like water off a duck's back. A couple of other guards joined him and one of them bent and tore off the woman's arm – just tore it off, with no visible effort, twirled it in the air and threw it away. It landed not very far from me and it was… it was a *real* arm, real flesh and blood, because when he did this I thought, it can't be, these people are not real, they are puppets or simulations, nobody can pull a human body apart like a paper doll. But they did. And the rest of the prisoners watched."

SEVERAL TIMES I WANTED TO CALL A DOCTOR. I could not be responsible for what was happening to her. And I admit I was squeamish.

But at the end I did not. I gave in. I became her assistant, chronicler, witness, and nurse. I obeyed her orders. She had this effect on me. Without love, without gratitude, commitment or obligation, she bound me to herself more securely than any other woman before or since.

Her nipples did not bleed after the first time. But when she crawled out of the sea for the second time and stood shivering as I threw a robe around her, I noticed angry red stripes on her back. The skin was puffy, as if she had been lashed with a belt.

"What is this?" I asked.

She shrugged.

"Does it hurt?"

"A little," she said reluctantly. I put some aloe gel on her back and tried to pretend it was the effect of the seawater. But the third time she came back with half her hair torn out by the roots, the bare patches on her scalp raw and bleeding. She cut off the remnant of her hair and shaved her head with my electric shaver. Were it not for the scabs, it might even suit her.

I thought that perhaps she had been discovered. I imagined her naked figure crawling in the ashes. Had she been gang-raped? I was afraid to ask. But that night she pushed herself against me with a startling desperation and we made love like two castaways on some bleak shore. This was the last time; when she returned the next day, she tried to hide her body from me but I could see how her journey had marked her. More than mere mutilation, it was as if her flesh had melted in the passage and then cooled into a ragged new shape. After that, she came back every time with a new brand, like notches on a gun to mark the killings.

She did not mind; she was preoccupied with more practical concerns. She wanted to spy on the camp. She was upset because she had not managed to approach it any closer: her way had been blocked by a giant pile of discarded clothing, suitcases, shoes, toys, all mixed together and dumped in the midst of the wasteland. Rooting in it, she found a teenager's pants and a man's khaki shirt that fit her, dug a little hole and hid the clothes, marking the site with a rock. Next time she would snoop around properly dressed in dead people's hand-me-downs. I was struck by the gruesome irony of it but she was not; rather, she was puzzled by the seeming senselessness of the dump.

She could not understand the economic logic of the camp, she said. I laughed when she first talked about it. But then I began to realize she was serious. She had to come to terms with the camp by squeezing it into the procrustean bed of her rationality. She was not content to turn away in disgust from the meaninglessness of atrocity; she had to force atrocity to make sense and then she could live with it. It made her abhorrent in my eyes; it made her admirable; and as distant as if we were denizens of different galaxies.

The prisoners were often marched around the camp, going nowhere. To me, it sounded familiar, almost mundane; there were the death marches after the camps had to be evacuated and the purpose of these marches was killing, pure and simple. This camp, however, seemed in no danger of liberation as there were no signs of war around it; no drone of warplanes or distant rumbling of the artillery. There were crematoria inside and they worked at full capacity. She saw the tall chimneys protruding into the yellow air, belching oily smoke and an occasional tongue of flame. Even the sickening stench of the burnt human flesh that she had missed on the first occasion was there, only masked by the piercing odor of unknown chemicals. So, she insisted, there was no point to those impromptu death marches.

"Perhaps the gas chambers and crematoria are overloaded," I suggested.

It was possible, she agreed reluctantly. There was a railway line that brought prisoners in: occasionally she could see a tiny train on the horizon. Still, there was something about the killings that puzzled her. When she came back after her fifth visit eager and excited, I knew she had solved the mystery.

"I know now!" she exclaimed.

She came across a heap of dead bodies, not very large, perhaps twenty people in all. Most seem to have died of sheer exhaustion; several were shot. The bodies were stacked together like firewood. Approaching them cautiously, trying not to breathe in the death-stink, she saw stirrings in the heap. She thought of rats; but the creature that wriggled out and plopped onto the cindery ground resembled a starfish. It was poisonous yellow, with a rough tegument and six radial arms that it proceeded to flex as it flopped around.

"Those patches," she explained, "are not sewed-on pieces of fabric but living organisms. They are parasites, feeding on the prisoners. I think that they need dead bodies for the incubators. This is why a certain percentage of prisoners are not burnt but killed outside the camp. I saw groups of inmates on the plain before, moving from one pile of bodies to another. I thought they were *Sonderkommando.* But now I believe they were harvesting the stars."

I stared at her. There is a threshold in horror beyond which lies sheer numbness and a kind of detached curiosity. I was at this stage but she – she was somewhere else. Her cheeks were flushed.

"Where do you think these creatures come from?" I asked.

"I think they've been made in the camp," she replied. "I think…" she hesitated slightly, "I think *he* made them."

Next time she came close enough to the gates to see the familiar inscription ARBEIT MACHT FREI. She was relieved; she had heard a prisoner scream something in a language she did not understand and was concerned about the possibility of miscommunication. This was also the first time she saw the guard dogs. They were large sleek brutes with naked pink paws like rats and semi-human faces, pug-nosed and slit-eyed. She was convinced they talked to the prisoners.

She refused to let me tend to herself but when she fell asleep I saw a pink growth, like a fleshy coral, on her thorax. I lay down on the couch, revolted and hating myself for my revulsion.

How to get into the camp? That was the problem she pondered incessantly.

"Most inmates wonder how to get out," I said sarcastically. She just shrugged but I began to consider whether this was true, whether there was, in fact, any place to get out to. It seemed to me that her stories of the camp world were growing more bizarre, more hellishly elaborate, as if that world was diverging further from our knowledge of the past. Perhaps by now there was no war, no opposition to the camp system, and no hope for the people who were used as hatcheries for monsters.

"There is a camp ecology I have to understand," she said. "The yellow stars I think are just larvae. Perhaps at the next stage they become the guard-dogs."

"What for?" I asked.

"I read his diaries," she said. "He really believed in what he was doing. He was a scientist, not a butcher. Perhaps here he has the chance to put his theories into practice. Perhaps in that world they are *true.*"

"How do you know he even exists in that world?" I asked.

"Oh, I know," she said unhesitatingly. "He's there, I can feel him. This is why…" she added after a while, in that contemplative tone that always gave me the chills, "this is why it all looks so familiar."

"Why don't you just walk to the gate, then, and say you have come for a family visit?" I asked.

She looked at me with those bulging eyes. Her face by now had the uncompromising look of a martyr.

"If I don't find any other way, I will do it," she said.

"I want to come with you," I said.

"No."

Of course, I could have argued. I could have followed her.

I did neither.

The last time I waited for her for the entire day. The brief violet dusk came and went and she was not back. I prowled the edge of the sea; the sounds of singing and laughter came from the new promenade.

Exhausted, I drove back to the bungalow. When I saw the light streaming from the windows I almost crashed the car.

Kirsten was inside, sitting on the bed, her head in her hands. She had put some clothes on but there was black water pooling at her feet.

"I've seen him," she said.

"How did you get here?" I yelled.

"I walked," she said vaguely. "Listen, I've seen him."

I don't believe she had walked up half a mile, naked and barefoot, from the shore to the bungalow. I suspect the worlds were bleeding into each other and she was the wound, the raw place where they rubbed. Her mutilations were signs of their contact; and the wider the zone of contact became, the more randomly was she tossed along the edge.

Apparently, she had taken my advice. She had simply walked to the camp entrance and announced herself. I imagine her standing at the bottom of the curving ramp, a tiny figure in the wasteland of ashes and poison, looking up at the towering ironwork of the gate.

Her description of the camp was rather vague but also surprisingly prosaic: prosaic, that is, in the sense that it was not all that different from the descriptions I have read since then in historical books. She talked about the barbed wire, the churned-up bare earth, rows of barracks, smell of excrement. Not too many inmates were around. Those she saw were shuffling *Musslemen*, living skeletons with extinguished eyes covered in filth and sores. They, however, were free of yellow stars, confirming her hunch that the creatures were parasites that needed relatively healthy hosts. The guards who escorted her did not speak and seeing them from close up, she decided they could not. The helmets were actually their real heads, covered with a shining black carapace like a beetle-wing. She tried to figure out how they fed and came to the conclusion that they had mouths in the palms of their hands. She was convinced now that the guard-dogs were their masters.

Brought to the medical barrack – she caught a glimpse of a room filled with small cots, a child in each – she was led into an office. There was a desk with a typewriter, a fringed Art Deco lamp, and a portrait on the wall. Not the familiar face with a tiny mustache. Not a human face at all.

She was left waiting in the company of a nurse, a youngish woman in a starched uniform. She refused to talk but gave Kirsten a sugar cube. And then her grandfather walked in.

They talked. There were no spy-novel attempts at disguise; she did not pretend to be a special envoy from Berlin. She told him she was his descendant from the future; she said she had traveled back in time. He was familiar with the concept; being an educated man, he had read H. G. Wells. However – and this indicates to me he had realized there was something fishy about the situation – he did not ask her many questions about the future, though he did inquire about his family. Instead, he seemed to be only too pleased to talk about his work in the camp.

It was, as she had suspected, an attempt to create a total ecology of death, in which the energy released by torture and extermination would be used to promote the malleability of the living flesh.

"Think about it as a fountain of youth, like the legendary spring of Eldorado," he had said enthusiastically. "There is no limit to improvements we can achieve. Total freedom from disease, physical perfection, mental acuity, all fertility problems solved once and for all."

The yellow starfish, the black-helmeted guards, and the talking guard-dogs were just experiments, she gathered (inside the camp, most personnel seemed ordinary enough but on her way out she caught a glimpse of a creature like a giant dun-colored caterpillar crawling on two rows of human hands). The prisoners were vermin whose extermination was a necessary hygienic precaution; it was the greatest boon to science that this simple public-health measure also opened a window of opportunity for the human race.

What else had passed between them at this family reunion, I wonder. What else was said, perhaps not in words but in exchange of looks, in the body language? She had spent her entire life in his shadow, thinking and dreaming of him, hating him, but perhaps also admiring his courage in stepping outside the bounds of the merely human. All she had ever wanted, she told me, was to separate herself from him. But is it really possible? The more she looked into the past that should have been dead but wasn't, the more the past looked back at her. The past had reshaped her in its image even before she took off her clothes that evening. Her white skin was festooned with hanging sacs of skin filled with milky liquid and there was a tiny dark core in each, a fetus-like form turning head over heels.

"I am going back tomorrow," she said. "I am going to kill him. You are a soldier; you will teach me how."

I took her with me, bundled in layers of my T-shirts, as we sped on the empty highway. It was pretty late to come knocking at the door, but the owner of the flat-roofed house in a small village owed me a favor. Arms are easy to come by in a country at war. The handgun could be hidden under her clothes. All she had to do was pull the trigger.

We were back at the Dead Sea just as the first rays of the sun broke over the Jordanian hills, turning the heavy water into a sheet of beaten gold. In that glorious light Kirsten's wasted skull-like face looked frightful. And yet I felt something close to adoration as I looked at her. We both knew she was not coming back. Heroism is the opium of fools.

I tried to postpone the moment, offering her coffee, keeping up the feeble pretense of normality. She refused and tucking the gun, carefully wrapped in a plastic bag, inside the waistband of her pants, walked to the sea edge. It occurred to me that it was the first time she was going there dressed.

I watched her as she paused with her feet planted in the viscid swell. I hoped she would look back at me. But she did not and I realized, once again, how little I meant to her. It had been between him and her all along.

She started walking in and the sea parted as usual. But something was different; there was angry churning and the water, normally so sluggish, rose in foamy billows that twisted as if whipped by a gale, even though the air was still. A piercing whistle assaulted my ears, rising to an unendurable pitch as the sea exploded into a harsh blaze. I fell down. Groveling on the ground, my eyes watering from the Hiroshima radiance that turned the flying foam into the hail of fire, I could still see Kirsten's dark silhouette. She must have screamed but her voice was drowned in the rage of the Dead Sea, offended at her presumption in carrying an instrument of death into its domain. I could see the metallic glitter of the sky through her body as the waves dissolved her flesh, eating holes in legs, buttocks, and thighs. An especially large wave broke over her and when it retreated a pristine skeleton was standing in the sea, its arms still raised in supplication. But the sea was already giving it new flesh, covering the slender bones with the coat of interlocking crystals that grew into a structure of surpassing beauty, as lacy and delicate as the rime patterns on the windowpane. This new creation, however, endured for an even shorter time than Kirsten's own fragile body, for the salt statue broke up and fell into the hungry water that swallowed it up and buried it in its own salty depth.

IT HAS BEEN FIFTEEN YEARS. I don't remember the days that followed but eventually the routine won, as it always does. I called her parents and told them their daughter had left me but I did not think she would be coming home soon. They were not surprised.

I make good money. I am married and have a three-year-old daughter. When she was born, I wanted to call her Kirsten. My wife was shocked by the idea. We called her Shirley.

Recently I took a day off work and drove down to the Dead Sea. I walked on the promenade in the pale silvery light of the late afternoon. A boy was sitting on the parapet, reading a book, resting his feet on his huge backpack. He was blond and blue-eyed. As I approached, he lifted his head and smiled at me.

"US?" I asked as I sat down beside him.

"Germany," he replied.

We chatted a little. His life was brand-new, untarnished by memory. He was highly complimentary about my command of Deutsch.

"History is a nightmare from which I am trying to awaken," said Joyce. But what if a nightmare becomes history? I imagine Kirsten and myself yoked together by elastic bonds that warp out of shape as they stretch back in time but never snap. Unless they are cut.

My wife kids me for working out so obsessively. But I have to be in top shape when I'm ready to cross the Sea of Salt and enter the undead past in order to put it to rest.

I will be ready soon.

Schrödinger's Gorgon

By *Keren Landsman*

Translated by Emanuel Lottem

K EREN LANDSMAN, M.D., IS A MOTHER, a medical doctor specializing in epidemiology and public health, and an award-winning SF author. In 2014 she volunteered to go to South Sudan to instruct local health care workers in epidemiology and public health. Landsman is one of the founders of Mida'at, a voluntary organization dedicated to the promotion of public health in Israel. She currently works at a free STD clinic, at the mobile clinic for women in prostitution, and at the Ministry of Health's Epidemiology Department. She now knows that being an epidemiologist in the midst of a global pandemic is not as much fun as she was led to believe.

Landsman started reading SF in school, in spite (or because) of the librarian's claim that "it's not for girls." Her interests come through in her works, from motherhood to friendship and coping with loss, all these and more find their way into stories that balance emotion, plot, and vision. Landsman published her first story in 2006. So far, she has won four Geffen awards: twice for best original short story and twice for best original book. *lgbtq+*, a social justice story, was published in English in 2019.

BEEP.

Beep.

Beep.

A short squeak. Red lights are blinking all along the station's round hull, my home in deep space.

I walk down the corridor, watching my shadow as it slides on the walls, getting distorted where two panels meet and interrupt the plastic's flow.

Beep beep.

Beep beep.

The squeaks urge me to hurry up, and I start running towards the sound that's getting ever stronger. The corridor ends abruptly with a closed door, soundproof, airproof, odorproof. That's why it has taken us so much time to find out why help hadn't come. I take a deep breath, pass my hand over the lock. A moment's hesitation, taking in another breath. Every time it's getting harder.

Beep beep beep.

The intervals between those squeaks are getting shorter. I count to three, with the beeps. The next gap, I hit the Open Door button. The smell hits me. I've cleaned the control room dozens of times, but death's thin arms still grasp at me, wafting on filtered air infused with pine odor.

The beeping becomes a continuous bleat. The whole station is screaming, and I shut my ears and enter the string of numbers that is its name.

Course change postponed, I see, green letters on a black screen. I still remember the first time I saw this line. We numbered thirty then. Tired, dirty, believing we were saved. This was the first time I've managed to sleep through the night. And the last time, too.

I abandon the keyboard and turn back, not looking at the row of empty chairs staring at me silently all along the wall. The bodies we cleared the day we'd broken into this room. But their stares remain, watching my every step and pleading with me not to abort their last action. Their last will and testament to the survivors. Two more ratings had died before we realized what the people who'd locked themselves inside the control room had been trying to do during the week we've spent trying to break in.

I drag my feet down the corridor back to the main galley. The chairs are neatly arranged by the tables, and I move two of them, sitting on one and laying my feet on the other. I order a meal for one and drinks for two. At first we instituted food rationing, but now there's no need for it. The station can support me till the day I die.

A single beep and a deep chime announce it's nighttime. The lights dim momentarily, and I get up. Time to sleep. I have just less than six hours before the course change sequence will be reactivated. The senior staff rewired the controls. After we'd broken in, we were told by Kard, the software engineer, that it's better not to abort the countdown before we make thorough software checks. He suggested a temporary fix until then, which would allow us to restart the countdown every six hours. "A temporary solution," he called it, and promised to complete his thorough checks in a week. He died two days later, and since then, our lives have been framed by six-hour watches.

I sigh, stretch, and return to my stateroom. When the station became empty, I thought of moving closer to the control room but couldn't get away from the memories filling my stateroom. Another day has passed. Maybe this time I'll have a good night's sleep. Perhaps this time, I won't wake up again.

I wake up at a start. My heart is beating against my chest. The siren sounds again, and I disentangle myself from my beddings. My limbs groan after a frequently interrupted, nightmarish sleep. I cuss when I hit a wall, and again when I hit a bed support. It's only after I've passed through three pressure doors that I realize that the sound is not the usual alarm. Instead of those blinking red lights, the familiar corridor is bathed in deep blue light. The sound is a rhythmic ding-dong I haven't heard for many a long month.

A friendly ship is approaching the station.

I stop short. My twisted shadow on the curved plastic wall looks like it's grinning at me and I grin back, a hesitant, fragile grin. The blueish ding-dong sounds again, and I keep running. I'm trying to recall the docking procedures I've memorized once, looks like ages ago.

Contact-sealing-insertion-pressure equalization-decontami-nation.

The hull shudders as the ship makes contact with the station. I must get to the airlock before sealing is completed. Decontamination won't do, not by a long stretch. I must warn them.

I reach the airlock. A metallic *clang*, then the slight hiss of air being pumped in. Lights start blinking on the other side of the door. For a moment, I yearn for the sight of human beings, but horror overcomes all other sensations. They must *not* come in. I press the palm of my hand to the separating wall. Automatically, the mechanism pushes back. A short beep for identification, and I activate the sealing sequence.

I hit two switches, and the hissing stops. A double locking takes over from my side. I breathe again. They won't be able to come in. They're safe. I can imagine them, on the other side, crowded in the airlock, trying to figure out why they can't open the door.

A sudden beep, then a human voice. "SB 5977. Docking procedure incomplete. Your airlock is compromised."

I clear my throat, press hand to wall again, searching. There. The intercom. "The lock is OK." My voice trembles, and I cough and force my vocal cords to produce the right soundbites. "You must not come aboard."

Crackling sounds. Another person gets online. "This is Captain van Oors. Who's speaking?"

"This station is quarantined. You must not come aboard."

Capt. van Oors huffs and puffs. "On whose orders?"

"Doctor Katala, sir." Deep breath, then, "me."

Cracklings on the other side. "We are responding to a distress signal sent out from this station. I'd like to talk to Commander Gorb."

"He's dead." This is the first time I have to say this to someone who hasn't seen the bloated body reclining in the command chair, a bullet hole dripping congealing blood in its eyeless head.

"Then let me speak with Lieutenant-Commander Shatooli."

I wet my lips. "Dead too."

I snivel, remembering Tooly, his face frozen, looking at the mirror and pointing at a reddish spot underneath his chin. "It's nothing," I told him at the time. "Just a pimple."

"You must not come aboard," I repeat for the third time, and my voice is stable now. "Isolation suits won't do any good. You should move on to SB 7796."

The intercom crackles, and a new, younger voice is saying, "This is Doctor Oleanz. No need to worry. We have new-type suits, resistant to any biological agent."

I ignore the hope that raises its head despite these last months of suppression. "Too great a risk. Quarantine procedures remain in force.

Anyone coming aboard will only be able to leave after an interval exceeding the longest incubation period."

"Alright," says the ship medic, "what's the longest incubation period?"

"Four months," I reply.

The speakers remain silent.

"Your distress call is dated to four months ago. Is there a carrier still alive?"

I breathe deeply. "Yes."

Silence. Then Dr. Oleanz says, in a slightly more gentle voice, "yourself?"

I nod. Too late, I remember that they can't see me. Another crackle on the other side, and Capt. van Oors says, "Doctor Katala, Lieutenant Oleanz assures me that the new suits are completely proofed, even against all known extraterrestrial agents."

"Not good enough," I answer. I feel again a burning sensation in my lower back, a reminder of those long days I've spent over the microscope. "I've made thorough checks. Even those I'd put in isolation were infected. I can't accept the risk." I'm thinking of Younar, dying in the repairs capsule, revolving eternally around the Jump point.

Yet another crackle, and then Dr. Oleanz says, "I know about the outbreak. We'll come aboard with a skeleton crew, remain in our isolation suits throughout our stay aboard your station, and then remain in full quarantine for a period of time to be determined by you. Even if we get infected, we won't pass on the disease. Is this acceptable?"

"But…" I'm grasping for a reason not to allow them to come aboard. It's been months since I last touched another human being, saw another human being.

"Yes." Reason gives way. I cancel the double locking and allow the click sounds on the other side to echo through the heavy door. They pump out the air between us, leaving a lifeless vacuum, supposedly impenetrable to pathogens.

Once we depressurized the entire station, in a last-ditch effort to overcome the disease. This was after we'd cremated all those bodies, since I'd given up trying to do so many post-mortems. We donned our pressure suits and opened all orifices to space. Waited outside for two hours, during which time we imagined these alien proteins dispersing in space, streaming towards the Jump point. A couple of days later Tooly got sick; in a week he was dead.

There was no rhyme or reason to their dying. Patients got infected in ways that seemed totally random. Within two months, only I was left. In retrospect analysis, I realized that most patients had complained of fatigue one week before presenting the disease's first signs. I included this in my last report to Earth, marking it as a frequent but not conclusive symptom, and relied on this when I determined the incubation period to be one week.

The door opens. Three huge figures appear behind it, clumsy in their blue standard spacesuits. A shining liquid film covers their faces. On their backs they carry disposable oxygen tanks. The first two are hauling a large suitcase, encased in brown foam.

The first figure salutes me. "Rating Goshen, ma'am."

I return his salute, wondering how I look to them. It's been months since I've last bothered to comb my hair or even look at a mirror. I push my fingers through my hair, trying to smooth it a little to look more presentable.

"Where's the main lab, ma'am?"

"Deck three, blue wing." We'd changed the regulation green at the request of Mishi, the station commander's daughter.

The figure passes on. The next one stops for a moment to salute as well. "Rating Gebil, ma'am," she says. They keep going, and I look at the third figure. Hard to see the man's face underneath the isolation mask.

"You Doctor Oleanz?"

He nods. "Doctor Katala?"

I offer my hand. After a moment of hesitation, he shakes it. For the first time, after these long months, I get to touch another human being. I breathe deeply. For him, this is so ordinary, to touch another person, a living one, and I adjust myself. The inner door closes between the station and the airlock, and the gentle pumping sound is heard again. Dr. Oleanz nods to a voice speaking in his ear and says, "Captain van Oors wishes us good luck."

I am too tired to smile, too despairing to hide this. "This way to the lab."

"Are you the station's original medic?"

I shake my head. "The medic assigned to this station got space allergy, and then Tooly got…" I stop and correct myself, "Lieutenant-Commander Shatooli was transferred here, and I joined him."

"Your husband?"

There's something gentle in Dr. Oleanz's voice, and I dare not look at him.

"We didn't have the time." I don't want to elaborate, and he doesn't ask.

Dr. Oleanz walks behind me. Once he's gathered enough self-confidence, he asks, "Where are the bodies?"

"There aren't any," I reply, "but there are tissue and cell cultures."

"And recordings?"

I shake my head. "Destroyed during a general power failure." Which happened after we'd made the course change, but I don't tell him that.

My shadow slides along the walls, in the company of some others, after all these long months. Dr. Oleanz wants to hear about the disease, the first cases, and I tell him. I make a point of focusing on the essential details, leaving out the emotions involved. I start by describing the long-bodied, long-haired reptile. He arrived from the Butterfly Cluster, M6 by Earth's old designation. He had six legs and his skin seemed scaly, making him look like an overgrown tailless crocodile. He spoke a strange dialect, breathing out strangely between puckered lips to produce sibilants. He showed up at the sickbay three days afterward, his hair twisted around his head, and his eyes, which had no eyelashes, were rolling rapidly. He said that he had a weird rash and that he was losing sensation in his lower body. Tests showed nothing, but I kept him in for observation.

Four days later, his body shook in a last spasm of agony. I sealed the case study in a classified file and sent it to Earth. Protocol required me to place the station under quarantine for twenty-four hours following any death for an unknown cause. Nothing happened during this time, and the reptile's stateroom was thoroughly sanitized. That night, Tooly laughed at me. He said I got too excited over unknown diseases and suggested that I find a cure for his cold instead. I'd sent queries to worlds visited by this passenger before arriving at our station, but none of them admitted knowing anything about such a disease.

Dr. Oleanz interrupts me. "We have this report. The next case was a pet, I take it?"

"Yes." I swallow. "A cat." Mishi's.

"And how did you make the connection between these two cases?"

The corridor ends with a couple of double doors. Ratings Goshen and Gebil are waiting by them. Their suitcase lies on the floor between them. I place my palm on the identification strip beside the doors, and we get into the lab. It is sparkling under the blue lighting, its floor spotless after weeks of autocleaning. Next to the corner biological hood, there are still dozens of test tubes containing blood samples from all crew members, neatly arranged, remnants of my futile efforts to find some vaccine.

The two ratings are quite experienced. They relieve their suitcase of small containers, portable computers, and glass slides, beside a portable tissue analyzer and a set of folding laser blades.

"We've got an unlimited budget," says Dr. Oleanz, noticing the way I look at all this. "We can't have an alien disease loitering within a Jump distance to the Solar System without us synthesizing an appropriate remedy."

I shrug. "Wish you success."

The ratings have already taken off their pressure suits; now they are wearing regulation lab coats. Dr. Oleanz starts to change in front of me. An alarm sounds, and all three freeze. I cuss voicelessly and turn to go. I'm farther than I usually am; usually, I try to stay nearer to the control room.

"Where are you going?" Dr. Oleanz hurriedly walks beside me.

"To the control room," I breathe. I am separated from it by three levels and four long corridors. The lifts are waiting for us – it's been long since anyone walked these corridors except me.

"What's in the control room?" he asks as we stand in the lift, making our way to the station's innards.

"Must restart the course change counter," I tell him. His skin is liquid under my glance. "Is this the new-type isolation suit?"

"A monomolecular film," he nods. "Blocks any agent that doesn't have the wearer's genetic load, with special filters lining the stomach and the lungs." I can see his face now, dark and confident. The doors open to a corridor bathed in a blinking red light. The beeps come faster now, and we run down the corridor, our boots hitting the floor in unison.

No time to dawdle in front of the door. I punch in the code and the lights go back to normal, following the announcement *Course change postponed.*

I turn back from the board and almost run into Dr. Oleanz, who is standing behind me. He's looking around. I wonder what he sees. His memories aren't mine.

I'm still breathing hard. "They… tried… to crash the station," I say. Dr. Oleanz's eyes are brown and deep. The monomolecular film covers his face, separating him from the contaminated air within the station, and from me.

"You managed to stop them."

I try to decide whether it was a simple statement of fact, or perhaps the medic facing me is really glad that I'm still alive. I turn my back on him and start walking towards the exit.

"What's this?" he's pointing at a flashing button, but then he presses it before I can stop him. Younar's face appears on the screen beside this button, his hair spread out in zero gravity, his eyes sunken.

"Ah, Medic, I… I'm… I'm sorry to be bothering you so much."

"It's only the second time, don't worry about it, Younar." My recorded voice is tired. So tired.

I don't want to look. I remember this conversation quite well. Younar was looking for the proper words, as he had always done when talking to me. My medical degree placed a vague wall between us. He was sure he'd done something wrong, and expected to be dressed down. "Since we spoke last, I can't see very well," he admits. His voice is shaking. "And I have weird spots on my knees."

My recorded voice sounds again, encouraging him to specify what's going on with him. I choke on my tears, hiding them from the stranger beside me. Dr. Oleanz bends over the screen. I recall that I'd thought Younar must have injured himself somehow. My voice is interrogating him, striving for the real answer, and then comes the response that had made my blood freeze in my veins.

"I don't know, Medic, but I can hardly feel my legs."

Dr. Oleanz hits the button again to stop the recording. The button is still blinking, protesting that the message was not played in full. He leans over the screen. I wipe my eyes, waiting. After a moment, he turns to me. His face is white.

"Petty Officer Younar Kishinev was a maintenance technician at the station," I say into his silent eyes. "Every six months, he used to go out for regular maintenance work on the Jump point." I wipe my eyes again. "He'd gone out the day the alien arrived. He'd never met him, but reported exactly the same symptoms."

"Are you certain he became sick?" Dr. Oleanz's voice is rasping.

"It's possible that he'd been injured. It's possible that the lack of sensation he reported had not been the onset of paralysis, but rather a side effect of a long time in zero gravity," I shrug. "I didn't want to put him in harm's way by recalling him to the station. At first, I'd thought I could contain this outbreak, and then…" I turn back. "And then there were no more messages."

He's looking at me, and I see in my mind's eyes Younar floating in space, waiting for the message calling him back home. "I didn't want to put him in harm's way," I finally repeat myself.

Dr. Oleanz nods his head. "I'd have done the same, I think," he says quietly. We get out of the room. After long minutes of silence he asks, "How *did* you make the connection between the cat and the alien?"

I blink my eyes rapidly, recalling Mishi as she held her little animal, its stiff body twisted, just like the alien's. She expected me to make her Kitty well again. "I gave him some soup, but he didn't lick it," she said, and I knelt on my knees and told her Kitty must rest now and she'd done well to bring him to me. After she'd left, I did the autopsy.

"Under the fur I found the rash, and analysis showed advanced decay of the peripheral neurons," I tell the medic walking beside me, not remembering the grayish animal lying on my operating table.

"Next – the child, not so?"

I nod.

He repeats my nod. "I've memorized your reports."

I can imagine myself in those reports, lost inside my isolation suit, my hair in ever-increasing disarray, the rings under my eyelids increasingly darker. Each one of my reports spoke of ever-higher mortality rates.

I grin. "I was so tired when I dictated them, I can't be sure the last ones conformed to standard."

Dr. Oleanz lays his hand briefly on my shoulder, an unexpected contact that makes me jump. "They were amazingly detailed. It's good to find on the frontiers physicians who can function well under duress."

"Thanks." I find it hard even to blurt this word.

"You're welcome." His gaze wanders around the walls, and the station seems suddenly warmer. "Progression was steady, if I'm not mistaken. Rash, neuronal decay, death." He counts the symptoms on his fingers as he speaks them.

"Only for the first ten victims," I correct him. "Subsequently, there was also internal bleeding. I imagine the agent has undergone a mutation that started affecting the coagulation mechanism as well."

"That, or perhaps the clotting mechanism had been involved from the start. Both rash and decay could have been due to embolism or localized hemorrhage."

"I've checked for this." We get out of the lift, making our way back to the lab. Remembering all this is painful, but it's nice to hear my ideas bounce off someone else's mind. "I'm convinced the agent has mutated."

He shrugs, a gesture more graceful than what I'd expected from a military medic.

I keep going. "I've managed to establish direct links among the first five cases – the alien had been given the CO's stateroom, where the cat must have caught it. It then mutated, started attacking humans. Child to carer, carer to the other three children, then their parents."

"And then"?"

This time, it's my turn to shrug and remain silent. By that time I was so swamped with patients, I was losing count. But this is not something he needs to know. On our way to the lab he interrogates me on the symptoms, rash formation and other details physicians hang on to when they don't know what their patients are dying of. As if finding the right detail will prove the key to solving the case, prevent the disease from spreading to Earth. I answer his questions, occasionally looking at screens for details that slipped my memory. It doesn't matter. The disease isn't going to break out of this station. It will die with me.

"So, what do you think?" He turns to me when we reach the lab. "Viruses? Prions? Phages? Nanobots?"

I place my hand on the wall, and the door recedes. Behind it, Rating Goshen is working on the abandoned tissue cultures, lining them up according to the logic of lab technicians. Rating Gebil takes out of the suitcase perforated boxes, stenciled with *Rodents. Handle with Care*. In a corner I see, in handwriting, *Canaries in Medcorps Service* and a sketch: a winged mouse in a birdcage.

"This is an alien disease," I say to Dr. Oleanz. "Its mechanism is different from everything we know." I've already looked into all these mechanisms, but I know he's going to reexamine my assumptions all over again. That's what I would have done in his shoes.

"Of course." He smiles, and his eyes suddenly lit up. "But you must start somewhere, and I don't know how to start at the end."

I return his smile.

It's only when I'm way down the corridor that I realize I've smiled twice in one hour, after four months of no smiles at all.

WORK BEGINS. They analyze the new cultures, working backward. Examine cell negatives, broken pieces of nucleic acids floating in a microgravity field. They joke occasionally. Rating Goshen says, "what's the difference between a bicuspid valve and a tricuspid valve?" Rating Gebil answers, "The tricuspid one doesn't need training wheels!" They both laugh. Dr. Oleanz smiles in the corner, recording his impressions from his autopsies of tissue residues. I just sit and look at them: enclosed in their suits, a thin liquid film preventing the disease from reaching them. I want to hate them, but I can't; they're too young.

It takes them four hours to rule out viruses and bacteria as possible pathogens. Dr. Oleanz raises his eyes and asks me if I'm interested in helping him examine the cultures. I decline. He doesn't insist. I've stared at enough cells to know what they're going to find. Nothing. There is no pathogen in those cells, or cultures, or the bodies we've cremated. At least, no pathogen we know how to identify. No staining locates it; no magnification shows it.

Six hours later, I go back to prevent the station from crashing into the Jump point. The station won't recognize Dr. Oleanz's authority, so I'm the only person allowed to stop the countdown. Once I'm dead, no one will protect this station.

After eight hours, I go to sleep. They rule out prions and keep working. After eleven hours, I'm back at the lab. Rating Gebil is sitting to one side, typing on a small screen. She raises her eyes when I approach. "Silg and Dr. Oleanz went to sleep," she says and turns back to the screen.

"What are you working on?" I come closer, and she flinches. An involuntary aversion to a carrier.

She turns her screen in my direction. "I'm sick and tired of looking at diseased tissues, so I took a tissue sample from one of the mice."

I shudder, thinking of the little critter squealing in her gloved hand. "Is it alive?"

The rating waves her hand. "Of course. We're not allowed to kill them."

Of course not. I'll be the one who'll kill them. I, and the plague I carry. On the screen facing me, red blood cells are flowing out of intact blood vessels. Platelets swirl in glossy plasma. I refocus the tissue analyzer and watch skin cells divide, tired old cells dropping off the healthy tissue. The rating is yawning behind me.

"I still have to go through all these cultures," she says, pointing at the pile of dishes waiting beside the machine.

I move back, return the screen to its original position. Accidentally, I change the lens's focus. Something at the edge of the field of vision catches my eye.

"Hold on!"

"What?" She stares at me.

I point at the cells accumulating at the screen's edge. "Was this here before?"

The rating looks at the screen. "I don't know. She yawns again. "Maybe."

I manage to get a hold on my shaking hands and breathe deeply. "Think. This necrosis, at the margins of the tissue, did it come from the canary?"

The rating looks again at the screen. She still doesn't get it. "I don't think so." She hesitates for a moment, then says, "No. I'm certain. The tissue was quite clean when I took it from the mouse."

I'm relieved. Tissues get destroyed when removed from the body. The necrosis I see, the damaged blood vessels, it's not due to the disease; it's just a normal tissue decay.

"Here." The rating touches a few points on the screen. "I'll show you." She loads the autopsy's recording. Focus changes again, until the lens is right on the object. The field of vision is full of destroyed blood vessels.

The rating flinches. "That's not what's happened. I wanted to look at a healthy tissue." She's pale underneath her liquid film of isolation layer.

I move around her, walking to the open cage. The mouse is lying there, rash spots are appearing on its furless body right in front of my eyes. I turn to the girl. She's holding her head in both hands, murmuring, "This can't be, this can't be."

I grab her arms and raise my voice. "Listen to me!"

Somehow, I manage to control my desire to shake her up. "Listen to me," I repeat, more quietly. "I know this disease. It spreads very fast in canaries. It's possible that when you placed this tissue in the analyzer, the mouse still looked healthy."

She nods her head.

"Get Dr. Oleanz. I'll go through the samples and see what's happened. Okay?"

She nods again and leaves the lab. I go back to the tissue analyzer. The disease is running amok on the screen in front of me. Platelets are sticking to each other ineffectually, helpless against the tears that keep appearing in the blood vessels. Plasma floods the tissues, carrying bunches of platelets underneath the skin. I go back to the mouse. Using a dedicated syringe, I take three more tissue samples from its hind legs. They're already paralyzed, and it feels nothing. I return to the tissue analyzer.

"Doctor Katala?" The sound of Dr. Oleanz's voice makes me jump and drop the test tube. Small nozzles emerge, spraying resistant foam where it hit the floor.

"Sorry," he says, looking at the foam. In a couple of hours, the bacteria in the foam will have dissolved whatever was in there, and then self-destruct.

"Civilian development, isn't it?"

I nod and turn back to the atomic analyzer. "The CO bought it after I'd showed him a report on job-related accidents in the past three years."

"A resourceful medic. Not many like you in the SBs."

I want to talk with him, get to know him, but I turn to the screen instead. "The first canary got infected."

Dr. Oleanz bites his lower lip.

"There's nothing you can do; they always die first," I repeat what I said to Rating Gebil, but with him, it won't wash. He knows our mantras. I move the sample, focus on another area. Both of us watch those blood vessels being eaten away on the screen, disintegrating before our eyes. It's less than fifteen minutes until the whole tissue dissolves. Cell debris spread all over the glass slide. I move my eyes away from it and sigh. "A waste of canary. You've got more in the ship, don't you?"

Dr. Oleanz nods. He's pale, wiping his forehead, staring at the screen. He's not used to such a fast propagation.

"Perhaps we should put a canary in a kind of isolation layer like yours?" I tilt the screen away from him.

"Not possible." He's looking at the cages along the lab's wall, where mice are dying out of sight. "It's a molecular isolation, tailored only to the antigens in human skin." He sighs and returns his eyes to me. His eyes are wet under the film. "I'd like to test apoptosis inhibitors."

His unabashed grief at the death of a mouse penetrates my defenses. I touch his arm. For a moment, he lays his hand over mine, then turns away. I put in the analyzer another tissue sample from the infected canary. Dr. Oleanz hands me a green solution, and I drip it carefully into the dish.

"Where did you study?" Dr. Oleanz breaks the silence, and I accidentally pour too much solution into the dish. The cells foam in protest, and he hurriedly hands me a disinfectant. Our hands meet over the test tubes. We exchange quick looks and go back to our solutions.

"New Delhi," I murmur quietly, but Dr. Oleanz responds. He has relatives there. He tries to tell me a joke in broken Hindi, and I laugh at the appropriate place and correct his convoluted syntax.

"You're very…" he starts, then adds quickly, "different. From other SB medics."

"Thanks, I think," I smile at him, and his eyes lit up in a smile.

We work quietly then, sorting out experimental drugs, stopping from time to time to take more tissue samples from the canary. Some hours later, we are joined by the ratings, and work speeds up.

Rating Gebil looks withdrawn, still beating herself over her mistake. She still maintains the sample she took had been a healthy one, even though the recordings say otherwise.

THE HOURS PASS FRUITLESSLY. The ratings keep trying to isolate the pathogen. Dr. Oleanz decides to try and look for something that could retard tissue decay. He remains in the lab, bent over test tubes containing various solutions. Some of these I've tried, when there were still people to cure. The rest seem too experimental for my taste.

Again I stop the station from crashing. This time Dr. Oleanz doesn't accompany me. Eat, sleep, wake up, go to the lab. In one of my visits to the lab, Rating Gebil complains that she's sick and tired of plastic boxes and food that tastes like cardboard, and Rating Goshen suggests that she eat the plastic and throw away the food. Dr. Oleanz and I exchange glances, and I can see that he's trying not to giggle. Shifts blur into one another. The ratings' eyes are sinking ever deeper into their dark rings. Dr. Oleanz's back becomes more bent by the shift. They inject stuff that encourages angiogenesis into one of the two remaining canaries. Dr. Oleanz believes that creating more blood vessels should allow more nutrients to reach necrotic organs, despite the ongoing decomposition of blood vessels' walls. After three shifts, Rating Goshen asks me to look at the canary that got this injection. The mouse is sleeping quietly in its box.

"Wasn't it supposed to get infected already?"

I shrug. "We've never tested for incubation period in animals. We only had one animal that got sick. All the other cases were humans." And for us, incubation periods ranged from a couple of days to four months. I'm still waiting for the disease to break out inside me.

After two hours, it's time again to postpone the station's crash, and then I'm back in the lab. Rating Goshen is bent over the tissue analyzer. Dr. Oleanz's beside him. They have the canary's box with them, and the mouse is peeping at the world outside through a transparent window. Dr. Oleanz turns to me; he's smiling. "Come see, Doctor Katala."

I come closer. "It worked?"

He nods. Rating Goshen is almost dancing in his seat. I come closer still. Dr. Oleanz makes room for me. On the screen, I see a perfectly healthy tissue. Eagerly, I magnify the image. No two ways about it, a healthy tissue.

I turn to Dr. Oleanz. He's handsome when he's smiling. His eyes are shining, and he has a dimple in one cheek.

"I think we should give it one more shot, then try it on the other canary. How about that?"

I nod and turn back to the screen. If it works, perhaps I'll be able to get out of here. Come back home. Hurriedly, I push this thought away, but some of it remains at the back of my mind. A strange sensation creeps up my throat. Happiness, I think. Long time no feel.

A healthy tissue. It's been so long since I've seen one. I bathe my eyes with the sight of these pinkish cells, wholesome blood vessels carrying nutrients to tissues. I touch the screen, changing focus, measuring capillary widths, watching red blood cells hurtling with the flow of plasma.

"Doctor Oleanz!" Rating Goshen's voice tears me away from the screen. "Something… there's something wrong…" His words die in his throat. I turn to the rating. The mouse is not running around in its box. It lies on its back, its front paws waving in the air, its hind legs folded tight against its belly.

The screen nearby displays the center of the tissue. I already know what it's going to show when I move the focus to the margin of the cut. Decay. Death.

Dr. Oleanz uploads the recording of the original autopsy. Rating Goshen's voice is heard in the background: "Autopsy, canary number four-two-eight slash cee. Despite the addition of angiogenesis enhancers, as of this morning an ongoing weakness is presented in the hind limbs. Following a complete physical check the decision is made to conduct an autopsy…"

"That's not what's happened," Rating Goshen murmurs. "It was completely healthy."

"Then how do you explain this recording?" Dr. Oleanz looks at him, drumming with his fingers on the mouse's box.

"That's not what I said." Rating Goshen's voice becomes louder. "I said it was healthy, and it was time to try and shoot the same stuff to the third canary."

Dr. Oleanz's lower lip trembles. "I'm not sure I understand what you think you are doing."

"No." Rating Goshen raises his hand to massage his forehead. "I'm sure… I think… I'm pretty sure it was healthy."

"One of us is wrong, and it's not me." Dr. Oleanz's voice slashes through the air. His eyes have narrowed. His body leans forward. Rating Goshen lowers his hand. His shoulders slump. He shuts up. The rings of fatigue show darkly in his pale skin.

I leave the lab without looking at them and don't come back anymore.

THE SECOND CANARY DIES, then the third one. Dr. Oleanz had tried 13 more substances on the canaries before they died. Once the three cages become empty, he arrives at my stateroom.

"I want to repeat our tissue tests." Prior to boarding an infected station, all crew members are required to provide tissue and blood samples for comparison in case of suspected infection. His eyes take a tour of my quarters, staying for just a little while on the neat shelves, the books lashed to the walls.

I clear my throat, and he returns his gaze to me, sitting in my unmade bed. I pass the fingers of one hand through my hair. My fingers become entangled in all those knots, and I give up on my attempt to look better.

"You mustn't remove your isolation suit."

He bites his lower lip. "We'll only be out for a couple of minutes. We'll remove our isolation suits in the airlock, take our samples, then re-don them and open the lock to space."

I shake my head. "And if you've been infected?"

"We were not. None of us removed their suits."

"The mice were completely isolated." I sit up in my bed.

"Not molecularly. Trust me –"

I shake my head again. "I won't take the risk of its getting out of here. You stay."

His voice softens. "Doctor Katala, none of us carries the disease. We've maintained complete isolation at all times. We won't make contact with anyone on board our ship. I promise you."

I wring my fingers while running scenarios through my head. They all end in death. Dr. Oleanz sits on the bed beside me. He understands. None may get off the station before we find a way to kill it. Whatever "it" is.

We sit together in silence. His hand finds its way to mine, settling on top of it. I wonder whether it's normal for me to notice the feel of his skin against mine. Its warmth, its softness.

Dr. Oleanz's hand communicator buzzes. He moves one hand to silence it. It buzzes again. Dr. Oleanz sighs and answers. A crying voice is coming through.

"I… I've got…" Rating Gebil's voice is broken by snivels.

"Sir," Rating Goshen bursts in, "Ayeli has a rash all over her face."

Dr. Oleanz and I exchange glances and get up as one. "We're coming," he says, and we both start running. I zip my coveralls as I'm running, tripping on a shoe left forgotten on the floor. Dr. Oleanz gives me a hand, and we keep running on down endless corridors, all the way to the lab.

We stand in front of the door. As I pass my hand over the lock, I notice it's trembling. I'm flooded with memories. Those people locked on the bridge, Mishi handing me her frozen cat, those nights beside Tooly.

"Doctor Katala?"

Dr. Oleanz's voice is soft in my ear, and I want to turn to him and urge him to get out, board an escape pod and run away from here with his soft eyes and warm, light-spreading smile. But I only breathe deeply, move my hand over the lock and open the door to see Rating Goshen bent over a folding cot on which Rating Gebil is sitting, crying.

I sit down beside her and caress her head. I can hardly feel her hair behind her molecular isolation.

"Let me examine you," says Dr. Oleanz. Rating Gebil raises her head and removes a strand of hair from her face. Her tears are glistening under the protective film, leaving bright, transparent trails. A red mark with irregular purple margins mars her right cheek. Another, smaller one, can be seen above her eyebrow.

Dr. Oleanz looks at me, and I nod. He lowers his head. "Perhaps there's something wrong with your isolation …"

Rating Goshen interrupts, "It must have been punctured, or scratched, or…"

Rating Gebil snivels, and they both shut up. I raise my head, and my eyes meet Dr. Oleanz's. He raises his chin and says, "We'll just have to work harder. We got very close with the last canary."

Rating Goshen sits up. "That's right! Don't you worry, Ayeli, everything's going to be alright!"

Rating Gebil smiles through her tears, and only I remain silent. We are no closer to a solution than I was the day that reptile came into my sick bay for the first time.

I decide to stay with her, as Dr. Oleanz and Rating Goshen return to the lab. I want her to be comfortable, and she chooses a stateroom closer to the lab, with a soft bed. In five hours, the rash spreads all over her body. She naps, and I attach her to a pulse oximeter, go out to stop the countdown, and then come back to the lab.

Rating Goshen is bent over culture dishes. Dr. Oleanz autopsies one of the canaries. His back is bent over the sparkling lab bench. He is biting his lower lip. I come closer and see the monomolecular isolation still shining on his skin.

He raises his head when I stop beside him.

"Her deterioration is faster than expected," I tell him.

"How long, do you think?"

I want to lie, but the answer slips out on its own. "Three days. Maybe less."

He nods and turns back to his autopsy.

"Anything new?" I ask, getting closer to the lab mouse underneath the tissue analyzer.

He shakes his head.

I quash a sigh and wait. After some minutes of close scrutiny, he lays down his scalpel and straightens his back. He looks at Rating Goshen, still busy with his Petri dishes, and leans toward me.

"There's nothing wrong with the isolation," he says quietly.

"Your isolation?"

He nods.

"Ayeli's as well?" It's the first time I use her first name.

He nods again. I take a breath.

Dr. Oleanz again bends over the cut body. "Three days," he murmurs to himself.

I want to hold him tight, promise him that everything's going to be alright, things happen, the rating just wasn't as careful as he is. But Rating Goshen is here, and I dare not come closer to Dr. Oleanz in his presence.

After some more minutes of silence I leave the lab, returning to my patient, who's whizzing away in her new stateroom. I send a message to the ship, and after a few moments, I see Captain van Oors's face looking at me on my screen.

"I need Rating Gebil's contact information," I say to this bearded face, so different from how I imagined it when we spoke over the intercom.

He raises his eyebrows. "This information is only available to her immediate superiors."

"I know." I wring my fingers behind my back. "But I'm not sure how long she's going to remain conscious. I thought it would cheer her up to see her family."

Captain van Oors rubs his chin. "Did you ask Daro's permission?"

It takes me a moment to realize he's talking about Dr. Oleanz. I shake my head. "He's too busy at the lab. Trying to find a cure before…" I don't complete my sentence.

"And you don't think they'll succeed?"

I remain silent, and Captain van Oors remains silent too. Finally he nods. "Talk to you soon."

I disconnect, and the screen darkens.

THEY'RE TRYING ON HER coagulation stimulators, apoptosis inhibitors, plasma replacements, and complement system proteins infusion. Nothing doing. In two days, paralysis spreads to her respiratory muscles, and she needs a mechanical ventilator. On the third day, Dr. Oleanz caresses her forehead and inserts a transparent solution into her IV line. She closes her eyes, then shudders and relaxes. I call her death. Outside, Rating Goshen leans his forehead against the wall. His tears flow silently. Dr. Oleanz stands beside him, whispering encouragement. I leave them to stop the countdown, then return to the lab, where Dr. Oleanz is sitting beside the now-empty tissue analyzer. His hands cover his face. I touch his shoulder, and he says quietly, "we'll have to do a post-mortem on her."

I nod, realize he's not looking at me, and say, "We can wait a little."

He shakes his head and looks at me. "We don't have the time."

The doors whisper and Rating Goshen steps into the lab. One glance at him, and I understand what Dr. Oleanz meant. He has on his neck a small red mark with undefined, purple margins. Must have developed shortly after I'd seen the rating in the corridor. We both get up.

"I'll prep the cadaver," I say.

"I'll recalibrate the analyzer."

Rating Goshen says nothing. He moves over to his bench, on which there are stacks of tissue dishes, sits down, takes an indelible marker, and starts marking the dishes. Dr. Oleanz takes his seat in front of the tissue analyzer and recalibrates it for humans. I leave the lab, back to Ayeli's stateroom.

The place is quiet now, absent the rhythmic sounds of the respirator, absent the dripping sounds of the IV. Ayeli is lying on her bed; her skin is reddish-brown. I remember Tooly, a moment after I'd told him it was just a pimple. He smiled at me and raised his hand to hug me, and our mirror fell down and broke. I told him it was bad luck. "It only means that next time we'll have to do a better job hanging it on the wall," he laughed and hugged me. One week later, his skin had the same color.

I kneel and caress Ayeli's hand. The isolation film sticks to my fingers, and I wipe them on my thighs. I breathe slowly as I stand up.

The standard cover over the bed is stretched, and I bundle her inside it. It sticks to her, outlining her contours, and Rating Ayeli Gebil becomes a plastic woman-like creature, ready for autopsy and analysis.

I press the appropriate spot on the wall, and an orifice opens up under the headboard. I type the destination and push the cadaver into the tunnel. Artificial gravity takes over, and it disappears from view on its way to the lab. There, Dr. Oleanz will feed slices of it to the tissue analyzer, in an effort to isolate the pathogen. The orifice closes up.

I leave the room and go to the command center. There, among blinking screens and ghosts of the dead, I can cry.

A week later, I repeat this procedure for Rating Goshen.

I look for Dr. Oleanz all over the station till I find him at last in his stateroom, curled up in a corner, his head between his arms. His screen is blinking – an incoming message. The door closes behind me in a slight *whoosh*.

"You didn't listen to the message," I say. He only shrugs.

I press the activation spot. It's a recorded message for Rating Gebil. Her parents are waving at the camera, both of them, holding a kitpuppy. I let the message run its course, then delete it.

Dr. Oleanz is still motionless. I kneel beside him and he moves a little, puts his head on my shoulder, and breathes out. We remain sitting like this till I think he's fallen asleep and try to get up. But his hand closes on my wrist.

"Stay," he says. "Please." I sit down. Bristles cover the lower part of his face; there are dark rings under his eyes. His lips are thin, pale. I turn toward him, lay my head against his, and close my eyes. His body shudders from time to time in my embrace, and I hold him tighter and tighter still. Finally, we both fall asleep.

That annoying beeping wakes me up, and I hurry to the control room to stop the countdown once more. When I'm back to his stateroom, he's no longer there. I try the hand communicator.

"I'm in the lab," he says. His voice sounds choked. I race out to the lab. Don't let him have the rash, I murmur, but I don't believe in what I say.

At the lab, he's sitting in front of a communications screen by the back wall, whispering to it. I come closer, and he looks at me. His face is free of spots. I want to hug him, relive last night's intimacy. I smile, but he doesn't smile back, only turns to the screen and ups the volume.

"Five patients so far," a rating I don't know is saying. He's wearing a lab coat over his orange uniform. "Two of them in a bad way. We've tried the compound you'd recommended, but as of now, there's no improvement."

"Perhaps you used the wrong dosages," says Daro. "Increase the apoptosis inhibitors, reduce the steroids. I'm sure it's not an immune problem."

He lies so smoothly to the rating he's talking with, as if he has a clue about how to combat this disease. I don't contradict him. False hope is better than despair.

When the screen darkens, he turns to me. His shoulders are slumped, the dark rings under his eyes look darker.

I try to think, to remember. Rating Goshen spoke of getting more canaries. Ayeli wanted to diversify our breakfasts. "Who broke quarantine?"

Daro shakes his head. "Nobody. They were here all the time."

"Not possible." My voice gets louder. "One of these two left the station and carried it to your ship."

Daro gets a hold of my arms. "No, none of us broke quarantine. And even if someone did leave the station, the first case was Captain van Oors. How could they have gotten to him? I don't understand any of this."

I remain silent, which Daro interprets as an invitation to go on. "If they'd gotten off to the ship, the first cases would have been among the decon crew. Rating Gebil had a partner. Should have gotten it way before the captain. It doesn't make sense."

He falls silent, looking at me. Silences reverberate off the walls.

I can't look him in the eye. "There must be a simple explanation," I mumble. My mind is racing, trying to tie up the clues. "It's probable that someone on the decon crew was the first case, and van Oors only got sick because he was older. This doesn't necessarily mean that he was patient zero."

Daro is hanging to my every word. "Really? You've noticed this pattern during the outbreak in the station?"

I run the first cases through my head. "The difference was in the duration of the illness," I say quietly. "Not in the order of presentation. Older people didn't get sick sooner."

"I'm not infected."

I shake my head, and the words come out on their own. "Just you wait."

Dr. Oleanz nods. He's paler than I'd thought. His eyes are dark.

I raise my hand to touch his cheek, and stop it. "I'm infected, yet – I'm not ill."

"You're special." He's smiling at me, but his smile dissipates before I can respond, and silence comes back to reign between us.

I open my mouth to give him an answer, but a thought bursts into the sentence that I haven't begun. "Younar!"

My cry is ringing back at me off the walls. Daro looks at me, bites his lower lip. "Younar?"

I nod vigorously. "Suppose he did meet the alien on his way out. Maybe the timeline report was wrong."

He taps his chin with one finger, and I continue. "He meets the alien, gets infected, dies in his repair capsule, and it drifts off course. Your ship finds the capsule and picks it up."

Daro nods. "They wouldn't have thought the quarantine rules apply to it as well, so they opened it and got infected."

"And surely the CO would be present when they open the capsule."

For a moment, we both glow in the light of this discovery. He takes my hand. "Let's check it out." My heart beats faster at the touch of his hand.

We hurry to the nearest touch screen. I type the code that allows me access to all station records. A name list rolls in front of my eyes, and I click rapidly at the screen's edge to speed up the autosearch.

"There!" Daro points at one of the lines.

"*Petty Officer Kishinev*," I read. "*Time of exit 18:54, Sunday, April 5th. No time of egress recorded.*"

"Now we just have to find your reptile," he says.

"Over here," I point.

"FD?"

"Foreign Diplomat," I explain. Daro nods.

"This line says, *FD – egress 22:37, Sunday, April 5th. No time of exit recorded.*"

"This means…" I start.

Daro interrupts me. "This means there was no contact between them." He sighs. "Even if the ship picked up the petty officer's capsule, he could not have been a carrier." He lays his head against the wall. "I can't figure it out."

I come to him, laying my head on his chest. His arms wrap me. I can hear his breathing, muted down through the uniform. We go to my stateroom, supporting each other. My bed is unmade. Daro takes off his shoes, sitting down on the bed. I sit beside him, put my hand in his, leaning my head on his shoulder. He puts one arm around me, pulling me closer. We lie together on the bed. I close my eyes. His insulation does not let his smell reach me, only the sound of his breathing. I can hear his heart beating next to mine.

"The captain seemed alright when I spoke with him," I say.

"You spoke with him? When was that?" Daro murmurs, turning to me.

I change position, adjusting my body to his. "About ten days ago," I reply, "when Ayeli got sick. I asked him to contact her family."

"The captain got sick the day before yesterday."

"One week after I'd spoken with him." The average incubation period is one week.

I stop his hand that is trying to caress me.

He releases his hand from my grasp. "So what?"

I breathe deeply. After all these months, I have it figured out. "For as long as we were enclosed in this station, we could blame the air, the isolation suits, the food. Too many factors, each of which could have been a potential carrier." I have the answer right here, staring me in the eyes.

Daro is looking at me. I can see the white of his eyes in the darkness of my room. He can't follow the flow of my reasoning. No matter. He'll understand soon enough.

"The mice had been perfectly healthy until I looked at their samples. This was what both Rating Gebil and Rating Goshen claimed, remember?"

He nods. "But the canaries must have been sick when the samples were taken. You said so yourself – the disease develops very fast." He moves closer to me.

I draw back from him. "Not *that* fast. I looked at the mice, and they got sick."

He doesn't reply. I keep talking. "Captain van Oors. He had been perfectly healthy. No one came out of the station to infect him. But he spoke with me, and now he's dying. Can't you see the connection?"

Daro shakes his head. "You don't make sense."

"Younar." I sit up. I wave my hand to switch on the lighting.

"What about him?" Daro sits up beside me.

I rub my forehead. "Younar. He was just as perfectly healthy. And then I'd told him to remain in the capsule. By the next time I called, he was already sick."

Daro bites his lower lip. "You said he'd been injured. You gave a perfectly reasonable explanation. It makes no sense."

I start laughing uncontrollably. "It makes perfect sense. I look at someone, and he or she or it dies."

Daro backs away from me. "Stop it. It's bullshit!"

I keep on. "The observer effect – the act of observation changes reality."

His lips waver between smile and rage. I am unable to get a hold of my laughter, until a thought penetrates my growing hysteria. "Ayeli's parents!"

"What?" his voice overwhelms mine.

I stand up. "Ayeli's parents – I watched their video message."

Daro gets up and grabs hold of me. "Listen to me, you're imagining things. There is no connection between these events. No pathogen works like that. It's some kind of bacteria, or virus, or prion, or a piece of an unknown enzyme. That's all. It managed somehow to work its way through the isolation and into our ship. We'll remain in quarantine, both station and ship, until we find a solution."

I nod. He lets go of me. "What we need to do now is take some more samples from you and try to figure out what makes you resist this disease."

I shrug my shoulders. I can't stand up to him. He's wrong, but I can't think of a way to convince him.

"Alright," he says as he walks to the door, "I'll finish with the samples we've taken from Rating Goshen, then I'll work through your samples again. Surely we've missed something last time."

I nod again.

He goes out to the lab, and I sink back into my bed. Why didn't I get sick yet? I run all my patients through my head, forcing myself to find the contexts, the linkages among these people. My legs find their way to the control room on their own. My shadow chases me down the corridor.

At the door, I stop. Daro was right. The mice were developing the disease too fast. There is an incubation period. It's not possible that the moment I looked at them, they got sick.

I repeat this in my head. It's not possible that the moment I looked at them they got sick, and yet, as soon as I looked at the sample, it started decaying, and the disease spread through it as if the mouse had been sick for a long time. There is an incubation period, but only for whole animals. I was looking at tissue samples. I force myself to accept this idea. As soon as I looked at the sample, the mouse has changed from healthy to sick. Reality has changed.

My hand still hovers above the lock. Observation changes reality. Everyone knows this. That creepy-crawly creature looked at Mishi's cat, and it got sick. The cat looked at Mishi, and reality changed accordingly.

I think of Ayeli's long hair, of Daro's beard stubble. She got sick, he didn't. I remember Tooly standing in front of the mirror and me being jealous because I hadn't had the time to put on my facial cream. At first I hadn't had the time, then I became afraid of finding a telltale blemish on my face, finally I've had no reason to do it. I've gotten used to living without taking care of my looks, and during my months of loneliness, I've left this habit behind me, never tried to resurrect it. This disease can't harm me. It needs me in order to survive. I got it from the reptile. I am the focal point, it was from me that it spreads to other people – by sight.

I take a step back, turning my back to the control room.

I think of Ayeli's parents. If Daro is right, we're dealing with a regular pathogen that we haven't been able to figure out as yet. It's enough for me to prevent the station from crashing, and the disease will die out here, with us. But if I'm right…

I move away from the control room, and the beeps are chasing me. I don't have much time, just a few minutes. That should be enough. I run down the corridors to Ayeli's stateroom, where I'm sure I'll find what I need.

Daro. I don't have time to say goodbye to him. For a moment, my legs falter, but then I push them to run harder. I didn't say goodbye to Tooly either. If I'm wrong, I'll say goodbye to him in a few moments more. If I'm right – he won't miss me at all.

The echoes of my footsteps come to me from everywhere. The beeps get stronger. A few more minutes, and the station will dislodge itself, dragging the ship with it into the Jump point's gravity well.

The mutation that had transferred the disease from the reptile to me made me its focal point. And all this time, I remained healthy.

I think of the mice that became sick the moment I looked at their tissue samples. I have to be ill and healthy at the same time, create a paradox that will change reality into a world in which this disease does not exist. This disease must self-destruct because, evidently, nothing else can destroy it.

Ayeli's room is closed, its silence uninterrupted for more than a week now. I get in, followed by the loud beeping of my dying station.

I stand in a corner, and the course-change alarm turns from punctuated beeps to one continuous scream, as I look straight at the mirror hanging on the wall. One last thought goes through my mind – will they miss me?

The Assassination

By Guy Hasson

Born in 1971, Guy Hasson is an author, playwright, and filmmaker who crafts plays in Hebrew and prose in English. His books were published in Israel (*Hatchling, Life: the Video Game, Secret Thoughts,* and *Tickling Butterflies*), the UK (*The Emoticon Generation*), and the US (*Hope for Utopia* and *Secret Thoughts*). He has won the Israeli Geffen Award for Best Short Story of 2003 ("All-of-Me™") and 2006 ("The Perfect Girl"). Since 2006 he has been focusing on producing original films, including the feature-length *Heart of Stone* and the web series *The Indestructibles.* Hasson's latest book in Israel, *Tickling Butterflies,* was released in Israel in 2017.

Eschewing Hebrew in his SF/F writing has served him well in accessing a broader readership. Still, it has also caused a modicum of confusion at home, especially when some of his work found itself translated back into his native Hebrew. However, in either language, Hasson is a force to be reckoned with, and his work has been translated into seven languages so far. His stories can be found in the various Apex World SF anthologies and Apex's *Horrorology.*

In 2013, Hasson created an independent comic books company, New Worlds Comics, and its flagship title *Wynter,* written by him, was hailed as one of the best SF recent comic book series. In 2015, Hasson created an online comic book store for the blind and the visually impaired, called Comics Empower.

London-based SF/F writer Lavie Tidhar says of Hasson: "In his refusal to compromise on commercial principles, and in his ongoing experimentation with various forms of media, it has become clear that he is following an intensely personal vision; one to which his commitment is whole."

In 2020 Hasson chose the route of self-publishing to maintain complete control of his new fantasy book series, *Lost in Dreams*. The first book, *The Forgotten Girl,* was published in 2021. The book series is an experiment in storytelling, which follows Joy Shelley, a girl born in her father's dreams, from birth to death, with each book jumping forward three years of her life. The daily podcast *The Squashbuckler Diaries* accompanies the books and describes the daily events in Joy's life between the books. "It is my life project," says Hasson.

HE WEARS THE STORY OF HIS LIFE on his face. That first second, looking at him in person, is a rehashing of everything I know about him: The hardships, the killings, the fight for freedom, the struggle against the British Mandate, the wars with the Arabs, and the cruel battles against traitors within. I can see four decades on his face: The 1930s all the way through the 60s. Decisions and fates had been carved in the stone of his skin more than fifty years ago. So much of a person's face is not captured on a TV screen.

His eyes move past my face, scan the large mirror behind me, then come to rest on the conference table between us.

"My name is David Sanderson," I offer my hand. "A pleasure to meet you, sir."

"I'm sure," he mutters, and rather than shake my hand, he moves to sit down. A ninety-year-old body moves slowly, and it still takes me a couple of seconds to notice that although he did not deign to give my organization the respect of a handshake, he had seated himself in front of the mirror.

I sit opposite him, making sure not to hide any part of him.

"You're recording this, I suppose."

"Yes, sir."

He shrugs and moves his head as if he's lived through this dozens of times before. "How many times do I have to be right," his mouth curls up in a slight smile, "to be right?"

"This is the last time, sir."

Something in the way I said that makes him look at me. He scans me up and down.

"How old are you?" he says. "Twenty-six? Twenty-seven?"

"Twenty-six, sir."

He looks down and laughs. "I have granddaughters older than you."

"I know. They're two very beautiful women."

"Their children are even more beautiful."

"That's right, sir."

He nods. He has five great-grandchildren, two grandchildren, and two children – a boy and a girl, all from marriage to Dinah Shamgar, his devoted wife. She was the one who helped him dress before he came here, no doubt.

I saw pictures of her when the two of them had met, two twenty-three-year-olds in the middle of a war for freedom. Oh, she was something. They met by accident. British Intelligence decided that Aryeh Shamgar had been the man responsible for the assassination of Colonel Tanner at the King David Hotel. Shamgar needed an apartment to hide, and the Underground ordered him to lie low at Dinah Gat's apartment. She was a bike messenger for the Lehi, the smallest and most militant of the resistance groups, passing notes from one officer to another and, of course, ready to lay down her life for our independence. Aryeh lived on the floor of her bathroom for six months, keeping quiet lest the neighbors hear. When she was out, he would store his feces and piss in glass jars in fear that someone might hear or smell the toilet. When it was dark, he would occasionally wander the streets of Jaffa wearing a false beard, dressed as an Orthodox Jew.

After the Nazis were beaten in '45, after the British left 'Palestine' in '48, and after the Independence War was won in '49, they were married. They have been married now for 60 years.

"Would you like some tea, sir? Coffee? We have mineral water here for you."

"Just get it over with. I won't be here more than ten minutes."

"Yes, sir. For the record, this is October 16th, 2010. My name is David Sanderson." As I talk, I see his eyes glaze over in impatience. "I am sitting here with Aryeh Shamgar in Tel Aviv. The time is –"

"You're a leftie, aren't you?" he cuts me off.

"Sir? I don't know what that has –"

"You're a leftie," he states.

"My job here has nothing to do with –"

"Your job here is to find out the 'truth' about how we drove the British occupation forces out of our country, how evil we were and how good they and the Arabs were."

"My job is to find out the truth about what happened, sir."

"And you happen to be a leftie."

"That has nothing to do with –"

"Why afraid to admit to the truth? Show some guts, show some balls. This is what our meeting is all about, isn't it? Guts. Guts and truth. Come on, tell me the truth."

I look into his eyes. He's sharper than the hi-tech geniuses I work with. He put me on the defensive on something I shouldn't be defensive about. The facts are on my side.

"Yes, sir," I say, not moving my gaze from his. "I'm a liberal."

"And lefties like you have been coming after me since the Seventies. Every two years, I'm invited to see another set of 'facts' or 'papers' that show that the assassination of Colonel Tanner was unjustified and cold-blooded. Every time they come in, all cocky. And every time, they are proven completely and utterly wrong."

"Yes, sir. That's right, sir."

"And every last one of them is a leftie. Imagine that. When they try to undermine my heroic act, they are actually trying to undermine the footing and legitimacy of the fight for this nation."

"Yes, sir. And although I am a 'leftie,' I would like nothing better than to realize that everything I learned about you in school was right. You are my hero, sir."

He thinks of answering, but after a second, he closes his mouth and locks his arms around his chest.

He *is* my hero, and has been my hero since childhood. He has been a hero for more than sixty years. A hero of the nation, given countless honors and citations, all because of this one assassination, the one that turned the tide of the British Mandate, the one that got the British government to decide they should relinquish their control over 'Palestine' and leave it for the Arabs and the Jews. On the waves of his public adulation, he was a Minister of Defense for ten years. When he left that office, he received countless offers from lucrative business companies. The successes he had had with the five he chose to run made sure he and his family would be set for generations.

This is the man whose life I have to crumble. This is the man whose heart may be too weak to withstand it. And I have to break his heart as a 'courtesy,' as requested by my bosses, before the news is released and the press does it to him.

"And like I said, sir," I continue, my voice even, "this is the last time."

His eyes watch me sharply, then, rather than be confrontational, he leans back calmly. "Dispense with the formalities, then."

"Ummm... all right, sir. This," I put my hand on a folder and spin it around so that he can read it, "contains information about our institute, Past Intelligence." He no more than glances at it. He doesn't have his reading glasses with him. "We are not a 'leftie' organization. In fact, most of our work is done for military intelligence and the Mossad." He raises an eyebrow with surprise and respect. "Though we *are* an independent foundation. This particular project, pertaining to you, is not military in any way, and therefore whatever facts we discover are not classified as Top Secret. The manner in which we uncover these facts, however, *is* so classified."

I move the folder to his side of the table. "What we do is, we use a new technology, developed at the Weizmann Institute, and available only in Israel so far." He squints at me, trying to see where I am leading him. "The technology deals with… Well, receiving information through time, from… the past. Basically, what it means is, we can 'hear' things that happened during a small window of time, between sixty-five and seventy years ago, and record them on…" I almost say a fancy word, and then I remember that I am talking to someone from a different era, "on tape."

"You can *hear* things from the past?"

"Yes, sir. Basically, we have a spy satellite… into the past. But always sixty-five to seventy years ago."

"And you… record those things?"

"Yes, sir. And everything's real. We are sanctioned, as I said, by the government and the military and the –"

"Sixty-five to seventy?" he cuts me short again, leaning forward. "Sixty-eight years ago, I assassinated Colonel Tanner."

"Yes, sir. And we have that recording. In fact, we have the recording of each and every conversation in British military circles that led to the conclusion that it was you who had been behind it and to the decision that you must be hunted down –"

"That can't be true," he says, but his eyes glisten with the memory of the past, a memory he has been living again and again every day, I'm sure, since it had happened. That long-lost past is his present still. He lives it daily. He breathes it. He speaks of it, and people speak to him about it. He is invited to other countries to speak of it. He makes the headlines when liberals like me try to discredit him. "You can't hear the past!" In this instant, I see in his eyes that the past I've listened to is his present.

"It *is* possible, sir, and we have put all the DVD's, uh... the *tapes* –"

"I know what a DVD is, and I know how to work it!"

"Yes, sir. We put all the DVDs of all the recordings in this folder for you. You can listen to them at home. They also include all the discussions in the top echelons of the Lehi that led to your hiding away, and even the first time you met Dinah, at her apartment. We hadn't known that that would be what we would hear, and we thought you would like to hear it, so we put it in for you. We didn't listen to anything else between you two that came later."

He puts his finger on the folder, "All that is here?"

"Yes, sir."

"And this technology is real? This is not a joke?"

"No joke, sir. Latest technology. Only we have it. And I trust you to keep it a secret."

He nodded, for an instant a dutiful soldier again, serving the interests of his nation, "Of course."

"Now... we also happened to record – and that is what we were actually looking for – everything that led up to the most famous assassination of a British soldier that the Lehi has ever carried out. We have a recording of the orders you received."

His eyes widen. "You do?"

"Yes, sir."

There is war in his eyes now. Something new appears there. It's as if he is fighting some urge. Then, in less than a second, it disappears, and age-old anger reappears. "If your recording does not match my version, word for word, then your entire institution is a sham!"

"No, sir. Our recording corroborates your version, word for word. It corroborates the version you've retold in dozens of documentaries and inquiries here and abroad about the orders you received and how you carried them out. All that is now corroborated by irrefutable facts."

His anger abates slightly. "Good." Then a sparkle appears in his eyes, "Can I see it? Is it on the DVDs?" That sparkle: It's young. It's like he's 23 years old again, talking to me with the energy of youth.

"Yes, sir. Of course we put it on the DVDs."

He takes a breath, and that breath feels cleaner and fuller than all his previous breaths. "Excellent."

"In fact, I'd like to play it for you right now, if you don't mind."

"No, no, not at all."

I nod and take the remote into my hand. There is a big HD screen to my right and his left. The HD is redundant, since there is nothing to look at. We only capture sounds, so we only play sound.

I press 'PLAY,' and the recording I have heard so many times before begins to play.

It begins with the sounds of the street. They aren't muffled by a closed window. This was the second floor in a stone building in Allenby Street, the temporary hiding place of Nathan Burnstein, one of the three Lehi leaders. This was in January of 1942, but the weather in Tel Aviv was unseasonably hot and humid. As Ben-Gurion had said, we were fighting the Nazis alongside the British as if there was no British occupation of our land, and we were fighting the British occupation as if there was no world war with the Germans.

You can hear the market outside: chickens, a donkey, and the occasional car engine sound – a sound that does not exist today.

His entire body perks up. "That sounds exactly like –" He looks at me. "You *do* have that technology?"

I nod and point to my ear, urging him to listen.

"Shamgar, come here," a man's voice urges.

Shamgar's mouth drops, and he slams his aged fist on the conference table. He immediately recognized the voice of Nathan Burnstein, his commander, the man who at that time led the military arm of the Lehi and would later lead a major political movement that would change the nation's history.

His voice doesn't sound like it was recorded sixty-eight years ago, because it wasn't. What we hear is the cleanest sound one can achieve with today's technology, because it was recorded by us only two months ago, as if we had a microphone in the room.

"Yes, sir, I'm here." This is Shamgar's voice. He sounds like a different person, his voice higher, his words faster, his rhythm different.

Shamgar doesn't react to this as powerfully as he did to his commander's voice. His body is frozen with intensity.

"Sit down, soldier."

"Yes, sir."

There is some scuffling of a wooden chair dragged on the floor tiles. Another car passes in the background.

"That's exactly what the street sounded like," Shamgar whispers, a tear in his eye. "I'd forgotten how much I remember."

I nod. The recording continues, "I have dire news and a great task, for which I need my best soldier."

"Yes, sir!"

"There is news from our intelligence about the latest plans of the Mandate Government."

"Yes, sir."

"Colonel Tanner has sent his recommendations to Churchill."

"That's exactly his voice," Shamgar's voice is a whisper. I press 'PAUSE.' "How did you do that?"

"It's the technology, I told you. I –"

"Turn it back on," he raps his fingers on the wooden desk. "Continue!"

I press 'PLAY,' and Burnstein continues to speak, "Our intelligence has intercepted a copy of it. The colonel believes a harder hand is required with the Jews. He requests full authority, so that following any violent action on our part, he will have complete freedom to arrest any Jew, guilty or not, and let them rot in jail. Guilty ones will be sent to prison in British East Africa. And the ones he deems most guilty will be executed."

Shamgar points at the screen. "Yes! That's right!" – I press 'PAUSE' immediately – "That's what he said! That's exactly what he said! I remember! That was it!"

I nod and wait.

He looks at me. "Did you stop it? Go on! Go on!"

I press 'PLAY.'

"But that goes against every principle the British claim to believe in," Shamgar's young voice booms. He was agitated and appalled.

"Yes, I would have said that!" the older Shamgar in front of me is riveted.

"Churchill would never approve!" The young Shamgar half shouts, sounding like a teenager whose voice was still breaking.

"Yes," Nathan Burnstein says. "These were my sentiments. But we have evidence, irrefutable evidence, that Churchill has sent word that Tanner's initiative is to be followed."

"What!" shouts the young Aryeh Shamgar.

The old Aryeh Shamgar nods. "That's right."

"Calm down, soldier."

"Yes, sir."

There was a sound of a wooden chair moving on a stone surface. Shamgar had apparently jumped out of his chair and was now getting back into it.

"Churchill is busy with the Germans and has no patience for us anymore. Are you following me?"

"Yes, sir!"

I look at Shamgar's eyes. It is as if he is having an epiphany.

"Churchill's message is so sensitive, and he was so afraid that it may find its way to us, that it has been entrusted to one man alone, a confidant. But despite Churchill's attempts, we had intercepted that message and received it before it got to Colonel Tanner. The courier will deliver the message personally to Tanner. In fact, it will be delivered later today." There is a slight pause. I always assumed Burnstein was letting Shamgar absorb the news. "We can stop this. It is up to you, Shamgar, to stop this. Colonel Tanner must die tonight. By your hands. Alone. Immediately after he receives the message. We will be sending a message of our own to Churchill that the Jews can be even more trouble than they have been so far, and that this new policy is unacceptable.

"I need a brave, fearless soldier. I need someone who can walk into the King David Hotel, into a ballroom full of British personnel, cool enough to appear as one of the help, cool enough not to be intimidated by anyone he sees there. I need someone brave enough to walk up to Colonel Tanner when he goes to the loo, put a bullet through his head, then walk out calmly through a room full of enemies. Are you that man, Shamgar?"

"Yes, sir!"

Every time I listen to this part of the recording, I keep thinking that the main difference between Shamgar's voice today and his voice then is that nowadays you can hear the past, you can hear the battles, the decisions, and the decades with which he had to live with those decisions. But back then, you couldn't hear any of that in his voice. His past was a child's past, a teenager's past, devoid of scars.

Burnstein continues. "Am I making the right choice by letting you take on this mission on which our independence hangs?"

"Yes, sir!"

"Good man. Go home, then. Prepare yourself. In an hour, a man will drop by with the plans. Open them when you're alone. Read them, memorize them, then burn them."

"Yes, sir!"

"An hour later, another man will drop off your escape plans. Open them when you're alone. Read them, memorize them, know them by heart, then burn them. This mission will be just you... alone."

"Yes, sir!"

"Dismissed, soldier."

"Yes, sir!"

I press 'PAUSE.'

"Basically," I say. "That ends this part of the recording. There are some noises, and you leave the room."

Shamgar is looking at me. He can hardly breathe.

"That's it!" he says, his voice filled with air. "That's the proof right there! You have the incontrovertible truth right there! That's just the way it happened!"

"Yes, sir."

He's looking around, trying to get a hold of his excitement, maybe even looking for more witnesses. "Every time I've claimed this was the reason we killed Tanner, the lefties and the British would say that that couldn't have been the case, that the British would never behave like that, that there was no such order. But there was, and they did! They did! That's the proof of everything I've been saying for decades!"

"Yes, sir." I want to add a 'however,' but he continues...

"Oh... Oh... That is unbelievable. I can't believe it... I was there again... I was there inside the room... This technology... I'm never going to have to justify my deeds again. I can go to my grave without a scandal hanging over me."

"Sir, I just –"

"You said I could have recordings of all of this?"

"Yes, sir. This, and all the other stages of the assassination and the escape. Of your and your wife's meeting. Of –"

"Amazing!" He is ecstatic. Suddenly, his entire life seems vindicated.

It hurts me that much more to bring him down from such a high to total abjection. "Sir, there is one more recording I need you to listen to."

"Yes, yes!" He is too excited. He is too happy. His guard is down.

"The following is a recording of events that took place thirty hours earlier, in Nathan Burnstein's hideout. In this recording…" I am losing nerve. I phrase it as delicately as I can, letting the recording bear the brunt of the blame. "In this recording, we can hear how Burnstein made the decision to assassinate Colonel Tanner."

"All right," Shamgar is energized. "Play it!"

"Yes, sir." I switch to the next track on the DVD, and it begins to play.

The street noises are different. They're quieter. There is no hustle. A muezzin is heard in the background – a call for the morning prayer from sixty-eight years ago. There is scuffling of a chair.

"Sit." This is Burnstein's voice. His tone is friendly, not at all the commanding voice he used with Shamgar.

Another wooden chair moves on stone. The muezzin's voice grows softer. A man is beginning to set up shop right underneath the window and calls out orders to his helper.

"What have you found out?" Burnstein asks.

"I followed the subject since yesterday afternoon until she went to sleep." This is another voice. Young – everyone was young in the Lehi – and serious and idealistic-sounding.

Shamgar straightens at the sound of that voice. "I know him! Who's that…?"

I don't press 'PAUSE.' The recording continues, "What did you find out?"

"The subject's day was quite routine, spending it –"

"Tsootsik!" Shamgar shouts. I press 'PAUSE.' "Zalman Berg! We called him 'Tsootsik'!"

That's right. Zalman Berg, a.k.a. 'Tsootsik' (which means 'pipsqueak'), was charged a year earlier to create Lehi's intelligence service from scratch, a task performed magnificently well, and was soon to become one of the Lehi's legendary leaders. Berg and Shamgar would be friends, though not close ones, for most of the 1950s, until Berg developed cancer and dies in 1962.

"Go on," Shamgar orders me. "This is unbelievable. Go on, go on!"

I rewind a bit and press 'PLAY.'

"The subject day was quite routine, spending at her home –" Berg was saying.

"Don't call her 'the subject'," Burnstein interrupts. "She's got a name, and this isn't about the resistance."

"Elisheva," the young Berg amends his statement, "was at her home all day and all the previous night."

" 'Elisheva'?" Shamgar whispers to himself. It sounds familiar to him, but he hasn't put the pieces together yet.

"At six o'clock, she began to dress for a night out," Berg continues to report.

"Yes?" Burnstein said.

"What are they talking about?" Shamgar whispers to me.

"Listen!" I say.

"At seven o'clock, she met with Colonel Tanner at Haled's fish restaurant on the Jaffa pier."

"She met with him?" Burnstein's voice is tight.

"They stayed there for an hour," Berg continues the report. "They seemed… amicable. Smiling a lot. Intimate in nature."

"Yes?" It is as if Burnstein was gritting his teeth.

"They left together and took a long walk on the beach to his home."

"Colonel Tanner's home?"

"Right."

Shamgar squints and looks at me. "There were two Elishevas?"

I shake my head and raise a finger, indicating there was only one.

"She stayed the night at his place… At their place."

Shamgar touches his cheek. "Why were they following the woman and not Tanner?"

"Listen," I say.

"At eight twenty-seven p.m. I took a risk and looked inside through the window. They were in the middle of a… sexual act. And then I –"

"All right, all right," Burnstein interrupts him. "Thank you. We got the data we wanted."

"We certainly did."

There was silence for a long time, then a chair was pushed back on the floor quickly: Burnstein got up suddenly, no longer able to sit down. "She told me she was never coming back to him. She told me it was over. She said she was revolted when he was near her. I felt she was…"

Shamgar looks at me, horrified. "Are you saying they had an affair?"

"I'm not saying anything. What we're hearing is what happened."

Shamgar listens. "Why am I not hearing anything?"

"They're quiet," I said. "Listen."

All we can hear is more and more vendors setting up shop in the street. The muezzin had finished his call for prayer. The silence lasts for more than a minute, in which I can see Shamgar's impatience growing.

Then, finally, we hear Burnstein's voice. "Tsootsik, Tsootsik… I can't let this happen. I can't lose her. I can't lose her to him. I can't let her do that. I can't have him… This is unacceptable…" There is another short silence. "I'm going to kill him! I won't let him be with my woman!"

"No," Shamgar, in front of me, says.

"You know I've always thought we should kill senior British officers," Berg says. "And who's more senior than Colonel Tanner? You're too fearful of killing the British."

"No no no," Shamgar shakes his head.

"Yes… Yes…" Burnstein says. "We *should* kill them. You're right. This will send a message to the Brits!"

"It will."

"That we're powerful."

"Yes."

"No!" Shamgar shouts. His eyes are screaming.

The recording continues, "That we're not to be messed with."

"Yes."

"All right. All right. Let me think. I need a devoted soldier, one who's willing to die for the cause. A brave soldier."

"No! False! No! False!" Shamgar is shaking his head almost uncontrollably.

"I've got just the man for you. Aryeh Shamgar."

"He's young, isn't he?"

"Not as young as the others. He's been around. He has nerves of steel. And he's been begging me for some real action. And… he's expendable."

"Lies! Lies! Lies! Lies!" Shamgar slams his open hands on the table, and then buries his face in them.

"Yes… Yes…" Burnstein is excited. "All right. I'll start making plans. I want Colonel Tanner's complete itinerary for the next few days. I need to know where and when would be the best place to strike."

"I'll have it for you in two hours."

"Excellent."

"We are not going to rest until that man is dead."

"No, we're not."

"No, we're not. Now go. You have a job to do."

There are noises of people walking on the floor, and then a door closing. Shamgar is looking at me. I look down. The recording isn't over.

Without warning, we hear Burnstein scream, "Whore! Whore! Whore! Whore!"

Shamgar's mouth opens in horror. "No! No! No!" And then Shamgar shouts at the screen, "What are you doing?!"

"Whore! Whore! Whore!" the screen shouts back, joined by the unmistakable sound of furniture being thrown against the walls and then kicked around. "Whore! Whore! Whore!"

I press 'PAUSE.' "This goes on for a while. Then there's a long silence. And then he begins to plan the assassination."

Shamgar's mouth is puckered tight, and he is shaking his head. He looks to the right. He looks to the left. His fingers begin to drum on the table. "It's a lie. It's a lie. It must be a lie. There is no way… You fabricated their voices somehow. You…"

"I assure you –"

He raises his hand to silence me. "I want to hear it again," he says.

His cheeks are red and puffy. I keep my calm. "All right."

I press a few buttons, and the recording is played all over again.

As he listens to it again, his eyes seem to sear through whatever they are focused on. I follow their gaze, but they are not focused on anything in the room. They are focused on the past. They are searing through to the past, just as our technology does.

"Again. I want to hear it again," he says once the recording has played through.

He listens again. And he listens again. And he listens again.

The more he listens, the more awake he seems. The more he listens, the shorter his breath becomes. The more he listens, the redder his cheeks become. A vein in his neck I haven't noticed before is making its presence known: His pulse is rising. I try to time it in my head. Around 130 a minute. Not good. Not for a ninety-year-old man.

After three times, in the middle of the fourth playback, he raises his hand and says, "That's enough."

Immediately, I fumble with the remote, find the button, and press 'PAUSE.'

He looks at me. His body is shaking. His fingers are shaking.

He looks away from me, at the table. He looks at his trembling hands. He reaches into his pocket. For a second, I think he's reaching for a gun. But of course, he isn't. He takes out his clamshell cell phone, opens it, is about to push a button – probably to call his wife – but he hesitates. Then he throws the cell phone at the wall. "Traitors! Fucking traitors!" he yells.

He looks down, gathering his breath.

Then he looks up, straight at me. His eyes are clear, not trembling, sharp – even sharper than when he had come in. Without moving his eyes, I can see that he is no longer looking at me but at the mirror behind me. "You've had your fun. You took your pound of flesh, and now you have your victory. Do you really need to keep filming this?"

I look behind me, at the mirror, and get a chill. It's true. Why do we need to film an old man losing his life cause? What historical purpose does that serve?

"Cut the feed," I say. "Stop the camera."

I hear voices on the other side.

"Stop the camera," I say.

A tiny red light, still seen through the one-way mirror, vanishes.

I turn to face him. "The camera is off."

"I'm sorry, sir," I tell him. "There was no reason to record this in the first place. I'll make sure it never gets used."

Shamgar looks at me with the eyes of a man who is lost. "It doesn't matter. You won the battle. Take your victory lap, and enjoy the applause…" he looks down, and there is a tear in his eye when he says, more to himself than to me, "While it lasts."

He puts his hands on the table, and it seems clear that he is about to pull himself up.

"Wait," I put my hand next to his, but do not touch him. "Stay. You don't have to go *immediately*." He looks at me. "Please. I meant what I said earlier, and back then, I had known what I was going to show you. You *are* my hero. You are still my hero. Take a couple of minutes to calm down. Drink some water. Have some coffee or tea. Breathe. Just… Stay here a couple of minutes more."

For a long time, he just thinks. Then he says, "I'll have some tea."

Even before the tea arrives – Wissotzky, no sugar, just the way I know he drinks it – Shamgar closes his eyes and sinks into his own world.

Within a minute, he begins to bang his open hand against the conference table in small baby slams. "The traitors…" – *slam* – "The traitors…" – *slam* – "The traitors…" – *slam* – "Such traitorous…" his fingers curl. "Such destructive… That something so filthy should be the cause for… The excuse!" He raises his voice on this last one. "Everyone who followed them… Everyone who believed in them… For *sex*?! Sex! … Such… traitors…"

Then he sinks into silence again, his eyes closed.

He drinks his tea in silence, his eyes far away from here. Suddenly, anger flares again. "He was my friend! My friend! For thirty years after we won our independence! For thirty years, until he died! Lied to me, embraced me, told me how brave I was. Looked me in the eyes. And never… never… said… anything…"

He takes another sip of his tea. "The treacherous bastard. Treacherous bastard!"

He raises his cup, but his hands shake, and some tea spills onto the table.

"I'm sorry." He looks aside, abashed.

"I can't believe it!" Five minutes later, he claps his hands together and gives me the look he had given me when we had met an hour ago. "I can't believe it! Not true! Fabricated! Great fabrication, but inconceivable."

"I assure you, the tech –"

"I don't need your words," he silences me. "Play it again. Then, after that, I want to hear something else. Play something else, something that can't be faked. I want to hear the time I met Dinah."

I nod. "All right."

I reach for the remote.

The track begins to play.

"Louder," he says.

His old ears probably heard only half of what I heard.

I turn up the volume.

Burnstein says a few more words, and Shamgar cries again, "Louder!"

And a few seconds later, "Louder!"

"Louder!"

"Louder!"

Then, almost at max volume, he is content. And he listens to the conversation again, to its very end.

I WAS PREPARED TO PLAY FOR HIM all the segments we had prepared, but it is his meeting with Dinah that breaks him. He listens to it, head bent over, following every sound. Then, once it is over, he raises his hand and says, "Enough."

I look at the remote and press 'STOP.'

When I look back up at him, he is holding his chest and leaning back. "Ow. Ow."

I leap up and run to the other side of the table.

"Is everything alright?"

"Yes."

I grab his hand to feel his pulse; he shoves it away.

"Stay away from me!"

"Shall I call for an ambulance?"

He shakes his head. Maybe he isn't able to speak. I reach for my cell phone.

He slaps it out of my hand.

"Enough," he says, still holding his chest. "Sit down."

I look at him. He looks straight into my eyes.

"Sit down. It's just pain. It will go away."

I freeze in place. I want to do what he said, but I am unable to move.

He looks away and takes a deep breath. With apparent effort, he lowers the hand that held his chest. I still don't move. He doesn't look at me.

His hand reaches down to his pocket, then up again. "I miss cigarettes," he says. His hand is at his pocket a second time, searching for something that hadn't been there in ten years. "I could use one right now."

Trembling, he brings his hand up. He leans forward, elbows on the desk. "This is a good time to start again." Without looking at me, he says, "Sit down."

Warily, I sit down.

HIS FINGERS ARE ON HIS FOREHEAD. He is licking his lips. Fifteen minutes have passed, and he is still hungry for cigarettes.

He hasn't looked at me in a few minutes. That's all right. I'm here for him, not the other way around.

"We died for them…" he suddenly whispers, maybe forgetting I was there. "We bled for them. I killed for them…"

He stares into space. Then he sighs. "No. We died for the nation. We bled for the nation. We killed for the nation. *I* killed for the nation. I killed… the wrong man for the nation."

A small, hollow laugh escapes him. "Ridiculous."

"You!" he aims an accusing finger at me. "You're probably happy. This fits so neatly into your political theories. We were all liars, weren't we? The entire nation is based on lies… That's what you think!"

"No, I –"

"Our entire nation is not based on lies. It is based on ideals and a need. There were a few bad apples… Some rotten, rotten apples. But they can't ruin it for the rest of us. The dream is just. The dream is true. And you can go to hell if you think that you can make a leftie out of me."

I shake my head. "No, no, I don't!"

"Rotten apples, and that's it!" He growls through his teeth.

MUSIC BEGINS TO PLAY.

He looks immediately sideways, I realize it's his cell phone, and then I remember it was on the floor where he had thrown it.

He tries to bend down to reach it.

"I'll get it for you," I leap up.

I grab the phone and give it to him, not looking at the caller.

He answers without looking at who was calling him. "Yes, Dinah…"

I'm sitting back down, and a sigh escapes me when I hear the name. This will not be over for him when he leaves this place.

"Yes, I'm all right. It's just taking too long… I promise, nothing bad… It might take a few hours, go to sleep. I'll take a cab."

"I'll pay for a cab," I say.

He shushes me with a finger. "I'm going to stay for a while, that's all. … Go to sleep. … Great… Thanks… Yes, yes, I'm all right. … Tell you all about it later. … Good… Good night."

He closes the cell phone, causing it to disconnect, and puts it on the desk.

His hand rests over it.

"Dinah…" he says softly and looks at me with soulful, twenty-three-year-old eyes. "I never would have met her if I wasn't on the run, if I hadn't assassinated…"

He looks down. His fingers touch the cell phone softly, and I imagine how he had touched his wife when they were young and had just met.

"I met his daughter, you know," he says after a ten-minute silence. He had been drinking one cup of tea after another for the last three hours.

I look up, the question in my eyes.

"His wife wouldn't meet with me. But I met his daughter."

"Whose daughter?"

"Colonel Tanner's," he says. His eyes are elsewhere again. He's reliving a meeting that had taken place decades ago. "He had a family, you know. A daughter. A wife. Who, evidently, he was cheating on. But a family, he had a family. I killed a man with a family for the Cause, not for a…" he trails off.

"I met his daughter, you know," he says again after a while. "Back in, uh, '64. She was just getting married, in her early twenties. I, uh… She wanted to meet with me. I immediately agreed. There were concerns she would try to kill me. I said, No, don't worry about it." He stops for a while. This is where he would have taken a great gulp of smoke.

"How was she?" I say.

"You know… Young… She understood… She wanted to hear it from me… She wanted to hear the why… She wanted to know how he was… how he was during those last minutes… She wanted a missing piece of her father."

He trails off again, then continues. "I told her he was a great and honorable man. That is why he was a choice target. I told her he died with dignity. I told her I was sorry for her private tragedy and that it wasn't personal."

When he trails off again and does not continue, I ask, "How did she take it?"

He shrugs. "All right. No anger there. She hardly even knew him. She just wanted to know."

"Did she say anything important?"

He shrugs. "No. His wife, her mother, never agreed to meet with me. That was all right. It's understandable."

"Yeah."

"But, the thing is…"

"Yeah?"

"He had a family. A daughter who is now a grandmother. And a wife who remarried. He had a family. I destroyed his family… for my commander's shag in the bed. That's why his family was destroyed."

I nod. I don't know what is the right thing to say now.

"Yeah," he says. "For a shag in the bed."

"Decades I spent on this. Decades.

"These last three decades, this is practically the only thing I did. Meetings like this. Invited to lectures and seminars. Answering hecklers and ill-wishers… The documentary they did on me… following me around for a year… needs to be revised. Nothing is true. No reason for it anymore." He looks down, ashamed. "I was wrong… I was mistaken… My cause was unjust… No, my cause was just, my deeds were unjust…"

"You couldn't know. As far as you were concerned, you had a just cause to assassinate him and protect your people."

"A man is dead. A family is dead. Bystanders were hurt. What does that matter?"

"The tide of war turned because of that event. The British Mandate began to lose its spirit."

"Yeah… That's good. It's good that it happened." He falls silent, no doubt thinking about that point. Then, after a while, he says, "The results were accidental, weren't they? It wasn't because…" He shrugs again and puts his fingers to his lips as if he is smoking. "Just a lucky accident."

His lips curl. "People think I'm brave."

I look up. He had been silent for something like twenty minutes. "You are brave."

"Pfah. I'm not brave. I just like to think I'm brave. No, no, I am brave." He waves dismissively at his own thoughts. "I'm rambling."

After five minutes of silence, he starts again. "*Other* people think I'm brave."

I don't respond this time. He already knows I'm one of those people.

"Other people…" he holds his forefinger tight against the desk and moves the rest of his hand this way and that way, like a child. "Other people… they thought I was brave… I got honors… honors on top of honors… There was a ceremony just last year… Golda had made me a minister. Do you think she would have done that if not for the…?"

He looks down like a chastened child. "I'm sorry."

WHEN HE DOESN'T SAY ANYTHING for a few more minutes, I ask him, "What are you sorry for?"

He looks at me with doe eyes. "I should call her."

"Dinah?"

"His daughter. Tell her I'm sorry."

I think about that. "Maybe you shouldn't do that. It was so long ago. It's history. We're just fixing history here, not people."

"I'm living it still, every day. She's living it still, every day."

He purses his lips, and tears begin to form in his eyes. "No, I'm not brave. I just like to think I am."

He sighs, and seems to deflate in front of me.

"I WAS A GOOD MINISTER, DAMN IT!" He slams his fist on the table, suddenly enraged again. Slamming his fist on something is a mannerism he had been famous for doing during cabinet meetings. "I was a good minister!"

"Yes, sir. I –"

"I did good. I helped build the nation! I fought for military acquisitions that saved us in wars, created connections that served our nation…" When he trailed off, more light seemed to leave his eyes. "What does it matter?"

And in his chair, he seems to deflate even more.

"NO ONE WILL REMEMBER anything of me. They won't remember the good I did. They won't remember I was an accomplished member of the Knesset. They won't remember I was a successful CEO of four companies."

"Five," I correct him.

He squints for a second, then nods. "Yes, five. I brought success to whatever I touched. Burnstein took that away from me. At that moment in time, when I was twenty-three, he handed me my future. But he also took away my future." His eyes begin to look here and there as if searching for something. "He took that away from me."

He shuts his eyes and puts five fingers on his forehead. "I would never have met Dinah if it weren't for this."

He opens his eyes, and he seems like a shy sixteen-year-old suddenly. "I wonder if she would have liked me if not for… She stood by me all this time… She believed in what I did… She believed in me… Our entire lives… Together… Together…"

He wipes a tear from his left eye, then looks at me as if he was caught stealing. I look away.

"Don't think that makes me a leftie," he isn't aggressive now. It's four-thirty in the morning. Most of his strength has left him. He is now completely deflated, and his voice is raw. And yet he sits there, unable to leave, running through thoughts in his mind, thoughts and scenarios I couldn't begin to guess.

"Hey!" he says, snapping me out of my own thoughts.

"Yeah?"

"You didn't make me a leftie, you know. Don't think this takes any of the emotional, intellectual, spiritual, historical basis on which we built this nation, on which I built myself." I shake my head, about to tell him I didn't think that, when he looks down, and in an even weaker voice, he says, "What does it matter? It doesn't matter."

"I remember one of my first missions…"

It's been eight hours since he had learned the truth. Neither of us has left the room. As he speaks, his eyes are floating, seeing a past that hasn't been there for more than seventy years. "We were lying down on top of one of the hills outside Jaffa's open-air market…" He speaks softly, dreamingly. "We thought we were snipers… Our mission was to shoot Arabs and cause as much mayhem as possible… I was the lookout. I wanted so much to be the sniper. … I wanted to kill Arabs… I remember thinking that: I wanted to kill Arabs… But no Arab adults came when we were there, only children… Then someone ran over, told us that the mission was aborted, that we had to leave… I wanted to kill so badly… We were children, playing children's games."

He looks at his right arm, deep in thought.

I'm afraid to move my hands or even shift my weight in my chair. He seems so fragile to me, so broken. Any movement on my part might cause him to snap out of it and leave. And then he would go through the rest of it on his own, at home.

I can't stop looking at him.

Suddenly, he mumbles, "Children's games… Children's games… I haven't been a child in…" and his eyes are suddenly infinitely fatigued, "…in *so* long."

"MY FATHER ALWAYS SAID… When you grow up… You have to work. Work is food. Work is respect. A man who does not work has no dignity… I kept true to that all my life… The minute the war was over, I got a job… Even during the Mandate, I was working for the freedom of the nation… The Knesset… Building a new nation, a good nation, working for the government…"

Suddenly he squints. "Why did I think of that? Why this talk about everything my father had told me? Why…" And then realization appeared in his eyes. And with it, almost immediately, there is light. A spark of light, for the first time in hours. "Ah! I was going to be a gardener! When I was just a kid, that's what I wanted to do. Yes!" He smiles, sadly. "My mother learned about this, so she waited for my father to get home. She spoke with him, and then he came to talk to me. I needed a real job, he said. Being a gardener, that is not a real job." And as he speaks, the spark in his eyes grows slightly brighter. "I'd forgotten about that."

"I ALWAYS HAD A GREEN THUMB when I was a kid. I had a small garden plot behind my family's home… I used to go in and look at it and take care of it every day. … I figured out how much shade each flower needed… I figured out when to water the plants and when it was best to keep them thirsty a bit… I took out books upon books from the library, telling me about the different kinds of plants. And when my Dad came to me and explained that I needed to be serious… I dropped everything about gardening… I never took another book from a library. Can you imagine that? Not one book."

He looks at me, and there seems to be a gleam in his eye.

For a second, I start to believe he was beginning to feel better. But it couldn't be. His world had collapsed.

He had been quiet for fifteen minutes, looking at his fingers as they moved on the table. It looks to me like he is playing a very slow piano or as if his fingers are playing some sort of game. His gaze follows his fingers with mild fascination, as if surprised by their action.

He breaks the silence, "I wanted a plant nursery… wall to wall with roses… daffodils… lilies…" his fingers are still playing on the table, and his mildly fascinated gaze follows them. "Persian alliums… the cyclamen, before they became a protected species, were fantastic… I love them to this day…"

He leans back, and I could swear that for a minute, he was resting.

"I haven't touched flowers in decades…" He hadn't spoken about anything that had to do with the assassination in forty minutes now. "I haven't looked at them… No, that's not true. I've looked. From afar, when I happened to come across… I never bothered thinking about it, but I remember my eyes getting stuck on the sight of a beautiful garden, and every time that happened, Dinah would ask me what's the matter, why was I daydreaming…"

He smiles. And there is a longing in his smile. Is that longing not sadness about all that he had lost today? For a split second, I think it might be. But, no. I'm wrong about that.

He looks at me, and his eyes are as sharp as they were when he came in. But they are also different. They are still sharp, but neither aggressive nor defensive. "So what if gardening isn't a vocation?" his eyes look at me, sharp but not searing. "I mean, so what? Who cares?"

I shake my head. I don't know what we're talking about anymore.

He leans back, and he seems taller and not as sickly-thin as when he came in. "I loved my childhood, Mr. Sanderson. I loved my childhood."

I don't understand what he's trying to say, but I have to say something. So I smile back at him and answer his words. "Me too."

"Did you?" he says, smiling. But my own smile cracks.

He slams both hands on the table, not aggressively, but to help him get up. "Well," he said. "Time to go home."

I stand up when he stands up. "Are you sure?" It's ten past six a.m.

He turns to face me with the briskness of a young man. "I'm sure. Thank you for all your work, Mr. Sanderson. And your honesty. And your understanding during this night."

He offers his hand, for the first time. I shake it heartily. "It was an honor to meet you, sir."

He shrugs it off. "If you say so." He doesn't care about that anymore.

I look at him as he leaves the room. If I didn't know better, I would say by his gait, from behind, that the man was forty years old. He's tall, his back is straight, and he is no longer dragging his feet. He walks with energy and lightness of foot.

Right before he disappears, as he goes out the door, he looks back at me and nods. And I notice that all his wrinkles have disappeared.

Five Four Three Two One

By Hila Benyovits-Hoffman

Translated by Rehavia Berman

BORN IN ISRAEL IN 1976, Hila Benyovits-Hoffman has been an avid bookworm from the moment she could read. Her teen experiments in poetry and prose were enhanced by a four-year course of art history and Western philosophy at Tel Aviv's Camera Obscura Art School. She went on to obtain an Arts and Education B.A. degree from Leeds University's Israeli extension and a graduate degree in Gender Studies from Bar Ilan University, where she wrote a thesis about modern witches, focusing on the mutual influence between Wiccan history and ideology and the second-wave feminist movement.

Hila's popular blog in Hebrew, "Van Der Graaf Your Sister," brought her widespread recognition and became a platform for her social activism and a vehicle for promoting a better understanding of mental health as well as feminist issues, based on her very personal experiences. She returned to writing prose in the speculative genre in 2012, publishing stories in various online and paper publications by the Israeli Society for Science Fiction and Fantasy. In 2014, her story "The Last Page" won the Best Story Award in the competition held by the Olamot convention. In 2015, she won the Geffen Award for best original story for the story featured herein. Hila's story "Open (Or: the Light that Shines through the Keyhole)" is shortlisted for the 2021 Geffen Award; the winners are yet to be announced.

Whenever she manages to take some time off her day job as a technical translator, Hila continues writing short stories for future publication. She hopes to venture into book-length speculative fiction, when circumstances permit.

OK, listen. Something happened.

I woke up in the bathtub with my robe and the sides of the tub covered in blood. There were thin lacerations on my wrists. I guess most had already closed, and the blood had clotted by the time I was fully awake. I felt a little dizzy and tired, probably from the loss of blood, but I managed to recover and get out, so I really hope that if any damage was caused, it wasn't too great.

Ariana, you didn't leave anything written in the diary. Why did you do it? I'm scared spitless.

I had no choice but to report this to the Oversight Committee. I'm just so worried about what will happen when Ariana comes back. Ariana, sweetie, I'm not mad. We all have tough days. I just hope that it'll all be much better by the time you return. I love you. We all love you.

Procedural note: Adam, tomorrow morning, you too have to appear before the Oversight Committee. They questioned me for hours today. They'll likely want to interview you too, and maybe the rest of us. Don't try to hide anything from them; somehow, they already knew about Rani and his fake bracelet, even though we hadn't told them anything. Damn,

I really didn't want to talk about Rani at the Institute, or anywhere else. Crap, I'm so stupid sometimes.

Yuli, I picked up your package from the post office with the fabrics you ordered. They're beautiful! Don't forget to take pictures to show me how it comes out. And if anyone doesn't like it, they can bite me. This means you too, Adam.

Avi, remember to let the cat back the moment you wake up, because it's already a bit chilly outdoors this time of year. Two weeks ago, you'd forgotten to let him in, and the poor thing huddled in the blankets in his kennel and made angry faces at Ariana when she finally let it in. Oh, and I also threw away your toothbrush. It's all worn out. Adam or Yuli, can you please buy Avi a new toothbrush? I didn't have the time today because of the committee and all, and it's already very late.

Ariana, sweetie, big hug, I'm waiting to hear from you.

"NAME?"

"Abigail Hydra."

"Hydra three, right?"

"No, two."

The clerk in the gray suit noted on the form before him: "Hydra 08\B; Sequence: 2; Name: Abigail."

"Very well," he said. "Please sit down outside Room 10. You will be called in."

Rooms one to five were the usual therapy rooms for Group A, and rooms six to ten were designated to Group B. *That's how it goes,* Abigail thought bitterly as she walked down the over-cooled corridor. *You become a number to them, part of a sequence, a cog in the machine. Everyone is thrown in, ground down, and thrown out as a confused mush, and then they expect us to collect all the smashed pieces and put them together somehow. You're Series 08 first, then Group B, then Sequence 2, and only lastly Abigail, a twenty-five-year-old person, or five persons, depends on who you ask. He didn't even notice that I was so afraid, so drenched in cold sweat; he just carries on filling in my details on the form with complete indifference. I'm just another cow in the herd. What does he care that this cow was almost slaughtered last night?*

Abigail stopped at the door to Room 10 and was about to press her identification bracelet to the automatic scanner. Something made her stop before she held her wrist up to the chip reader. *Actually, that's not true,* she thought. *After all, the clerk asked for your name before all the other details, and to be honest, you yourself have no idea what his name is. He's been working here for six months now, and all you know about him is that he's the clerk in the gray suit with the Institute's logo on its sleeve. He too is a kind of cow in this slaughterhouse.*

Abigail dropped her trembling hand to her side and glared defiantly at the door, as though the board of wood and metal was to blame for it all. She stared at the number "10" on the door for another moment, then turned on her heel as firmly as the lump in her throat permitted and walked back to the clerk in the gray suit.

The clerk looked up at the young woman returning to his counter. "What's wrong? Is there no one in the room?"

"I don't know; I haven't gone in yet," replied Abigail. "I just wanted to ask, what's your name."

"Ask what?" the clerk's eyes widened in surprise.

"What's your name. You've been here for months, and I've never asked."

The clerk was silent for a moment. "Yoel," he finally answered. "My name is Yoel."

"Nice to meet you, Yoel. I'm Abigail."

"Erm... yes," replied the gray clerk, whose name was Yoel, still slightly bewildered.

"Abigail Hydra?" said Abigail, as though trying to jog his memory.

"Yes..."

"Also known as '08\B\2'...?"

Abigail and Yoel stared at each other for a few seconds, and then started laughing. Yoel extended his hand. "I'm sorry, it's just that none of the Hydras has ever asked my name. It's a bit hard to know here..."

"... what is and isn't allowed," Abigail completed the sentence.

"Yes, exactly," smiled Yoel. "But I suppose we're allowed to exchange names. Very nice to meet you, Abigail."

Abigail continued to shake her new friend's hand a few seconds longer than required by proper etiquette. Now, when he was no longer just the clerk in the gray suit, it was as though an invisible cloak of distance had been removed from him. She could notice things she'd missed before: a dimple that appeared only in his right cheek, never in his left, laughter lines in the corners of his eyes... and his eyes, of that elusive green shade that sometimes seems brown and sometimes blue, depending on the time of day and the rays of light hitting the retinas. She stole a glance at his wrist, just to be sure. There was no bracelet there and no thin lacerations that scabbed over just a few moments ago. A chill went down her spine, as though she had been rudely thrown back to the moment she'd awoken to a night of pain, confusion, and a burning sense of betrayal.

"Abigail?" A woman in a blue robe, with the familiar Institute logo on her sleeve, poked her head around a bend of the hallway. "We didn't see your call on the scanner. Would you prefer not to come in?"

"No, I just stopped here for a moment," Abigail replied. "I need to talk to you."

"So come in," said the woman, gesturing down the hallway. With a nod and an apologetic smile, Abigail took her leave from her new friend, formerly the clerk in the gray suit, and hurried after the woman to Room 10.

Orna, who was walking briskly in front of her, was one of her favorite inspectors. She wasn't a hyperreactive or hysterical type, like some of the other inspectors. This was why Abigail hoped that the complicated news she was about to deliver would be received with understanding, and handled with sensitivity and moderation. That wasn't always the case. There were quite a few stories floating around about homes in which dozens of cameras and microphones and motion detectors were planted, about secret agents from the Institute who shadowed Hydras suspected of abnormal behavior, following them day and night. The Hydras from Group A of Series 08 liked to spread a story – it may have been nothing more than a myth – that Hydras of Series 04 to 06 hadn't died young because of medical complications, as they were told. Instead, they mysteriously disappeared after they'd started to act contrary to the Institute's directives. The Institute's inspectors were dismissive of such stories, but the rumors still floated around and refused to die.

Now Abigail will have to sit before the inspectors and explain, as calmly as she could, how she had woken up bleeding this morning. How concerned she was for Ariana's safety. And how she has no way to know what happened because Ariana will only return in five days and did not leave any explanation. Is this a mistake to report to the Oversight Committee? Perhaps it would have been better to deal with it among themselves, without worrying whether they'd all be locked up in the hospital until Ariana returned and could be questioned, and who knows what they'll decide to do with them in the end?

In all her twenty-five years, Abigail has never been afraid for her life. When she sat down that morning at the long, familiar table of the Oversight Committee, she was engulfed by an overwhelming urge to survive. She must tell. Should she cease to exist in a few days, at least they would know why.

"Good morning, everyone," said Orna with a radiant smile. "Abigail, you remember Yaron and Dan," she said, pointing at the inspectors who sat to her left and right – "We're glad you've come to visit. It's been a while since we'd had a report from you."

"Yes," Abigail replied, "I've been a little busy." She placed her hand on her right leg, which began to tap on the floor of its own accord, as though wishing to flee the room.

Orna studied the tense young woman for a moment. "Abigail, there is no need to be so nervous. We already know, and we're glad you've decided to tell us."

Abigail's heart missed a beat.

"How do you know? It only happened this morning..." her voice trembled.

"This morning?" wondered Dan, the inspector sitting to Orna's right. "I thought it's been going on for two months now."

"What... what are you talking about?"

"What are *you* talking about?" the inspector retorted. "What only happened this morning?"

"One moment," Orna raised her hand. "I want to set things straight. First of all, Abigail, we know that for two months now, you've been seeing a young man posing as a Hydra. He managed to obtain a fake ID bracelet. The bracelets are monitored, and following on a report we received from another Hydra regarding an unidentified man passing himself off as one, we have located him and put an end to his deception."

Abigail remained silent and fixed her gaze on the floor.

"I understand that it's difficult, but it's imperative to report such cases to us. This guy didn't mislead only you. Every day he picked on a different girl, peddling this lie to worm some favor from her. I don't know how he persuaded you not to turn him in, but it's important to me that you know that even if you don't report to us, someone is looking out for you."

Abigail raised her eyes.

"Looking out for me? Following me, you mean."

"You're all too important to us," said Yaron, the third inspector. Then he added, in a softer tone, "We understand the sacrifice you're required to make, so it's important for us to protect you from people like that."

"Who told you? Which Hydra? I want to know."

"Does it really matter? A Hydra who cares about you, just like we do," said Orna.

"It's not her decision. Rani... this guy... at least he didn't treat me like a number, and he..."

Orna sighed.

"I understand that he was nice to you. These are hard enough, the relationships between Synthetics and Normals, even without basing them on lies."

Abigail quickly wiped her cheek to prevent her teardrops from falling. "It wasn't all a lie."

Orna looked at the tearful young woman. "I'm sorry, but that's not true. He posed as a Hydra to gain your trust him so that you'd agree to..."

The rest of the inspector's explanation died on her tongue. She understood. It wasn't easy to deal with the first time, especially when you realize you've been used, like plenty of other women, by a charming fraud with no scruples. She would need time to grieve and recover. Perhaps it's best to change the subject. Orna cleared her throat. "Okay, enough about that man. He has been taken care of and will never harm anyone else. Tell us, what happened this morning?"

Abigail swallowed her tears and breathed in deeply. Then she raised her head and looked straight at the inspectors.

My head aches. I've had a terrible day, so here's a short recap. I went to the Oversight Committee. They gave me a load of crap about how important it is that we remain alert to anything that could happen with Ariana because it affects us all. I told them that I have no idea what happened, but Ariana, I trust you one hundred percent and won't for a minute accept the idea that you would want to hurt us, so let them be alert to whatever they want. I'm not playing that game. I think we should have kept it all between us, and above anything else, we should have given Ariana a chance to explain.

Procedural notes: Yuli, you too, of course, will have to go to the committee, so the first item on your agenda in the morning is a visit to the Institute. And try to wear something that doesn't look like a curtain with unicorn puke. Oh, and Abigail, remove all worry from your mind. I bought Avi a new toothbrush. And I'm guessing he'll tell you, in two days, exactly what you can do with this toothbrush as far as he's concerned.

Rereading the recap, I come across as kind of angry – it really has been a tough day. Seriously. Try explaining to your partner that the committee got all up in your ass because they think that your sister may be trying to kill you all. Abigail, do you see why we should keep things to ourselves? I'm not mad at you; I get that you were scared. But can't we show a little more patience?

Yuli, I am so sorry. I think you're going to wake up with a migraine from hell. Wear whatever you want, my dear lunatic. Big, big hug for all of you. We'll get through this, you'll see. Love you.

"I'M JUST SAYING IT'S GOOD that you wore a long-sleeve shirt."

Doron passed his finger gently over the thin red lines stretched across Adam's wrists.

"Your mother would most likely have reacted hysterically to someone trying to kill her son."

Adam growled in response, turning around so that he spooned Doron from behind. "My mother loves Ariana very much. It's best if she doesn't think of her like that." He laid his head in the crook of Doron's shoulder. "All our parents get along well, except for Ariana's; they are a bit snobbish, always ducking dinner parties."

"Have you thought of talking to them? Maybe they know something about what happened to Ariana?"

Adam growled again.

"That's it, you switched to growling? You forgot how humans speak?" Doron teased, gently pinching Adam's thigh. "Or are you just not in the mood for me?"

"Sorry," Adam replied tiredly, "I think I'm developing a headache. I've been running around a lot today. The Oversight Committee this morning was a nightmare, then lunch with my parents..."

"Then sex with me, which is a surefire recipe for a headache."

Adam counterattacked with another growl and a tickling offensive, which turned into a friendly wrestling bout. In the end, Adam pressed his forehead to Doron's and sighed again.

"I'm sorry. Nothing's going right for me today."

"That statement is not only fatalistic but factually incorrect to boot," replied Doron and gently stroked his lover's neck. "Why don't you tell me already what happened at the Oversight Committee? Instead of growling at me like a bear with chickenpox?"

"How do you know what a bear with chickenpox sounds like?"

Doron remained silent. Then he rolled onto his back and detached himself from Adam. For a few seconds, the only sound in the room was that of paws digging in the litter box in the other room after the cat had finished its business.

Adam turned on his side, imploringly stroking the black curls lying on the pillow. "Don't be mad at me. It's not you. It's just hard for me to talk about it."

"Start from the beginning; after that, it'll be easier," his partner replied encouragingly and stroked his chest."

"OK," Adam sighed. "I got up, saw Abigail's report. Obviously, she panicked and told the committee everything without thinking that maybe it would be best to deal with it among ourselves. So I went to the committee this morning, prepared for a little more panic."

"Maybe not panic, but don't you think there's some cause for concern?"

"No," replied Adam decisively. "Ariana's not stupid. As I see it, there are only two possible scenarios: One, it was an accident that happened just before the changing of the shifts on the first day. Two, she had a bad moment and wanted to pass it on to Abigail and the rest of us, and for some reason, couldn't write it down in our shared journal."

"And there's no way, you think, that she really tried to kill herself?" Doron challenged him."

"To kill yourself by slitting your wrists, you cut along the arm, not across," argued Adam.

"Maybe she didn't know that?"

"It's Ariana. She knows everything. She's the smartest person I've ever met."

"Technically, you've never met her."

Adam gave his partner, who was still stroking his chest, a sad look. His eyes were always so warm, so embracing.

"You understand why it's so hard for me to talk about it? I don't want to write, like Abigail did, that everything will be alright, and we all love her and all that babble. I want to hold her, and I can't. I have no idea what she's going through, but I know for sure she would never harm her brothers and sisters. Not consciously."

"And that's what you told the committee?"

"Yes."

"And what did they say?"

Adam growled again.

"Stop with the growling already... My boyfriend is a Hydra, not a wild beast..." Doron chided him.

"We're both Hydras. Not just any, we're Sequence 3 Hydras. Imagine if I were 2 and you were 4, or *vice versa*. We'd never meet," Adam joked. Then he turned serious.

"Well, the committee. They answered that 'my loyalty to a sister Hydra is most commendable,' and that it was really touching that I trust her one hundred percent, but 'we have to prepare for all eventualities,' including the possibility that Ariana will have to spend her next shift, maybe her next few shifts, in a locked room under around-the-clock observation. I told them that if that happens, I'm cutting my wrists as well."

"Adam!!!"

"Of course I'm not going to do it. But they refuse to get it through their thick heads that I'm a lot closer to Ariana than they could ever understand, no matter how many cameras they stick in her face."

"And now they may stick cameras in your face too," Doron got angry. "What did you have to threaten them for?"

"So they'd understand that this decision is also ours, if not *only* ours."

Now it was Doron's turn to sigh. "Great. I found myself a partner with principles, full of piss and vinegar."

"Good for you indeed," Adam winked at him. Doron tried to keep his reproachful face straight, but in a moment, his angry expression dissolved into a burst of giggles.

"OK, smartass, it's ten-thirty, and we both have to prepare to change shifts."

After Doron left, Adam quickly changed the sheets and then rushed into the shower. Under the running water, he tried to imagine that he was also washing off any lingering thoughts, so that no shred of them would pass on. He felt a twinge of guilt for hiding from Doron his real reason for not turning to Ariana's parents. The Oversight Committee told him that morning that the inspectors had already tried to involve them, and they were uncooperative and asked to cut off all contact. *They've never truly appreciated their amazing daughter,* Adam thought.

Maybe they had a nasty fight. My wonderful sister, how did you wind up with parents like these? You deserve better.

It was already five minutes to eleven, and Adam was now clean, combed, and dressed in a white robe. He finished writing his report in their shared journal, massaged his aching temples, and returned to the bedroom. Suddenly he remembered something and turned with a colorful curse to search the house frantically for the cat.

"Hercules! *Pssst pssst*, Hercules, come here!"

A black cat with a white bib and white paws peeked from one of the rooms. Adam used leftover tuna from the fridge to coax the whiskered creature to the kennel in the yard and closed the back door. Then he hurried to the bedroom, lay down on the bed, and closed his eyes. He had only a few seconds left.

MAY I SAY THAT THIS was the best day I've ever had?

OK, let's start from the beginning. Adam, I found the note you left in my pants pocket. Thank you... It gave me a smile to start the day with. And the suit doesn't look like something a unicorn threw up on, you dummy. It's called variety. You should try it sometime, instead of all your black and gray clothes. If you annoy me too much, one day I'll dye all your pants fuchsia purple.

Abigail, thanks for picking up the package for me! Would you like me to sew you a skirt from the green cloth with the birds-of-paradise print? I think it would look great on you, and the color really goes with your eyes. Ariana, sweetie, when you come back, I'll design something for you too. Just take your pick. I owe you a huge thank you as well. You know why.

The committee experience today was totally different than usual. For the first time, they called me by my real name. Not to humor me, but officially. You know, Orna is terrific, not at all intimidating like I always thought. I'm no longer afraid to write everything here, so you too can treat me as I am. Anna only exists now in my file at the Oversight Committee, as a birth identity and nothing more. Thank you for your efforts in coming together to defend me. You won't have to do it again, and I have no words to express what a relief that is. I'll never be exactly who I want to be, but at least I won't pretend to be someone I'm not.

Procedural notes: Avi, I'm sorry if you have a runny nose tomorrow. I couldn't resist temptation and went out to pet Hercules. Such a cutie. He was so shocked! Then I wiped my nose for hours, but it was absolutely worth it. Abigail, a nice man named Yoel who works at the Oversight Institute asked me to say hello to you for him today. He seems to really like you, and unlike that previous piece of – well, you know what I think of him – who lied to you, he impressed me as a sincere and forthright person. And he's cute too... I'm all for it.

By the way, Avi, your Magic is already here. She asked, sweet as always, to sit here by my side and wait for you to arrive. Of course, I agreed. I'm so happy for both of you!

"Meow!"

"That won't help you."

"*Mrrrow...*"

"Hercules, you're adorable, but I can't let you inside. I'm allergic, and I've just finished vacuuming the house for the day. Take a short nap on your pillow in the kennel."

"*Meowwwwww!!*"

Yuli sighed. The stubborn creature had been adopted two years earlier and still hasn't got used to the idea that he should be left outside every five days. Brain the size of a peanut, what can you do. Why do cats always want to cling to those who most want to get away from them? And why the hell was he standing in the living room having a conversation with a cat through a glass door?

The chime of the doorbell interrupted his train of thought. "Damn," he muttered and slowly shuffled to the door. *Who comes to visit at such an hour? Whoever it is, I have no time for chitchat. I have to go to the Oversight Committee, and what's more, with the remnants of a migraine from last night.* He pulled the door wide open, all prepared to decline the unexpected visit politely, and then froze. At the door stood Orna, the inspector from the Institute, meticulously dressed in a skirt and jacket suit.

"Good morning Anna. How are you? I'm sorry to barge in on you like this. I hope I'm not interrupting anything important."

"No, not at all," Yuli answered quickly and ran his fingers through his messy bangs. "Come in, please."

The inspector followed him into the living room. Bright clothes strewn on the sofas, a half-finished cup of coffee cooling on the table.

"Sorry," said Yuli and quickly picked up the clothes and the cup to give the room a semblance of order. "I was just trying to decide what to wear today."

"No problem. Your clothes are always so colorful," Orna replied graciously and sat in the armchair. "It's really nice. You sew them yourself, right?"

"Most of them, yes."

"And your combinations are always interesting and creative. Embroidered vests over flouncy pants... and the wonderful outfit you wore last week. A sort of coat combined with culottes. A really innovative design."

"Thank you very much. Would you like some coffee? There's a great cake; Abigail baked it. She always bakes when she's stressed..." Yuli quickly shut his mouth when he realized what he was saying.

"No, I'm good, thanks. And it's quite understandable that Abigail is feeling stressed. It's been a tough time for her. On that matter, we owe you our thanks. You did a good job, exposing that guy who tricked her and pretended to be a Hydra so she'd fall for him."

Yuli lowered his eyes.

"I don't feel comfortable going behind my sister's back. But I didn't want to wait for her to return so that she wouldn't have to confront him. She's so sensitive... That's why I told you first."

"Understandable, and quite commendable. By the way, how did you find out that he's an imposter?"

"Abigail took a snapshot of him in secret, to show us his picture. Two days later, I saw him in the street."

"And he looked exactly the same."

"Precisely. Meaning, he's no Hydra."

"I think it's wonderful that you wanted to protect your sister. Even if you had to bite the bullet and use our help to do so."

Yuli blushed. He avoided meeting the inspector's eyes; instead, he gazed out through the glass door.

"It's not as if I have anything against the Oversight Committee, of course... It's just that we like to keep things among ourselves."

"I know. But sometimes you have to involve someone from the outside too, right?"

"Right."

Orna crossed her legs and smoothed an invisible crease in her skirt.

"Good. I'm glad you agree with me, Anna, because another sister of yours has done the exact same thing, only for you."

"What do you mean?"

"The last time Ariana was here, she came to speak with the Oversight Committee. She argued that we have to stop following the Hydras covertly and start relating to you, more than we used to. I explained to her that the surveillance might be unpleasant. Still, it's necessary, because your physical and mental well-being is important for this ongoing research, and therefore we have to know every detail about your lives."

Orna lowered her foot to the ground and leaned forward, her fingers laced on her knees. Her gaze caressed Yuli's profile, while he continued to stare through the glass door at the cat in the front yard.

"Ariana showed us that we're wrong, that all the covert surveillance in the world won't stop you Hydra siblings from communicating with one another in ways we'll never understand. When the head of the research department told Ariana that there's nothing we don't know about you, she said that for many years we've been following the progress of a Hydra 08\B Sequence 4, a woman named Anna, when all this time we were dealing with a man named Yuli."

Yuli's fingers fastened at once around the coffee mug. His eyes locked on Hercules, who was sharpening his claws on the trunk of the poplar tree. It was as though he'd been nailed to the cat's body by the mighty blows of a sledgehammer.

Orna got up and moved to sit by Yuli's side on the sofa. Then she took the cup from his shaking hands, placed it on the table, and took his hands in hers. Her glance fell on the Hydra 08\B ID bracelet fastened around his right wrist. *Do they sense,* she wondered, *that it's not just an ID bracelet but also a surveillance transmitter?*

"We knew that the others had begun to call you Yuli because we read your shared journal," Orna said. "You pretended it was just an endearment, and you managed to convince us. But this change is troubling, and we completely missed it. That's why it's so important that Ariana came to us about it."

Yuli remained silent. He could think of nothing that would improve his situation right now.

"Yuli, I don't know how much they told you about the first generations of Hydras, but there is a basis for our concern regarding Hydras who are uncertain about their sexual identity. Did they teach you when you were children some of the history of the experiment? It was most probably just the official, abridged version that jumps from the first experiments in fetal cells to Series 07 and 08, which is you, right?"

Yuli bit his lip, his eyes still fixed on the oft-scratched tree trunk. He swallowed hard before trying to speak.

"Is it true that... all the Hydras from Series 04 to 06 were euthanized?"

Orna shook her head. "No, not at all. I know that there are rumors, but they're simply not true. Let's go over everything from the start, so you can understand why we're worried about you."

Yuli removed his gaze from the cat's antics in the front yard and turned his head slowly to meet Orna's eyes. Only then did he notice the dark shadows under her eyes. She looked as though she hadn't slept for days. The inspector stroked his cheek as she had used to do years before, when he was a toddler, and began to speak softly.

"I wish we knew how to conduct ourselves better, as a species. Unfortunately, we have failed in this. By the end of the twenty-third century, too many people were on the planet and not enough resources. There was no choice but to reduce drastically the number of babies born; stringent and limited quotas were introduced. They were based on a random lottery performed by supercomputers to prevent a black market for baby permits from developing. Nobody could crack the computer code."

Yuli nodded. There were plenty of stories about people who tried to hack the supercomputers to insert their own names as winners in the lottery. The best hackers in the world met with utter failure. The algorithms were too complex and defeated even large groups of experts armed with the most advanced computers, let alone mere individuals desperate for a child, who've tried their luck with the impenetrable machine.

"Those who tried to defy the quotas – or who got pregnant by accident – were given a choice: immediate termination of the pregnancy or participation in the Hydra experiment. The genetic material of five fetuses scheduled for abortion would be combined into a single fetus that would gestate in an artificial womb. When it reached a steady metabolic rate, after nine months, it would undergo a controlled decanting."

Steady metabolic rate, thought Yuli. *Maybe your scientists took the concept of "biological clock" just a little too far.*

"The combined DNA double helix was constructed so that each time another part of it would be triggered, to express one of the children that had been fused together. Each child is active for twenty-three hours, and then a transformation mechanism is activated, initiating the code sequence of the next child, while the body itself enters a temporary comatose state for one hour."

"When we were kids, we sometimes tried to stay awake beyond twenty-three hours," Yuli reminisced, "and then the den mothers would find us sprawled out in a corner with clothes that didn't fit us."

"I remember," Orna smiled. "Once Adam insisted on not taking a shower after running around all day in the yard and getting all muddy, and then you woke up after him and started crying because you were so filthy and bruised. You still had pigtails back then..."

"It's scary," Yuli interrupted, "waking up with scratches on your knees you didn't get. But things like that taught us to be considerate of one another." He stroked his knee where there was still a faint trace of a scar. Then he thought for a moment and added, "Do you have any idea what it feels like to think twice about every choice you make, every action you take, throughout the day? To think that if you overeat, the person who follows you in the sequence will suffer from indigestion? Or if you don't drink enough, the next person will be dehydrated? Pardon the pun. If you catch the flu, by the time you're back it will be gone, but the people who'll follow you will be sick then and recover for you? And that's before we get to everyday chores. Abigail took out a package from the mail for me today because she knew the post office would be closed on my day. Adam wanted to buy his boyfriend a gift, and Avi bought it for him because they spent the whole day together on their sequence day, and Adam couldn't buy it for him without ruining the surprise. And me – I'm the only one of us who's allergic to cats, so poor Hercules spends one of every five days outdoors. I can't take anti-allergy medications because their effect is long-term, and with us, there's no such thing as 'long-term.' There's only one day at a time, and that lasts only twenty-three hours. For us, the earth rotates a little faster."

Yuli was a bit short-breathed after unburdening himself. Orna leaned back on the sofa and sighed.

"You're right. There are many drawbacks to the system, but the experiment still allows us a reasonable continuity of the human gene pool. Even with the scant allotment of new babies. You undoubtedly pay a heavy price. That's why we try to protect you, and when one of you shows signs of falling apart..."

I am not falling apart, thought Yuli furiously. *I just want the right to determine for myself who I am.*

"You asked what had happened to the Hydras before you. Series 01 through 03 didn't make it past the initial stages of fetal development. Their DNA collapsed, and they didn't survive. Series 04 through 06 reached an age of about one year, and then, during one of the switches, they went into a coma and eventually died. Understand this, Yuli: One of the first signs of the collapse in the early Hydras was a breakdown of the X and Y sex chromosomes. It took us time to understand that full interbody regeneration is what causes the breakdown. We found a way to leave part of the body as is and to perform a transformation – a partial change that expresses only the sequences vital to each of the five's identities."

"But none of my chromosomes have broken. I'm just trapped in a body that doesn't fit with who I am."

"Yes," Orna agreed, "and that's exactly what Ariana explained to us three days ago. Did you know she's studying the structure of DNA? She really is brilliant. Without our knowledge, she mapped the entire

DNA of each of you and fully checked it, too. All is in order. No sign of breakup. She showed us the findings of her research and begged us to stop... what did she call it? 'Stop treating us like a clump of cells under a microscope and start seeing us as complete human beings in every respect.' For the experiment truly to succeed, she said, we – that is, the research and development team – have to let you live without fear. She told us what you were going through, not to 'snitch' on you but to demonstrate that your personality has developed independently and wasn't determined by your DNA. She also argued that this is a great success for the experiment. You, just like your Hydra siblings, are a strong and complete individual in and of yourself."

Yuli remained silent. He had no idea that Ariana had made such an effort to defend his right to self-determination.

"To my great regret, your allergy to cats is not the only thing we can't help you with," Orna continued, sorrow evident on her face. "Obviously, any sort of surgical procedure you undergo would not last and would be reset with the next transformation. And any sort of hormonal treatment would affect all five of you, and even then, its effect will diminish over time. We can't give you a man's body."

"I know," Yuli mumbled.

"But... what we can do is stop calling you 'Anna,' start calling you 'Yuli,' and address you as a man. As far as we're concerned, if this is what you want – be a man, to all intents and purposes."

Yuli blushed with excitement.

"Really? You can do this?"

"Of course we can. You're sound in body and mind, and it's your right to decide who you are. The only thing that bothers me a little is your choice of name."

"What do you mean, my name?" Yuli stammered.

"Well, with every Hydra, the names begin with the same letter, as part of the numbering. With you, the names begin with A. Now we'll have Avi, Ariana, Abigail, Adam – and Yuli, instead of Anna. Very inconsiderate of you. Couldn't you pick a name that begins with an A?"

Yuli opened and closed his mouth a few times, his eyes wide.

"I'm sorry... I didn't think of that... I..."

Orna broke out laughing. "I was joking! Don't worry. There's no problem with changing your name." Then she turned serious. "Actually, I was hoping you knew something about what's going on with Ariana. It's obvious that she feels very close to you, and it's strange to think that she tried to hurt you and the others."

"We *are* close," Yuli confirmed, "but I don't know what exactly happened to her. Adam and I both think that there's no way she'd want to kill herself and all of us. She loves us. I can feel it."

"If so, we'll just have to wait and see. I'll ask Avi to undergo his transformation in one of our rooms, under medical supervision."

"You won't lock her up in a ward or something, right?" Yuli asked, now concerned.

"I'll do my best, but I can't promise anything. I don't know how serious Ariana's condition is. We'll do what we can to help her and prevent her from hurting herself – and all of you."

Yuli walked the inspector to the door. Before leaving, the inspector turned back and gave Yuli a penetrating look. "What if your sister really was trying to commit suicide? What if she broke down and tried to kill herself and all of you?"

"Then we'll deal with it. Just like we deal with all our other difficulties."

"It won't be easy."

"It never is. But you know what? Like with everything else in our lives, we don't really have a choice."

The inspector nodded her understanding. Then she smiled.

"I enjoyed talking with you, Yuli. Now I have a wonderful task, to update these details in your file. By the time you show up at the Institute, everything will be ready. See you soon."

Yuli stood rooted to the spot and stared at the door for a few minutes, as though it, the protector of their home, was responsible for this sudden change in his life.

Then he turned on his heels, went back to the living room, and opened the glass door wide. When he lifted the cat and hugged it to his chest, bursting with joy and relief, he could no longer tell tears of joy from tears of allergy.

The cat, for its part, protested with a loud wail, and not for lack of sympathy. It just didn't like to get wet.

NEVER A DULL MOMENT with you, brothers and sisters. Not a single dull moment.

Yuli, my dear sister – sorry, dear brother, I'm just used to call you this – I'm so happy for you. I don't even care that I sneezed on Jasmine the moment I woke up. I'm happy you're happy, but that's no reason to sniff the cat.

Abigail, sweetie: Next time you throw away something of mine, be it a worn-out toothbrush, a cracked cup, or a used rag – I'm throwing away all your clothes, including shoes, socks, and stockings. Jasmine is reading what I write and pointing out that your intentions were good. Well, I promise both of you that I, too, will have the best of intentions when I dump your clothes in the trash. So seriously, a little respect for other people's belongings, please.

Adam, you're alright. You really, really are alright. Jasmine, too, adds that you're alright. She's even punching my shoulder to correct that she didn't say that, she said you're terrific. Thank you and thank Doron as well.

Procedural notes: I threw all of Abigail's clothes in the trash. Just kidding!

Ariana, you'll wake up in a room at the Institute under observation, not at home. Orna asked this, and I agree with her.

I trust you and love you, but I prefer you to be there, just to be safe. Orna is really amazing, and does want what's best for you. I don't believe you'd want to ruin all our lives; I do think you had a rough moment, and I'm waiting to hear just what happened so I can send you a shiver of love the next time you wake up.

Speaking of shivers of love... Well, as you've probably guessed, I proposed to Jasmine, and she said yes. I have no idea why – I wouldn't marry me, but she said yes. We discussed some of the details today with the Oversight Committee, and they were excited, because this is the first time a Hydra will be marrying a Regular person. I have a feeling they're going to get in our hair a little, but we're already used to that anyway. Isn't that right, dear spies from the Institute who never ever read our journal? We'll save you a slice of wedding cake.

And you, my dear siblings – you better not bail on the wedding, got it?

Ha ha ha.

Take care of yourselves, please. I'm going to kiss my fiancée, and I hope it's not our last day together.

JASMINE LOOKED AT THE FIGURE lying on the bed, washed, clean, and wrapped in the familiar robe. The transformation was always a gradual process, very subtle to the eye, although the change required enormous amounts of energy from the body and would most likely be painful if the subject of transformation were conscious when it happened. Jasmine shuddered at the thought of such a radical change while being fully awake.

But the process taking place before her eyes looked like a play of shadows and light, one body morphing into another, like clay in the hands of an invisible potter. Had she looked away for a moment and turned to look again at the unconscious face, she would have discovered that the shape of the eye had changed completely, or the ears looked different. On previous occasions, she tried to stare and not avert her gaze so as to catch all the tiny nuances of the switch, but these took place in such a precise, smooth flow that she was sucked into the process and didn't notice the changes until after they had taken place.

There, the hands already looked less like Yuli's and more like Avi's. Avi had longer and skinnier fingers. The familiar laugh lines at the corners of the eyes were there, but still not deep enough to be his. The nose lengthened slightly... and the depression under the nose, which gave Avi's fleshy lips the shape of a round heart, manifested bit by bit, as though by gentle, cautious dabs of a paintbrush.

Jasmine smiled to herself. The hour has almost passed, and it was time to bring tea and cookies to bed for a quick night snack, and then to snuggle together till morning. She got up from the bed and went to the kitchen.

Avi stretched slowly, then yawned. The sounds reaching his ears gradually grew louder. *Magic is here!* He thought to himself with sleepy joy, *it was really nice of Yuli to let her stay at the end of his day.* Then he sneezed loudly.

"Bless you," came a feminine voice from the doorway. "I think those are leftovers of Yuli's allergy."

Jasmine entered the bedroom carrying a tray with two cups and a plate of cookies. Avi smiled and turned on his side, while Jasmine reclined by his side and arranged the tray straight on the blanket. Upon the end of the ceremonious placement of cups and cookies, the two laid their heads on their hands and looked at each other for a few wordless minutes. When Avi felt alert enough, he leaned forward and kissed his beloved.

"Thanks for coming to be with me," he said softly.

"The thanks go to Yuli," she replied. "It's the second time he's let me stay. I know it's not easy for him. But it looks like he had a good day... It's good to see him smile at long last."

"He does deserve it," said Avi, taking one of the teacups. "Sometimes I think he has it harder than the rest of us. All five of us are stuck together in this body, but at least while we're here, we feel like we belong to what we have. With him, it's more complicated."

"Speaking of 'while we're here,'... How about coming with me today to pick a closet for our bedroom?"

Avi sighed.

"Magic, I love you, but you're complicating our lives. How can we split our time between this shared house and our house?"

"Just like we did over the past year, with me still living with my parents," Jasmine insisted. She bit into a butter cookie, adding with a full mouth, "For a year now, you've been unsuccessfully trying to discourage me, Magic. You think it's going to work now?"

Avi smiled and wiped the cookie crumbs from his cheek. He had discovered Jasmine's tendency to speak with her mouth full the very first time they met. They had to share a table at the local café, which was packed that day. He asked her to pass the sugar, she said, "Sure, here you go," and then, too, a few stray cake crumbs reached his face. She apologized and passed him a napkin, and a light conversation began. Yes, it's a Hydra bracelet. He has two brothers and two sisters. Yes, if he drinks too much coffee, the next one in the sequence has a hard time falling asleep. No, he's not angry about the study. He understands that there was no choice. Yes, it's true that the mental and physical maturation process is shared. No, it doesn't feel weird, mostly because he doesn't know what it feels like to be Normal.

"You seem completely normal to me," she noted then.

"Does it seem normal to you that someone wakes up only once every five days, and on the other four, they're busy being four different people?" he needled her.

"It sounds like magic to me," she replied, "that you're one person and five different people at once."

"Sounds a lot more magical to me to be just one person."

"It's not magic, it's just boring. I've always been just me, and sometimes I'm kinda sick and tired of me. Want a bit of my cake? I'm full."

From then on, they called each other "Magic" and saw each other every five days, on Avi's sequence day. The Oversight Committee followed the affair, at first with some amusement – since relationships between Hydras and Normals have never lasted long – and then with increasing concern, because the two became a couple to all intents and purposes. When Magic, that is Jasmine, introduced him to her parents, Avi was sure they would be scared by the thought of their daughter throwing her life away on a Hydra, a walking science experiment with questionable quality of life. To his surprise, they accepted him with open arms and great affection.

Gershon and Leah, Jasmine's parents, even expressed a desire to meet his brothers and sisters. "We can't all meet together," Avi replied, embarrassed. "That's okay; family is family," Leah replied, smiling from ear to ear. "Every family has its quirks." Avi was happy to discover that his partner had inherited not only her mother's tendency to speak with her mouth full of crumbs, but also her contagious *joie de vivre* and endless tolerance.

Thus Jasmine's family joined the circle of the parents of the Hydra siblings. *In fact,* Avi thought, *they came just in time to replace Ariana's parents.* Ariana's mother and father had stopped visiting them and attending the family dinners. From the few times he had spent in their company, Avi's impression was that they were an altogether repulsive couple, and their continued absence didn't bother him especially. Jasmine's parents, by contrast, adored Ariana, and Jasmine herself fell head over heels in love with her.

"I'm telling you," said Jasmine, briskly shaking the remnants of the cookie from her shirt, "there's no way Ariana tried to hurt you, or any of you. She's too smart for that."

"Smart people, too, make mistakes sometimes," argued Avi. "It's very unlike her to break down like this. I trust her, really, but I can't help worrying."

Avi glanced at his wrists. The bleeding cuts from five days ago had already turned into unobtrusive scabs. Something about seeing the wound that he had not caused himself reminded him just how fragile his life was, thrown arbitrarily into a Petri dish and poured into a test tube with four other doomed souls like him, reduced through no fault of their own.

On the other hand, he reminded himself, *not everyone finds love like you did.*

He turned over to the other side and opened the bottom drawer of the chest near the bed.

"Magic, what are you looking for?"

"Just a second, Magic."

In the drawer waited a small black box, with a note attached: "Good luck, fingers crossed! Adam and Doron." Avi smiled to himself, hid the box in the palm of his hand, and turned back to Jasmine.

"Magic of mine," he said softly, "I want to tell you something."

Jasmine raised an eyebrow, but listened without interrupting.

"I didn't believe it would last, our relationship. Not because I don't love you. You know I do, and if you don't, I guess I haven't done enough to prove it, and I deserve you even less than I thought."

Jasmine's lips began to tremble.

"Avi, you..."

"One moment, sweetie. Just one moment."

Avi cradled Jasmine's cheek with his free hand.

"No one knows how long they have to live, but I began the countdown with even less. Magic, my love, I only have one-fifth of a life. Only seventy-three days a year belong to me, and that's all I have to offer you. But all that I have, and all that I am – is yours. If you want me."

Avi opened the box in his other hand and showed Jasmine the ring it contained.

The moments that followed were a joyful storm of hugs, shrieks, and kisses wet with tears. Hercules, who had enjoyed his slumber on the linen box until that moment, awoke in fright and ran for his life. He found a new resting place on the living room sofa, where he shook his head in annoyance at the strange noises the bipeds were making. Then he let out a tiny feline sigh, closed his eyes and fell back asleep within seconds, curled up like a hairy pretzel.

"I'd rather have a fifth of a life with you than five hundred lifetimes with someone else," Jasmine said quietly, once the two managed to calm down somewhat and lay entwined, their breathing synchronized.

"Not only do you have to settle for one-fifth of a life, but you're also marrying four other people," said Avi with a note of sadness, kissing her hair.

"Who are all wonderful, and I'm guessing one of them bought this ring for you. Am I right?" Jasmine completed the sentence with a smile.

"Adam. He has excellent taste, I must say."

"How did you manage to ask him to buy a ring without writing it in your shared journal?" Jasmine asked curiously.

"We have our ways..."

"Now that we're getting married, you'll have to tell me everything!" Jasmine said gleefully, cuddling in his arms with a joyful sigh.

Now that we're getting married... Ariana, you can't ruin this for me, Avi thought, and a sudden, unbearable wave of despair flooded his chest. *I can't leave Magic now. I don't want to die... I may have only one-fifth of a life, but I want to live every moment of the life I do have with her.*

Jasmine fell asleep, a slight smile of happiness on her lips. Avi gently pulled her closer, buried his face in her hair, and inhaled her scent deeply. He stayed awake for a long while after, offering prayers and supplications, silently beseeching a woman who wasn't there.

FORGIVE ME.

That's the first thing, forgive me.

Especially the first and the last of us.

I'm so ashamed of myself for making you all so worried and scared. I thank you for trusting me.

And again, I apologize. Especially to you, Abigail, who woke up into a world of blood and confusion, and to you, Avi, who went to sleep under the watchful eyes of the researchers at the Institute, falling asleep into the unknown.

Let me tell you what happened, hoping that this will help you understand what led me to do such a terrible thing.

Five days ago, after the meeting with Orna and the committee at the Institute, I went to visit my parents. They hadn't come to our joint meetings in a long while, and I wanted to ask them what happened. It's true, our relationship has never been very good, but they are my parents, and they're important to me.

Mom opened the door, gave me an apprehensive look, and immediately turned her head back to tell Dad, "She's here." In truth, it sounded more like a warning than a greeting. We sat in the living room, trying to pretend we're simply having a nice cup of coffee together and making small talk. They've just been busy, was how they put it, nothing in particular had happened. They have to go away soon, for quite a while, maybe even years. Work-related, Dad quickly explained. We'll keep in touch by phone. We can talk by video as well.

Mom kept stroking her belly, avoiding eye contact.

I laid down my coffee mug and asked them straight out, "You won the lottery, didn't you?"

They both kept silent.

I repeated the question: "You won the lottery, you'll have a Normal baby now, and you're leaving. Right?"

They said nothing.

I got up, picked up my coat and purse, and walked to the door. Mom followed me, and before I left, she mumbled at me, "It's not your fault. I do think it's best for all of us. We don't know how to be parents to a..."

"A...?" I asked.

"An incomplete person," Mom replied, eyes deep into the keyhole of the door, her hand shaking as she stroked the handle.

"Complete or not, I'm still yours." I choked on these words.

She didn't answer.

Dad didn't say anything either. Just sat in the living room and stared at the wall.

I closed the door behind me and left.

I don't cry much, but I cried that night. I sat in the bathtub and bawled my eyes out like a little girl. I was mad at myself for not being able to stop the tears. After all, I knew what kind of parents I have. Since I was a kid, they've looked at me like I was a monster. When I was twelve and showed Mom the scar on our knee from the time Yuli climbed too high up the tree in the front yard and fell, she looked like she was going to throw up. I have always been too strange for them, too grotesque. Different.

So I sat there and cried because although I have you, and I have friends, and the researchers at the Institute who trust me, and I even have Hercules, I still needed their approval, embrace, understanding, and love.

And I realized I shall never get it.

At that moment, mere seconds before the switch began, I took a pair of scissors and slashed my wrists. I wanted to feel lesser pain, and a smaller bleeding wound than the one I felt inside. I wanted to see the blood pour out, to realize that I was still alive. Even if they didn't want me, I'm still alive, and I'll get better, and recover, and move on.

At that moment, I was selfish. The only excuse I have is that the sorrow and pain numbed me so much that I couldn't think clearly. It's not good enough as an excuse, and I know full well that I'll have to work very hard to make it up to all of you.

And so... I started doing this today, in fact. I've been doing biochemical and genetic research for a long while now, as you know. Today I signed an agreement with the Institute researchers, which formalizes a critical right we've had coming to us for a very long time. Congratulations are in order! I, we, are the first Hydra to be accepted as a full-fledged researcher with the Genetic Research Oversight Committee. The committee accepted that allowing Hydras to participate in researching their own lives makes a lot of sense. After all, who knows us better than we do?

I want to know exactly how to make things easier for us; how to make the transformations smoother. I want to understand the mechanism that allows us to feel each other across transformations. After all, more than tummy aches and headaches pass between us. Sorrow, joy, pain, fear – and what's most fascinating to me – the little messages we manage to plant in one another's thoughts. I knew that Avi left me a letter in the drawer without him mentioning it in the journal. Adam knew that Avi wanted him to buy a ring for Jasmine without him writing it in the journal. Abigail knew that Yuli was supposed to receive a package in the mail that day, and Abigail, you know... yes, you know. Without us writing it in the journal. Jasmine said it all: we *are* magic! And we are entitled to take part in discovering this magic. I promise to do everything necessary to become the best researcher at the Institute, for us. For all of us. And then, maybe I'll deserve forgiveness.

Procedural notes: I filled the pantry with everyone's favorite snacks. It's a rather childish part of my asking for forgiveness, but it's the least I can do.

I bought everyone new toothbrushes. You don't have to use them... They're in the bathroom closet.

In the wardrobe, on the other hand, you'll find Institute uniforms in everyone's sizes. I insisted that if I'm a member of the Institute, that means we're all members. They had to agree with me. Yuli, you're more than free to make changes according to your own taste. I know you hate clothes that are too "standard."

Avi, I booked the garden venue you and Jasmine wanted for your wedding, on the date you wanted. Your sorrow and fear that you may not live to see the day drilled a hole in my heart, which I totally deserve. Don't worry. You'll make it to that wedding, even if I have to take our genome apart and put it back together again three times by then. Did you know that our genome is a little like a Rubik's Cube, only with five sides instead of six? It's fascinating. Well, anyway, it's fascinating to me. And to Hercules, who's playing here on the floor with a plastic model of the double helix.

One last procedural note: If you ever hear a knock at the door, and there's a boy or a girl there, saying that I'm their sister – please explain to them that it's not my day, but if they wait a little, I'll be glad to meet them.

Love you, and I'm so proud to be your sister,

Ariana.

ORNA LEANED BACK IN HER CHAIR and looked at the screen in front of her with evident satisfaction. The screen showed the feed from the security cameras at the Institute's lobby: A guard speaking to a young woman, a few researchers in white robes coming in at a brisk pace, and the systems engineer from the third floor, her lunch partner, going out for a much-needed smoke. It wasn't a particularly good week for Orna's attempts to wean herself off her nasty vaporizer habit, as evidenced by the packet of disposable vials peeking from her robe pocket. "Vaporizer Extract, Nicotine Flavor, Strength Grade 10," read the label. There was no Grade 11.

However, at this moment, the veteran researcher did not need the comforting vaporizer pipe. She drew more than enough contentment from the sight of the Institute guard, Yoel, speaking with Hydra 08\B\2. Orna pushed a button to zoom in and focus on the two of them. He was talking excitedly about something and she... Orna smiled to herself... she was slipping a lock of hair behind her left ear, in that familiar gesture of embarrassment and interest in another which words cannot express.

Another researcher entered the room.

"Good morning, Dan," said Orna, still smiling, without looking away from the screen. "Ready to begin another sequence?"

"Do I have a choice?" her younger colleague replied, glancing at the screen. "Who is that, Abigail? Good, I gather the matter with 08\B ended well?"

"Absolutely. It ended optimally, I would say."

Dan took his seat by Orna's side.

"Was it really necessary to hide the truth from 08\B\1? After all, she accepted the fact that her parents were leaving."

"Yes, but she needed a reason. If they had just upped and disappeared, leaving her behind like trash, a failed experiment as they saw it, it would have hurt her much more. I don't think she could have taken that. And she's smart enough to have found a way to really kill herself."

"So you made up a scenario of them winning the baby lottery. Why did they even go along with it?"

Orna shook her head.

"Because we threatened them that if they didn't cooperate, we'd never let them leave. We could have forced them to keep meeting with

Ariana. Despite their alienating behavior towards her, these meetings were of value to her. We had to give her something to hold on to, to believe they weren't that horrible, that they don't hate her so."

Dan nodded.

"I understand. The problem is that she's smart enough to find out the truth sooner or later. Especially now that she'll be working with us."

"There is no report on this in the official files. I took care of that. If Ariana finds out some other way, I hope it happens when she's strong enough in her new position that it won't break her. In any event," said Orna, pointing at the door, "it seems that we have a visitor."

She pushed a button, and the view from the security camera switched to the other side of the door, where Abigail was pressing her ID bracelet to the electronic scanner. The scanner beeped, and she entered the room and smiled at its occupants.

"Good morning, Abigail," said Orna with a broad smile. "Your day started much better, didn't it?"

Help! I am Dr. Morris Goldpepper

By Avram Davidson

AVRAM DAVIDSON (1923–1993) WAS BORN in Yonkers, New York. Between 1941 and 1945, he served in the U.S. Navy as a medical corpsman in the South Pacific and China. From 1948 to 1949, he served with the Israeli Army as part of its *Mahal* foreign volunteers corps. With the conclusion of the war, he remained in Beersheva, where he worked at a local hospital as a male nurse until 1951, submitting, during that time, articles to the American woman's magazine *Hadassah*. While he never opted for Israeli citizenship nor, as best we can tell, submitted to naturalization, the editors have decided to bestow upon him sufficient standing to appear in this anthology.

Davidson spent most of his life writing and editing. In 1958 he won the Hugo Award for his story "Or All The Seas With Oysters." Between 1962 and 1964, he served as the executive editor of *The Magazine of Fantasy and Science Fiction*, editing three volumes of the digest's annual *"Best From"* series. He won a second Hugo in 1963 when *F&SF* was chosen Best Professional Magazine. Over the course of his career, Davidson published over a score of books and hundreds of stories. From a Jewish perspective, two stories are noteworthy. In his 1955 tour de force, "The Golem," a threatening android finds himself outwitted by an old bickering Jewish couple and ends up mowing the lawn. The story has been reprinted ad infinitum. Less well-known is "Help! I Am Dr. Morris Goldpepper," a hilarious account of the travails of the eponymous hero who is enslaved by toothless, blue-gummed aliens. We are pleased to reprint it here.

ONE

FOUR OF THE MEN, Weinroth, McAllister, Danbourge and Smith, sat at the table under the cold blue lighting tubes. One of them, Rorke, was in a corner speaking quietly into a telephone, and one, Fadderman, stood staring out the window at the lights of the city.

One, Hansen, had yet to arrive.

Fadderman spoke without turning his head. He was the oldest of those present – the Big Seven, as they were often called.

"Lights," he said. "So many lights. Down here." He waved his hand toward the city. "Up there." He gestured toward the sky. "Even with our much-vaunted knowledge, what," he asked, "do we know?"

He turned his head. "Perhaps this is too big for us. In the light of the problem, can we really hope to accomplish anything?"

Heavy-set Danbourge frowned grimly. "We have received the suffrage of our fellow-scientists, Doctor. We can but try."

Lithe, handsome McAllister, the youngest officer of the Association, nodded. "The problem is certainly not worse than that which faced our late, great colleague, the immortal Morton." He pointed to a picture on the paneled wall. "And we all know what he accomplished."

Fadderman went over and took his hand. "Your words fill me with courage."

McAllister flushed with pleasure.

"I am an old man," Fadderman added falteringly. "Forgive my lack of spirit, Doctor." He sat down, sighed, shook his head slowly. Weinroth, burly and red-haired, patted him gently on the back. Natty, silvery-haired little Smith smiled at him consolingly.

A buzzer sounded. Rorke hung up the telephone, flipped a switch on the wall intercom. "Headquarters here," he said crisply.

"Dr. Carl T. Hansen has arrived," a voice informed him. "Bring him up at once," he directed.

"And, Nickerson —" "Yes, Dr. Rorke?" "Let no one else into the building. No one."

They sat in silence. After a moment or two, they heard the approach of the elevator, heard the doors slide open, slide shut, heard the elevator descend. Heavy, steady footsteps approached; knuckles rapped on the opaque glass door.

Rorke went over to the door, said, "A conscientious and diligent scientist —" "— must remain a continual student," a deep voice finished the quotation. Rorke unlocked the door, peered out into the corridor, admitted Hansen, locked the door.

"I would have been here sooner, but another emergency interposed," Hansen said. "A certain political figure — ethics prevent my being more specific — suffered an oral hemorrhage following an altercation with a woman who shall be nameless, but, boy, did she pack a wallop! A so-called Specialist, gentlemen, with offices on Park Avenue, had been, as he called it, 'applying pressure' with a gauze pad. I merely used a little Gelfoam as a coagulant agent and the hemorrhage stopped almost at once. When will the public learn, eh, gentlemen?"

Faint smiles played upon the faces of the assembled scientists. Hansen took his seat. Rorke bent down and lifted two tape-recording devices to the table, set them both in motion. The faces of the men became serious, grim.

"This is an emergency session of the Steering Committee of the Executive Committee of the American Dental Association," Rorke said, "called to discuss measures of dealing with the case of Dr. Morris Goldpepper. One tape will be deposited in the vaults of the Chase Manhattan Bank in New York; the other will be similarly secured in the vaults of the Wells Fargo and Union Trust Company Bank in San Francisco. Present at this session are Doctors Rorke, Weinroth and Smith – President, First and Second Vice-presidents, respectively – Fadderman, Past President, McAllister, Public Information, Danbourge, Legal, and Hansen, Policy."

He looked around at the set, tense faces.

"Doctors," he went on, "I think I may well say that humanity is, as of this moment, face to face with a great danger, and it is a bitter jest that it is not to the engineers or the astronomers, not to medicine nor yet to nuclear nor any other kind of physics, that humanity must now look for salvation – but to the members of the dental profession!"

His voice rose. "Yes – to the practitioners of what has become perhaps the least regarded of all the learned sciences! It is indeed ironical. We may at this juncture consider the comments of the now deceased Professor Earnest Hooton, the Harvard anthropologist, who observed with a sorrow which did him credit that his famed University, instead of assisting its Dental School as it ought, treated it – and I quote his exact words – 'Like a yellow dog.'" His voice trembled.

McAllister's clean-cut face flushed an angry red. Weinroth growled. Danbourge's fist hit the table and stayed there, clenched. Fadderman gave a soft, broken sigh.

"But enough of this. We are not jealous, nor are we vindictive," President Rorke went on. "We are confident that History, 'with its long tomorrow,' will show how, at this danger-fraught point, the humble and little thought-of followers of dental science recognized and sized up the situation and stood shoulder to shoulder on the ramparts!"

He wiped his brow with a paper tissue.

"And now I will call upon our beloved Past President, Dr. Samuel I. review of the incredible circumstances which have brought us here tonight. Dr. Fadderman? If you please…"

The well-known Elder Statesman of the A.D.A. nodded his head slowly. He made a little cage of his fingers and pursed and then unpursed his lips. At length he spoke in a soft and gentle voice.

"My first comment, brethren, is that I ask for compassion. Morris Goldpepper is not to blame!

"Let me tell you a few words about him. Goldpepper the Scientist needs no introduction. Who has not read, for instance, his 'The Bilateral Vertical Stroke and Its Influence on the Pattern of Occlusion' or his 'Treatment, Planning, Assemblage and Cementation of a 14-Unit Fixed Bridge' – to name only two? But I shall speak about Goldpepper the Man. He is forty-six years of age and served with honor in the United States Navy Dental Corps during the Second World War. He has been a widower since shortly after the conclusion of that conflict. Rae – the late Mrs. Goldpepper, may she rest in peace – often used to say, 'Morry, if I go first, promise me you'll marry again,' but he passed it off with a joke; and, as you know, he never did.

"They had one child, a daughter, Suzanne, a very sweet girl, now married to a Dr. Sheldon Fingerhut, D.D.S. I need not tell you, brethren, how proud our colleague was when his only child married this very fine young member of our profession. The Fingerhuts are now located on Unbalupi, one of the Micronesian islands forming part of the United States Trust Territory, where Dr. Sheldon is teaching dental hygiene, sanitation and prosthesis to the natives thereof."

Dr. Hansen asked, "Are they aware of –"

"The son-in-law knows something of the matter," the older man said. "He has not seen fit to inform his wife, who is in a delicate condition and expects shortly to be confined. At his suggestion, I have been writing – or, rather, typing – letters purporting to come from her father, on his stationery, with the excuse that he badly singed his fingers on a Bunsen burner whilst annealing a new-type hinge for dentures and consequently cannot hold his pen." He sipped from a glass of water.

"Despite his great scientific accomplishments," Dr. Fadderman went on, "Morry had an impractical streak in him. Often I used to call on him at his bachelor apartment in the Hotel Davenport on West End Avenue, where he moved following his daughter's marriage, and I would find him immersed in reading matter of an escapist kind – tales of crocodile hunters on the Malayan Peninsula, or magazines dealing with interplanetary warfare, or collections of short stories about vampires and werewolves and similar superstitious creations.

"'Morry,' I said reproachfully, 'what a way to spend your off-hours. Is it worth it? Is it healthy? You would do much better, believe me, to frequent the pool or the handball court at the Y. Or,' I pointed out to him, 'if you want to read, why ignore the rich treasures of literature: Shakespeare, Ruskin, Elbert Hubbard, Edna Ferber, and so on? Why retreat to these immature-type fantasies? ' At first he only smiled and quoted the saying, 'Each to his or her own taste.'"

The silence which followed was broken by young Dr. McAllister. "You say," he said, "'at first.'"

Old Dr. Fadderman snapped out of his revery. "Yes, yes. But eventually he confessed the truth to me. He withheld nothing."

The assembled dental scientists then learned that the same Dr. Morris Goldpepper, who had been awarded not once but three successive times the unique honor of the Dr. Alexander Peabody Medal for New Achievements in Dental Prosthesis, was obsessed with the idea that there was sentient life on other worlds – that it would shortly be possible to reach these other worlds – and that he himself desired to be among those who went.

"'Do you realize, Sam?' he asked me," reported Fadderman."' Do you realize that, in a very short time, it will no longer be a question of fuel or even of metallurgy? That submarines capable of cruising for weeks and months without surfacing foretell the possibility of traveling through airless space? The chief problem has now come down to finding how to build a take-off platform capable of withstanding a thrust of several million pounds.' And his eyes glowed."

Dr. Fadderman had inquired, with good-natured sarcasm, how the other man expected this would involve him. The answer was as follows: Any interplanetary expedition would find it just as necessary to take along a dentist as to take along a physician, and that he – Dr. Goldpepper – intended to be that dentist!

Dr. Weinroth's hand slapped the table with a bang. "By thunder, I say the man had courage!"

Dr. Rorke looked at him with icy reproof. "I should be obliged," he said stiffly, "if there would be no further emotional outbursts."

Dr. Weinroth's face fell. "I beg the Committee's pardon, Mr. President," he said.

Dr. Rorke nodded graciously, indicated by a gesture of his hand that Dr. Fadderman had permission to continue speaking. The old man took a letter from his pocket and placed it on the table.

"This came to me like a bolt from the blue beyond. It is dated November 8 of last year. Skipping the formal salutation, it reads: 'At last I stand silent upon the peak in Darien' – a literary reference, gentlemen, to Cortez's alleged discovery of the Pacific Ocean; actually it was Balboa – 'my great dream is about to be realized. Before long, I shall be back to tell you about it, but just exactly when, I am not able to say. History is being made! Long live Science! Very sincerely yours, Morris Goldpepper, D.D.S.'"

He passed the letter around the table.

Dr. Smith asked, "What did you do on receiving this communication, Doctor?"

Dr. Fadderman had at once taken a taxi to West End Avenue. The desk clerk at the hotel courteously informed him that the man he sought had left on a vacation of short but not exactly specified duration. No further information was known. Dr. Fadderman's first thought was that his younger friend had gotten some sort of position with a Government project which he was not free to discuss, and his own patriotism and sense of duty naturally prevented him from making inquiries.

"But I began, for the first time," the Elder Statesman of American Dentistry said, "to read up on the subject of space travel. I wondered how a man 46 years of age could possibly hope to be selected over younger men."

Dr. Danbourge spoke for the first time. "Size," he said. "Every ounce would count in a spaceship and Morris was a pretty little guy."

"But with the heart of a lion," Dr. Weinroth said softly. "Miles and miles and miles of heart." The other men nodded their agreement to this tribute.

But as time went on and the year drew to its close and he heard no word from his friend, Dr. Fadderman began to worry. Finally, when he received a letter from the Fingerhuts, saying that they had not been hearing either, he took action.

He realized it was not likely that the Government would have made plans to include a dentist in this supposed project without communicating with the A.D.A. and he inquired of the current President, Dr. Rorke, if he had any knowledge of such a project, or of the whereabouts of the missing man. The answer to both questions was no. But on learning the reasons for Dr. Fadderman's concern, he communicated with Col. Lemnel Coggins, head of the USAF's Dental Corps.

Col. Coggins informed him that no one of Dr. Goldpepper's name or description was or had been affiliated with any such project, and that, in fact, any such project was still – as he put It – "still on the drawing-board."

Drs. Rorke and Fadderman, great as was their concern, hesitated to report Dr. Goldpepper missing. He had, after all, paid rent on apartment, office and laboratory, well in advance. He was a mature man, of very considerable intelligence, and one who presumably knew what he was doing.

"It is at this point," said Dr. Danbourge, "that I enter the picture. On the 11th of January, I had a call from a Dr. Milton Wilson, who has an office on East 19th Street, with a small laboratory adjoining, where he does prosthetic work. He told me, with a good deal of hesitation, that something exceedingly odd had come up, and he asked me if I knew where Dr. Morris Goldpepper was…"

The morning of the 11th of January, an elderly man with a curious foreign accent came into Dr. Wilson's office, gave the name of Smith and complained about an upper plate. It did not feel comfortable, Mr. Smith said, and it irritated the roof of his mouth. There was a certain reluctance on his part to allow Dr. Wilson to examine his mouth. This was understandable, because the interior of his mouth was blue. The gums were entirely edentulous, very hard, almost horny. The plate itself – "Here is the plate," Dr. Danbourge said, placing it on the table.

"Dr. Wilson supplied him with another. You will observe the perforations on the upper, or palatal, surface. They had been covered with a thin layer of gum arabic, which naturally soon wore almost entirely off, with the result that the roof of the mouth became irritated. Now this is so very unusual that Dr. Wilson – as soon as his patient, the so-called Mr. Smith, was gone – broke open the weirdly made plate to find why the perforations had been made. In my capacity as head of the Association's Legal Department," Dr. Danbourge stated, "I have come across some extraordinary occurrences, but nothing like this."

This was a small piece of a white, flexible substance, covered with tiny black lines. Danbourge picked up a large magnifying glass. "You may examine these objects, Doctors," he said, "but it will save your eyesight if I read to you from an enlarged photostatic copy of this last one. The nature of the material, the method of writing, or of reducing the writing to such size all are unknown to us. It may be something on the order of microfilm. But that is not important. The important thing is the content of the writing – the portent of the writing.

"Not since Dr. Morton, the young Boston dentist, realized the uses of sulphuric ether as an anesthetic has any member of our noble profession discovered anything of even remotely similar importance; and perhaps not before, either."

He drew his spectacles from their case and began to read aloud.

TWO

Despite the fact that our great profession lacks the glamour and public adulation of the practice of medicine, and even the druggists – not having a Hippocratic Oath – can preen themselves on their so-called Oath of Maimonides (though, believe me, the great Maimonides had no more to do with it than Morris Goldpepper, D.D.S.), no one can charge us with not having as high a standard of ethics and professional conduct as physicians and surgeons, M.D. Nor do I hesitate for one single moment to include prostheticians not holding the degree of Doctor of Dental Surgery or Doctor of Dental Medicine, whose work is so vital and essential.

When the records of our civilization are balanced, then – but perhaps not before – the real importance of dental science will be appreciated. Now it is merely valued at the moment of toothache.

It is only with a heavy heart that I undertake deliberately to produce inferior work, and with the confidence that all those to whom the standards of oral surgery and dental prosthetics are dear will understand the very unusual circumstances which have prompted me to so to do. And, understanding, will forgive. No one can hold the standards of our profession higher or more sacred than I.

It must be admitted that I was not very amused on a certain occasion when my cousin, Nathaniel Pomerance, introduced me to an engineering contractor with these words, "You two should have a lot in common – you both build bridges," and uttered a foolish laugh. But I venture to say that this was one of the truest words ever spoken in questionable jest.

Humility is one thing, false pride another. Those who know anything of modern dentistry at all know of the Goldpepper Bridge and the Goldpepper Crown. It is I, Dr. Morris Goldpepper, inventor of both, and perfector of the Semi-retractable Clasp which bears my name, who writes these words you see before you. Nothing further should be needful by way of identification. And now to my report.

On the first of November, a day of evil import forever in the personal calendar of the unhappy wretch who writes these lines, not even knowing for sure if they will ever be read – but what else can I do? – shortly after 5:00 P.M., my laboratory door was knocked on. I found there a curious-looking man of shriveled and weazened appearance. He asked if I was Dr. Morris Goldpepper, "the famous perfector of the Semi-retractable Clasp," and I pleaded guilty to the flattering impeachment.

The man had a foreign-sounding accent, or – I thought – it may be that he had an impediment in his speech. Might he see me, was his next question. I hesitated.

It has happened to me before, and to most other practitioners – a stranger comes and, before you know it, he is slandering some perfectly respectable D.D.S. or D.M.D. The dentist pulled a healthy tooth – the dentist took such and such a huge sum of money for new plates – they don't fit him, he suffers great anguish – he's a poor man, the dentist won't do anything – et cetera, ad infinitum nauseamque. In short, a nut, a crank, a crackpot.

But while I was hesitating, the man yawned, did not courteously cover his mouth with his hand, and I observed to my astonishment that the interior of his mouth was an odd shade of blue!

Bemused by this singular departure from normalcy, I allowed him to enter. Then I wondered what to say, since he himself was saying nothing, but he looked around the lab with interest. "State your business" would be too brusque, and "Why is your mouth blue?" would be too gauche. An impasse.

Whilst holding up a large-scale model of the Goldpepper Cap (not yet perfected – will it ever be? Alas, who knows?) this curious individual said, "I know all about you, Dentist Goldpepper. A great scientist, you are. A man of powerful imagination, you are. One who rebels against narrow horizons and yearns to soar to wide and distant worlds, you are."

All I could think of to say was, "And what can I do for you?"

It was all so true; every single word he said was true. In my vanity was my downfall. I was tricked like the crow with the cheese in the ancient fable of Aesop.

The man proceeded to tell me, frankly enough, that he was a denizen of another planet. He had two hearts, would you believe it? And, consequently, two circulatory systems. Two pulses – one in each arm, one slow, the other fast.

It reminded me of the situation in Philadelphia some years ago when there were two telephone systems – if you had only a Bell phone, you couldn't call anyone who had only a Keystone phone.

The interior of his mouth was blue and so was the inside of his eyelids. He said his world had three moons.

You may imagine my emotions at hearing that my long-felt dream to communicate with otherworldly forms of sentient life was at last realized! And to think that they had singled out not the President of the United States, not the Director-General of the U.N., but me, Morris Goldpepper, D.D.S.! Could human happiness ask for more, was my unspoken question. I laughed softly to myself and I thought, What would my cousin Nathaniel Pomerance say now? I was like wax in this extraterrestrial person's hands (he had six distinct and articulate digits on each one), and I easily agreed to say nothing to anyone until the question of diplomatic recognition could be arranged on a higher echelon.

"Non-recognition has its advantages, Goldpepper Dental Surgeon," he said with a slight smile. "No passport for your visit, you will need."

Well! A personal invitation to visit Proxima Centauri Gamma, or whatever the planet's name is! But I felt constrained to look this gift-horse just a little closer in the mouth. How is it that they came inviting me, not, let us say, Oppenheimer? Well?

"Of his gifts not in need, we are, Surgical Goldpepper. We have passed as far beyond nuclear power as you have beyond wind power. We can span the Universe – but in dentistry, like children still, we are. Come and inspect our faculties of your science, Great Goldpepper. If you say, 'This: Yes,' then it will be yes. If you direct, 'This: No,' then it will be no. In respect to the science of dentistry, our Edison and our Columbus, you will be."

I asked when we would leave and he said in eight days. I asked how long the trip would take. For a moment, I was baffled when he said it would take no longer than to walk the equivalent of the length of the lab floor. Then he revealed his meaning to me: Teleportation! Of course. No spaceship needed.

My next emotion was a brief disappointment at not being able to see the blazing stars in black outer space. But, after all, one ought not be greedy at such a time.

I cannot point out too strongly that at no time did I accept or agree to accept any payment or gratuity for this trip. I looked upon it in the same light as the work I have done for various clinics.

"Should I take along books? Equipment? What?" I asked my (so-to-speak) guide. He shook his head. Only my presence was desired on the first trip. A visit of inspection. Very well.

On the morning of Nov. 8th, I wrote a brief note to my old and dear friend, Dr. Samuel Fadderman, the senior mentor of American

Dentistry [on hearing these words, the Elder Statesman sobbed softly into his cupped hands], and in the afternoon, so excited and enthralled that I noticed no more of my destination than that it was north of the Washington Market, I accompanied my guide to a business building in the aforesaid area.

He led me into a darkened room. He clicked a switch. There was a humming noise, a feeling first of heaviness, then of weightlessness, and then an odd sort of light came on.

I was no longer on the familiar planet of my birth! I was on an unknown world!

Over my head, the three moons of this far-off globe sailed majestically through a sky wherein I could note unfamiliar constellations. The thought occurred to me that poets on this planet would have to find another rhyme, inasmuch as moons (plural form) does not go with June (singular form). One satellite was a pale yellow, one was brown, and the third was a creamy pink. Not knowing the names of these lunary orbs in their native tongue, I decided to call them Vanilla, Chocolate and Strawberry.

Whilst my mind was filled with these droll fancies, I felt a tug at my sleeve, where my guide was holding it. He gestured and I followed.

"Now," I thought to myself, "he will bring me before the President of their Galactic Council, or whatever he is called," and I stood obediently within a circle marked on the surface of the platform whereon we stood.

In a moment, we were teleported to an inside room somewhere, and there I gazed about me in stupefaction, not to say astonishment. My eyes discerned the forms of Bunsen burners, Baldor lathes, casting machines and ovens, denture trays, dental stone, plaster, shellac trays, wires of teeth, and all the necessary equipment of a fully equipped dental prosthetic laboratory.

My surprise at the progress made by these people in the science at which they were allegedly still children was soon mitigated by the realization that all the items had been made on Earth.

As I was looking and examining, a door opened and several people entered. Their faces were a pale blue, and I realized suddenly that my guide must be wearing makeup to conceal his original complexion. They spoke together in their native dialect; then one of them, with a rod of some kind in his hand, turned to me. He opened his mouth. I perceived his gums were bare.

"Dentical person," he said, "make me teeth."

I turned in some perplexity to my guide. "I understood you to say my first visit would be one of inspection only."

Everyone laughed, and I observed that all were equally toothless. The man in the chair poked me rudely with his rod or staff.

"Talk not! Make teeth!"

Fuming with a well-justified degree of indignation, I protested at such a gross breach of the laws of common hospitality. Then, casting concealment to the winds, these people informed me as follows:

Their race is entirely toothless in the adult stage. They are an older race than ours and are born looking ancient and wrinkled. It is only comparatively recently that they have established contact with Earth, and in order that they should not appear conspicuous, and in order to be able to eat our food, they realized that they must be supplied with artificial teeth.

My so-called guide, false friend, my enticer and/or kidnaper, to give him his due, had gotten fitted at a dentist's in New York and cunningly enquired who was the leading man in the field. Alas for fame! The man answered without a second of hesitation, "That is no other one than Morris Goldpepper, D.D.S., perfector of the Semi-retractable Clasp."

First this unscrupulous extraterrestrial procured the equipment, then he procured me.

"Do I understand that you purport that I assist you in a plan to thwart and otherwise circumvent the immigration laws of the United States?" was my enquiry.

The man in the chair poked me with his rod again. "You understand! So now make teeth!"

What a proposition to make to a law-abiding, patriotic American citizen by birth! What a demand to exact of a war veteran, a taxpayer and one who has been three times on jury duty since 1946 alone (People vs. Garrity, People vs. Vanderdam, and Lipschutz vs. Krazy-Kut Kool Kaps, Inc.)! My whole being revolted. I spoke coldly to them, informing them that the situation was contrary to my conception of dental ethics. But to no avail.

My treacherous dragoman drew a revolver from his pocket. "Our weapons understand, you do not. Primitive Earth weapons, yes. So proceed with manufacture, Imprisoned Goldpepper."

I went hot and cold. Not, I beg of you to understand, with fear, but with humiliation. Imprisoned Goldpepper! The phrase, with all the connotations it implied, rang in my ears.

I bowed my head and a phrase from the literary work "Sampson Agonistes" (studied as a student in the College of the City of New York) rang through my mind: Eyeless in Gaza, grinding corn… Oh, blind, blind, amidst the blaze of noon…

But even in this hour of mental agony, an agony which has scarcely abated to speak of, I had the first glimmering of the idea which I hope will enable me to warn Earth.

Without a word, but only a scornful glance to show these blue-complected individuals how well I appreciated that their so-called advanced science was a mere veneer over the base metal of their boorishness, I set to work. I made the preliminary impressions and study casts, using an impression tray with oval floor form, the best suited for taking impressions of edentulous ridges.

And so began the days of my slavery.

Confined as I am here, there is neither day nor night, but an unremitting succession of frenum trims, post dams, boxing in, pouring up, festoon carving, fixing sprue channels, and all the innumerable details of dental prosthetic work. No one assists me. No one converses with me, save in brusque barks relevant to the work at hand. My food consists of liqueous and gelatinous substances such as might be expected would form the diet of a toothless race.

Oh, I am sick of the sight of their blue skins, bluer mouths and horny ridges! I am sick of my slavish serfdom!

I have been given material to keep records and am writing this in expectation of later reducing it in size by the method here employed, and of thereinafter inserting copies between the palatal and occlusual surfaces of the plates. It will be necessary to make such plates imperfect, so that the wearers will be obliged to go to dentists on Earth for repairs, because it is not always practical for them to teleport – in fact, I believe they can only do it on the 8th day of every third month. Naturally, I cannot do this to every plate, for they might become suspicious.

You may well imagine how it goes against my grain to produce defective work, but I have no other choice. Twice they have brought me fresh dental supplies, which is how I calculate their teleporting cycle. I have my wristwatch with me and thus I am enabled to reckon the passing of time.

What their exact purpose is in going to Earth, I do not know. My growing suspicion is that their much-vaunted superior science is a fraud and that their only superiority lies in the ability to teleport. One curious item may give a clue: They have questioned me regarding the Old Age Assistance programs of the several States. As I have said, they all look old.

Can it be that elsewhere on this planet there is imprisoned some poor devil of a terrestrial printer or engraver, toiling under duress to produce forged birth certificates and other means of identification, to the fell purpose of allowing these aliens to live at ease at the financial expense of the already overburdened U.S. taxpayer?

To whom shall I address my plea for help? To the Federal Government? But it has no official or even unofficial knowledge that this otherworldly race exists. The F.B.I.? But does teleporting under false pretenses to another planet constitute kidnaping across State lines?

It seems the only thing I can do is to implore whichever dental practitioner reads these lines to communicate at once with the American Dental Association. I throw myself upon the mercy of my fellow professional men.

Dentists and Dental Prostheticians! Beware of men with blue mouths and horny, edentulous ridges! Do not be deceived by flattery and false promises! Remember the fate of that most miserable of men, Morris Goldpepper, D.D.S., and, in his horrible predicament, help, oh, help him!

THREE

A LONG SILENCE followed the reading of this document. At length it was broken by Dr. Hansen.

"That brave man," he said in a husky voice. "That brave little man."

"Poor Morris," said Dr. Danbourge. "Think of him imprisoned on a far-off planet, slaving like a convict in a salt mine, so to speak, making false teeth for these inhuman aliens, sending these messages to us across the trackless void. It's pitiful, and yet, Doctors, it is also a tribute to the indomitable spirit of Man!"

Dr. Weinroth moved his huge hands. "I'd like to get ahold of just one of those blue bastards," he growled.

Dr. Rorke cleared his throat. All present looked at their President respectfully and eagerly.

"I need hardly tell you, Doctors," he said crisply, "that the A.D.A. is a highly conservative organization. We do not go about things lightly. One such message we might ignore, but there have been eleven reported, all identical with the first. Even eleven such messages we might perhaps not consider, but when they come from a prominent scientist of the stature of Dr. Morris Goldpepper –

"Handwriting experts have pronounced this to be his handwriting beyond cavil of a doubt. Here" – he delved into a box – "are the eleven plates in question. Can any of you look at these clean lines and deny that they are the work of the incomparable Goldpepper?"

The six other men looked at the objects, shook their heads.

"Beautiful," murmured Dr. Smith, "even in their broken state. Poems in plastic! M. G. couldn't produce bad work if he tried!"

Dr. Rorke continued. "Each report confirmed that the person who brought in the plate had a blue mouth and edentulous ridges, just as the message states. Each blue-mouthed patient exhibited the outward appearance of old age. And, gentlemen, of those eleven, no less than eight were reported from the State of California. Do you realize what that means? California offers the highest amount of financial assistance to the elderly! Goldpepper's surmise was right!"

Dr. Hansen leaned forward. "In addition, our reports show that five of those eight are leaders in the fight against fluoridation of drinking water! It is my carefully considered belief that there is something in their physical makeup, evolved on another planet, which cannot tolerate fluorine even in minute quantities, because they certainly – being already toothless – wouldn't be concerned with the prevention of decay."

Young Dr. McCallister took the floor. "We have checked with dental supply houses and detail men in the New York metropolitan area and we found that large quantities of prosthetic supplies have been delivered to an otherwise unknown outfit – called the Echs Export Company – located not far north of the Washington Market! There is every reason to believe that this is the place Dr. Goldpepper mentioned. One of our men went there, found present only one man, in appearance an old man. Our representative feigned deafness, thus obliging this person to open his mouth and talk loudly. Doctors, he reports that this person has a blue mouth!"

There was a deep intake of breath around the table.

Dr. Rorke leaned forward and snapped off the tape recorders. "This next is off the record. It is obvious, Doctors, that no ordinary methods will suffice to settle this case, to ensure the return of our unfortunate colleague, or to secure the withdrawal of these extraterrestrial individuals from our nation and planet. I cannot, of course, officially endorse what might be termed 'strong-arm' methods. At the same time, I feel that our adversaries are not entitled to polite treatment. And obviously the usual channels of law enforcement are completely closed to us.

"Therefore – and remember, no word of this must pass outside our circle – therefore I have communicated something of this matter to Mr. Albert Annapollo, the well-known waterfront figure, who not long ago inaugurated the splendid Longshoremen's Dental Health Plan. Mr. Annapollo is a somewhat rough person, but he is nonetheless a loyal American…

"We know now the Achilles heel of these alien creatures. It is fluorine. We know also how to identify them. And I think we may shortly be able to announce results. Meanwhile –" he drew a slip of paper from his pocket – "it is already the first of the month in that quarter when the dental supplies are due to be transported – or teleported, as Dr. Goldpepper terms it – to their distant destination. A large shipment is waiting to be delivered from the warehouses of a certain wholesaler to the premises of the Echs Exporting Company. I have had copies of this made and wrapped around each three-ounce bottle of Ellenbogen's Denture Stik-Phast. I presume it meets with your approval." He handed it to Dr. Hansen, who, as the others present nodded in grimly emphatic approval, read it aloud.

"From The American Dental Association, representing over 45,000 registered dentists in the United States and its Territories, to Dr. Morris Goldpepper, wherever you may be: DO NOT DESPAIR! We are intent upon your rescue! We will bend every effort to this end! We shall fight the good fight! "Have courage, Dr. Morris Goldpepper! You shall return!"

Dragon Control
By Rami Shalheveth

Translated by Rehavia Berman

BORN IN JERUSALEM IN 1971, Rami Shalheveth grew up in a homeful of books of all sorts. For his Bar Mitzvah, he was given *A Connecticut Yankee in King Arthur's Court*, which' along with *I Robot* that he got from his homeroom teacher, and *The Lord of the Rings*, which he decided to read on his own at the same year, opened up his imagination to the wondrous spaces of fantasy and science fiction realms.

In 2000, as a graduate student of communication at the Hebrew University in Jerusalem, he started an online SF/F magazine called *Bli Panika!* (*Don't Panic!*), which he has kept going ever since. Since then, he has been editor of translated and then original fiction for the ISSF&F's fanzine, *HaMemad ha'Asiri* (*The Tenth Dimension*), and a short-lived magazine called *Leprechaun*, all in print. When *HaMemad* closed down, Shalheveth led the launch of the literary yearly *Hayoh Yihyeh* (*Once Upon a Future*), which has been going on since 2009. Shalheveth also translated several SF/F books and stories.

His day job is contents editor for the Davidson Institute of Science Education, the educational arm of the Weizmann

Institute, which focuses on making science accessible to the general public. For most of the time, Shalheveth writes about science and speculative literature, but takes greater pleasure and satisfaction in editing what other people wrote. "Dragon Control," a winner of the 2004 Geffen Award, is one of the very few stories he has written.

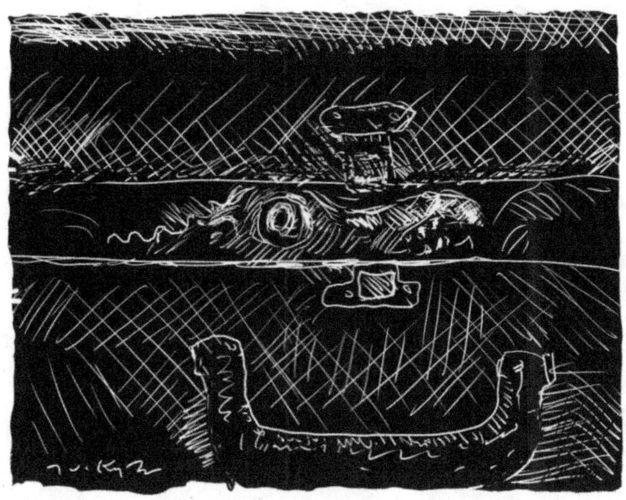

Hello, sir.

Did you pack on your own?

Are you carrying a weapon?

Did someone give you anything to deliver to anyone?

Will you open your suitcase, please?

Excuse me, why not? Are you having a laugh at my expense? What is a pocket dragon, anyway?

I understand.

Uh-huh.

Even has a license? You don't say…

The District Veterinarian? Nice.

No, you can't move on. I need to check the regulations.

Okay, I see we have a problem. How old is it?

Excuse me, sir – it's absolutely my business. The instructions say that dragons are considered a security risk once their fire glands have developed, at age 5.5 to 7 months.

A year and a bit? I'm sorry, then, you won't be able to take it with you on the plane.

Huh? There's nothing in the regulations about a standard muzzle.

Oh, right. Then I suppose that's alright. Now, what about the rest of the documents?

What do you mean, what documents? It says here that to fly with a dragon, you must have a municipal pet license, a pet flight license, a predatory animal flight license, a fire safety certificate, a wing tax receipt, a clean bill of character, five large moths, and excuse me, miss, can't you see there's a line here? Wait for your turn like everyone else.

Yes, everyone here is waiting patiently, you'll have to do the same. Now, where were we? Moths?

Yes, that's a new regulation following the unfortunate incident on the Air France flight. We don't want a hungry dragon on board, do we?

Okay, but take the suitcase with you. You can bypass the line when you're done.

Hello, miss, you see? You didn't have to wait long.

Welcome back, sir. I'll be right with you. I see you brought the moths.

Haha. Two moths and three grasshoppers. You're killing me. Okay, fine. Prepare the paperwork meanwhile.

Okay, got the paperwork?

I see. Two signed flight licenses, a fire safety, a visa for a human with an animal, the moths I've seen… and what's this document?

No, I don't think you need a weapons license for a dragon.

Okay, and what about the municipal license?

Giv'ataim? What do they have to do with it?

They don't require a license there? Hang on a moment.

You're right, sorry. Have a good trip.

Hello, sir.

Did you pack on your own?

Are you carrying a weapon?

A troll? One moment, let me check.

The Word Farmers
By Lili Daie

L ILI DAIE IS A LAPSED LIBRARIAN with academic degrees in Cognitive Science and Communication Studies, who found herself working in Israel's booming High-Tech industry to finance her habit of writing short stories on high-quality notepads (the kind with thick, creamy paper) that she carries around wherever she goes. Before this, she'd spent several years in academia studying the unconscious mind, which she often draws on in her writing.

Daie was born in Jerusalem in 1983 to immigrant parents from Iran and the USSR, grew up in a home that celebrated multiculturalism, acceptance, and literature, and as the daughter of a fantasy writer and a science fiction fan – started writing about other worlds almost as soon as she could write. She won the 2008 Geffen award for the best short story for her story "Where Books are Lost." She spent a few years on the Israeli Society for Science Fiction and Fantasy executive committee. She now volunteers as the fiction editor for the society's online magazine and on the judging panels of several of the society's short story contests.

"The Word Farmers" is her first attempt at writing in English. It was born while traveling abroad, as she was staring out a plane window. A Hebrew translation of this story was published in the annual anthology *Once Upon a Future* in 2019.

IN AN INFINITE UNIVERSE, RAPIDLY EXPANDING, you come in the fullness of time to expect the most unlikely things.

"Agriculture and Astronomy? Isn't that a strange combination?" he asks. I shrug. I've already forgotten his name, if he'd ever told me.

That the pattern of fields and forests on planet Earth, random blocks of color as defined by historical, socioeconomic, and geographical conditions, would resemble a form of alien writing which may just briefly surprise anyone with any kind of understanding of the cosmos, but nothing more. Don't ask me how I know this. I just do. But why would anyone here have any kind of understanding of the cosmos? And it's not like I can tell them. Still, I bow my head slightly to allow the cover of my dark, earth-colored hair to hide my eyes, allowing myself to answer. My eyes, I've soon learned, are my greatest flaw, always attracting unwanted attention – appearing normal for most of the time, they acquire a golden hue whenever I speak of the Book, radiating a faint light. A warning from my creators, probably: don't expose your knowledge to the Farmers, don't imagine for a second that you belong.

With my head bowed and a screen of dark hair covering my narrowed eyes, it is as safe to answer the innocent-seeming question as it can get.

"My two great passions," I say, "the earth and the sky. You could say that this way, I study everything."

When the light fades and my vision clears again, when I look up to see the effect my words had, I find him staring at me in wonder. Did he see it? I can feel the panic starting to rise within me. Did he notice the light escaping between my eyelashes, trickling down my skin like tears of molten gold? I don't want to hurt him. I've never wanted to hurt anyone. I think I understand the logic behind this light, which seems to make my work so much more difficult: my mission does, at times, require death, pain, destruction. You are *not* one of them, warn my creators with this light; your very survival demands ruthlessness. Were they just being kind? Did they think it would be easier for me if I couldn't look a Farmer in the eyes?

"And what do you want to be when you grow up?" he asks, and I am relieved – he's just hitting on me, he probably didn't notice my eyes at all. Adopting the habit of wearing low-cut shirts, I found early in my existence, makes talking to men far less dangerous. I give him one of my stock answers – NASA, or farming, or both. It doesn't matter. I won't ever grow up.

To the Bai, Earth is an open book – an ever-changing assemblage of words morphing with the changing of the seasons and the onset of droughts, whole sections of the text disappearing as progress takes place and cities emerge. The apparent meaninglessness in word order has always been a subject of much discussion, as were the occasional meaningful messages that cropped up when the wheat turned gold, or the climate shifted. "DO NOT SHOUT," it once said, and then "DO NT SHAW," which received dozens of exegeses. For the past hundred years or so, a plain in China has been saying "GATHER." But who knows where to gather, or when, or why, or what? A general, philosophical gathering, some suggested – become a more united species, show love and understanding, be open, truthful, allow others into your life and soul. A gathering of minds, as it were. Most Bai think this is rather silly, really, but try not to say so in the presence of the Gatherers – the poor, sweet, deluded souls that they tend to be.

I confess that I'm feeling a little distracted – it is, in a way, my birthday. It is ten years to the day since I became, and I have accomplished nothing. The Farmers are polluting the Book more than ever, but what could I possibly do about it, all alone, a single human-like girl among billions? My creators put so much knowledge in me – but not that. I feel so useless, so very, very lonely, and therefore I allow him to take me home, close my eyes and let my mind wander, hungry for distraction. The next morning, he gives me a ride to the university and asks if he could see me again.

For thousands of years, the Bai have been reading, analyzing, discussing the Book. They have come to know the human race, to realize that the Book was not a result of humanity attempting to communicate. When the humans started gazing at the stars, the Bai learned concealment. When they found their vision of the Book obscured by smoke, they found new ways to observe. The Planetary Book is regarded by many as sacred, by others as ridiculous, or a random trick played by chance, or an enigma, or an unexplained yet beautiful natural phenomenon – no two Bai seem to agree. Those who return from the Observatories, now popular tourist destinations, tend to have a haunted, bewildered look about them, as though they have perceived a meaning they cannot quite comprehend, that lies just slightly outside their reach. Don't ask me how I know this. I just do.

WHEN WILL HE SEE ME AGAIN? What can I say to that? That I'm only ten years old and not ready for a relationship? That I can't have a relationship anyway because eventually, he will notice my eyes and I shall end up hurting him? That I only *look* human? In the end, I give him a fake phone number and run off to class. This isn't one of my proudest moments.

It's not as easy as you may have expected, to learn something you already know. I need to be noticed, to reach a position of influence, without giving myself away, and more importantly, without influencing human science beyond an acceptable yet unspecified level. I must show potential but never fulfill it, never make any crucial discoveries, constantly guard myself against accidentally revealing essential information given to me by the Bai; it slowly unfolds within me when it becomes relevant. It won't be long before I am done here, at the university, and it is time to find my place in some space program, or perhaps in politics. I shall miss it here. For a while, it was as if I belonged. Perhaps, I think sometimes, I could really belong in one of the space programs, perhaps I shall meet my family there – more and more accidents have been happening these past two years, spacecraft crashing or burning during reentry, others failing to launch altogether. I am sure this is the work of others like me, ones who adapted faster than me. They will understand me. Accept me. Know me completely. There will be no lies between us, we will fulfill our purpose together, my brothers and sisters and I, and I shall never be alone again. I study the night sky in search of a sign, but it remains empty, empty and clear and silent as ever.

And as the technology of the humans – affectionately dubbed the Word Farmers – kept evolving, the social order of the Bai destabilized rapidly: contact them, said some, make it easier to study the Book, simply ask them what they think about it. Keep away from them, said others, do not interfere with this race or you will affect the Book, denying it the freedom to share its wisdom with the universe, with the Bai. And so, eventually, the impossibly complex project of Book Preservation began.

It is easy to study the sky. The machinery is amazingly accessible. The Book Farmers scan the night sky obsessively, although they never find anything of note. They visit the moon, send probes and messages into deep space, shout into the universe without ever hearing back, remain lonely in the silence that engulfs them. Forever ignorant of the thousands of Bai slaving away to keep the space surrounding the Book pristine. No, the Farmers' probes are never intercepted or interfered with; they are simply accompanied on their journey, fed data of emptiness where emptiness is not, a perimeter of one hundred light-years in every direction wiped of all artificial signals. This small-yet-talkative planet is sheltered, isolated, its inhabitants allowed to continue their existence without interference by or awareness of the rest of the universe. Sometimes the Bai try to intercept and analyze all these communications, looking for some understanding or meaning, a key to the Book's mysteries, but if there is one, it is yet to be deciphered. You may ask me how I know this, but I cannot explain. How do you know where the world ends and you begin? And yet, somehow, you do.

"I've talked to some people," says my professor, a nice old man who practically adopted me as his daughter these past two years. "There might be room for you here in the department."

I smile. I take his hand. My very existence is a betrayal of everything he believes in, the old dear. "You know I'm looking for something more… something less theoretical."

"Always the diplomat, eh?"

I shrug.

"You can't blame an old man for trying."

"I would stay if I could. For you. I love working with you. But it just… isn't who I am," I answer, more honestly than I intended.

"I'll name a galaxy after you," he winks.

"Are you calling me fatso?" I retort.

"I can find you a place in one of our more practical labs."

"Their projects are years away from practical."

"Are you in a hurry?"

Yes. Yes, I am.

I thank him, but I leave. In my room, there awaits a board displaying most of the space programs on this planet. The bigger ones are the obvious choices, but they are also harder to influence, and likely to already have been infiltrated by siblings. I don't want to waste my efforts. But then, what if we all follow the same logic? What if none of us arrived at NASA simply because we all believed someone else was headed there? And what if they really are already there, my family, would it be so wrong? Our combined efforts could…

No. This line of thought is never fruitful. I collect my thoughts and carry them to the observatory, where I always go when my mind is overwhelmed.

There was probably nothing to distinguish the Day of Choice from any other day in the Bai calendar, which is complex and bewildering at the best of times. I believe it was simply the culmination of a long process, a point where a decision could no longer be postponed, an opportunity for an ambitious politician to declare that the Day of Choice is Upon Us. My knowledge fails me in this, though. I am left to imagine it as best I can: The Farmers evolving beyond the Bai's abilities to contain them from the outside, the ethics of limiting a species of sentient beings on account of the planet they inhabit being once again weighed against the existence of the Book, a horrible, barbarous thing to do, and will the Farmers not retaliate if ever they learn of it? Will they not interfere with the Bai through manipulations of the Book? There is much profit to be had by making subtle changes to this protected planet. The decision had eventually been put to the vote – every Bai, everywhere, was facing the Choice in fear and hope and agonizing indecision. And, eventually, I became.

I remember becoming conscious of myself, of my surroundings – seemingly flat but curved, I knew instinctively, on a scale beyond my processing abilities, forming an imperfect orb, the great Planetary Book. My two hands shielded my two eyes against the bright light. My two lungs gulped the sharp, clear air. My surprisingly symmetrical body pulsed and gasped, a well-designed machine that my Creators are still unsure whether it evolved here naturally or was explicitly designed to Farm Words.

But I, unlike these miserable creatures I resemble in body, knew my purpose – I was to study the Book and its Farmers and protect them from all threats, themselves included. I am the Choice, I am the Solution. I and others like me. For there are others like me – mending the damages made by humankind and interfering with its various space agencies, altering the species' future in subtle, non-violent ways, without damaging the Book. It is an impossible mission, some may say, but it is not my place to ask – and if it were, I'd have no one to answer me. I am alone here, on Earth, my siblings strangers to me, my creators distant and unreachable. All there is, all there will ever be, lies around me in the fields.

"Beth." Daniel acknowledges my coming in without looking up from his work.

"Hi, Daniel, am I interrupting anything?"

"No, do come in. Wanna have a go at the old telescope?"

Of course I do. Don't I always? I move to the all-too-familiar telescope, staring at the darkness between the stars like a dog staring at a closed door through which his masters may enter at any moment. Daniel works on the more modern equipment, for once refraining from remarking on my old-fashioned taste in telescopes. Who is he kidding, anyway? He looks at the sky while he's waiting for his code to compile, the same as all of us. No one who can withstand the temptation of an old telescope finds himself here.

"So, how goes the farming?" he asks, and I, without thinking, without even realizing, answer him.

"Oh, you know, it's farming," an automatic response, no real meaning behind it, but still, my eyes fill with light. I'm facing away from him, it should be safe, but the light coming out of my eyes hits the mirror, reflects into the room. I shut my eyes tight, too late, too late.

"Are you OK? What the hell was that?" Daniel pulls me away from the eyepiece. Poor Daniel, always so friendly, ever since I first came here, attracted to the gigantic antique telescope but too shy to ask, and he came up to me to explain all about it. "You want that one, don't you?" he asked, knowingly. "We have more sophisticated equipment, you know… you're a romantic, I can tell. Go on, have a look." There was such kindness about him. We were never really close outside the observatory, but we spent many a night talking, gazing at the sky together. It has always been just a matter of time, I realize now.

"Are you alright? Beth?" He leans over me, but I can't open my eyes to see him, not yet. "Did that light hurt your eye? What was it, did you see?"

For a moment, there is hope, but only for a moment – soon he will find out that no one else saw anything, soon he will figure out that light came from somewhere in here, there will be questions, questions I can't answer. The protocol is clear, more instinct than conscious thought, the Bai reach out with my hands, it is the Bai who lock my fingers around his neck, squeezing, the light has faded from my eyes long ago, but I don't dare open them, if I don't see it maybe it never happens, the look in his eyes, the surprise, the betrayal, I have to get out of here, and still I squeeze and squeeze until the struggle is over, and his weight is crushing me. I have to get out of here. Poor Daniel. I've never killed anyone I liked quite as much. Poor, poor Daniel. I want to feel sick, but I don't – this is how I was made; this is what I was made for. I liked him, I killed him, and now I must leave him. Now. Before anyone else comes in. I open my eyes, push Daniel off me, run. I want so badly to cry for him, for myself, but I'm pure instinct now, there will be plenty of time for hating myself later.

The next day, I'm shocked to hear that Daniel is dead. I go to the funeral. Talk about him in a hushed, quivering voice. Tell the story of how we ordered pizza one night, and he accidentally smudged one of the instruments, the panic and the hilarities that ensued, listen to everyone else's stories as we get totally drunk, honoring his memory. For a few weeks, I show the same irrational fear of going to the observatory as any other student, as if the killer is still lurking there in the shadows. It doesn't help that the killer has never been caught. There are new locks on the door, new entrance codes, personal ones for anyone allowed to use it. The guilt isn't new, it's been there ever since my first kill. Fourteen by now, most of them in that first year, when I was young and careless, still learning the ways of this strange world. I try not to think about them. I try to concentrate on finding a job, on getting out of here. Poor Daniel… I'm sorry, I'm so sorry.

The Bai are murderers. It was they who killed those fourteen innocent souls, not me. I didn't want to; I didn't mean to hurt them. The Bai built me as a killer. Sometimes I imagine myself confessing, going to the press, telling them all about the universe and the aliens. But what evidence do I have? My body is all but identical to a human's, apart from the eyes, which could be explained as a minor mutation or defect. The Bai gave no clues. I shall end up as the convicted killer of fourteen people, possibly deemed insane, certainly locked up for the rest of my life. Lonely. Miserable. And even worse, even more unthinkable, defeating my purpose, unable to serve my masters in any way. It won't take my body long to deteriorate, I'm sure. Not that it matters – the words simply won't come out. I know it even without trying.

No, I was never given a choice. And therefore, I cannot be blamed for what I've done. I still feel guilty, though. This world is overwhelming. Sometimes I wonder – what if there is just one other like me? Placed far away, on the other side of this planet? What if none of the others survived? What if the space programs' failures and malfunctions are just accidents, and I only want so badly to see them as evidence for my family's existence somewhere out there? I am not alone. It would be too great a responsibility, it's impossible that I'm alone, but what if there are only two of us, and I shall never meet the only entity in this endless universe that is like me?

I am always gloomy after a kill. And Daniel's death weighs heavier on my mind than most. I am so very hopeless, lonely, lost. Next month I shall leave and never think again about this place – always look to the future, to the mission. I ask myself why they made me this way, those Bai. How is this crippling despair good for the mission? Or is it all a mistake – did they wire me the wrong way? Did some technician slip? How can I tell whether I am who I was meant to be? And where does this line of thinking end? Perhaps I should forget all about this. Find someone who will love me, glowing eyes and all, and spend the rest of my days never once looking up at the sky.

And then, suddenly, I realize – I don't want to join some space program, sabotage shuttles and watch them crash and burn, killing all those people. I just don't. But there is another path open to me: the desert. I shall study the desert, strive to understand the shifting climates, deforestation, desertification, the changing Words, and maybe through them, understand myself. And if my eyes glow, anyone who would notice will assume it's just too much sun making them see things. Let others solve the problem of humanity. I shall never again kill in the Bai's name.

It's not easy finding the right program, but I refuse to compromise. Somewhere out there is the right place for me – remote, as far from civilization as I can get, a small, diverse group that will be too busy with their own work to take too much notice of me… I search for what seems to be forever until I find it. Getting in is even more difficult than that, and as I make my way to the other side of the planet, I'm still not sure whether I'll be allowed to stay. A personal interview by the group members themselves is a non-negotiable condition for acceptance, I am told. But I'm willing to travel, I'm used to uncertainty, and there he is, the first of the bunch, sitting in front of me. I'm sweating and tired. He seems impervious to the heat. His eyes are hidden by a pair of oversized sunglasses despite the relative darkness here in the shade. He is coolness and conceit embodied. They're not going to accept me, I realize. I've come all this way for nothing.

"So, this is a unique combination you majored in. What made you choose…"

I stare at the floor, my eyes are just slits, and hope that whatever sunlight is getting in through the windows will conceal me as I answer.

"…Astronomy and agronomy?"

The narrow stretch of desert I can see wears the familiar, oddly bright glow as I speak, head bowed, and suddenly I feel his hand on my chin, forcing my head up. Startled, I allow my eyes to open by sheer force of instinct, eyes filled with panic. I see the golden light reflected from his large, trusting eyes. Reflected? Reciprocated, more like… this flow of liquid light, the last thing too many people have seen, is so beautiful, mesmerizing, I never realized. I laugh, flutter, my instincts and thoughts fill my head with fireworks, I fall on my hands and knees, struggling for air. And suddenly, his hand is on my back, searching, prodding, pressing… the world is bright with searing pain, and then everything is clear again.

"Beatrice figured it out. She calls it the Panic Button."

"How many?"

"With you, four."

I want to meet them, I want, where are they, I want… I want to sleep.

"It's the button," he says. "You'll be OK. Don't worry." His voice is fading as I let go of my struggle for consciousness, let go of the world, of all worries, succumb to my bed of sand in the safe, unfamiliar knowledge that my brother is watching over me.

When I wake up, they are sitting nearby, three dark figures in the night, their eyes a faint glow – I wonder if it's me they're talking about. I get up, walk towards them and stand there, looking down. They seem so close, so familiar with each other, I feel a stranger more than ever before. And then the girl – Beatrice, is it? – is up, her arms around me in the protective hug of an older sister, and I know that she, too, has missed me all her life, not knowing whether I existed.

"It's so nice not to be the only girl anymore," she whispers in my ear, and I find myself giggling like the child I never was. "This is Brian. You already met Ben."

They stand up to greet me, starting with awkward handshakes and quickly warming up to hugs, they make room for me in their circle, and that is that. I belong. The conversation flows free and wild, all the forbidden topics broached, our combined light fills the night with more gold than I could imagine.

"The first one to glow does the dishes!" declares Ben eventually, as if it were nothing but a party trick.

My face must betray my dismay, for my newfound sister is quick to explain the game to the newcomer: every player is asked a question by each of the others. Using a glowing term, in either question or answer, means losing the game.

"Even here, we have to deal with… them, sometimes." She clumsily avoids referring to the outside world as either humans or Farmers. "We mustn't neglect our survival skills. What did you study, sister?"

They all turn to me, anticipation and smiles mixing in their eyes. My mind is racing to find an answer that will circumvent any words or topics that would light up my eyes. I fail, completely and utterly. They laugh. I do the dishes. Is this what having a family feels like?

I am young, I learn. The youngest of the bunch, and it doesn't take long for them to start babying me. I don't resist. I can't seem to get enough of their smiles, their teasing, their cuddles, and their affection. Beatrice and Brian are almost ten years my seniors, veterans in their own eyes and mine, and they take to teaching me – everything from survival skills to diplomacy, anything that might come in useful. I'm a quick yet reluctant study: I was made to learn, analyze, understand, yet I resist the idea that they might leave, so fast I've grown used to their protection.

And Ben… he claims to be older, certainly, but girls mature faster, and the age gap between us isn't so big that it cannot be bridged. His know-it-all attitude aggravates and annoys me beyond anything I've imagined possible. Beatrice and Brian can hardly keep us from each other's throats. He thinks I'm spoiled, perhaps even that I took his place, no longer the youngest, and he takes an odd pleasure in bossing me around, teaching me the ways of the group, gleefully pointing out each mistake. At night, he sits by me until well after the stars come out, tells me stories of the Book and beyond, makes up wild fantasies about our creators, stays with me long after I drift off, to protect my sleep and chase away my frequent nightmares. He is every bit the older brother that I've always known I had, somewhere, out there, waiting to be found, and I hate him and love him for it, stupid and annoying and kind though he may be.

We move about a lot – to explore, to avoid the humans ("Not Farmers," warns me Beatrice time and again, "humans. People. As if you are just one of them."), to remain always adaptable to circumstances, to surprises. To Survive. At least until the night of the fire.

I wake up to the smell of smoke. It is faint, at first. Anyone else would have missed it. Anyone not hardwired to be a smoke detector and a fire extinguisher rolled into one, who was not created to identify and exploit any opening, to run into the flames and come out again with the Words as intact as possible. Fire, my brain screams as I switch from asleep to awake in an instant, skipping all the phases in between. Fire! Spreading through the Book, eating away at it! I spring into movement, and my whole body whiplashes back as something grabs me. I struggle to free myself, Beatrice and Brian have already passed me by, running into the flames, nothing but shadows now as the blaze becomes visible. I scream as the urge to move tears at me, struggle in my brother's terrible grip.

"It's perfectly contained!" He's yelling in my ear now. "Just a bit of a Rewrite, nothing to worry about. And a good one, too."

I sag in his arms as the understanding sinks in. A Rewrite. The knowledge is both fresh and familiar, startling and expected, ingrained as deep into the fiber of my being as the nature of the Book. Yet only now it becomes relevant, accessible to me. A Rewrite. Religious? Political? Commercial? He probably doesn't know the answer to that either. The fire is a minor danger, being handled, born to be contained. I do not run to put it out when he releases me. The light in his eyes is flaring with terrible joy as he fulfills his purpose, making his subtle changes, corrupting the very thing I was made to protect, in the service of masters as distant and cold as my own. How like me he is. How beautiful in the flames of his insanity that are no fault of his own. How easy it will be for us to join forces against them, cancel each other out and live, just live, purposeless and free. Easy and impossible.

I stare and stare and stare at the fire reflected in his burning eyes, turned up to his invisible masters in pride and hate, his body shaking with their manufactured joy as he longs for a freedom he will never have. Yes, how like me he is, the Rewriter, how beautiful and terrible and like me, how still at my feet as I finally release my grip from around his throat, no longer a threat to the living, growing, ever-changing, sacred Book that is all I shall ever know.

The Thirteenth Fairy

By Nadav Almog

Nadav Almog was born in 1978 in the north of Israel and relocated to the country's central region as an adult. Currently, he resides in Giv'atayim. The first book he read on his own was a children's retelling of J.M. Barrie's *Peter Pan*, and he has been "hooked" on fantasy ever since.

At the age of 14, Nadav received two fantasy books in English, and there began his infatuation with English literature. It was then that his dream of earning a Ph.D. in the field was born. This dream has recently been granted by the Haifa University. Titled *Home and the* Unheimlich *in Children's Fantasy Literature*, his dissertation explores elements of the uncanny and the home in popular works of fantasy fiction for children throughout the 20th century.

During his studies for a master's degree in English Literature, Nadav started writing fiction again, and also created a genre news website called *The Fantastic Library*, under the pseudonym The Night Librarian. Established in 2008, it is one of the longest-running independent genre websites in Israel.

Nadav's stories have been published in sci-fi and fantasy magazines, such as *Bli Panika* and *Halomot BeAspamia*. His stories usually explore the darker themes of folk tales and mythology. "The Thirteenth Fairy" is his first work to be translated into and published in English.

FORBIDDEN!

That was the word that ruled her life. She was forbidden to play with her ball near the well, forbidden to mix with animals and dwarves, forbidden to make any promises, or stand by the window and sing. Forbidden to talk to strangers, or stray from the path, or flirt with the servants. Forbidden to appear too intelligent in the eyes of potential suitors, or roam about on her own. But above all, she was most strictly forbidden to go anywhere near pins, needles, spindles, or any other sewing devices that could prick her delicate skin.

In short, most of the knowledge Princess Thalia had acquired about life until she reached her fifteenth birthday involved all the things she had been forbidden to do.

In accordance with her royal status, the princess lacked for nothing. The King and Queen showered her with love, attention, and gifts, for she was their only daughter and the apple of their eye. They lived in a magnificent, ancient palace, which has been enlarged and rebuilt over generations by countless monarchs, each seeking to outdo their predecessors. The palace towered proudly over its surroundings, and it seemed as if its splendor alone was enough to push back the forest that girdled it; majestic trees were replaced by vast green swathes of grassland which served as pasture ranges in times of peace.

Closer to the palace, enclosed by a high stone wall, were the renowned royal gardens. On special occasions, in times of festivities or holidays, the kingdom's subjects were allowed to visit the gardens and enjoy their beauty. But during such days, the Princess was strictly prohibited from leaving the palace, forbidden to meet with them.

"Everyone loves you very much, and you will undoubtedly be a wonderful queen one day, but in the meantime, we wouldn't want anyone to get the wrong idea, would we?" her parents tried to comfort her. On those days, all Princess Thalia was allowed to do was sit by the window and favor the commoners below with an occasional wave of her hand.

The inner rooms of the palace contained all imaginable riches, and its stone expanses served as the Princess's kingdom. But even that kingdom, rich as it may have been, wasn't enough to quieten her heart for, from the day she was born, at each and every moment, in each nook and cranny, she was constantly observed. The eyes of the King and Queen, or their servants, watched her every step, her every move. During her childhood, following the princess about the palace was no simple task – its vast size offered a curious and mischievous girl plenty of opportunities to disappear into any number of hiding places. But the Princess was never able to get far, or to remain hidden for very long, for not a moment would pass before the King or one of his servants would appear to accompany her back to the main living quarters with all the necessary pomp and circumstance.

"Sometimes, I think you deliberately seek out these places," her mother would scold her.

"Why can't I walk around the palace or in the royal gardens by myself? When will I be able to see the outside world?" Princess Thalia defiantly asked. But each time she tried to ask about the thing her parents seemed so afraid of, she encountered a barrier of silence, a silence as solid as the stone walls of the ancient palace. Over the years, she had reluctantly learned to accept the walls that governed her life, and her protests had diminished, much to her parents' relief and gratification.

Because of the attention she had been subjected to all her life, the Princess was extremely surprised to wake on the morning of her fifteenth birthday and discover that she was alone in the palace. At first, when no one came to wait on her, she was not sure what she should do. While she waited, she occupied herself with thoughts of her birthday and the presents she was bound to receive. But time passed, and the regular knock failed to sound on her door. Her surprise slowly turned to curiosity.

Princess Thalia swung her feet over the edge of her magnificent four-poster bed and lowered them to the floor. Slowly she stood up. At that moment, just as she inclined her head to think, something on the floor twinkled and caught her eye. She saw a silver thread, as fine and thin as a single hair, stretching away under her feet from the leg of her bed. She followed it with her eyes and saw it alternately gleaming and vanishing under the gentle touch of the sunlight shining through the window. When touched by a ray of sunlight, the thread became almost invisible, but against the background of the shadows on the floor, it very nearly shone. The Princess extended a slender finger, plucked the thread like a violin string, and listened to the satisfying sound it produced.

A thought suddenly flashed into her mind. *The thread must be leading to a surprise of some sort!*

Thalia was filled with renewed joy. She dressed as well as she could on her own, put on her sandals, and, for the first time in her life, hesitantly opened the heavily ornate door and left the room on her own. A thrill ran through her slender body as she began to follow the trail of the silvery thread that led her through the palace. The excitement was a living thing in her; after all, who wanted to waste her birthday in bed, locked in a bedroom?

Much to her surprise, she found the long corridors deserted too. She had never heard the palace so utterly silent. *This must be some sort of prank,* she thought, and continued following the thread. The Princess was enjoying herself. The game was fun, mainly because the thread did not discriminate against places where she was not usually allowed and those which she had been forbidden to enter.

The Princess wanted to explore some of the rooms more closely; for instance, dressing rooms containing attractive garments or rooms showcasing fascinating artifacts and weapons the likes of which she had never before seen. The temptation to linger and explore increased the more she drifted, all unknowing, away from the palace wings she was familiar with, and soon she found herself walking down corridors she had never set foot in before. But each time she felt some stirrings of unease, she was distracted by the silvery thread that was glinting in the corner of her eye, reminding her of her birthday.

What a thrilling adventure. This will be the best birthday ever! She thought. And so, step by step, she moved away from the safe, illuminated, familiar rooms of the vast palace.

Perhaps somewhere, deep in the corridors of her mind, the Princess suspected something. Perhaps one of the King's prohibitions even echoed softly in her thoughts, but no one was there to stand in her way, and fifteen years of living under the burden her parents imposed on her have left her hungry for new experiences. The light of the silvery thread seemed to shimmer ever brighter in the unfamiliar, dimly lit corridors, making it even more magical and inviting than ever.

Not long after she set off following the thread, the faint, silvery light led Thalia through an opening hacked in an old wall. In such an ancient palace, it wasn't rare for walls, even entire rooms, to surrender to the erosive weight of time and crumble, especially in the older wings. To Thalia's surprise, the opening she was about to step through had not been boarded or blocked, as was usually the case with such occurrences.

This certainly doesn't look like something my mother and father would have come up with. It's… too… adventurous! thought the Princess.

She was about to turn about and retrace her steps, but something stopped her – that same rebellious spark she thought she had left behind in her childhood. The shadowy hole in the wall looked like a gaping maw, and although it was still and silent, Thalia felt it calling her, as if announcing it was time for her to decide. She knew her parents had planned to surprise her, knew she should pretend to be genuinely surprised for their sake. But now, despite her sense of guilt about her ingratitude, she also knew that nothing her parents had prepared for her could ever equal the adventure she might now create for herself.

Thalia placed both hands on the edges of the hole and steadied herself. Then, with a graceful bound, she allowed the darkness to swallow her. On the other side of the wall, she found herself in another world. There was an immediate, sharp shift. At the other side, there was a cozy-looking room beyond which gaped a silent, shadowy expanse. The scrubbed marble of the palace behind her had given way to coarse, rough-hewn stone, and the comfortable warmth she has known all her life was suddenly replaced by chill and darkness.

With just the silvery light of the thread to see by, the Princess strained her eyes to look around. She was standing in a spacious hall. From somewhere close to the ceiling, a faint light seeped in through distant windows. Thalia could feel the ancient history of the place with all her senses. As she walked on, she pictured in her mind's eye the balls, the loves, duels, disappointments, and triumphs its walls must have seen. Roaming about that place, where the silence was disrupted only by occasional gusts of wind, was both thrilling and chilling. A sharp smell that permeated the hall felt to her like something tangible in itself. The obviously abandoned relics of this place looked to Thalia like mere shadows of the grandeur that must have once filled it with life and light. And for that reason, the spark of defiance that had led her through the hole in the wall now called to her to disturb the silence that must have pervaded the place since long before she was born.

I can always turn back and retrace my steps using the thread, she convinced herself.

The Princess walked on and eventually found herself standing at the foot of a winding staircase that snaked up into impenetrable darkness. The silver thread stretched back and forth over the middle of the stairwell, softly glowing, a complex warp and weft pattern.

Thalia stood silent and unmoving. She felt as if time was standing still with her at that place, as if the staircase had been awaiting her arrival since the beginning of time. She looked up, her eyes transfixed, slightly glazed, as if she had been hypnotized. The circular pattern of the stairwell seemed to extend an invisible hand to her that sought to pull her up. At the same time, feelings of doubt and fear tried to pull her in the other direction, back to where she had come from. She bit her lip and placed her foot on the first stair. It was, she realized, a challenge to her old world. She glanced over her shoulder, giving anyone who might be there a last chance to emerge from behind some wall or pillar, as they were wont to do, and stop her. A moment later, when nothing happened, she turned her gaze upward and began to climb.

Every few moments, she stopped, expecting to hear the sound of footsteps rushing after her, but all she could hear were the echoes of her own steps ringing through the darkness before her. Higher and higher the tower stretched, and before long, the hall floor was lost in the depths of the black abyss below. Thalia was able to peek through the occasional narrow crack in the wall and see the grounds and the roofs of the palace drifting away. The whistle of the wind and the sight of the trees swaying down in the valley below stood in complete contrast to the utter silence and darkness of the tower.

A different world…

Finally, the Princess reached the end of the stairway. Her breath had quickened and her heart was pounding, more from the thrill of doing such a forbidden thing than from any physical strain. Her eyes followed the silver thread which made its way along the straight corridor in front of her, finally disappearing under a small door at its end. It was an old wooden door with a rusty key poking out of a keyhole wreathed in abandoned cobwebs. If it hadn't been the last door at the end of the last stretch of the last floor of the ancient tower in the most remote wing of the grand palace, it might not have looked so unique or inviting. But that was exactly what the door was, and so, Thalia simply had to draw near and examine it closely. Even as she thought how even this small, curiosity-driven act must also be forbidden, her hand was reaching for the key. She twisted it and heard a loud, satisfying click. Thalia recoiled sharply, her hand flying to her face to cover her mouth as the door slowly opened a crack.

From the shadows beyond the threshold, a moisture-laden gust of cold air chilled her face. A pale, tattered drape hung in the doorway, flowing sinuously, slowly. The Princess stepped forward and cautiously peered into the room. She reached out with a hesitant hand and pulled back the curtain. Something cold squeezed her heart as her fingers sank into the fabric, which clung to them like a kind of sticky membrane.

Spiderwebs! She shivered. Almost involuntarily, she jerked her hand back until her fingers were free of the clinging cobwebs. The sudden movement caused her to stumble backward. She stood still. Something inside her was urging her to turn around, to run back into the light and seek her parents. But no!

Forbidden, forbidden, forbidden! Their voices reverberated in her head.

Haven't I come all the way here? If I go back now, will I ever be able to find this place again?

Thalia steeled herself, chasing fear away from her mind. She wrapped her hand in the sleeve of her dress and split the webs in the doorway with a resolute thrust. Beyond them, she was now able to see a murky, damp-smelling corridor, gently inclining up into the dark. The Princess took a deep breath and walked inside, through the doorway…

The passageway she had entered was lit by a wide beam of light penetrating from an open aperture carved into the upper end of its back wall. Only when she reached the end of the passage, when she was standing in the very opening of the room, did she see the beam of light illuminating the figure of an old, bent woman, clad in tattered, faded rags. She was sitting down, completely immersed in her work. Thalia was so shocked to see her there, in the heart of the darkness, that she almost turned and ran for her life. But it appeared that the crone hadn't noticed her, and she stood there watching, fascinated by the unexpected sight. The light coming from the ceiling left the crone's face in shadow, and only her reedy, nimble hands were distinctly visible, wrapping fine thread around an enormous spindle. Thalia watched in admiration as the skillful hands seemed to move on their own, from here to there, tugging, twisting, stretching. Round and round the old woman spun the spindle, rapidly winding around it the thread that gleamed with a silvery light. Thalia gazed at her, mesmerized.

"Hello, old mother," she said, having finally found her tongue. "What are you doing?"

The crone slowly raised her head. "Hello Princess!" she said. "I'm glad to see you've finally decided to pay me a visit. I was wondering when you'd come."

The Princess's heart leaped into her throat. How could it be that the old woman has been waiting for her arrival? She had heard stories of elderly women who could foretell the future and cast spells. "Are you a witch?" she asked.

"Don't be foolish, child," the crone scolded her, yet her voice was laced with amusement. "I am merely an old woman, a spinster *and* a spinner, all roll-rolled into one." She chuckled lightly. "But it is impolite to speak to someone from such a distance. If you'd like to see what my work is like, please come nearer and see for yourself."

"Tell me what it is that you're doing first!" the Princess insisted. The anger she heard in the echo of her voice frightened her. How could that old woman, that stranger, know who she was?

"My, my, Princess, I see that you've left your manners somewhere downstairs…" The crone stopped working and turned to Thalia. Two piercing eyes peered from a face as furrowed as the bark of a tree. "That's all right, I happen to like obstinate girls who know how to stand their ground. I thought you might have already guessed, though, child. Your parents asked me to prepare a birthday present for you."

Thalia felt that the old woman was mocking her, but her words did make sense.

Today really is my birthday… And what if I have shamed my parents again by asking all these questions?

She took a deep breath, raised her head, and stepped forward hesitantly. "What kind of present?" she asked.

"A breathtaking one! You have never seen its like. Your parents have spared no expense to get me here," the old woman answered, honey coating the aged voice. "Come a little closer so you can see for yourself. I'm already accustomed to working in the dark. But you must close the door behind you, to stop those cold drafts."

Thalia glanced at the door from the corner of her eye, but she did not move. In the murky darkness of the room, she could not see clearly the crone's face, but could feel her reassuring smile and expectant gaze. She turned back to the door and closed it almost completely, leaving it open a tiny crack, just in case. She forced herself to smile when she turned to the crone again.

As if in reply, the spinster picked up the thread and returned to toil at the spindle. While she worked, she began to hum a pleasant tune, her head swaying with the music that fitted in perfect harmony the movements of her hands. At first, her voice sounded as thin as the finest of threads, but gradually, the tempo intensified, the old voice grew in strength, and the humming rose until it became singing. In front of the Princess's astonished eyes, the crone spun her silky string faster and faster, the thin, skeletal fingers moving with ever-increasing speed, and the silver thread gradually took the form of a garment.

The sound of the old woman's singing filled the room now. Her voice echoed off the walls, weaving into the threads of the enchanted fabric in perfect harmony. The words were in some foreign language Thalia did not recognize, but she still listened to them, enraptured. Faster and faster the garment grew, until it began to take the form of a beautiful dress. And still, the crone continued to spin and sing. The dress grew longer and longer, and the crone's hands moved faster and faster. And the echoes of her voice embroidered themselves into beautiful patterns entwined into the fabric of the dress.

The Princess looked on impatiently, her eyes wide with awe. Just as she thought the dress could not possibly be any more perfect, she saw that the pace at which the crone had been working had begun to slow down. Finally, the crone stopped singing just as her hands stopped moving. For a brief moment, the last notes of the crone's voice echoed in the gloomy chamber, but having no new sounds to support them, those echoes died away, and the magic unraveled as if it had never been there.

The crone lifted the dress, presenting her handiwork to the Princess.

Thalia clasped her hands and drew closer. Then she extended her hands as if she was longing to stroke the fabric of the dress, touching without touching.

"I see that you like your gift, my pretty one," the crone whispered in her ear. "Now, you must try it on. Take off your clothes!"

The princess shook herself as if waking from her thoughts, "What?"

"Take off your clothes!" the crone repeated. "I will help you put on the dress. Don't worry, just take off your clothes!"

The princess looked at the crone's age-ridden face and wrinkled her nose. All her maids were young, and the thought of undressing before the prying eyes of an old hag was distasteful to her. But then she saw the hag's bony fingers stroking the fabric and knew she could not leave the dress in her hands for a single moment longer. She turned her head away from the crone and undressed, feeling as she did so the ancient eyes piercing her back. Naked, she waited for the spinner to hand her the new dress. Thalia put it on and waited patiently while the crone tightly laced it up around her body.

The Princess had never worn such a snug dress. It fitted her slender body perfectly. She looked around, looking for a mirror.

"You look wonderful!" the crone said. "The fairies have blessed you with grace and a beauty that is second to none. What a pity I don't have a mirror for you to see yourself."

The Princess truly did feel she needed a mirror. She spun around, enchanted by the sight of the dress swirling out and the magical lights that sparkled from it. The light, it seemed, surrounded her body with a supernatural glow. She felt the softness of the dress, rubbing the fabric between her fingers, stroking the lace of the shoulder straps and the silvery strips of light embroidered down her chest and hips. Her eyes followed the cascading waves of silk swirling as she moved her feet and the flickering patterns she made on the floor as she spun around and around. Only when her head began to spin as well did she stop. She lowered her head to examine the hem of the dress.

It was then that her eyes caught a glimpse of something glinting on the floor, the edge of a silver thread, as fine as a single hair, that sloped down from the edge of her dress and rested on the ground.

She quickly raised her eyes, anxiously seeking the silver thread that had led her to this room at the top of the tower. But she could see no trace of it. She turned, and her eyes met those of the crone. The smile peeled away from the wrinkled face as though it was nothing but dry bark that was now crumbling to expose an entirely different visage, malicious and evil. The crone held the end of the thread that hung out of the dress. She tugged at it in a single smooth motion. The dress tightened like a noose, caging the Princess's arms and pinning them to her body. She remained on her feet for a brief moment, then she lost her balance and crashed on the bare floor. The violence of her fall squeezed the air from her lungs, and her head struck the unforgiving floor.

Thalia felt that she was about to lose consciousness. She was barely able to raise her eyes and focus. In a series of awful spasms, the terrifying transformation Thalia had seen in the old hag's face spread until it encompassed her entire body. Her bent back began to stretch upward like a growing tree, and she shook off the rags that had covered it. The wrinkled, emaciated skin peeled away and joined the rags on the floor. A towering figure now, the woman shook off the last slivers of her skin. Now her slender body was covered with an armor-like brilliant black substance. The tangled white hair mutated too. It now became silky, flowing down to her shoulders. Her face was smooth and unblemished; the skin stretched tightly over high cheekbones. Was it a smile on her narrow lips, or a grimace of pain?

Terrified, Thalia stared as the woman was wriggling and changing before her eyes until two pairs of legs stretched behind her back. "Much better," the woman sighed. She hunched down to the floor.

The Princess expected the monster hag to turn on her at any moment; but just as she looked ready to pounce on her, a thread shot from her hips toward the ceiling. The creature grabbed the line with her legs first, then with her hands as well, and began to climb up with quick, skillful movements. A moment later, she had disappeared.

The Princess allowed her head to sink to the floor, her breath gently stirring the dust that coated it. Her entire body ached, and her heart threatened to burst from her chest.

Forbidden! Forbidden! Forbidden! The words echoed in her heart with every pulse, and she felt the tears welling. *Will it hurt to die?* She wondered. *Could it possibly hurt more than this terrible sense of remorse?*

She heard a liquid, sucking sound, and then felt a slight tremor. Her eyes darted quickly around the chamber, looking for the source of the sound. She heard it again. She began to panic as she felt her legs being tugged upward. She saw the silvery webs now stretching from her feet up into the darkness of the ceiling. Thalia squirmed as hard as she could, but more and more webs shot down from the darkness to hold her. Before long, her waist was rising from the floor, then her shoulders and her head, until she found herself suspended upside-down in the air. A brief moment later, she stopped squirming.

"You lied to me! You told me you were not a witch!" the Princess cried as she hung there between heaven and earth. Her desperate complaint echoed from the walls.

"I didn't lie. I truly am the fairy spinster!"

The voice was distant, coming from somewhere high up in the dark recesses of the ceiling. It was accompanied by a dry, venomous cackle of laughter. "I spin many things. I spin threads, I spin stories and legends, lies and falsehoods…" And all the while, the princess was being pulled up with excruciating slowness.

"I spin shadows and the nocturnal darkness between the stars. I spin the webs of sleep, the dreams – and the nightmares…"

Now Thalia was approaching the aperture that illuminated the floor of the room. Her body, hanging, spinning round and round in the air, continued moving upward toward the opening. She shut her eyes against the blinding light. When she spun away from the light, she opened them again, and then she discovered how all the denizens of the palace had vanished, where they had gone. All around her, in the air, hung dozens of cocoons, large and small. From some, obviously spun in haste, shriveled limbs poked out, or faces – petrified in eternal expressions of horror or surprise – stared out. More cocoons lay on stone and wooden shelves. And, as if resting on magnificent thrones, two bodies were seated, the crowns of the King and the Queen placed carelessly on their heads, adding a touch of mockery to the terrible sight. An insufferable stench filled her nostrils.

The blood that was rushing from her upturned body to her head, and the sights before her eyes made her senses swim. She began to breathe quickly, hysteria setting in to overwhelm her rational mind. A powerful tremor rippled through her entire body as she heard the monster's voice again, whispering in her ear. "I spin the destinies and endings…" A hand, a claw, she knew not which, grabbed at her and spun her into place.

"And sometimes, when I am tired of being a spinster, I braid. One way or another, I'm very good at what I do."

Those final words seemed to hang on in the air between the young girl and the creature that had been a crone. She too was hanging upside-down. A pair of unnaturally large eyes blinked in front of Thalia's face. Then another pair, and another, and then one final set of eyes.

The Princess wanted to scream, but was paralyzed with fear. She averted her gaze from the monster's many eyes to the familiar sight of the two crowns entangled in the close-knit webs. Something in her soul darkened. Was this how her brief, restricted life was to end? She bit her lip, and her heart ached as she recalled, not without resentment, the litany her parents so often recited to her – *You must not talk to strangers!* Tears trickled from her eyes onto her forehead, then gathered in rivulets in her hair until a single teardrop fell silently to the floor far below. When she opened her eyes again, she saw the creature gazing at her with a sickeningly sweet smile and hungry eyes.

"Still with me? You're stronger than I anticipated." She smacked her lips with obvious glee. "You must be wondering why all the drama, Princess. You must think all this has been cruel and unnecessary, especially on your birthday. But you see, one should meticulously observe the way a meal is served, and I've had plenty of time to plan this meal." The soft voice hardened. "For fifteen years I've waited for this day. Your parents thought they could protect you from me." The thing brought one pair of eyes closer to Thalia's. "You see, they thought they could trick me, rob me of the honor I deserve! Surely they have told you how they had dreamed of having a child and how happy they had been upon your birth; a genuine fairytale. But have they ever told you that magic actually exists? Have they ever taught you its cost? Or the fact that it cannot be fooled? The finest of virtues, beauty, wealth… those were the things with which the other fairies had blessed you. All rubbish! None of that foolishness has anything to do with real life. I would have blessed you with pain. I would have given your life a sting. I would have breathed meaning into it! But no one wanted my gift, oh no… Twelve seats! There were only twelve seats at the royal dinner table! So I ended up having to teach them an important lesson, the lesson of pain." She chuckled venomously. "You should have seen their faces when I told them you were dead. But that, of course, was impossible. For fifteen years I have waited, and now the time has come for me to satisfy my hunger, and to *my* feast, as you have probably seen, everyone is invited!"

"Who are you? I don't understand what you want from me," Thalia blurted desperately, trying to gain time, to delay what now seemed to be her inevitable death. But the monster's words had struck at her heart like a dagger. In a blink, she was able to picture in her mind's eye the faces of her parents, bound and helpless, as the crone had lied to them about their daughter's death. In her head, she heard an inner, mocking voice: *What difference does it make? The lie will soon become the truth.*

The spider woman took her time before replying. She gazed at her captive princess with her many eyes. Although the eyes weren't human, Thalia could still tell that the thing was enjoying the sight, gulping down her plight, her every fear, savoring them as appetizers that would soon lead to the main course.

"Who am I? Who am *I*?" The monster cackled again, but there was no humor in her laughter. "You really don't know? I am old Mother Arachne, the fairy who dwells in the dark. But for you, child, I am the thirteenth fairy. I have no intention of giving you anything! But still, I am a fairy, obliged to observe the rules of protocol, so humor me. Do you have a final wish?"

All her life Princess Thalia had been shielded, protected, and guarded against pain or harm, but now her life was nearing its end in the most outrageously pathetic way. Once more, she looked at the webbed cocoons gently swaying in the light breeze and knew there was no one left to miss her. She looked into the face of Mother Arachne, the spider woman – a powerful predator, a being the likes of which she had never met. A resolution formed in her heart.

"Please… teach me," she whispered hoarsely.

"What?" The dark fairy asked impatiently. Then she drew nearer, until her repulsive face was almost close enough to kiss the Princess. "What would you like to learn?" She tilted her head, her gaze inquisitive. A reddish spark burned in the dark pupils.

"I want to… become a spinster too," replied the Princess. She struggled not to divert her gaze from the creature's many eyes.

"But my dear, you are too young and sweet to be a spinster," Mother Arachne mocked and worked her pale chops in hunger and anticipation.

Thalia shook her head. "Please. I want to learn how to spin, to weave… like you do."

Thalia watched curiosity seeping into the spider woman's clusters of eyes. The monster retreated and silently stared at the Princess for a long moment. Her fingers fluttered restlessly in the air, as if weaving an invisible thread. Then, all at once, her pupils widened as she tilted her head back with a squeal that transformed into ear-splitting laughter. "You are clever! How ironic, yes. Poetic even. This might actually work! Good girl!"

The fairy drew closer and stroked Thalia's face. Before she fully understood what was happening, she found herself clutched between the monster's arms. The she-spider pressed her to her bosom in a close embrace, then bent to kiss her forehead. She looked at the girl's face and smiled her sickening smile again. "It looks like I'll sweeten your punishment and fulfill your wish after all," she said, almost in wonder. Then her smile widened more and more, revealing two formidable fangs extending from her mouth. "This won't hurt… much. Good night, my beauty. Close your eyes. Don't be afraid; I'll weave some sweet dreams for you…" she whispered.

The Princess felt a sudden sharp pain, and she sensed her body slackening. The world sank into a dark horizon.

How EASILY IS the candle's light forgotten once it has died…

"AND THEN I SAW HANGING on one of the trees… I can't even bring myself to say it! It's a forest of death. They hang there from the branches, just skin and clothes, and their bones…" The drunkard paused to down the contents of his glass in a single gulp.

That was how the Prince had learned of the existence of the palace. While traveling in search of adventure and riches, he has heard many stories of enchanted treasures and tales of princesses in distress whose fathers were willing to pay their rescuers a handsome reward. Most of these stories had turned out to be fictitious – nothing but fables. But others held a grain of truth, and that grain was worth much more than its weight in gold – or diamonds. The Prince bought the blathering man another drink, and another, gradually unearthing the details of his story.

The locals, so the Prince learned, believed there was a cursed palace hidden in a nearby forest with all its denizens behind a shroud of mystery. The palace, so the story went, contained unfathomable riches, and if that wasn't enough – a Princess whose beauty was legendary. But woe to the man who would try to pillage the palace and its riches, for a curse had been cast on it, bringing an excruciatingly painful death to anyone who tried. Most of the locals doubted the truth of this tale but still took care not to enter the forbidden forest, and some even refused to speak of it. Every few years, some young adventurers would set out in search of the haunted palace. Most returned empty-handed; others were never seen again.

The man in the tavern spoke of a haunted forest, a place littered with corpses and skeletons. He had found the palace, so he said, but his way was blocked by a deep, impenetrable ditch covered by thick webs through which he could see the remains of more corpses.

In the deathly stillness, so he said, all his dreams of the wealth he could find in the cursed palace were forgotten. When he'd noticed a movement in the shadows, his unstrung nerves had overcome any rational thought, and he had run for his life. The shadows, he swore, had given chase, rushing after him among the trees. He had run and run, he said, until he had been ready to collapse from fatigue. But then he got lucky and broke out of the forest into the open air.

"I'll be taking no more risks like that!" he said, a haunted look in his eyes. "I dare not keep going in the dark of night, but I'll be off and away from this place at the crack of dawn…"

The Prince spent all night thinking of the young man's story. He tended to believe him because, even if he had invented his tale, he was still very convincing. But should he believe him? After all, the man was only a commoner from some far-off kingdom. The sort of superstitious peasant who was afraid of his own shadow. These people's tall tales were always outrageously exaggerated. But the promise of an abandoned palace full of treasures pervaded the Prince's thoughts until he knew, superstition or not, he had to go and see for himself.

As the first light of the new dawn broke over the village, the Prince set out to find the young man who had told the story of the mythical palace, but there was no trace of him. None of the villagers knew where he'd gone, or if they did, they simply refused to tell. Realizing he could not gather more information from them, the Prince paid the innkeeper, mounted his horse, and headed towards the enchanted forest.

Several hours later, the Prince entered the palace gates. He had nothing but his armor, sword, and an empty sack that he hoped to fill with gold and jewels. He had left his horse behind when it had refused to enter the forest whose the trees were garbed in tangled layers of cobwebs. All his coaxing, threats, and attempts at bribery had failed. In the end, he tied his horse to a tree outside the forest and continued on foot. Other than the enormous curtains of spider webs silently swaying in the wind, he saw nothing menacing. As he walked deeper and deeper along the ruined road, he saw mounds of human bones piled around some of the trees. The Prince walked on, his sword drawn and ready, but other than the webs that occasionally blocked his way, easily torn asunder with his sword, the way to the palace was open for him. When he finally stood outside the heavy door, he was sure that whatever had killed those miserable souls whose bones were scattered among the trees was no longer there, no longer a threat. Perhaps time had simply taken its course and removed whatever it was…

When he had heard the stories of a vast palace, the Prince had imagined that years of tall tales and overwrought hyperbole had exaggerated the true grandeur of the place. But now, having walked the deserted corridors and huge halls for long hours, he realized that the villagers had actually forgotten the full extent of its size and magnificence with the passage of time. His sack remained almost empty. He had repeatedly filled and then emptied it to make room for even more precious treasures, or because it had become too unwieldy with the weight of riches. Finally, he decided to fill the sack only on his way out.

He decided that his final investigation of the palace would be at the tallest tower. Although he had arrived at the palace early that morning, he had spent so much time exploring its labyrinthine corridors that it was already late in the afternoon. The Prince reached the straight corridor at the top of the tower, completely out of breath. At the end of the corridor, he saw an old wooden door with a keyhole. If it hadn't been the last door at the end of the last stretch of the last floor of the ancient tower in the most remote wing of the grand palace, it might not have looked so unique or inviting. But that was exactly what the door was, and the Prince simply had to discover what was hidden behind it. He was worried by the fact that all the time he had been in the palace, he had encountered no threat or challenge. Even foraging animals that would usually have turned such a desolate place into their nests and dens were nowhere to be seen or heard.

The Prince took hold of the door handle and distractedly turned it. If the miraculous success he had enjoyed in the palace so far had caused him a slight tremor of guilty anxiety, that uncomfortable feeling suddenly multiplied a thousand-fold. He knew it was because the handle had willingly yielded to the touch of his hand, and the door offered no resistance as it opened, other than to produce the grating sound of rusted hinges. A gust of cold, damp air blew from the shadowy space beyond the threshold. It made him flinch and pause as it wafted unpleasantly against his face. The Prince lifted his sword, strengthening his grip on the hilt. He entered.

The small room was shrouded in darkness; only a single beam of light coming from an aperture in the ceiling penetrated the heavy blackness. The ray of light illuminated what looked to the Prince like an altar. Only as he drew closer did he see that it was, in fact, a bed on which lay a shape covered with a blanket as fine as silk. His heart beat a little faster. Was it the Princess of his dreams?

He approached the top of the bed and moved his sword closer to the fabric. Then he covered his mouth and nose to prepare for what might follow. Skillfully, he used his sword to cut a slit through the cloth. He pulled the slit open and carefully, cautiously peered in. His breath caught in his throat, and he gasped aloud when, instead of the skeleton or shriveled corpse he had expected to see, his eyes settled on a beautiful face. It was illuminated by a soft light that imbued it with an enchanting, mysterious air. He stared down for long moments, mesmerized, trying to decide whether the Princess was alive or dead. His gaze moved downward, from her face to the contours of her covered breast. Carefully, he again gripped the two sides of the slit he had made in the covering fabric. He looked again at the girl's perfectly shaped face and, seeing that it remained still, unmoving, he took courage, tightened his grip, and pulled both edges of the cover aside. The soft material yielded, the slit gaping open to expose more of the body beneath it.

The Prince looked at the result of his handiwork with surprise. An apology froze on his lips, for there was no need. Slowly, he lowered his eyes to look down the neck until he found himself gazing at the girl's naked chest. The ray of light from the aperture in the ceiling lit the perfect, unblemished fair skin, accentuating every curve and contour. He felt the first glimmerings of shame as he became aware that his loins were awakening. It was only then, to his horror, that he noticed the beautiful chest was rising and falling with the gentle movement of the girl's breathing. He bent over her face, and indeed, he felt her breath, light and fragrant on his cheek. He shook the maiden with increasing urgency. It seemed to him that the girl, whoever she was, was sunken deep in an enchanted sleep, in some peaceful place between life and death. She offered no resistance or objection as he peeled the gleaming fabric away until the magnificently naked body was entirely revealed. Nor did she react when he laid down his sword, shed his armor, took off his clothes, and climbed into the bed beside her.

MOVEMENT.

From abysses immeasurably deep, somewhere far off in the thick, enveloping darkness, there was movement. This was so novel and surprising that she couldn't help but focus her attention on it. And once she had done that, she felt herself being pulled upward. It seemed to be a long journey up; rising, rising from the warm, enveloping darkness until she finally began to sense other things. Now it was cold. Within the darkness and movement, she felt cold. And with that realization came another, that of her own boundaries. She had skin and a body! A body moving in a continuous, rhythmic motion.

A strange noise assailed her ears. She tried to focus on it, and the more she did, the more she felt herself rising upward further and further to fill her own body. She was suddenly conscious of a smell, some sort of sharp scent. She followed it with absolute concentration, and in an instant, all her senses returned. Within a moment of panic, she became aware of herself and her body, and she felt a deep, irresistible urge to open her eyes. A stranger's face filled her vision. His eyes were closed, his head pulled back and up, his face contorted as in a grimace of effort. But he must have felt the sudden change in her, because he lowered his head and opened his eyes.

A scream pierced the silence, and she knew not whether it had emerged from her mouth or the stranger's. Dimly, she felt him trying to pull himself away from her. Was he surprised by her wakefulness? Was he afraid?

Only then did she notice she was pinning him down to her body with her arms and legs. The man squirmed and struggled to release himself from her grip. An overwhelming passion claimed her, urging her to tighten her grip and pull the naked body to her. The man, trying to rise, struck at her face as hard as he could. Something in her back bothered her. She swayed from side to side, feeling more arms and legs breaking free of the confines of her body. They extended naturally to clutch the man's hands and head. The strange sensations engulfing her brought a smile to her face. The man's face became a mask of surprise and terror as her hips moved in a rhythmic motion under his pinned body.

Desperation gradually claimed the stranger. His resistance lessened, but her own appetite increased. His eyes closed, and he shook his head helplessly from side to side. Tears trickled down his cheeks, and she felt an overwhelming urge to put out her tongue and taste them. The man's body stiffened. He seemed to struggle in her grasp for a long moment, and then he went limp. The stranger's eyes closed again. She felt the heat of his body oozing, dripping, flowing into hers. Immense gratification suffused her as she absorbed the man's essence.

An unbearably piercing pain in his chest made the man open his eyes again. He looked at her face in disbelief at the sight of her gaping mouth, its teeth running red with his blood. But his vision began to cloud until his eyes were utterly glazed, enveloped in darkness. She lifted him over her body and placed him beside her. Her entire body ached from a hundred-year-long hunger, but she knew she couldn't sink her teeth into the man now. Instead, she dragged him across the bed until his body was beneath her. She leaned over him. His body was still warm, his heart throbbing its last despairing beat as she began to spin a web him around. Over and over, dressing him, wrapping him with a gleaming silver thread. Her senses had revealed it to her before, but it was only now, now that the deed was done, that she raised her head to look.

In the corner of the room, she saw the image of an old lady. She was standing, watching her with powerful, compelling eyes, thin lips stretched in a chilling smile. When the crone finally opened her mouth, all the Princess heard was a brief series of clicks. To Thalia's surprise, she understood their meaning.

"GOOD MORNING, BEAUTIFUL!"

Above the Clouds,
Above the Mountains,
Above the Sky...

By Pesach (Pavel) Amnuel

Translated by David Reid

Pesach (Pavel) Amnuel was born in 1944 in Baku, Azerbaijan (then in the USSR), and became known as both an astrophysicist and an SF writer. Amnuel predicted (in 1968, with O. Guseynov) the existence of X-ray pulsars, which was later confirmed by the American Uhuru satellite. Their catalog of X-ray sources was considered the world's most complete.

Amnuel first began publishing SF/F in Russian in 1959, his first story appearing in the *Technology for Youth* magazine. His first story collection was published in Moscow in 1984. Since 1990, he has lived in Israel, where he has taught at Tel Aviv University and edited several Russian-language newspapers and magazines, including *Aleph* and *Vremya*. Since emigrating to Israel, he has published several novels: *Men of the Code* (1997); *Three-Universe* (2000), the latter involving social satire and kabbalistic mystery, with events transpiring in a mid-21ˢᵗ century Moscow run by the Russian Mafia and Israeli rabbis; *Revenge in Dominoes* (2007); *Flight of Five* (2014); *Pure Scientific Crime* (2018); *The Worlds We Choose* (2020); and *Bias* (2021) — as well as sundry SF/F collections, short stories, and detective novels.

His work appears regularly in Russia, where he continues to claim a large fan base. He has won multiple awards, including The Great Ring, for achieving the greatest popularity among contemporary Russian writers, the 2009 Bronze Icarus Award of Russian Science Fiction, and the "Aelita" (the Russian equivalent of the Hugo) in 2012.

The story I am going to tell you happened a great many years ago, but that is all the more reason for telling it, before it is completely forgotten.

Hans Christian Andersen, *The Nightingale*, 1843

THE TRAVELER CAME TO THE VILLAGE in the evening of the Day of the Harvest. He went from house to house, sought refuge and found it with the carpenter Valens. Logue learned about the Traveler when it was already dark, and there was nowhere else to go. His mother had sat him down to rock the babies to sleep while she herself was busy in the kitchen. Logue was nervous – in his short seventeen years of life, he has never spoken with Travelers, those strangers who came in smelling of fields and distant wanderings. Logue had heard many strange stories, strange as an autumn drought, from Lepir, who was now old and sick, not wanted by anyone any longer. Lepir had once been a Traveler too; he had come to the village long before Logue's birth. Logue had heard his stories a hundred times, but these stories were overgrown with fictional details. Logue wanted to know the truth.

After the babies fell asleep, Logue lay in his corner and waited for the morning. He knew that he would not be able to sleep. Excitement mounted; he had never been so excited, even after a quarrel with Lena. The Traveler. There's a really brave man. As far as Logue could remember, no one in the village dared leave home without a safety rope, simply putting one foot before the other in the fog, surrendering to chance. Once, when Logue had been two years old, his father left and has never returned. Then his mother took on his stepfather; babies were born. His stepfather was a serene man, not making any move to leave. He lived for Logue's mother, for the children, for their home. But alas, this was short-lived. Recently, just last spring, a beam fell from the rafters, and his stepfather was no more.

The Traveler seemed to Logue an ideal man. Logue had quarrels with Lena over this. He and Lena usually met at an abandoned house that stood on the outskirts of the village. Nobody lived there; the house had a bad reputation as being haunted. Nobody has seen the ghosts, of course, but many have heard them. In the night fog, one could hear well.

"Can you imagine," Logue said that evening, "getting to know new settlements, new people, new fields. New voices, strange and mysterious. And smells. In good weather, you can climb a tree and see the leaves. When I was a child..."

"You still climb trees," Lena interjected in a strange voice. "I know, and everybody knows, and someday you will be punished. I do not want you to break your neck, okay?"

"What are you on about, my dear?" Logue replied affectionately. "I will not fall from the tree, even in the thickest midnight. Go ahead, you can touch my toes... they're prehensile."

Lena pushed him and walked away, instantly disappearing into the fog. Logue heard how she went to her house; he ran after her, stretching out his hands, out of habit, so as not to bump into anything.

"Lena, dear," he pleaded, "I'll never climb trees again, do you hear me?"

Lena stopped and asked Logue: "And you will not tangle up the rope to confound others when you leave the village?"

Logue froze. *She knows,* he thought. *Does she really know? And what shall I do if she tells?*

Lena was gone, and Logue had stood there, wondering what to do next. Since that night, they have not seen one another. Was Lena angry, or has she lost interest in Logue? True, he has not sought to meet with her, although at first he had terribly missed these meetings. He was afraid to be found out. No one was supposed to know that Logue, going from village to field, purposely jumbled up his belay rope. He used to make sure it was hard to find, so that no one would know where he was going and what he was doing. Nobody. Not even Lena.

The Traveler wore a long beard; his clothes were old, patched many times, and had so many swag holders that it seemed that there was only one of them.

Logue came across the Traveler one day. Having knocked at the door of carpenter Valens's door, Logue entered into the dark hallway. The morning fog had thinned out a bit, though, of course, still not to the level of yesterday's clarity. But coming close, Logue still managed to see the Traveler. It was good that the carpenter could not see the look on Logue's face; otherwise, the carpenter probably would have run to the Chief Elder. The Traveler saw and understood; he retreated from the doorway, silently gesturing Logue to enter. The carpenter was watching them, but waited for Logue in the studio. Then he left, muttering something to which Logue paid no attention and which the Traveler did not hear.

The Traveler took Logue's knapsack off his shoulders, then sat next to him on a broad bench. From it came a smell of something unfamiliar, distant and attractive. Logue was able to tell apart thousands of odors, but this one was uncommon; it was not like anything else he knew.

"My name is Logue," began the youth, with tightness in his voice.

"And I am Petrin," the Traveler said calmly. "I have little time; I want to go as far as possible before dark."

"You... you, sir..." Logue was confused. What he was hearing just didn't fit into his consciousness.

"Yes," the Traveler grinned. "I'm leaving. I never stay in the same village for more than two or three days. Since your village is so small, I decided to limit my stay to a single night."

The Traveler pronounced his words very correctly and constructed his sentences as if he were building a house from close-fitting logs. Logue got goosebumps when he imagined how every morning the Traveler put his knapsack on his shoulders and went out into the fog, the gray nothingness, not knowing whether he would spend the night under a roof or in the field, or even whether he would reach any human habitation. He couldn't know whether that day would be a day of failure, whereby he would finally get lost in the fog, remaining marooned forever among the trees and haystacks. From then on, he would be wandering around, screaming and cursing fate until he would die of starvation. Then, many days later, by harvest time, someone from the nearest village would accidentally step on his bleached bones and be instantly horrified. He would be just as terrified as Logue had been when, once, his foot touched something hard and round – something which, as Logue saw when he squatted down, a skull. Logue had reacted by grabbing and pulling the belay rope, making sure that it was still firmly tied to one of the many security posts on the outskirts of the village.

Nobody – Logue was sure of it! – dared to Travel twice. The best one could hope for would be to go from one village to another, coming across a path by chance. But this same path could stretch from one day to many weeks, so exhausting that a Traveler might then remain forever in the village to which he worked so hard to get. How could you go if you did not know where you were headed, if you did not see your way, or even know whether you had continually returned to the same place, straying in the fog? The cold would accumulate in your heart because the farther you went, the worse it would become, as you become conscious that there was no hope to arrive anywhere. But to set out again, having once reached a destination, it's... You had to be crazy...

"Don't look at me like that, child," the Traveler said, smiling affectionately. "I left home two years ago. I have been in eleven villages; yours is the twelfth." (Logue leaned toward the Traveler to catch every word.) "Several times I thought everything was completely lost. But I kept going, and arrived each time. Once I did not eat for almost a week; I ran out of supplies. But I arrived. In that village, I spent a month and almost stayed for good, but then something called me, and I set out again... Everyone lives for something, child. Logue, right? Everyone. Logue lives for something. Women live to ensure that the family does not wither. To ensure that the home is cozy and quiet. Men live in order that tomorrow people do better than yesterday, and even better after that. In order that no question remains unanswered. In order that no one be afraid of anything."

The Traveler paused, and Logue suddenly wanted to tell him everything. The Traveler was due to leave that very day; he just did not have time to explain everything to Logue. In any case, he would not do so because that was how he was, and he alone could understand.

"Petrin," said Logue – the sound of the name seemed unusual, as the Traveler himself was. "You... you are not afraid of the Heavenly Voice?"

"I'm afraid of everything that I do not know. And what this Voice is – I do not know. As you do not. I'm afraid of the Heavenly Voice only because of this reason, although I know that no one has ever suffered from it."

"Why?" Logue spoke hastily; he knew about this, as it was drummed into him daily in the House of Prayer. "The Voice can be kind, giving us a good harvest. The Voice can be evil, and then someone in the village dies. The Voice recently called Antora, the baker, and he was not very old."

The Traveler suddenly laughed.

"Say, Logue, how many times a year do you hear the Heavenly Voice?"

"Well… twenty."

"The harvest happens twice a year, and people don't die so often. Hence, in most cases, the Voice is an empty sound, not so? Indeed, do people die immediately after they hear the Voice? It happens before or after, even after a long time. Yet one blames the Voice…"

Logue wanted to protest, but the door creaked as it opened, and he remained silent. The carpenter returned.

"I have to go," said the Traveler, lifting the heavy knapsack from the floor. "Valens will lead me to the last house. Further, I will go by myself. Goodbye, child. It was my pleasure to speak with you."

With a rapid movement, Traveler pulled Logue to him and whispered in his ear, tickling it with his coarse hair: "Have you ever seen a blue fog with yellow veins? It pours out from the shade, and you think you're inside a huge toy… A yellow fog? It smells bad, and your head hurts from it, and your legs shake. Beware the yellow fog. How about orange? Have you ever seen an orange fog?"

Logue was shocked, shaking his head. He has never seen such things; he did not dare to admit, with the carpenter standing nearby, able to hear every word, that this was his dream, the meaning of his life – to see the bright orange fog, to see the yellow and blue fog. Anything other than the usual dull gray. Logue held on to the Traveler's elbow and did not want to let go. If he could have, he would have gone with him. But he could not. His way, Logue's path, was different, but he did not dare to confess this now.

"Do you know," whispered Petrin heatedly, "how fog is different from air?"

"They're not at all different." Logue was surprised.

"Then why are there the two words, not just one?"

"Who knows?" Logue shrugged. "Words often repeat each other. 'Lies' and 'deceit.' 'Correct' and 'true'."

"Think, child, and you'll hear the difference in these words. A lie can be unintentional; deception is always intentional. But what about 'fog' and 'air'? If these words are different, then someone came up with them and invested them with different meanings, right?"

"I don't know," said Logue distractedly, not knowing what the Traveler wanted to convince him of.

"Well, get on with it," shouted the carpenter, who was assuredly listening to the whispers as he stood in the corner. "Come on, Petrin. And you, Logue, go out to the field."

The Traveler lightly pushed Logue and followed the voice. Steps stomped down the street, and all was quiet.

Logue sat himself down on the corner of the bench. *How wonderful it is*, he thought. *From village to village. Through the fog. Nothing to see ahead, not knowing what awaits you the next moment, and still going. Ever striving to reach a new village, not stopping, but moving on.* Since his childhood, when they had told Logue about his father going away, Logue has often thought about where he was now. A dream emerging: to see another fog. An Orange one. Somehow Logue favored this color above the others, perhaps because Lena loved all things orange. Maybe an orange fog was more transparent than the gray fog. Here in the village, even on the best days, you could see no further than three to four cubits, and there... Maybe there, talking to a person, you always saw his face, so it would not be only from the tone of voice that you could guess about the other's mood... But old Lepir, who was the only one in the village who had come from afar, had seen no orange fog. And he came most likely from the nearest village; according to him, he wandered a lot and almost died. But that one could stray yet remain in one place – such is the property of fog, its law.

Having said that to himself, Logue walked away. The Traveler Petrin did not fit into his mindset. No, on the contrary, he fit; how well did he fit! The first confirmation that his dream could come true. He, Logue, could learn more about the world in which he lived. He would see such beauty, which nobody else had seen…

Logue rushed out into the street, feeling the rope that led to the field. It differed in thickness from the others stretched along the road. Logue walked quickly, turning the rope with his fingers. He would find a way; he used to go to the field every day for two years, ever since the Elders had announced his coming of age. But now, he did not want to go at random. Afraid? Yes, he was afraid, too, because his goal was at hand. He would not risk it for anything in the world.

Before evening fell, Logue cut the lithe stalks and folded them along a ridge in straight strips so that boys who followed him would collect the stalks and heap them into stacks. The work was monotonous and did not interfere with his thinking or even with talking with neighbors, whom he had never seen, of course, but nonetheless he has heard them, and knew them well.

When the gong sounded to mark the end of work, it was getting dark. Logue was tired and hungry and thought that he could not carry out his plans on that day in such a state. He just went back and checked whether all was intact, and no one accidentally found his plot of land. He was expected for dinner at home. Later, as the babies lay in his arms, his mother, invisible in the fog and evening dullness, said: "Logue, the Chief Elder asked that you go to him."

His heart leaped. He was asked to go. Ordered, more like it. The last time the Chief Elder summoned Logue was three years ago, after he had gone with the other boys to throw stones at the haunted house. Nothing happened to the house, but Logue and the others were punished.

After hastily eating, Logue rushed out of the house, and barely noticeable signs known only to him showed him the way to the road — nicks which he knew by groping with his hands, even before he could see them. He reached the outskirts of the village, and after sitting down for a long time, started searching for the end of the rope he had left the day before. He found it some distance from where he had expected. He hurried into the thickening darkness, certain that he would not find anything in the plot. He was sure that the summons to the Chief Elder had to do with that terrible event and would destroy all his hopes and plans. He was in such a hurry that he bruised his leg on something. But at the plot, all was in order; all he had left yesterday was still there; nothing budged, nothing was lost.

Logue took a deep breath. He went back, hurrying to get to the Chief Elder before he went to sleep – the Chief Elder used to go to bed early – to avoid further punishments. He did not think about the reason for the summons. The main thing was that no one had found the plot – everything else was irrelevant.

At the Chief Elder's door he stopped and listened, but all was quiet. In the back of the room, lamps were burning, dispersing yellow light – three round spots on a gray canvas. The Chief Elder lived alone; if he was not praying at the house of prayer, he was usually lying on his bed, resting after a busy day. The Chief Elder never had an easy day. He was not young, and had plenty of cares.

"Come here, Logue," said the Chief Elder, recognizing Logue's footsteps. "Do not worry; I did not summon you for punishment, even though you deserve it."

Logue groped for the bench by the table and sat down. Straw rustled under the Chief Elder; he stood up, knowing what Logue was feeling. Afraid of punishment. Everyone fears punishment.

"The Traveler impressed you," said the Chief Elder, "and I want to warn you. You, Logue, are hungry for anything unusual; it's in your blood. It pulled you to the haunted house, then to the Traveler. And you did not realize that the Traveler is stupid."

Logue made a motion, almost knocking over the table on which a mug of water rested.

"Yes, stupid." The Chief Elder raised his voice. "A clever man would not wander from village to village, where all life is hard and the same everywhere. Doesn't the Law teach this? Is it not to serve the Law that a person lives for? For you and for me, for both of us. Logue, you know this well, because you were the best student of the Elders' teachings. How far can the eye see? Up to an arm's length. How far can the ear hear? All the way to the neighboring houses. That's it. You need to live the life that is close to you. Blue fog... Even if there is such a thing, looking for it is unworthy; this is heresy. To live is to work and work. And to think about your neighbors: the mothers of babies, that leaky roof on the house and, therefore, the need to make repairs. This is life. You're clever. Logue, Petrin is stupid and will die somewhere in the fields from hunger and exposure to dampness. You will be remembered; he will be forgotten. You have time to do many good things, but he did not even manage to do evil. Do you understand, Logue...? The Elders want to punish you, but I'm not going to do this. Think, Logue, about what I have said. Now go..."

So, the Chief Elder knew of the last words of the Traveler? Logue thought as he left the house. *Carpenter Valens heard everything?* The Chief Elder had given him a warning. Logue knew it was the teachings of the Law, and it was correct – but not for him.

Old Lepir did not live alone, unfortunately. He rented a small room in a house where three other families lived. When Logue spoke with the old man, the noise – voices, laughter, and even cries – from the other side of the wall always made conversation difficult. In addition, those on the other side of the wall could hear anything they wanted to listen to, even whispers. Logue did not know what part of his conversations with Lepir was known to the Elders. Lepir has not left his room for more than a year, because he became blind in his old age. Blindness did not bother Lepir – he could find his way around perfectly well – but the sight of the veiled whites of his eyes was unbearable for Logue.

"I thought you were not coming today," said Lepir, hearing Logue's footsteps.

"There was a Traveler," said Logue.

"I know," whispered Lepir. "I heard all about that day. He came and then went. You talked to him?"

Logue recounted the conversation, trying to remember not only the words but also the intonation.

"Once upon a time I was like that," sighed Lepir. "But to leave so quickly, immediately... He's a reckless man, this Petrin. He will die. Orange fog, yeah... Beautiful. And to think that people are killing themselves for the sake of beauty. What's the difference what color the fog is?"

Logue was struck silent. It was a day of amazement. Now it hit him that Lepir was old; Logue remembered how Lepir had enthusiastically recalled his one unique journey, which lasted eight long days.

"Yeah," whispered Lepir, "you think I'm crazy in my old age. No, I just think... For the sake of beauty alone, it is not worth going out. If you are looking for the beauty of the unknown – orange mist, you say, you know what you want to find. Really? Imagine it. And then it is not necessary to look for it. Imagine for yourself an orange mist, and you probably would imagine it to be more beautiful than it truly is. Right? You need to go only when you do not know what you will find. That's why there are so few Travelers. Everyone knows everything. They know that the day is light, that it is dark at night, and that this is so everywhere. They know that the Heavenly Voice takes a part of the crop, leaving enough for us not to die of starvation. And this is so everywhere. Right? They know that new knives and axes appear on the road when the Voice so desires. Why there? You know why: the Voice gives them as a reward for our crops. We all know this. Then why go? Huh?"

"To search for beauty," said Logue with utter conviction. "I can imagine an orange mist, but what if what I would find will be unimaginably beautiful?"

"In the end, what you are looking for is not beauty but knowledge," Lepir said, barely audibly. "New knowledge. This could be a new knowledge of beauty. But what you want is to learn something new. Logue, is it necessary to go anywhere? Tell me, here in the village, can't you satisfy your thirst for novelty?"

"I know everything here," Logue grinned, "and by the way, it was with your help, Lepir."

"Yes, I have taught you what I could. But what is deep underground, deeper than the deepest wells? But what is in a grain of sand, so small that our eyes cannot see?"

"Yes," said Logue. Now, finally, he decided to reveal to Lepir some of the mystery – not all, not so much that the old man would know anything, but enough to hear the answer. "I do not know. And I do not know what there is high above our heads, above the trees, above the houses."

"The Voice," said the old man. "The Voice, the sky, and light. If it weren't for the Voice, we would not be alive; there would be no light, the earth would be barren."

"And what if there, where the Voice is, where all this comes from and where light dwells, what if the fog there is not gray, but orange?"

"You keep going on about that," said the old man irritably. "You have grown up, Logue. Before, you used to listen to me, and now – only to yourself."

Logue fell silent; it seemed to him that there was some movement behind the thin wall. *We talk too loudly,* thought Logue. *And we should not talk about that. It was decreed that such conversations must not take place in the village. Instead, discuss plowing and sowing. Repairing the house. Crafts. But definitely not the beauty of the incomprehensible.*

Touching the thin old man's shoulder and coming closer to him in the dark, Logue whispered: "Traveler Petrin is a brave man, but he was not out there looking for beauty. And you, Lepir, were not out there looking for knowledge. There was nothing new in two, three, or a thousand days of Travel. You were a Traveler yourself, and Petrin said the same thing. And under the ground, there is nothing new. And you, and Petrin, and my father – you all repeat going in each other's ways. One was looking for new beauty, the other – new knowledge, and yet another one – a better life. And no one has found or could find it because they went the same way as so many before them. There is another need. Quite different, you know? To see the beauty of what has not been seen, to learn what no one knows, above all, a need to do what has never been done."

"What are you thinking, Logue?" Said Lepir in an anxious whisper. "I do not understand you. You say strange things; it is alright if you say them only to me. But do not forget about the Law, Logue…"

They came for him early in the morning. Logue had had time to feed the babies and get dressed to go out into the field when several people entered the house, one of them, to judge by his voice, the Chief Elder. Logue never even thought about hiding.

"Honestly, Logue," said the Chief Elder, tying Logue's hands together, "you are foolish, like a baby. I warned you… The punishment, I think, will not be severe, because this will be your first time before the Court of Elders."

And then came the Voice. It came out of the morning silence, out of the thick fog. Within a few moments, it became coherent, gained strength, and finally roared deafeningly over his head, bouncing off the walls, the ceiling, everything that was in its way, including Logue's head. The Voice was reflected and repeatedly reinforced, deep and powerful, irresistible and frightening. The Heavenly Voice.

Everyone froze. The Chief Elder's words were barely audible in the din of the shouted prayers, and Logue's throat became parched. He kept silent, fearfully thinking: *Whose turn is it now to die? It is not for the crop that this Voice came in this odd hour of the morning! Maybe for old Lepir?* Logue didn't even think about himself. Only after the Voice had fallen silent and vanished into the fog did one Elder suddenly grab him firmly by the elbow and drag him to the door, invisible in the fog, leading him outside. Only after a mother screamed, and children, stumbling under their feet, shouted almost as loud as the Voice, only after he was in the street, did Logue think that the Chief Elder and the others interpreted the appearance of the Voice as a sign that Logue was to be justly punished.

Just in front of the pit into which were thrown the guilty and the unrepentant, Logue came to himself. He knew the way better than the others. The fog thinned somewhat, and Logue saw the shoulders of two people walking beside him. Logue allowed himself to be pushed into a cramped space, where there was room enough for just a bed, with a hole overhead into which you could barely stick your hand and head, but go no further. The door slammed, the bolt creaked, and the voice of the Elder said: "You will be judged tomorrow. Think and repent, Logue. Your charge before the Law is that you aspire toward that which is forbidden and trespass on the Foundations."

The steps receded. Logue dropped onto the bed; it was damp, but there was nowhere else to sit. *Of course,* thought Logue. *Yesterday's conversations had reached the ears of the Elders. My talks with the Traveler and with Lepir.* But the punishment for seditiousness was only one month, and then he will continue to work. Unless... no, it can't be that they have found the site. But who had betrayed him? Who had heard their conversations? With the Traveler, that would be carpenter Valens. But with Lepir?

The day passed. Logue was not bored; he pondered. He was not rush his thoughts, counting his free time not by handfuls but by whole bunches. In the evening, the Chief Elder came, sat down by in the window through which the soup was provided, and waited until Logue had had his fill.

"Tomorrow, the Council of Elders will convene," said the Chief Elder. "If you repent, then you certainly will be treated with indulgence, and the worst thing that you will face will be a year in jail."

A year? A year in this earthen pit, being let out only to work in the field – because everybody has to work. But what about his mother? How about old Lepir? And his plot of land? If they find it, there will be another punishment, even harsher. It's all over. Everything is over. To live with people who need to be just as they are, all alike. And if you want something different, something which must not be, and you think about it? Then – into the pit with you. Did he want orange mist? It will indeed be orange, and mottled green. In his dreams.

The Chief Elder left, not waiting for any clear answer from Logue. The Voice and its traces had faded away long ago. Logue sat entirely motionless, as if frozen, even though the summer night was warm. *I should have left,* thought Logue. *With the Traveler Petrin, or even alone.* What a fool he had been! He had wanted too much at once and therefore had lost everything. After a year, he will not be able to go anywhere; they will watch his every step – they will learn to recognize his footsteps in the thick fog – everything will become immediately known to the Elders. A lost dream. A lost life.

"Logue," he heard a muffled whisper. "Logue..."

It was Lena's voice. Logue instantly shook off his drowsiness. He jumped onto the bed and pulled up with his hands. His palm rested against the low ceiling; Lena's thin hot fingers groped for him through the window and found him. She dragged his hands out of the opening.

"Lena," said Logue, "Lena..."

Lena was crying plaintively, as she did at that moment when he had kissed her for the first time, against her will, when he had pulled her to him, not expecting himself to do such a thing, and then feeling her tender responsive lips.

"Don't cry, Lena," he said, wincing and trying to sound full of confidence which he was not experiencing at all. "Consider… it's only a year. After the next harvest festival, we'll be together, forever."

Together, forever, he was thinking. *Well, the 'forever' part, at least, will be true.* He wanted to cry too; her lips trembled, and his fingers scraped the earthen ceiling so that pebbles and sand fell on his head. A vague idea flashed in his mind, and for a moment, Logue even held his breath so that the thought would not be lost.

"My dear, kind Lena…" he said.

"I brought you what you need," Lena said, with a voice suddenly clear and calm.

"You brought…?"

"An ax and a shovel."

"You'd thought about it even before I did," muttered Logue.

It was the only way, and that Lena had thought about it before he did, made Logue understand a simple fact that was probably clear to everyone but him – the idea that more than orange fog, more than the dream of beauty, more than wandering and searching unknown truth, more than all this, there were things that made life worth living. Love, for instance. Love – that, his heart could understand; Logue knew that without it, life with the feeling of emptiness in his heart, with only the need to exist, subject to the Law – that would not be a life worth living.

Logue thought about it, and tears flowed down his cheeks for the first time in years. He had forgotten that he could cry. He cried not for himself but for his Lena, who would remain in the village and would love him even when he might already be dead somewhere in a field or in a foreign country. Logue thought about it while his hands did everything necessary of themselves. They picked up the tools and began smashing the roof with the ax. They dug through sand and stone with the shovel, expanding and opening the window as sand and stones rained down on Logue and got into his eyes, mouth, and throat. During the night before the trial at the Council of Elders, no one needed to guard the prisoner – Logue would remain a captive of the Heavenly Voice. And if he did not take advantage of this opportunity now, it would be impossible to escape later. And Lena, dear Lena, she realized that even before Logue himself had.

The hole over his head was finally large enough. With Lena's help, Logue climbed out of the pit and fell to the ground panting. Lena brushed the sand off his face and clothing – something that was very necessary at that moment – and kissed Logue's dirty cheeks.

"Here," she then said. "These bags are full of food. This one is yours, and this is mine."

Only after these words had been said did Logue understand that what she did was much more reckless than it had seemed at first. Lena wanted to Travel with Logue. To be with him – if not here, then there; if not there, then anywhere else. Logue hugged her to him, whispering words that he had long wanted to utter but had not dared; words that had been true a moment ago, but that now became merely a means to lull any suspicions Lena may have had, because he could not take her with him. He did not want to become a Traveler, repeating the meaningless feats of Lepir and Petrin. His path was different. It was now or never.

He hoisted the two knapsacks onto his back, trying to remember the way to his belay peg. He crouched low, groping in the dark vicinity of the trails. Lena walked behind him, holding the end of a rope tied to one of the knapsacks.

The village was quiet as people slept through the fog; not a single ray of light penetrated. To Logue it seemed like a very long time, while he was groping for his peg and could not find it; they would start looking for him at dawn. Lena was silent, and Logue knew that one question was puzzling her: what were they looking for? After all, one can Travel in any direction, from any place, as long as it's away from the pit.

Here it is, the peg. That's it. Logue saw the nick, the harness rope leading to the plot. Logue breathed and turned to Lena. The time has come to betray her, since it was the only chance to save them both.

"Lena, dear," said Logue, hugging her and feeling his resolve weakening. "Lena, my dear, I cannot go just yet; I need to go home for a moment. To get something. You should also go to your home and return at dawn. Everything will be fine. Take time to eat. And... remember the peg and the road."

Lena felt something odd in Logue's words, but said nothing. Since she had decided to be with Logue, she had to do as he said, without asking questions and without thinking. When Lena's steps ceased echoing in the darkness, Logue allowed himself a moment to relax. He sat down on the wet ground, leaned against the knapsacks, closed his eyes, and rested. *Now,* he thought. *Now that for which I have lived these last six months will happen.*

Six months ago – it was wintertime, everything around was matte white from the frost which had settled out of the fog – Logue strolled casually in a deserted field. The land here was not fruitful; the stunted stems that grew there were unpalatable, and the field had been abandoned, although each section had been duly registered. A belay rope unrolled after Logue as he slowly let it out from the coil around his waist. It was the winter harvest festival, and everyone had been staying at home, baking pies, getting ready for the evening prayer. The silence had been immense, almost sonorous, bottomless.

There was frost all around, but for Logue, this was a good thing. He didn't want to return before the prayers began. Taking out of his many pockets bits of stocked chips and silicon, he made a fire, fanned it and squatted, stretching his hands over the campfire. The fire was purple, and the fog through which it shone seemed orange. An orange cloud, swirling and bursting upward. His arm also felt the movement of the fog. Logue thoughts were clear, for the first time not constrained by anything. He noted that the upward movement was a kind of reality.

Upwards, he thought. *To move up. There's something to that.* He had in his bag a dirty piece of cloth. Logue straightened it in his palm, held it over the fire, and let go. The fabric began to fall, but then stopped for a moment and started rising lightly upward, slowly, slowly... until it fell down. It disappeared into the flames and shriveled. Logue watched as the fire died out. *So this is it,* he thought. *Fire – that's the force that pushes up the cloth. No, not the cloth. Fire somehow pushes up the fog, which then drags the piece of cloth with it... Has no Traveler thought of that? Upwards. To move upwards.*

That was six months ago; since then, Logue has led a strange double life. A mystery had begun to unravel, which he has not shared with anyone. At first, Logue experimented with fire and canvas. He cut pieces of cloth of various shapes and sizes and thrown them into the fog above the fire. Once a fairly large piece of canvas arched suddenly into a dome and hovered there, trembling, slowly moving up. Then it took off, flying away from his hand, ascending into the fog overhead. In his delight, Logue became careless and put out the flames by accident. He stood there in the darkness, and for the first time, thought that this was reality. This. Strange, incredible: nobody had yet invented it; he was the first. Logue saw it, and it was now real, very real. It will be necessary to try it again and again, because if you could fly up with such a large piece of cloth and then fly away further, you needed more than just a small campfire. If the fabric could fly, it would be able to carry with it something else. Yes, a larger fire will be needed, he thought. A huge bonfire and a huge piece of cloth.

What purpose could the cloth be serving? If it was the fog that was dragging up the cloth, then you needed... Yes! You needed to make sure that your particular fire will generate enough fog and remain directed, not flowing every which way...

The following evening he deceived his mother, telling her that he needed to make himself a new shirt. Logue sat behind the decrepit sewing machine – his mother's favorite comfort, which has been at home since time immemorial, inherited by his mother, apparently, from her great-grandmother. He sewed an awkward but light bag with a neck, which could easily be tightened with a string. The younger children interfered with his work, and the machine rocked back and forth and threatened to break down to pieces, but nonetheless, Logue completed his task and went to sleep satisfied, exhausted, and curious. The next day he worked poorly in the field, counting time from the first to the last bell. That evening he took his awkward construction (Logue came up with the resonant – to his ear – name, "foggy ball") and hung it over the fire. It began to rise, pulling the string on which he had hanged a reasonably heavy stone.

While days passed, or rather, dragged on, the evenings flew by, full of worries and anxiety. Logue was worried that someone might track him to his plot, find in the fog the safety peg to which his invention was attached. A harness string could be found purely by accident, but people came by only rarely to this part of the village, where the abandoned field began. When his mother asked about his absence in the evenings, Logue would say something unintelligible, and mother believed that perhaps he was meeting with Lena and did not try to pry any further.

After a month of this, Logue already knew that the big bag, the largest of the foggy balls he had sewn, could lift and hold a stone at the height of about ten cubits for half the evening. Then everything had ended. The fog created by the fire has, for some reason, lost its unusual properties, and the bag fell down – slowly and hopelessly. It was not a tragedy – Logue was not keen to experiment with the fog's unusual property on himself.

Once the fire had been extinguished and the folded bags gathered and put under a stone – against the wind – Logue heard a quiet crackling in the silence of the night. The frost that had covered the soil was gone, exposing a wet, sticky and cold ground, and tiny bubbles were coming out of it. The bubbles burst, disappearing into the mist and leaving that unpleasant bitter smell that Logue remembered from his first time in the pit. Because of this smell, the field had been abandoned many years ago, but it never occurred to anyone that the smell somehow was associated with the bubbles.

As he listened to the crackling, he understood what it meant. Logue suddenly realized that in fact, the bubbles were the same as the fog, originating somewhere underground, breaking up and merging with the air, no different from it; only the smell betrayed their presence. Logue discovered a place where there were lots of bubbles, and found that some pieces of cloth were lifted by the bubbles; they pushed it upward. This discovery so fascinated Logue that he forgot that he had to go back home. While in a state of torpor, as he listened to bubbles bursting, he heard the growing Heavenly Voice. Logue started running, almost losing his way, and came home dirty, nearly collapsing from fatigue. His mother scolded him, but he did not listen to her. He ceaselessly thought about these bubbles – they must be light, otherwise they would not have raised the canvas – so if you collected a lot of them, and could stuff them into a foggy ball...

All these things merged for Logue into a single, concentrated venture, interrupted only by the need to work in the field, to deal with the kids, to help his mother, to bring old Lepir his food – the usual chores, but for Logue, all this seemed gratuitous. Logue's mind was somewhere up there, amidst the marvelous beauty of orange fog that was easy to breathe, swirling around him, making life easy. Yes, it could happen, because the very first experiments with bubbles had already shown that they could raise considerably more fabric than the fog generated by fire.

Logue was unable to sew a bag that could lift his weight. Not because it was impossible; he simply could not have avoided his mother's questions. He could not have hidden his unusual sewing. He had made five foggy balls, not very big, and had hung them over bubbling places. Gleefully, Logue considered this a great success: the lifting property of the bubbles in the foggy balls did not disappear with time. Moreover, by midsummer, with the Day of the Harvest approaching, bubbles began to erupt out of the ground more intensively, as if under concentrated, invisible, and constant efforts by some mysterious creatures that were showing kindness to Logue.

Logue carried the knapsacks – to Lena they would be useless, but it would be great if two foggy balls could lift them. He stepped into the field, keeping hold of the belay rope.

In the plot, nothing has changed: five sacks hung low to the ground, feasting on bubbles of smelly fog. Logue let out the rope to its full length and jerked the balls, which were hanging invisibly somewhere overhead. He pulled back one of the foggy balls. He managed to do it, albeit with difficulty, but refrained from showing his delight. He tied a rope to a bag of provisions, and the foggy ball easily lifted the load. Logue tied another rope to the other bag, and only then pondered a question that was, in fact, quite fundamental. Indeed, he had no idea what awaited him up there. There were uncertainties and risks in any journey on foot, but at least there was the sure knowledge of what food was useful to a Traveler to keep him from dying of hunger, and how to make a bed so as not to sleep on the damp ground. But there, high above, where there was nothing but fog and the Heavenly Voice?

I just have to make sure, thought Logue. *I must see the orange fog for myself, and then I will cut off one or two bags and lower myself into the field. Having finally learned true beauty, I will have become a Traveler.*

So, convincing himself that a bag of food and bedding was still useful, Logue started attaching ropes. Foggy balls were linked together. A few days earlier, he had fitted straps to hold his shoulders under the armpits; now, a strong rope was tied underneath, but sitting on it was uncomfortable because the rope dug into the body. It was necessary to make a more comfortable seat. *There is bedding in the knapsack,* he thought. *I can use that.*

Logue felt a slight jerk of the harness rope that was still attached to the ring on his waist. He froze. Did he imagine that? The rope jerked again, tangibly, almost pulling Logue off the seat.

Lena is coming, he thought. *She will now be making her way here, and I will have to calm her down and persuade her to go back. Or even threaten her.*

But it was not Lena. Logue listened more carefully to the voices he heard now. People were moving in the fog along the rope. The strong bass belonged to one of the Elders, a man of great height and unpleasant, bearded face. The second voice, mumbling something in response, belonged to the Chief Elder.

Had Lena, instead of going home, told the Chief Elder everything? And in betraying her, had Logue merely made her a traitor? Not a savior, but a foe?

Logue detached himself from the end of the safety line. He sat tight, so that an occasional spurt wouldn't dump him out of the seat. Logue could barely reach the ground with his feet, and therefore could not bend down to release the rope linking the five foggy balls to the stake driven into the ground. The voices drew nearer; Logue made his seat as comfortable as possible, and slashed the rope with a pocket knife.

Everything remained the same; only the seat swayed slightly. His feet, no matter how much Logue extended them, did not find support. And then he heard the voices – from below, as if from underneath him.

It was only then that he realized that he was flying.

He felt a fleeting moment of fear but then calmed down, because the foggy balls were pulling him up easily and almost imperceptibly. But most importantly, the reason Logue knew that he was not hanging in the same place was a growing sensation of cold. On the field there was summer warmth, whereas here it was cold as on a good winter morning. Logue could not have foreseen this, and now shivered and cursed, using all the bad words he knew. But how could he have prepared for something he had known nothing about?

Logue distracted himself by trying to answer different *why* questions that came to his mind: Why is it cold up here? Why, even though the morning is still far away, was there something vaguely greenish overhead, barely visible yet distinguishable, as a distant glow of burning lamps? And why, when he lifted his suddenly wet hand to his eyes, he saw huge snowflakes on them?

Logue stretched out his hand into the fog to catch more of these snowflakes that unexpectedly appeared in the summertime. He then felt how his back and even his hair suddenly started sweating. Then, above him, he saw what seemed to be the fingertips of an extended arm. Even in this darkness, illuminated by those almost indiscernible lamps, he saw in the fog things that he could hardly have observed even on the clearest days! He looked up, and with the utmost clarity, as if before the very eyes, saw all his five foggy balls and the food knapsacks linked by all those ropes. In the background there was fog which, for some reason, radiated a greenish glow. It was impossible to take all this in at a single glance.

"Why are 'fog' and 'air' different words?" Logue remembered.

He looked up, twisting his neck; overhead, the fog thinned more and more, clearly revealing a huge glowing circle. It was not obvious how it stayed up in the sky. The fear Logue experienced on seeing this was soon replaced by an altogether inexplicable horror. Approaching from afar, crushing the night silence, was the Heavenly Voice. Something invisible was coming at him, tearing the air, the fog, and everything around, to shreds. Logue swung, nearly falling off his seat, as the Voice roared. It was the end of everything. It was the anger of Heaven, and it was awful.

Completely paralyzed, Logue waited for his death. But the Voice quieted down, diving into the depths somewhere. Then, somehow, Logue heard it beneath him, where he dared not look. Only much later, when the Voice finally melted away, did Logue look down to see the white field of rolling snow, with bright, crisp shadows, a field that stretched as far as... Logue could not compare it with anything, and he knew only one thing: he could see. Not just five, not just twenty, not just a hundred cubits, but more. Maybe even a thousand.

His eyes hurt. They were not used to this kind of work, to look into the distance. Logue closed his eyes for a moment. When he decided to open them again, he directed them not downward but rather upward.

The fog has disappeared.

There was a black, absolutely soot-black dome. And on the dome shone sparkling dots, some brighter than the others: white, blue, and yellow dots, perhaps snowflakes. It seemed to him that they were changing places and dancing. Logue's consciousness was no longer able to process this experience; he did not realize that the dots in the sky were, in fact, completely motionless. A stream of these dots flowed along, taking Logue far away from his native village and all earthly problems, which were forever dead to him.

Before Logue's eyes, a vast greenish face appeared with some spots on it, eyeless and noseless, and with a fractured cheek somehow. At first, it was a lamp that shone through the fog; then it turned into a face, a clear, terrible face, surrounded by snowflake spots. The face drew Logue to it. He opened his eyes wide and could not restrain the cry torn from his throat as he felt the approach of inevitability and despair.

The abyss of the dome grew deeper as ever weaker sparks appeared out of the darkness, joining the general dance. They become more than snowflakes in the field. When Logue turned his head, snowflakes rushed at him, falling on his shoulders as a stinging rain, bringing sickening nausea to his throat.

He felt neither his hands nor his legs; he was dying among the lights, gasping for breaths of air, sparse at this altitude. He did not realize that it was not the anger of the Voice that was killing him, but rather a simple lack of oxygen. It was not Heavenly eyes looking into his. Under him, there was no snow but rather the same fog from which he had filled a bunch of balloons with light gas to take him up into clear and open heights.

Logue did not see all this splendor as a usual summer night; instead, he saw only something he could not understand. He could not recognize that which his eyes were seeing.

Fog lay on the rolling plain, illuminated by the smooth and indifferent light of a full moon. Between the fog and the sky, unruly bunches of balls, not at all part of the fixed dome, swept in the airstream, throwing a strange shadow onto the surface of the fog.

Logue understood nothing of what he saw, as if he were an infant newly arrived to this world. Just as if he were an infant, nothing but feelings lived in his body – "nice" and "light," "cold," and "hungry." He wasn't thinking in these concepts; he was not *thinking* at all. A given moment came, and he became sated. Another moment came, and he remembered his name. Yet another moment came, and he began to distinguish parts of the external world, and saw something that was familiar to him from his previous life. Table. He remembered the name. Bench. Window. Light. People. That was something strange for this "infant" who did not understand the purpose of objects he has never seen before.

Logue's attention now focused on the man who sat at the head of his bed. He managed to focus on the human face, and this allowed him to escape infancy. He grew up almost instantly and remembered everything. All his former life and the horror of the last few moments, as the world had opened, were so incomprehensible that Logue was unable to accept it. But to not accept it would mean not to live.

Dizzy, Logue clutched a soft blanket with his fingers. Air! The room had no air! He saw a table and a bench near the opposite wall, a window facing into the blackness of the night, a dazzling bright lamp under a high ceiling – he saw everything at once! His eyes, accustomed from birth to look up only to an arm's length, did not perceive the bulk of distant objects, and the ceiling in this room with no air could be ten cubits high, or it could be a hundred thousand.

A man sat on his bed, silent and smiling. His face was cleanly shaven, like a young boy's, but it was full of fine wrinkles, undoubtedly belonging to an old man. The man looked familiar, although this impression could be deceptive.

"Child," said the man. "Child, your name is...?"

"Logue." The word felt like a bubble in his throat. Child. The man looked like a Traveler, resembling Petrin. It could not be Petrin, but Logue's wish that it be Petrin and no other proved stronger than reason. Logue, finding himself finally able to think rationally, or if not, then at least to speak coherently, asked: "Why?"

"Why what?" asked Petrin.

"Why do I breathe? There is no air. Why do I see? Everything is spinning, but I see. Why?"

"Are air and fog the same thing? These are different words, and they represent different things."

"Petrin!"

"My name is Yarin... I'll be your mentor, Logue, in your new life. Until you become independent. I'll tell you right away: you're alive. You've been unconscious all night; not too long. You're on the Mountain. And now it's your home. The remains of your airship lie in the next room, with your other belongings. Yes, you can really see for many ells around you. Eyes are the gift given to man to see the world. All at once. Here and there, far away. Remember that, Logue. Repeat that until you get used to it, until it enters into you, won't you? You've lived in a fog and did not know that the fog was not air but a barrier. But you were unhappy, right? You were looking for something new. You could not live like everyone else. And you discovered a way to go and find out. You know this. Not everything – only a tiny fraction of it. You breathe air. It is around you, invisible and imperceptible. Air opens your world, whereas the fog had closed it. There is no fog here, Logue. It remained at the bottom. You rose above the fog. You rose above yourself, Logue. Think about it. Logue. Accept this as fact. That's how it is."

Before Logue could utter a word, the deep, rumbling, menacing Heavenly Voice came from the window. There was no mistaking this sound. The Voice was angry with Logue; it had nearly killed him there in the night fog; it would overtake Logue here.

Yarin also heard the Voice, but remained quite calm. Maybe Yarin was a god? Yarin said something, and Logue even heard it, but did not comprehend; the words did not fit into a mind ruled by the Voice.

"That is a vintolet," repeated Yarin.

Logue calmed down. This word, which bore the stamp of the inanimate, of the invented, reassured him, as well as the indifferent way Yarin said this strange word, "vintolet."

"A vintolet," repeated Logue. "That is the Heavenly Voice…"

"Ah…" Yarin shook his head. "Yes, for those who are in a fog, this is the Heavenly Voice. Again, fog… We have to fly above the fog. We rarely descend into it; even with our navigation instruments, it is difficult and dangerous. If you have never seen a machine, then it becomes a legend. You have a lot of myths. More than knowledge. We also have myths and parables. But they are quite different…

"What rises above the clouds?

"Mountains.

"What extends above the mountains?

"Sky.

"What is beyond the sky where the planets and stars shine?

"Thought and Knowledge."

Logue understood almost nothing of what was said to him, except for one thing: the Heavenly Voice was there. He sat up on the bed. His arms and legs obeyed him completely; they were no longer trembling. Logue decided to stand up. But his eyes refused. Everything spun, turned upside down. Yarin grabbed Logue's shoulder, but Logue did not lie down. He sat, waiting with closed eyes, feeling nauseated. A voice sounded, coming from afar. When he opened his eyes, Logue saw that all things remained in their places. He asked, "It can be seen...?"

"Good for you, child," said Yarin. "You're just a boy, Logue. Of course you can see the vintolet, and even touch it. And then fly in it if you want. Soon the sun will rise, there will be light, and you will see the city and the vintolet and the plants, and the people who already love you... And now, so that you do not have to suffer any longer from quenched curiosity, it is up to me to tell you the story of our poor planet."

Logue shook his head. He did not understand half the words. *City. Plants. Sun. Planet.* Empty sounds.

One step, thought Logue. *One step and one stab at stretched ropes. And a new world. One step – and a new world.* Logue repeated these words, forgetting that before this step, he had taken many others. A lifetime of steps. He wanted the unusual, something he could understand and imagine, because people simply cannot want what is not. And he got it, though it was not what he had expected. Now he must step through the absurdity – not the absurdity of the world, only his own absurdity. His own preconceptions.

"Vintolet," Logue repeated. "The city, the planet... everything is spinning in front of my eyes, Yarin."

"That's natural," Yarin said. "It will pass. Close your eyes, Logue. Listen..."

And Logue learned.

Several thousand years ago, this had been a lovely green planet, with a high and clear green sky ("not orange?" Logue interjected), where white clouds floated. ("What?" asked Logue, but afterward, he no longer interrupted, only remembered the parts he did not understand.)

People had lived on the planet – a tribe of farmers and craftsmen, with flying birds and animals in the woods.

And then came the fog.

In the bowels of the planet, there were processes that none of the people of that time understood. Gradually, very gradually, the air, the beautiful, clean, and clear air, began to thicken. Almost everywhere, gases and vapors came out of the ground, ejected by underground reactions. They were harmless to humans, but birds had died from it almost immediately. The fog penetrated everywhere; to get away from it, one could only climb higher. The fog was heavy; it crept along the ground, and people lived in this milky prison.

They had fled to the mountains; not everyone, only some of the people. Others remained on the plains, in the familiar, albeit changed, environment. Those that remained have planted and gathered, and continued with their lives. They did such work as has been necessary not to die of starvation; such had been their life. They haven't seen anything in the fog, but they have not wanted to see because they had forgotten what there was to see. They have gotten used to it. Just a few millennia of such a life, and they probably would have developed a new sense of, say, infrared vision or sonar. But only a short time has passed – a little less than a thousand years. And in the valleys of the tribes of the blind, they have created for themselves a comfortable belief that what there was, was this world, and the world was this village. And life consisted of the work in the field, home, family, children, and nothing else, and should be nothing else, because that was the Law.

"That was your tribe, Logue…

"And then there were the others, those who had fled to the mountains. The fog kept overtaking them, and they kept going higher. It was hard for them, because in the mountains there was little food. Nonetheless, they did not want to give up – they wanted not merely to survive, but also to answer the question: *Why, why did such a disaster happen?*

"The fog has risen, slowly but inexorably. Only four peaks were higher when the fog finally stopped encroaching. Only four groups of people – a handful – remained, living separated from each other by thousands of kilometers. At first, they knew nothing about each other. Four islands in an ocean of fog. But they have protected themselves.

Moreover, they have retained knowledge. They built villages in the mountains, and when they did not have enough space, they blew up the rocks. The best among them became scientists and engineers. To move along the mountain slopes, they invented all-terrain vehicles. To communicate with the three other cities, they came up with radio and aeronautics. But they always lacked one thing: food. The yield of the mountain fields has been meager, and after two or three centuries, the fields could no longer feed the increasing population.

"Facing us, or rather, our ancestors, arose a problem to end all problems. That's when they had to go down into the fog-covered valley," Yarin said. After a pause, he quoted, "...And the sky was angry, and the Voice appeared, and a storm began, which lasted for many days and nights; when the Voice stopped, people left their homes and went out into the fields to gather the harvest into their barns, but found that the Voice had punished them, taking half the ricks to the sky. And when the people prayed, the Voice answered them, and so it will always be...

"Taking part of our harvest, leaving us guns in return," said Logue, who understood only the essence of Yarin's story, not the details.

"Yes," nodded Yarin. "The guns that you could not make yourselves, because you did not have the foundries."

"The what?"

"We were gods for you, mighty, disembodied, and loud." Yarin took a breath. "You are our brethren whom we cannot help, mainly because you do not need our help. You would have rejected it without understanding. You are happy, oddly enough. You are foolishly happy, knowing nothing about either yourselves or about the world. What does a man need to be happy? Poverty of imagination and certainty that happiness is achievable. The fog of ignorance hides the world from you. Fog has slipped into your mind. Each thought has been separated from the others; thoughts were weaned from the chain of reasoning. You are satisfied with what you have. You just have no imagination. Fog. Damned fog..."

"Maybe it's all for the best?" Logue muttered. He thought about his mother, about the babies, about Lena and Lepir. All at once, in a single glance, he somehow saw all his life and the life of the village from this new perspective. "You, Yarin, you have not lost the ability to strive for what you do not have. I also wanted to... I want to do the same. Orange fog. And now that I know that the orange fog is stupid, I want something greater. I cannot describe it; it seems to me that now I want so much that I am bursting with impatience. And I am so sad. And they are happy, those who remained in the fog. Therefore they are better off than you... than us."

Yarin paused, gazing into Logue's eyes.

"Would you like to go back down?" he asked. "To live like the others...? You see it. This is a great disease of the mind – the desire to know and to act. Like any disease, it is painful. But if you recover, your mind will be extinguished. Fortunately, this disease is incurable. But one so rarely gets sick..."

"The Travelers," said Logue.

"This is just a mild case of the disease," Yarin said. "It's no longer a mind which is completely asleep, but it's not yet wakefulness. It is a mild slumber, a slow awakening. A vague feeling of discomfort, entailing a sense that there is mystery in the world."

"How do you know so much about us?" Logue asked, already knowing the answer. "You have never come to us."

"And how do you, Logue?" Yarin smiled. "There are just a few Travelers. They go out into the fog. At present, that is the way information is exchanged between the villages of your world. Like an unanswered letter... But one in a thousand Travelers vaguely understands the need to do things very differently. These are the imaginative ones. They come to us. Rather, fly to us. They discover the law of thermal expansion, or like you, Logue, fill balloons with light gases. Such people are very few. Among those few, only a handful of individuals over the past century have managed to keep their sanity when the fog dissipated and they saw suddenly that the world is huge. They saw the distant horizon, the wind-strewn fields of fog, and above them, that which is for us inaccessible so far: sun, moon, planets, stars... Their minds, just awakened, were unable to withstand such a test. But there are exceptions. The last man who came to us from below did it seventy-nine years ago. He died long ago. Such people are quick to burn themselves out, their brains lit with the fierce desire to learn and understand... and now you have come, Logue."

Listening to Yarin, Logue looked out of the graying window. It wasn't dark; daylight was seeping in. A day was being born, and Logue headed for the window. His legs obeyed him, though the room still swayed before his eyes. But the move was made. The second step, the third. Leaning on Yarin's shoulder, Logue's fingers clutched the sill to keep from falling. He looked straight ahead into the world, which unraveled itself to him from horizon to horizon.

The house stood on a steep cliff. A dazzling white carpet lay beneath. The sky around blazed scarlet, orange, yellow, all shades, and something was born between the fog and the unimaginable beauty of the play of light. Something more bright and dazzling than flame.

"Sunrise," Yarin said. "The day is starting."

Logue recoiled. The idea that he was going to die was a fleeting one; it burned up in the flames of the sunrise. Logue felt this flame in his chest.

"The sun," repeated Logue. The flame in his breast did not fade, and Logue thought that it would remain with him until his death, that it would burn and burn. But before his thoughts turn to ember, he would learn all that these people knew. And above all, what they know now.

"Fog smothers," Yarin said, realizing the state Logue was in. "It extinguishes the flame in your chest. The fog... it's rising, Logue. Several decades ago, the eruption of gases from the soil increased again. Fog rises, and in two or three generations... the fog will be here."

"No!" said Logue, with an instant horror at the picture that his imagination drew for him on hearing these words. *No*, he thought, *no one should live as people live down there do. Nobody. Ever.*

"Unfortunately, the fog is stronger than the sun," Yarin said sadly, and Logue thought that Yarin was already half lost in the fog, in his own fog, if he was able to utter these words. Yarin continued. "To win against the fog, it is too little just to conquer oneself. One must conquer the world. Who can do that?"

"I CAN," said Logue.

Me and Nana Go Shopping

By Hamutal Levin

Translated by Emanuel Lottem

HAMUTAL LEVIN HAS BEEN AN AVID READER since she was five years old. She became a science fiction and fantasy fan when she came across Frank Herbert's *Dune* at the tender age of ten. It was then that she fell in eternal love with the world of possibilities that she'd discovered, and started reading every SF/F book she could lay her hands on. In 1999 she first joined an SF/F web forum and dove into it head-on. There she met her future career, her future spouse, and some of the people who've changed her life. It was there that the story presented here was written, directly into the unreliable user interface of the time – in one fell swoop, with no editing and no interruptions.

Levin has a master's degree in journalism and communication from the Hebrew University in Jerusalem. In the past, she has written on science, health, and culture for several Israeli newspapers. Now she lives in Tel Aviv and works as a translation editor of SF/F books, fiction, young adults, and novels, for several major Israeli publishers. At home, she has a spouse, two children, a cat, and a library of some 2,000 books, including 500 that she has edited.

NOBODY MESSES WITH MY NANA, and I pity anyone who ever tries. She'll slam the perp down real hard, just like she learned to do as a girl during the Biowar Riots, which around here are called simply the Mess at the End of the World, and which few remember as well as she does. Nana, who was 13 at the time, joined the group that controlled her hood and learned how to loot, bargain, beat the living crap out of people, set broken limbs, and use an electric knife. The people in her gang also helped people get rid of the bacteria and build new homes.

My Nana is a hero. That gang produced many of the leaders of the Post-Mess world, and Nana knows them all. The gang leader was someone everybody called the King, and I think Nana kinda liked him. Occasionally, they post a story on some news site asking, "Where Did the King Disappear To?" and they always want to interview Nana. She never agrees. In secret, she told me that the King went to the unrestored part of the world-before, where he's working on a plan that will help restore all the places and bring all the refugees back home, but we can't tell anyone about that. The King is a hero, and when he comes back with his plan, there won't be bacteria anymore, and everyone will have a home. That's what Nana says.

I think it's nice of him to work so hard for the refugees, especially since they're such scary criminals. Nana says that I don't understand, that the refugees are people like everyone else who just had worse luck at the End of the World Mess, but I know the truth, because Mom and Dad told me. Mom and Dad think Nana is a bit of a barbarian, and they don't really like to have her over, but when she offers to take me shopping, they don't dare say no.

I like getting around with her. My Nana is a scary woman, and when we walk together, nobody dares bother me. Everyone remembers what happened the last time Nana got pissed at some refugee thug, and everyone thinks she was right. Even the thug came back to shake her hand once he was able to walk again.

We drive in Nana's Volvo jet, a '31 model they should have decommissioned years ago, and she curses all the other drivers, who barely manage to flee the speeding Volvo left and right. Nana's autojet has been in so many accidents that by now, there's not a single driver in the airspace who doesn't recognize it.

We drive to town 'cause Nana doesn't like the mall in the gatecom, as we call our gated community. At the mall, you can't haggle with the vendors, and it only has certified brands, no knockoffs. Nana prides herself on getting everything cheaper than anyone else, and she's not afraid of refugees, so she shops in town.

The city excites me as it always does. None of the kids in my class has a grandmother who dares take them there. We have kids who've never left the gatecom in their lives. I think even Mom hasn't been there in at least two years. The last time she had to go to town because of some lawsuit filed against her food-control company: Someone got food poisoning from stale mayonnaise and sued Mom, saying that being sick scared him so much, he lost two years of their life expectancy. She was so scared that Dad had to rent an armored autojet and two gorillas to go with her. But Nana's never scared. She says that anyone who's been through the End of the World Mess can never be afraid again.

We get into an actual store, with a door out to the street that anyone can walk through, and Nana lets me try on any outfit I like, even the kind Mom would freak out if I wanted to buy it: A jacket with special pockets for weapons and a shirt with a bacteria shield print. Mom goes nuts when I ask for clothes like that. She yells at me, "I don't understand! Why would you want to wear such rags? what are you, some refugee girl?" Mom doesn't know the first thing about fashion. Nana doesn't mind what I wear, and when I finally choose something I want (a blue shield shirt and spike shoes), she happily haggles with the saleslady, who eventually gives in and knocks twenty bucks off the price.

When we go out to the street, we're both happy. I'm happy because I have the coolest outfit in the gatecom, and Nana's happy because the saleslady made her a deal. Mom says it's not civilized to haggle like refugees, but I don't tell Nana that. I don't need her getting mad at me too.

Nana wants us to go eat at a real restaurant, one with a door to the street, but that I don't dare to do. Mom won't even let me eat the food they sell in the gatecom, because everything could contain bacteria. She only trusts her own tests, so I tell Nana that I'm not hungry and only sit across from her as she eats something called an eggroll that comes on a plate just like that, without even a sterile package. I think Mom is right about the food, and I hope Nana won't get sick from being so reckless.

When we leave the restaurant, I'm in such a hurry to get back to the gatecom and show everyone my new clothes, that I start running towards the jetpark. Nana walks behind me, not too far, making sure that nobody bothers me.

I stop to wait for Nana by the jetpark. On the floor sits some dirty old refugee, asking people for money. I try to stand as far away from him as I can, so I won't catch the bacteria I'm sure he has, but he looks at me. I see that this refugee is not just a beggar like all the rest of them.

He tells stories for his handouts. Some people stand around him and listen, but he's wasting his time; most of them are refugees who don't have any money to give anyhow.

The old man talks anyway. He tells them about the world before, all kinds of stories about how once everybody had homes, and everybody could go wherever they wanted, because there were no restored and unrestored areas. He also says something about how it's wrong that there are bacteria-free gated communities that don't allow refugees in them. He tells the refugees standing around that in the world before, everybody used to be equal. He tells them that they're just as good as the people in the gated communities. That's nonsense. I know this because Dad told me so, but I don't disabuse him. Instead, I huddle in a corner and look for Nana, surprised that she's not here yet.

But then I see Nana, standing not far from the refugee beggar and looking at him strangely. I want to call her, I'm afraid she'll catch his bacteria, and then I'll have to drive with her and the bacteria in the sealed Volvo jet, but she looks so strange that I keep quiet.

The refugee beggar finishes his story, and the other refugees around him leave. Some of them even give him money, which they undoubtedly stole from other people. Too bad there's no cop here to arrest them. Everyone knows refugees only have money if they steal it. But Nana and I are alone here with all the refugees, and I just huddle even tighter in the corner and pray that Nana will come already and we'll go home. But Nana still stands looking at the refugee beggar. I see her moving closer to him, and I want to shout to her about the bacteria, but at the last moment, she stops. She won't take her eyes off him, like there's something special to see in the face of yet another dirty beggar, and she quietly asks: "King?" And then I get really terrified – 'cause for the first time in my life, I see Nana crying.

Life in a Movie

By Yivsam Azgad

Translated by Emanuel Lottem

YIVSAM AZGAD IS A WRITER, editor, journalist, and art curator. Born in Ra'anana, Azgad is a second-generation Israeli. He began his journalistic work as a youth, writing for a children's newspaper. During his military service, he was a producer, scriptwriter, director, and cameraman of training films. Later on, he turned to abstract photography, exhibited two solo art-photography exhibitions.

His journalistic career began with two personal columns in the daily *Yediot Ahronot* on futurism and a column on child-rearing, which included comments by his 8-years-old daughter. It was then that he began writing science fiction, appearing regularly on the pages of the seminal *Fantasia 2000* magazine. Later on, he was to publish two SF/F novels. In 1989, Azgad moved to another daily, *Haaretz,* where he edited a weekly science supplement; in parallel, he also published a science column in *Yediot's* children supplement. His writings on science won him in 1993 an international prize and a special scholarship from the German Max Planck Institutes.

Azgad went on to the Weizmann Institute of Science as Head of Communication and curator of the institute's art collection.

Having retired in 2020, he became an advisor to the institute's president, and kept his position as an art curator. He is still busy in the field of science communication within the frame of the Israel National Science Foundation.

On a certain morning, a person did not get up in the morning. The morning this person did not get up, the birds did not sing, the wind did not blow. A hushed, even hum was blowing from the end of what is to the edge of what is not. Beyond the wrap, members of his household slowly gathered at his home's living room. Grinwald, the neighborhood lawyer, was there too, with the remains of toothpaste holding on to the bristles of his beard. And also Yonathan, the new neighbors' young son, the only one who could have been talked with truthfully in the last years.

When one is really first in line for death, the oldest among one's siblings after their parents have passed away, people start tiptoeing around him. Treat him with deliberate tolerance, as if he is already a goner. No, you're not going to die, don't talk nonsense. Yes, your future lies ahead of you, why don't you go study something or other. But now they don't look surprised, he noted to himself as a plain fact, as though recording a matter-of-fact observation, keeping his distance, as objectively as possible, in a lab experiment.

They had no reason to expect a great deal. Still, nowadays, after the great trade war that had been raging from the second decade of the third millennium to the middle of the current decade, after the first coronavirus pandemic, after the wave of COVID-21, after the closure of borders, after the collapse of all "financial instruments" and high-tech industries, after the comeback of low-tech – every item of physical property one can lay one's hands on is valuable. A chair, a blanket, kitchen utensils – everything. The rest had gone to rest. Everybody became a bag lady, or gentleman. Beyond the wrap, it looks like a failed recreation of that Bouboulina scene from *Zorba the Greek*, except that Nikos Kazantzakis' Madame Hortense had still been alive, whereas here… well, never mind. Let's drop it.

The family gathering lumbered on from can-I-get-you-something-to-drink-here-have-some-of-the-dates-and-nuts-cookies-that-Hava-baked to the next stage where everyone's eyes were focused on Grinwald, who hurriedly stuffed the remains of his sandwich into his mouth, pulled a document out of his briefcase, and cast his glance upon those seated facing him. Shortly afterward, most of the legal beneficiaries had already left, each holding something they've lawfully won. His brother, the next in line ("now he's first in line for death" / "now I'm first in line for death") closed the door behind Grinwald, having paid his fees with a bag of oranges that was left in the house.

Relax, you idiot, relax. Sit down and be quiet. Everyone's gone, no audience and no reason left for making a scene. You're not in the outpatient clinic now. The anger raging in your blood is not good for your health.

What was it that he wrote in his book, Yoram Yovell, about anger and punishment? Something about how, if you let go, and take things as they come, and don't really mind coming out like a sucker, it is you whose blood becomes full of the love hormone, oxytocin, rather than the testosterone which is responsible for primitive male aggression; and in doing this, you choose to live. And everyone else can jump into a lake. So relax, tell yourself that everything is alright, flow on. So you didn't get the three-legged round table, nor the large mirror, nor the juicer, nor the electric cooker. So instead of all there, despite your seniority, you got a small envelope with a key and a note that soon, when you put on your glasses, you'll be able to read. So your brother didn't think of what you wanted or needed. Again, as ever, he was, eh… well, never mind. Let's drop it.

Only trouble, this brother of yours. And enough with this never-speak-ill-of-the-dead business. This must be the only building in town with five floors and no elevator. And I'm not young anymore. First in line for death. A whole gallon of oxytocin won't help now. And, if he's so wise, I wonder how he would have flowed on now, in my shoes, up the fourth floor. What went on in his head when he decided to give me this key? And what's more, a note with instructions for immediate action. Swap magazines as you're shooting. I'm the only one he could trust, for crying out loud. If these are not beads and trinkets for Indians, like the ones with which those bloody colonialists bought the whole of Manhattan, then I don't know what beads and trinkets for Indians could be.

There it is, the Studio sign on the door. Key. This gate for the Lord, into which the righteous shall enter. So what do we have here? A large screen, split into smaller screens. Each one running a different video. An airport. A street corner, Dizengoff and Yirmiyahu. A field of blooming anemones near Be'eri. Some neighborhood in an unidentified locale. The windblown top of a Mediterranean cypress. A bus stop. A supermarket. Kids playing ball outside a school gate. A slight movement of the navigation ball, and the screens slide away to be replaced by others. Go back. Sonofabitch. What's this supposed to be, this clip? What's it doing there, in the middle of the video? Our cousin, Yohanan, with the copper vase he got less than an hour ago in the session of… eh… well, never mind. Let's drop it.

And it gets stuck. And Yohanan just stands there, frozen, with this kind of a look, like he's pleading for help. Stuck in the middle of life. A sound wrap began to hum in the background, opaque, unchanging, very quiet. Something evil, ominous, final. In the inbox at the bottom of the screen, under the *Files for Today* column, there was one item marked *unscreened*. The sender's name was obliterated by a series of gray x's. No surprise there.

No, it's not stuck. It restarts. In a loop. There's Yohanan, leaving home in the morning. The sun is yet to top the building in front, and a great gray shadow lies over the street. Here we go again. Soon we'll get to the family session with Grinwald. And then? Another loop? A story with a no-end known in advance. Although there's still one unscreened file in the inbox.

Yohanan, getting off the bus in the street corner for the umpteenth time, who knows how many, with his pleading look. Why should he mind going back and forth all over again? It's a wonderful way to be forever young. Perhaps not the most interesting one. But it seems that he is somehow aware of what is going on. That's good. A rational, reasonable person would let it be. You want to turn the world 'round in circular loops? Go ahead. It has nothing to do with me. But the oxytocin, Yoram Yovell's cherished oxytocin. This won't be the first time love makes people do things they'll regret. In the end, and in the beginning, everything is chemistry. Wonder what the folks in the outpatient clinic will have to say about this. Where's the navigation ball? It seems the sonofabitch didn't make a mistake. Found the right sucker to give the key to.

The unscreened file goes into the processor headfirst. Today will be a new day.

Dress

By Gail Hareven

Translated by Adriana X. Jacobs

G AIL HAREVEN WAS BORN IN 1959 in Tel Aviv to celebrated author Shulamith Hareven, and to Israeli intelligence and senior Mossad officer and, later, Foreign Ministry official Aloupf Hareven. Dr. Yitzhak Epstein, her great grandfather, emigrated to Palestine in the 1880s. He was one of the founders of the Academy of the Hebrew Language, to which Hareven's mother and then Gail herself were subsequently inducted.

Hareven grew up in Jerusalem, where she now resides. After receiving a BA in behavioral sciences at the Ben Gurion University of the Negev in Beersheva, she spent five years at the Shalom Hartman Institute in Jerusalem, reading Judaic Studies and Talmud.

Hareven made her mark in Israeli SF/F in 1999, when she published an unabashedly genre-infused short-story collection called *HaDerech LeGan 'Eden* (*The Way to Heaven*). "The Slows," published in *Zion's Fiction: A Treasury of Israeli Speculative Fiction*, was placed in *The New Yorker* through the efforts of translator and researcher Dr. David Stromberg, an editor at the cultural journal *Zeek*. It was subsequently adapted into a short film, directed by Nicole Perlman. The collection's title is telling, since the loss of paradise recurs as a theme in much of her work. Her access to the fantastique, in contrast, is joyful, profusive, and infused with a sense of wonder.

A journalist and book reviewer, she has written for most of the major Israeli media outlets as well as for *Tikkun, Lilith,* and other progressive American publications. In 2006, she was a guest lecturer at the University of Illinois, teaching writing, and in 2012, a guest lecturer at Amherst College.

So far, Hareven has written 17 books: story collections, children's stories, novels, a thriller, and one non-fiction book. Her 18th novel is due to be published shortly. Major Israeli theater companies have staged five of her plays. *The Confessions of Noah Weber: A Novel* (2009) garnered the Sapir Prize in Israel, as well as rave reviews in the US and elsewhere. In 2015 she published *Lies, First Person*, earning similar accolades. Her work has been translated into English, Russian, Spanish, Italian, Serbian, Czech and Chinese. She is also a recipient of Israel's Prime Minister's Prize.

MY DAUGHTER IS WEARING A BROWN DRESS with a pattern of yellow keys. It isn't a pattern meant for ten-year-old girls, but my daughter didn't say anything when I showed her the fabric I'd bought at the market – she didn't even grimace at the spinsterish brown and the childish print. My good girl comes into the kitchen in jeans and a blue shirt, and she's already settled into her chair when this bad feeling comes over me and I take her back into the bedroom. For several long minutes I look into the closet, until my subconscious moves my hand, and my hand moves me toward the brown and yellow.

Now she sits across from me in composed silence, her braids beauti-fully woven, dipping a cookie into her tea. Today is a clear day, cool and clear; through the blinds the sun sketches light grilles over the tablecloth and over my daughter's hand. Sewing the dress, I did the best I could to make up for the fabric: a fitted waist, a flowing skirt, and a pair of small pockets along the chest, one above the other. I copied the pattern from a dress worn by one of her friends. As they'd opened their notebooks to do their homework, my daughter had marveled at her friend's sky-blue dress. "A fairy's dress," she'd said. It's still chilly out, too cold for thin fabric and sleeves above the elbow. But the generous praise that my daughter lavished on her friend pulled at my heartstrings and I yearned to make her happy.

Now I'm no longer sure about the brown. A clear day like this highlights the essence of things and makes everything painfully beautiful, and it is possible that a sky-blue fabric like the one her friend wore would have blended much better into this radiant background. Though sometimes it's the faded and blanked-out things that are taken.

THE DAY THEY TOOK N, I was wearing a red and brown floral dress and a short gold necklace. N, as always, wore dusty beige. Everything about N was dusty beige: the dry skin on her neck, her bespectacled eyes, her ragged shoes, her socks, her way of speaking in the teacher's lounge. Her hair, pulled tightly back, revealed a white streak, and a faint pallor sometimes appeared around her lips. But maybe I'm imagining this whiteness, which in literary texts signifies illness, fear, and death. Maybe I never really noticed this whiteness around her lips and it's my imagination that gives it this color now. The car was waiting for her next to the gate – not right next to it, a little farther on – a man blocked her path on the sidewalk, another man rested his hand on her back as she bent over to enter the back of the car. There were three of us on the staircase, three teachers on their way outside. There were children there, as well, busy with their own things. A ball rolled past us, bouncing down the stairs, and I turned around to scold the one who had thrown it.

MY DAUGHTER STIRS HER TEA IN SILENCE, raising up clouds of cookie crumbs. She's not much of a morning talker. Even when she was a baby she would wake up without crying, and when I would lean over her crib with a pounding heart, her black eyes would be wide open, calmly taking in what they could see. By the time she could walk, she would make her way to our bed, nudging herself between me and her father, and the feeling of this warm body carefully nestling up against mine used to rouse me from my sleep. When her father had to leave us, she quit coming to our bed. I'd imagined that his disappearance would increase her attachment to me, but she matured beyond her years and her gestures grew more restrained. By then she was six. What do children know? What does she know?

WHEN THEY TOOK N, the children in the courtyard didn't notice, and those who did saw an older, unpopular teacher, a beige, unstylish teacher, disappearing into a large car. By the next day they had a new teacher. What's there to remember? Actually, for me this memory is wrapped in shame. Of course, there was fear, but I don't remember it, or maybe I'm wrong and there wasn't any fear at all. By the time we noticed the car, the bald man was already blocking N's way. And it was already clear the car was there and who it would take away. When it left, we stood there, the three of us, our faces frozen, as if we were each having our own mad episode and trying not to reveal what we had seen, not to give in to the insanity. What am I ashamed of? That I uttered the first word and scolded the child who had thrown the ball. Even if there is nothing to be ashamed of, I'm ashamed nonetheless, and my body stiffens with loathing recalling that shrill voice, that turning motion toward the child.

WHAT DOES THE GIRL KNOW? It's possible that my daughter knows a lot and that her morning silence is not the same as before – it feels now like the silence of a secret. She never argues with me when I send her to change her dress, and her patience doesn't waver when I stand frozen in place in front of the wardrobe, my hand hovering in the air. With endless patience, she sits on her bed, folds her hands over her knees, and waits.

Beige is the color of camouflage, but beige doesn't protect. There are days when one is safer in an intense red or bright orange. The boy on the railroad tracks was also beige, a pulp of beige and brown, and a dark red spreading all over. I didn't know who he was until it was written in the newspaper: the son of… decadent in life and art, an alcoholic. Witnesses say he wandered about and collapsed. It happened on a gray afternoon, the same day they took N. I never exchanged more than a few words with her. The one time she confronted me was when I unintentionally sat down in her usual spot in the teacher's lounge, far from the blazing radiator. And I didn't say a word, just quickly gathered my notebooks without looking her in the eye. But I caught the slight smiles of two young colleagues who observed us from the hot water dispenser. She belonged to a different generation. She had taught at the school when I was a student there. I once heard that she had a daughter, a wild child who got involved with some foreigners and ran off at a young age, but for some reason I can't picture her as a mother.

IF ONLY I HAD KNOWN MORE ABOUT COLOR — but how can one know, when nothing is certain anymore? It can't be that there is no system, that there is no law one can identify. Like in nature. Someone gives the order, someone decrees: "You will take them today and let the rest go," and so the decree hangs down, branches out, sends its arms out to bring car after car full of today's "them."

The style of my daughter's dress is better suited to a younger girl — three, five years old. My daughter is ten, and according to the new constitution she reached the age of criminal responsibility two years ago. Maybe dressing like a toddler will allow her to slip under the radar.

Then again, maybe the color and style don't determine this. Perhaps there is another law entirely that I can't pinpoint. At night, when my daughter is asleep in her bed, I comb the newspapers, striving to find some logic in the melody of names that I contemplate out loud. No rule ever crystallizes from this humming, but for a moment my heart lifts with a feeling of enlightenment: a guttural syllable at the beginning of a name, a weak syllable at the end, a letter in the middle of a word. But right away, always, one after another, the exceptions emerge, and everything fogs up again, and once again my body wanders about in terror like a pagan approaching what his eyes perceive as a caprice of nature. Nature has no whims. Nature has law.

One night I gave up humming the names, and instead I focused on each individual name. Maybe this way I could decipher the code. First I memorized each name as it appeared and then switched the letters around. In the end, I calculated the total numerical value: first name, last name, and the two together. Against all probability, the first fourteen first names came up as multiples of three. My hands started to shake as I moved along the row, from name to name, number to number, up to the fifteenth name, which resulted in an even number, as did the three numbers that followed.

There are stories told of great scientists who make their discoveries in dreams. When my mind can't take any more, I lay my head on the pillow and go over the names one last time with my eyes closed. Maybe my dream will reveal something. Even though nothing comes to me in my dreams, I sometimes stir, gripped by a panic that I have forgotten something more important, that it has slipped by me unnoticed, something tangible like a real presence in the room. And when my breathing returns to normal, I am once again unaware of what has slipped by me, and I no longer feel its presence.

It is possible that the error is on account of dividing this search into days. Maybe the rules are exposed over time, in some sequence of weeks, months, or years, but even if I had a way of coping with so many names, I wouldn't have courage to save the list. And memory, wretched memory, retains so very little.

It is possible that I am inflicting an injustice on my daughter, and that for no good reason I am wrapping her in fabric for toddlers. One time, on television, I saw three people held at the border, the three of them wore dark-blue sweaters with a rhombus pattern in a color that I could not identify, a sweater just like the one our poet used to wear, and whom we gathered to mourn on the day of his sudden death. Aside from this, there were also the two in dusty beige whom I saw taken off the street, but I didn't know, and I have no way of knowing, what the others were wearing when they were removed: teacher, teacher, engineer, farmer, farmer, student, teacher, sailor, journalist, driver, chemist, laborer, builder, driver, watchmaker; thirty, twenty-eight, sixty-two, thirty, forty-three, fourteen. Maybe I'm wrong and there is no correlation between someone run over by a train and a woman taken by a car, and maybe it was days or weeks before she was loaded onto a railcar. Two coincidences don't make a rule, and only this heightened intuition, which is sometimes a sign of insanity, causes me to grasp at them as if they make some kind of rule.

Anyone who, like me, was a young girl during the Great War knows that you can't disregard intuition. The street you chose to cross; the street you avoided for no apparent reason on a certain day, at a certain hour; the sudden feeling that guided you at a certain moment to keep going and leave, and at another hour to wait. Dozens of times I followed my intuition, and if I survived it was thanks to that ancient voice that rises from the deepest recesses of the mind.

In those days we knew who the enemy was. The people, like a sick body, rose against themselves and attacked their own cells. Teacher, teacher, engineer, farmer, farmer, a thirty-year-old, a twenty-eight-year-old, a sixty-year-old. They say that one must amputate a limb before the gangrene spreads. Diseased cells disguise themselves as healthy ones, and the ones closest to the sick cells must be excised before they endanger the entire body.

My daughter is already ten years old, and her body has yet to reach that awkward stage that hits girls right before puberty. Warm and perfect, poised, she sits in her blue underwear and watches her mother's hands dig around the closet like a pair of skittish rodents. Sometimes I think that her passivity speaks to her maturity, and other times I think the very opposite: my daughter seems very childish to me. Either way, her passivity suits me, and yet there are moments when I glance back at her and yearn for an outburst of anger that would detain the mad movements of my hands. For it is madness—madness that provokes me to torture her in this way, every time she is ready to leave the house. If she were to burst out, to cry, to refuse to change her clothing for the third time, if she were insolent and yelled "you're crazy" to my face – maybe then I would recognize this madness, I would instantly recognize it and gather my daughter into my arms, and let her choose whatever she wanted to wear, and I'd even sew her a sky-blue dress, even though I'm not allowed to wear sky blue to school. The point is that if my daughter is taken, she'll be taken without me.

My first class begins at ten. In the meantime, I sit in my thick robe, putting on my work clothes only after my daughter has left. Choosing my own clothing doesn't require much thought. It's obvious that I can't wear a brown dress with a print of yellow keys, but in my closet there is a similar brown dress with a print of yellow circles, and from a distance the two dresses look alike, as if they had been cut from the same cloth. My daughter's dress is long, about twenty centimeters below the knees, and it will definitely fit her in the summer and fall, maybe even next spring. Because my daughter is growing fast and needs new clothes every season, I spend hours looking for clothes that look like mine, and when I can't find any, I sew something for the two of us.

Intuition sways me in two directions, and I can't decide which is the safest. Sometimes it swings this way, sometimes that way. In our closets hang pieces of clothing made from basic patterns, which you see often on the street, but there are also items that I have sewn from less readily available fabrics, fine, multicolored fabrics, the kind that you might find only at the theater. It was the second kind that earned me the reputation of a master seamstress. Often my colleagues would inquire where they could get a certain pattern, dropping hints that maybe I could make them something, but I wouldn't take the bait, and I also wouldn't reveal where I had purchased the fabric.

My daughter is done fishing cookie bits out of her tea and now, like the well-mannered girl that she is, she gets up to wash the cup, soaps it scrupulously inside and out, rinses, dries it off, and checks it against the light.

I sip my coffee and hide, try to hide, the sharp pain that seizes my stomach. Such a little girl – and such gravity in all her movements.

When I was my daughter's age, actually a little bit older, two years before the outbreak of war, my thoughts used to revolve around what I secretly called "the perfect movement." I wasn't graceful like her, and my self-conscious pride kept me from participating in ballet classes. I knew that I was not, and never would be, like those charming nymphs of lithe movement and body whose locks come undone, cascade, and prettily frame their cute faces. And despite my mother's anger, I refused to be one of those stubborn, clumsy dancers who fall over themselves.

Even though I didn't study ballet, I thought a lot about movement. Every movement, even the most quotidian movements—like combing one's hair or washing one's hands – could be executed in an ugly or less ugly way, in a regular way, or in a more beautiful way, and of course in a more perfect way. The perfect movement is the right movement. The hand rising in the air passes an endless line of imaginary points, the right points – not straying one millimeter – and as it approaches its goal, it traces this line with the right rhythm, without haste but also without slowing down, for there is a rhythm, everything requires the right rhythm. One simple and perfect movement, I thought, can change reality, like opening a door into another world, like turning on a light. The right movement isn't just a beautiful movement, it is beauty itself, and when it is revealed, it is impossible not to notice. In my mind I saw myself at a train station, lifting my hands to tighten the ribbon in my hair. At first, only a few people notice the movement, it attracts their gaze and illuminates their face. But this focused observation leads more and more heads to turn in my direction, and the station begins to quiet down, and as soon as I lower my hand, the last voices fade. I don't imagine any applause, shouts of praise, or people approaching me. The silence continues for some time after the perfect movement comes to an end. With a pensive turn, people continue on their way, reflecting on that revelation of perfect beauty. Everyone saw it, and even if they didn't know how to describe it, they felt as though their life had changed.

The perfect movement requires great practice and a complete lack of self-consciousness. It comes by chance, its awareness crystallizes only in the act, for too premature an awareness may distort it. With my hand driven by some internal mechanism that to this day I don't understand, I would enjoy long periods of time focused intently on one quotidian movement. Sharpening a pencil: the back is straight, but not too straight, the elbows lean on the table, the fingers grasp the metal sharpener, the palm of the second hand moves in delicate semicircles in front of the pensive face. The lips touch one another. One must not wrinkle the brow.

Over and over again, I would put on a coat, just to practice taking it off, like throwing a robe over one's shoulders. For some reason it seemed to me that in the removal of the coat, more than in putting it on, there was the potential for beauty. Sometimes the right movement was so close, but a sudden deviation – of millimeters, of excess awareness – would cause it to be lost and I would be forced to start all over again.

I don't remember how much time passed in that search, months it seems, until gradually the impulse to search vanished like a fleeting name. Sometimes, when I was already a university student, a flicker of that old feeling returned, when I focused the microscope in order to observe the structure of a cell, carefully guiding my fingers toward the perfect focus, and suddenly blurring the picture with a careless movement. Yet this was little more than a pale shadow of what dominated my existence when I was a child.

Now my daughter, with a dreamy expression, threads her hands slowly through the straps of her school bag. Right before she leaves the house the focus is perfect, and my girl with her braids, the edge of her slip peeking out, my girl with her brown dress, is the epitome of beauty, but beauty does not break open the world.

"Can I go?"

When I kiss her on the top of the head, I hold my hands, so that they won't grab her fiercely and bring her back to me.

I will stand next to the window and wait a bit. Through the sunlight, I see my little daughter appear, crossing to the sidewalk on the other side, turning right, passersby hiding her from my eyes. She disappears at the corner of the street, emerges again for a moment, and then moves farther away under the canopy of trees that have just begun to turn green.

And then, a few minutes later, terror will strike – maybe the brown dress is a mistake, a mistake that can never be repaired, and by making this one wrong choice, I have sealed the fate of my daughter.

CellShock
By Assaf Gavron

Assaf Gavron was born in 1968. Son of English immigrants, he grew up in a small village near Jerusalem and currently lives in Tel Aviv, Israel. He has lived in the US, UK, Canada, and Germany. He published six novels (*Ice, Moving, Almost Dead, Hydromania, The Hilltop,* and *Eighteen Lashes*), a collection of short stories (*Sex in the Cemetery*), and a non-fiction collection of Jerusalem falafel-joint reviews (*Eating Standing Up*). His fiction has been translated into 12 languages. He teaches creative writing in universities in the US and Israel.

The awards he won include the Israeli Prime Minister's Creative Award for Authors, the Israeli Bernstein Prize, the DAAD artists-in-Berlin fellowship in Germany, the Buch Fur Die Stadt award in Germany, and the Prix Courrier International award in France. His fiction was adapted for the stage at Habima – Israel's national theatre – and five of his novels were optioned for film or TV by Israeli and international film producers. As a translator of fiction, Gavron is responsible for the highly-regarded English-to-Hebrew translations of J.D. Salinger's *Nine Stories*, Philip Roth's *Portnoy's Complaint,* and Jonathan Safran Foer's novels, among others.

Gavron is the founder of Israel's national writers' and poets' soccer team. He is also the singer and principal songwriter of cult pop group The Foot and Mouth. So far, the group has released five albums.

A DOT APPEARS ON THE SCREEN. And disappears. And reappears. The first three times it appears, it is accompanied by the thin squeak I chose for her. The title of the squeak is "A Hungry Fledgling," and I know this is the sound of a real hungry fledgling, as it was recorded in nature. I work with real sounds only.

The squeak accompanies the first three flashes and then fades out, but the dot remains, coming and going. This requires me to press two buttons on the side of my handset in a specific combination. It brings up a screen on which the new message is displayed, the message for which the dot flashed and the fledgling squeaked. The message is written in red, warm letters: "I am here, in your zone. What RU wearing?" My head tilts up slowly from the screen so that she won't notice me. In situations like these, I always prefer to be the first to see the other. Not because I could then avoid her in case I don't like her looks – the deep tint of the red letters tells me she is too close to avoid – but this way, I am more prepared than her for the moment our eyes first meet. This way, she can't see my expression at the moment I see her.

My head tilts up slowly from the screen and observes. It is the end of a long day. A man next to me lowers his glass firmly to the bar, and

I feel droplets on my arm. I lower my eyes back to the screen, and two droplets are glowing on it. I wipe them with my sleeve. Three "Hungry Fledgling" squeaks announce a new message. I press the button and read: "Come on?? Who RU? U can't chicken out now!"

I beam: "Not chickening out. One minute."

My head tilts up once more and observes. It's crowded in here today. The bald heads of the men look from above like eggs laid in trays. The black wigs of the women. When this sight hits the eyes, the sounds hit the ears. Hum of conversations, message beeps, melodies of incoming calls, a pounding beat from the miniature speakers spread all over the ceiling. I hate it when men look at me when they are speaking to their mouthpieces.

I beam: "I'm the one with the bald head and the silver tie." Ha ha, like everyone else here. "And how do I recognize U?"

The name "Zloti" appears on my screen next to a flashing blue ax, and in my earphone I hear a locomotive I haven't heard in a long time. This is not good. Zloti is in my zone, which means that he has just entered the bar. I can identify a pretty acoustic guitar in the background through the ceiling speakers – I live for moments like these. In the entrance, where my glance is directed, stands Zloti, looking for me. His baldness shines brighter than his tie. This is very bad.

Hungry fledgling screams. The letters are red, "U will identify me by my green earphone." I lift my head and look for her. There are too many people.

Locomotive. A light blue text, signaling a secondary distance. "Remember me, Nikanor?"

Lowering myself, pushing my way through the crowd; around a corner, there's a corridor leading to the washrooms. In the corridor there are doors to the washrooms, and opposite them there is another door, to a narrow closet containing cleaning equipment.

I sit on top of a Hoover that can also mop the floor if needed.

Next to me is a wiper, upside down, on its head a new hi-end synthetic cloth, with the no-hairs-stick-to-it formula. When I close the door on myself, the bright light from the corridor breaks through the shutters onto my suit. For a moment, on my silver tie, it looks like sunlight breaking on water. My screen radiates an orange light onto my face. In my earphone, a fledgling squeaks. "Coward, coward, coward. Should I go home? Should I look 4 someone else?" her red text is paler now; I am not as close to her as I was. Zloti's ax is still blue. It is still flashing.

It's not as much as it sounds.

I work with Zloti. I mean, used to work. I mean… we did a project together three weeks ago. We are free agent programmers, digital warriors for hire, to anyone who can afford us. We met on this project, a large company that was hysterical, as all of them are, as always, to meet a deadline. A two-day job, $5,000 each. I made friends with Zloti. At the end of the second day I told him, "Let me bill them for the whole sum, this month I have a lot of expenses and I need it for my taxes. Next week I'll give you $6,000 instead of $5,000." This is what I always do, and programmers are naive. Then I disappear. For a week, I walk about with the handset turned off. The second week I turn it on only for calls and disable all the find and recognition functions. The third week I mark the other person, in this case Zloti, as an ax. This means I get messages regarding him with the highest level of urgency. At the end of the third week, I collect the money and move to another city.

Tomorrow the third week ends. I have a ticket.

The blue of the ax deepens. A locomotive penetrates my brain. "RU in the washroom? I thought U would be more creative than that."

I don't answer him. I type to her, "Don't go. Give me 5 minutes. I'm with U."

Three weeks is the shortest wait to receive the money in cash, at the offices of the company for which we worked. I don't have a bank account. – If I had one, they would give me a cheque after sixty days. If I had one, they would be onto me easily.

I said it's not as much as it sounds. But still, it shouldn't have ended in this broom closet, with the bright light breaking through the shutters and the orange gleam from my handset. A fledgling squeaks, "Don't get mad. I give U 2 minutes".

Life is made out of mistakes. Only today, one day before I'm out of this city for good, I opened my handset in full operation mode. Call me careless, but I had to find a red woman for tonight. And I found a red woman. And Zloti had to pass by my zone and recognize me.

A red woman is a woman who announces to handsets in her zone that she's looking for sex.

I was looking for the same thing this evening. So I'd opened all search and recognition systems on my handset and announced across my zone that I am red. She sent me a red text back. We shared profiles and a few messages. She looked good in the pictures she'd sent, if they were indeed pictures of her. We arranged to meet in this bar. Now I am cringing in the chemical smell of floor shampoo, and I can hear water flushing.

Heavy steps in the corridor. Water running in the sink. Someone passes in front of the closet and stops. A hot-air hand-drying machine starts up. I peek through the shutters and breathe into myself in silence. Zloti's gaze is on his screen. The door to the washroom opens. I see a green earphone.

My mother and father called me Nikanor. He was the minister of elephants in ancient Rome. They liked the name. Zloti puts his head through the door and sings in a high-pitched voice, "Nikanor? Nikano-hor…"

The green earphone turns around and looks at Zloti's back.

I type: "go away! Go back 2 the bar, I'll come in a second."

I press the button to send the message, and a second later, I can hear my sound coming out of the green earphone on the side of her head. She really is pretty, like in the pictures she sent me. The sound is so clear in the naked corridor that I fear Zloti will hear it. It is my sound. A cry of a shofar, rising, descending, then breaking. She lowers her head to her handset and then lifts her eyes.

I can hardly breathe. I lean back and close my eyes. I rub my temples and touch sweat.

The sound of her steps down the corridor. I can see behind her back that she is busy with her handset. Immediately after that, a hungry fledgling squeaks on my side. The dot appears and disappears, coming and going. The orange screen tells me, "Bye-bye… have fun… bastard…"

I have no control over things.

Her footsteps stop suddenly. And then I can hear them again. But are they getting closer now? They get stronger. And Zloti comes out of the washroom, he didn't find anything in there, he stares at his handset. She stops in front of him. His eyes look up.

She pulls a white-headed match from a thin box she took earlier from the bar, on a line of sulfur. "Tell Nikanor I was looking for him," she tells Zloti. She breathes in the fumes coming from the flame.

Zloti raises both his hands, confused, his smile troubled, his eyes don't understand.

I see how everything is happening. But she can't see his face, she turns back and walks down the corridor towards the bar, I can hear her steps on the white floor.

Zloti walks after her. He types into his handset. I wait for the locomotive and hear it a second later, trampling into my brain. I don't want to look at my screen.

I stay in the closet for another two minutes. Finally, I turn off my handset.

My father and my mother told me that everything has a price.

Composting

By *Galit Dahan Carlibach*

Translated by Ronnie Hope

Galit Dahan Carlibach was born in the border town of Sderot in 1981, and grew up in Ashdod and Jerusalem. She studied scriptwriting at Jerusalem's Ma'ale school of cinematic arts, and soon afterward started publishing short stories and essays in various newspapers, magazines, and websites in Israel and abroad. Her first novel, *Ahoti Kala vehaGan Na'ul* (*My Sister Is a Spouse and the Garden Is Inclosed*), was published in 2010 and won her the National Library's Pardes scholarship for young authors.

Subsequent novels and short stories won several awards, such as the AKUM Prize, the Prime Minister's Creativity Award for Authors, and the Fulbright Scholarship for participation in the University of Iowa's International Writing Program.

Dahan Carlibach's writing encompasses a variety of genres and themes. She once noted that the editor of one of Israel's leading literary supplements has consistently rejected dozens of her stories, essays, and poems, until she sent him a poem under a fictitious male name, whereupon it was immediately printed…

The following story, so characteristic of her unique blend of fantasy, horror, and humor, appeared previously in the *Tablet* online magazine.

I NEVER WANTED to reach this state, on my back, spreadeagled.

Not that it was so great out there, but being a zoology museum exhibit wasn't in my plans.

Hi there, come and see, close-up, the "Aerobic Compostization Processes."

I inhabit a mucous world. Paradise? Forget about it.

The animal world is creeping and crawling all around me: red worms, black worms, roly-polies, slugs.

A bone. That's all I'm asking. Two hundred units of osteoporosis pills, or whatever.

I am concentrating on one strong, solid desire: to repel, destroy, and finally rid myself of all the creepy-crawlies.

I'll smite them hip and thigh. Bones again. Assembled and joined together. In the compost world, there is no plaster to join broken legs together. Here, you don't get stronger or more rigid, you don't solidify.

Here, the key phrase is "get flexible."

My longing for the bone, for the hard and fast.

Coffins? They're only for Christians, not for Jews in Israel, unless they happen to be blown-up soldiers. The rest of us get only shrouds. Forget about the dignity of the dead. Until the time when an archaeological expedition will excitedly discover the dignity of the dead, it'll be at the mercy of the creepy-crawlies.

Energetically, the red worms sing along. Aah! The cells are guzzled up. Aah! The molecules disintegrate. Aah! Biological bonds are destroyed. Aah!

No, I never wanted to be in this state. Slowly decomposing, my body prey to industrious tone-deaf worms. I never had any desire to blend with the earth.

Life as ecology. Life as zoology.

And after all, there are better candidates than I in the ecological-communal community of Shorshon.

Candidate number one is my husband, Avishai Ben-Or. He's in the business – CEO of Compost Guard. His resumé is first-rate: conventional studies at the Weizmann Institute, and on the side, apprentice composter at the Kadesh Barne'a composting site. Here and there, with other women, supplementary courses at ecological seminars.

And what about Yiftah Graetz, our neighbor? While I'm being consumed by the tone-deaf worms, he's complacently breeding the enemy.

Red worms, 80 shekels, delivery to all parts of the country included.

Or why not Mira Goor, our number one composter – she wouldn't have been lying here like me, doing nothing. She would have done something, making fertilizer of herself, giving herself to the creepers.

Or perhaps Ahava Luria, who runs the Mother Earth workshop.

Yeah, Ahava, she should have been guzzled up. Fragile and brittle like her name, which means love. It used to be Hofit, which comes from the word for beach, but that name never felt right to her. Too sharp at the edges. When she changed it, she threw a big party near the spring, where she skinny-dipped and spread love around, enough to attract all the eco-testosterones in the vicinity. Ahava's crazy about the abstract. She yearns for anguished eyes, longs to roam the mazes of the soul, desires to touch the I.

"Mother Earth is great and hugging," I overheard her once as I jogged by on the path. At first, she'd persuaded me to join her yoga class. "You must stop running," she said to me. "Running jolts the soul," giving her own excuse for her terrible laziness. But Ms. Luria doesn't know that even breathing is connected to bone. A deep, deep inhalation, and the air is trapped between the lung bones – lungs belong to vertebrates. A long, long exhalation, and carbon dioxide finds its way out. Another breath. Hold the air in your diaphragm, push the ribcage out, and exhale.

If I still have some of my soul, I'll swap it for a lungful of air. I'll give my life.

Once I agreed to come in. The girls were all there, solemn-faced, sitting in a Buddha position, I sat down, and just then, my foot itched. A scratch that was sheer pleasure: One firm rub of the skin, peeling off the cover, and blood masks the bone. Scratching my foot cost me the determination of my I: It turned out that all my chakras were blocked and opaque. I got up and laughed, and my cigarette was already there, between my fingers.

I went back to jogging. (Remembering: Rigid bones jolt the asphalt, clean bone wrapped in red meat.)

As a Jewish woman, I have some basic rights. But in Shorshon, they haven't heard yet of the Final Grace.

We've already heard all about this True Grace of yours: To let Mira Goor, our number one composter, wash my dead body. You call that Grace? With vengeful force, she scrubbed my lungs. Don't let her think I didn't feel it.

However, alas, Netta Baraban didn't have lungs anymore. Netta Baraban loved her cigarettes dearly.

Netta adores cigarettes! Blessed be the manufacturers. Blessed be the tar. Blessed be the deposits of pitch in my soul. Blessed be thee, O cigarette. And may you all be blessed, carbon dioxide, nicotine, formaldehyde.

To hold a cigarette as it should be held: between forefinger and thumb.

No dignity of the dead, no Final Grace. No heap of compost, no worries about that damned methane gas.

Just fine ash scattering in the wind. L&M Lights, that's what I'd like to be. To hover in space, as a lot of lovely, pleasant particles.

Back at home, my husband is having a ball. Cleansing his car (galvanized iron, 2,000 cc, carbon monoxide, sulfuric oxides, lead) of Netta's cigarettes. His snooty women will lie there in comfort now. There's nothing like getting laid in detoxified air.

Avishai is tossing the microwave into the garbage. He realigns the recycling bins. Slaps our gardener on the back, a foolish man who likes talking to plants. Once, I slapped him across the face because he was standing there scattering cardboard pieces all over our garden plot. With his green angel face, he said: "That's to prevent evaporation of water." I roared at him: "Water. I want a lot of water. I don't care about the drought, or Lake Kinneret, or evaporation. Moisture everywhere!"

At home, they ignored my instructions. They didn't do our laundry in the machine. They didn't heat stuff in the microwave.

My little girl Roni is very quietly burning pita bread on the gas stove. Even the cats spit out the schnitzels that I fry. No vegetables, no eating.

Everyone cried at my funeral, and not because of sadness. Because of irritated tear glands. I know. Because of "letting the pain out." I know.

But your sigh of relief has made it all the way to the guzzlers of my flesh.

For who's going to sabotage consignments of earthworms to Yiftah Graetz? Who'll poison the green bench with puffs of smoke? Who'll kill the compost with their eyes? Who'll irradiate with the microwave?

No one. Netta Baraban is gone. The world shall not be irradiated. The bench shall not be poisoned. The earthworms shall not be sabotaged.

Netta has paid her debt to society. A rotten-from-within body has been given as a gift to the earthworms.

They won't cremate my body. They won't consign it to the deep. They won't vaporize it. My body is toxic; it releases heavy metals and kills fish.

The body will be given to the tone-deaf worms. Ahh. Ahh.

THE INVERTEBRATES AROUND HERE are hard workers. They salivate jelly. They compensate for their lack of bone by guzzling and multiplying. Don't underestimate them. Today's single earthworm is tomorrow's colony.

Compost, compost, compost. All living things decay.

Today my nose crumbled. This was where I broke down. My sonar is gone. Dead. A procession of worms was chanting, and a sucking noise was added to the sound of digging. They were drinking my nose through a straw. Each nostril served as a hall for these talented creatures.

Their audience, the erstwhile Netta, lay on its back, and gave no applause.

I should have been standing now in your organic communal dining room, eating without smelling. With what remained of my imagination, I enjoy the show: chewed roots and odorless juice sucked out of them. The flesh of chemicals-free fruit chomping in my mouth, with my nose blocked.

What a pleasure!

The animal world: A hierarchical world. Now it's my turn to be eaten. My bones lying horizontally, my soul swinging its legs: Watch me. I'm not finished off. Not yet.

In the community classes at Shorshon, they were lecturing: how to plant without chemical fertilizer and grow a vegetable garden based on friendship, how long a tin can lasts.

And only I will never reveal to you how much time it took for me to disintegrate.

Oh no, you never bothered to respect Netta Baraban when she was alive. You didn't listen to her. You conspired with her husband against her.

You played tricks on her: You hid her microwave. You robbed her of her garbage bags, blue plastic bags, tightly closed. You invaded them. You separated.

You kidnapped her kids and beat composting into them. You didn't allow her to close in a veranda with roof tiles. When she smoked cigarettes outdoors, you called in the media.

You got wise to Roni's adolescence. You opened up your hearts to her. The heart, you discovered, is not just another muscle.

You shook your heads in pity: Mum isn't ecological. Drop by drop: Mum is a bad one.

You stole my synthetic laundry off the line, don't think I didn't see it. And after I'd left your homes, you sprayed them with lavender oil so that my smell wouldn't cling.

And on a mushroom, Nature sits and smokes, smiling: Blessed is that Nature of whom this is true.

No. I won't tell you the rate of my decay.

The brain, I once read, is the last to be gobbled up.

Nature is cruel: It allows you to follow the processes right to the end. The last supper: to feel how the nerves burst, how the layers of skin melt, how the dermis recedes. And only white sticks are left after the banquet. Would that I could insert a bone into a worm.

I didn't want to reach this state, but who's asking me, who?

My funeral was horrendous.

My eyes were shut, as befits dead bodies that Mira Goor handles.

In another minute, I sensed, we'll reach my burial place, and there I'll lie in eternal repose. The cypress at the gate will then bow its head. Kids will happen to get here, looking for a thrown ball. Boredom, I'm telling you.

In the dining hall, a committee will convene and rule stringently on the matter of compost. In the club room, the tone will soften, and will become melodious in the compost workshop.

Compost, compost, compost. All that is living rots.

And of all people, I didn't expect Avishai to start off with, "She was a good student." Why bring up forgotten things that even the teachers prefer to forget?

They brought a teacher to attest that I had been a lively one. An abundant profusion of catchphrases and witticisms.

If only I'd had a megaphone, at least, to shout out my last speech. I was always good with the last word. Hello there, can you hear me? I have for you a prepared speech in my pocket.

"On this festive day, we celebrate the marvels of ecology. Ecology has spoken, and ecology has triumphed: Cigarettes *are* carcinogenic. Sewage water *is* polluted. Unseparated garbage *does* wreak havoc with the air. And asphalt, its grains *do* plug in the soul. That's assuming cynics have a soul.

"And there lies Netta. Her body was already rotting away in hospital. Do you hear the noise? That's cancer, gnawing at her body. Her mouth stinks of cigarettes, even at a distance.

"Netta abused the environment, and the environment has paid her back, with compound interest.

"We are taking leave of you, Netta. Another lump of humus is being added to the soil to enrich it. And who knows? In the fullness of time, perhaps some soil contractor will be able to make use of it. Do become good soil, Netta."

That's the speech I'd put in the pocket of my jeans. Jeans? Forget about it. They wrapped me up in an ugly shroud. Even a flag would have been better.

But the kind of speeches they belted out for me here. If not in my life, then in my death. Avishai proclaimed, "She was a good wife." Across the grave, five veiled-looking women fluttered their eyelashes at him.

Ahava: "At last, Netta has connected up with Mother Earth." And she added an ad: "Our workshop anticipates death and teaches how to cope with it." (I'll tell you how: Come with some worm food in your pocket.)

Mira Goor stifled a yawn: "When all is said and done, Netta, you were our living, funny, and delightful spirit." Roni came from the army, and with all the sensitivity of a personal-affairs NCO, she wept. She really loved me, the fool. And little Kotchi clung to her, looking frightened. Compost or not, I won one victory – mother's love is not ecological.

WHAT A SHAME that you can't choose your death. Death in the sea, the blue and serene sea. Eternal sailing among open-eyed creatures. Finned swell. Diving. When everything is underwater, I am not so frightened. And anyway, my nose is not functional.

I AM LAID TO REST. Seeing is out of the question. Outside, dulled voices. Perhaps it's a memorial gathering. Perhaps the yahrzeit, could be anything. My nose is already long gone, and all that's left is my longing to hold a cigarette between two bones and have a smoke, with no lungs. No-lungs will expand and draw in the smoke. No-lungs will contract, and the smoke will steadily escape from them. Look, Avishai would say, my righteous husband. There's her punishment. For all of her sins. Smoking, fractiousness, non-separation of garbage.

"Your sin, Netta," he would say, "is that you don't know how to blend in. Lie down in the earth and blend in. Your body will divide over and over. Particles that are good for the soil."

So here I lie.

SOMETIME, PERHAPS IN ANOTHER HOUR, my brain will drain out of my skull. From compost came I not, but to compost shall I return.

Set in Stone
By Yael Furman
Translated by Sarit Shalhevet

BORN IN RAMAT GAN ON 7 OCTOBER 1973 (a day after the outbreak of the Yom Kippur War), Yael Furman began publishing work of genre interest with "Hatzva'im haNechonim" (The Right Colors) in the online magazine *Bli Panika* in 2001. For the next few years, she published several well-regarded short stories in Israeli genre publications, such as the *Halomot beAspamia* (*Pipedreams*) and the annual anthology series *Hayo Yihye* (*Once Upon a Future*), for which she was nominated for the Geffen Prize a remarkable nine times.

Her novel *Yaldei Beit haZchuchit* (*Children of the Glasshouse*, 2011) is notable as a genuine example of Israeli Young Adult science fiction. Set in a future Israel, the novel concerns humans genetically modified to live in water, who exist in conditions somewhat reminiscent of Cordwainer Smith's Underpeople or James Blish's underwater inhabitants in "Surface Tension." Though the book's theme is not unusual in SF, the Israeli setting is uncommon, and in a nice use of location, at the end of the novel, the water people are transferred to the Sea of Galilee, where they are now free – or at least freer. The book was illustrated by artist Yinon Zinger and was based on Furman's earlier short story, "Kirot Reikim" (Empty Walls), winner of a first prize in a 2009 Olamot Convention short story contest. Her second novel, *Kir'ei 'Olam* (English title *The Portal Diamond*), was published in 2017, telling the story of two teenagers who find themselves in a real fantasy land very similar to the land in their computer game.

HE SCRUTINIZED MY FACE. He was so close that I could see his black pupils and colored irises. Two gray rings around each iris, the inner one wider than the outer, and I could see the red blood vessels in his eyes. They usually observe me from a distance, nod their heads and move on to the next exhibit. But this guy scrutinized me in every which way. And I can't avert my eyes, so I continued to stare at the exact same spot.

He bent down and moved out of my field of vision. What was he doing there? I knew he didn't go away. He was nearby. I got used to the numbness a long time ago, but now I felt acutely distressed. I couldn't see him, and I had no idea what he was doing. Then a woman stepped into my field of vision. She wore a light blue blouse with a blue scarf around her neck. She stared at my body, and a disgusted scowl replaced her smile.

"Tzahi, what are you doing?" she asked.

"Just looking at this statue," replied the man. His voice sounded quite nearby.

"You're patting her boobs," the woman said loudly. If I could feel, I would have felt sick.

"No, no," said Tzahi, and I could hear his voice moving farther away. He came back into my field of vision, and when he turned his back on me, I could see his black hair.

"So what were you doing there?" asked the woman suspiciously.

"There's something really weird about this statue," said Tzahi.

"There's something weird about this entire museum," said the woman.

"This statue feels alive," said Tzahi.

He approached me, and again he came too close: my eyes were transfixed onto his right cheek. I saw a short, dark stubble and a red pimple beneath his cheekbone. He stepped back, and the woman came closer and stood next to him. She took reading glasses out of her pocket and leaned in to take a better look at me. She examined my lips, and I saw the roots of her red hair. Dyed. Of course it's dyed, I could see that her roots were black. I used to dye my hair too, once. I wanted to be blond. Now I'm all white.

"She's carved out of stone," said the woman.

"Definitely stone," said Tzahi and knocked on my cheek with his finger. I could hear the knock.

"It doesn't sound hollow," said Tzahi.

I heard the footsteps of one of the guards arriving. Soon they'll get this pair of snoopers away from me. They'd better take them away, before they discover something.

"I can see what you mean," said the woman. "There really is something… it's hard to explain."

The guard's voice boomed next to me, "Don't touch the exhibits!"

The pair took one step back.

"We're only looking up close," said Tzahi.

"I saw you touch the statue. Please move on," said the guard.

The woman turned to look at him. I could see every detail of her ear, with an earring made of red beads strung top to bottom. "We didn't do anything," she insisted.

"Come, Esty," said Tzahi and took her hand. He must have seen the threat in the guard's eye. They always looked threatening, these guards.

They continued to the next exhibit, and the guard approached me. He scrutinized me, made a short, pleased hum, and walked away. I continued to look straight ahead at the same point on the wall, at the picture of a boat moored in the middle of a flowering meadow. Up until recently, I was in another room and looked at the statue of a young boy who always stood leaning forward with his hands outstretched, as if he was trying to get a candy that was beyond his reach. When they rearranged the exhibits, they moved me here, to another room full of statues and paintings. I don't know where they moved the boy to. They removed the metal displays to one of the rooms in the western wing. The museum staff went past me when they carried them there. Sometimes I hear the visitors complain that there's no rhyme or reason to the arrangement of the exhibits in the museum. Had they known the Curator, they would have understood. Sometimes I imagine a sign at the entrance to the museum which reads: "Please check your common sense at the cloakroom."

Tzahi and Esty walked past me again before the end of the day. They seemed troubled, and they walked quickly. One of the guards followed them. Were they being thrown out? But I only saw them for an instant, and then they were gone. I'll probably never see them again.

No light was coming in through the window now, and the glare from the ceiling fixtures has become harsher. The visitors began moving toward the exit. They all passed by me as they made for the doors. Soon the janitors will arrive, wash the floor, dust the statues and paintings, polish the benches, and empty the trash cans. And then they will leave too, and the lights will go out. Darkness will flood the museum. Only the guards will continue to walk among the rooms, holding flashlights, to guard against invaders. And then *he* will come, and the magic hour will begin.

The Curator. During the day, I rarely saw him. When he did come down for a moment from his upstairs rooms, he was meticulously dressed in a dark suit, his hair tied back and his face clean-shaven. He would walk around wearing the self-important expression of an artist aware of his genius. Usually, he would be conversing with a journalist or an art critic, and occasionally with a colleague from another museum. They would pass by me, the Curator talking, waving his hands, and his visitor listening attentively. Terms like "combination," "artistic daring," or "brave choices" would reach my ears. They never lingered long enough for me to hear any of the conversations. They were always on the move, always walking briskly.

But at night, he would turn into a different man. At the magic hour, the museum would become a different world, disconnected from reality. The colored lights come on one after the other, imparting a dreamy ambiance. In the silence, I would hear his footsteps. Not the brisk tapping of daytime shoes, but the patter of soft-soled ones. And then he would arrive, his hair flowing, wearing loose-fitting clothes topped with a white cloak. The guards would retreat to the corners, invisible, as silent as the exhibits. The Curator would stroll along, inspecting each piece closely, as if he were seeing it for the first time.

Choose me, I begged in my mind. I loath him, but as in every night, I hoped he would choose me. He passed my room and continued to walk, but I knew there was still a chance. He always walked through each room of the museum before making his choice.

It's been a long time since he had last chosen me. Maybe that's why he returned to my room and approached me the night of the day I saw Tzahi and Esty.

"Arise, my beauty," he said and touched my forehead.

A wave of sensation began at the fingertips of my hands that were clapped together above my head, and descended all along my body down to my toes. I took a deep breath. His familiar fragrance entered my nostrils. I put my hands down. I could move. Tonight, the magic hour will be mine.

He gave me his hand and said, "Let's dance."

Music, a big band was playing a waltz tune. I held his warm hand, and we danced. We moved from room to room, twirling among the statues. The main doors were locked. Only the music and us. I was finally moving my body after such a long time of standing still. The Curator looked at me, caressed me with his eyes. And I danced, spun around myself, my long hair flying around, grazing my face. For many a night I had watched him dance with others, and I waited. Now we moved among the rooms, visible only to the statues and guards, who all stood still, silently watching.

Finally, we stopped in front of the stairs leading to his private chambers. We walked up the stairs, holding hands. The music faded behind us, and the colored lights went off. Tonight, the magic hour was mine.

We walked along the corridor of the second floor and entered the Curator's large apartment. A table was already set for a light meal for two. The large canopy bed stood to the left. I lingered for a moment in front of the mirror at the entrance, stood in front of it naked, white as a stone from my hair down to my toes. I am a statue, a statue that got its life back for one night. The Curator wrapped his hand around my shoulder and led me to the table. When I sat down, he poured me a glass of red wine. Tonight, we had fresh rolls with an enticing bakery aroma, soft butter, apricot jam, small cakes, and a fruit salad. I spread jam on half a roll and bit into it – the taste of heavenly. We sat there and ate silently. I savored every bite of the food and every sip of the wine. I knew it would be a long time before I'll get this chance again.

After we finished eating, we rested for a while. And then he came closer, held my head with both hands, and leaned in to kiss me. And even though I hate him and loathe him, I kissed him back. This rare night was my only chance to feel. When he carried me to the bed, I recalled the guy I saw earlier, Tzahi, and it occurred to me that sometimes the Curator would choose boys. What does he do with them? And then he kissed me again, and my thoughts focused on one thing only.

Later, when I lay in bed and saw the darkness beginning to recede, that question came to my mind again. My time was running out. He sat cross-legged with his back to me, next to my legs, and stretched. I hadn't said a word to him since the moment he woke me up, but I felt I had to ask.

"What do you do with the boys?"

He turned his head and brushed off the long hair that hid his face.

"What do you mean?" he asked.

"Sometimes you wake up boys," I said. "What do you do when you come up here?"

He smiled, "I don't sleep with them."

He looks quite nice when he smiles.

"Not that I reject the idea out of hand," he continued. "But so far, it hasn't happened. I also don't sleep with all of the girls I wake up."

"I thought you did," I said.

"I don't tell the others what I do with you. There's no reason for me to tell you what I do with them."

I was glad to hear that he doesn't sleep with everyone. There were some children among us. He got up and began to dress leisurely. Outside it was almost daylight.

He offered me his hand, and I rose from the soft bed and took it. We walked down to the ground floor together, strolling from room to room. We passed several guards, who nodded their heads in greeting. We entered my room, and I climbed onto the low pedestal and turned again to face the painting of the boat moored in the meadow.

"Did you have a good time tonight?" he asked softly.

"Yes," I said.

"I'll choose you again, don't worry."

I lifted my hands above my head and joined them together, like in a Bollywood dance move. He wrapped them with his warm hands and arranged my posture as it was yesterday. He moved my hands back a little, straightened up my shoulders, arranged my hair behind me, and laid a finger on my lips to close them.

"You're lucky," he whispered. "You'll never grow old."

He moved his finger across my face, as if trying to make sure that my expression will return to be like it was yesterday.

"Time to sleep, my beauty," he said, and touched my forehead.

I felt a wave of numbness going up from my toes to my fingertips. I became a statue again. The magic hour was over.

IN THE MORNINGS, most visitors arrived in organized groups. Tourists speaking in foreign languages, retirees on a trip, students, a high school art class. The guides explained the various exhibits. The high school students walked around wide-eyed and stared at the paintings and statues. They stared at me.

"Don't touch the exhibits," yelled the guards. For most of the kids, one threatening look was enough.

The guide stopped by my side, and the students gathered.

"This statue, *The Indian Princess* by Pimper Monish," he said, and continued with his boilerplate lecture. Pimper Monish, the artist, the Curator. That wasn't his real name. I've never heard his real name. He made most of the museum's artwork himself, but he bought some from others as well. The painting facing me, for example, was created by an artist from Haifa.

"The greatness of this statue, and of course of Monish's other creations, lies in how real it appears," continued the guide. "If you observe it carefully, you'll notice the attention to detail, the delicate stonework. They don't make sculptures like this nowadays. Monish brings back the old art form its best period."

And so on and on, words that I've heard many times before. One boy scrutinized me with a penetrating gaze.

He interrupted the guide and said, "She looks sad."

"Part of the artistic design," replied the guide.

They continued to the next statue, but the boy lingered for another moment before rejoining the group.

At noon, as the angle of the light behind me showed, the Curator passed by my room, wearing his dark suit, accompanied by someone I never saw before, probably a journalist.

"I felt the galleries weren't treating my creations well," I heard him say, and he moved his hand around the exhibits in the room.

"And then you established this museum?" asked the journalist.

"I felt that I had no choice," said the Curator. "This is my art, and I have to express it most accurately. I couldn't bear interventions by strangers. Even when I buy other people's artwork, I make it a point to respect all their requests regarding the way their pieces should be exhibited."

"But where does the money come from?" the journalist asked. They had already passed by, and their voices were fading away. I managed to hear him ask, "Does the revenue from entrance tickets really…?" and then his voice trailed off.

I probably sleep from time to time; there are times when my awareness turns itself off. I'm not sure of this, but it seems to me that sometimes there are lapses in time, by how light comes in through the window behind me. A lapse like that happened after the Curator and the journalist had left, until I suddenly saw Tzahi sticking his face into mine. Yes, the same Curious George from yesterday. He stood in front of me and stared.

"She's moved," he determined.

"That's impossible," I heard Esty's voice from my left.

"Look," he said and moved to the right. Now Esty's face entered my field of vision as well.

"Looks the same to me," said Esty.

"Not exactly," said Tzahi. "Look here." He pointed a finger at my face, careful not to touch me this time. "She has a tiny wrinkle on her forehead that wasn't there yesterday. The eyes are a little narrower. And the hair, I'm sure it was not tied back as tightly. Either they made changes to the statue, or it moved."

Esty pulled out her reading glasses and again stooped to scrutinize me.

"You may be right," she said. "The lips do look slightly more compressed." She stood up and removed her glasses, folded them gently, and put them in a case that was in her bag.

"But we didn't notice this on any other statue, did we?"

"No, she's the only one." Tzahi wrinkled his brow and scratched his head.

"It doesn't make sense," muttered Esty, "The statue couldn't have moved, and there's no reason for them to replace the statue overnight."

They both went silent, and I immersed myself in observing the minute details of their faces and clothes. I already knew the painting very well. It's always good to look at something new.

"Camera," said Esty, waving her hand in front of Tzahi. "We have to photograph any suspicious statues."

"They don't allow cameras or phones inside the museum," he reminded her.

"There are tiny ones, like those used by spies," said Esty. "Let's go and get one. We'll come back another time."

They turned and walked away. *If somebody catches them photographing…* But I couldn't warn them. I can't move, and even when my next magic hour comes, which could be days away, I won't be able to do anything.

I KNEW HE WOULDN'T choose me the following night. He never chose the same statue two nights in a row. He passed by me, his hair untied, his body wrapped in a cloak. After a while, the music began again, this time an Irish dance tune. And then I saw them, the Curator and the statue of the shepherd boy who once stood in the eastern wing. They danced and spun around each other, and I saw in the face of the boy what the other statues saw in my face yesterday. The joy of movement, the pleasure of mobility. They danced, their feet tapping the floor in rhythmical steps, and then went out of my field of vision. After a while the music died, and the colored lights went off.

The morning light crept up behind me and began to light up the room. The only living things were the guards, moving from room to room, watching over us. The Curator and the shepherd boy passed by me, slowly making their way back to the boy's current place. The statue was smiling peacefully, his body relaxed. Why don't we try to escape? I thought. After all, none of us enjoy standing in this frozen posture for days on end. Yet, when this rare magic hour is over, we obediently return with the Curator to our places, stand in a posture of his choosing, and allow him to turn us back into stone. Is it because we have no chance to escape? Or do we fear he won't choose us again? Or maybe something inside us wants to return to our relaxed, peaceful stillness? This night is a wonderful vacation, but we long to return to our real, stony existence when it is over.

The Curator passed by me on his way back, walking alone, his head lowered, ignoring the statues, ignoring the guards. He will go to sleep now on the soft bed with the beige sheets to gather his strength for the following night.

"I think she didn't move this time," said Tzahi.

The two sleuths stood again facing me and staring. Esty leaned forward, her reading glasses up her nose.

"She looks the same to me, too," she said.

"I'm sure that artist who's running this place has something to do with all this," said Tzahi. "Tell me, what normal person would call himself Pimper?"

"A pimp?" asked Esty.

"Or someone who's insane. I smell something's fishy here."

"Tzahi, go keep the guard busy."

Tzahi turned around and went to talk with the guard who was standing at the corner. Meanwhile, Esty pulled out a tiny camera, turned it toward me, and snapped a photo. She lowered her hand to the height of my belly and repeated the action. She moved on to the next exhibit and photographed that one as well. From the corner of the room, I heard the faint sound of a conversation. Tzahi rattled on, and the guard replied in short barks. I prayed they would give up and go. The Curator does not like people meddling in his affairs.

What if they succeed? They'll photograph everyone and return day after day and photograph everyone again. They'll be able to prove that every night one of the statues has moved. Whom could they tell that? What will become of us if outsiders intervene and take the Curator away? They'll throw us in some godforsaken warehouse where we won't even be able to see the visitors. Or maybe they'll send us to other museums, and we'll remain statues forever. We won't even have our magic hour, and no one will know who we really are.

And I can't tell that to the Curator until he chooses me again, and that could be days away.

THIS NIGHT HE CHOSE the statue of a little girl. I never saw her in a statuesque posture, but I've seen her dancing with him many times before. She was one of the metal statues, with a copper-colored body and short curly hair. They twirled around each other to the sound of bells, and her loud laughter rang throughout the museum hall. The children always laughed. They danced for a long time, passing through my room four times. But eventually the music died, and the lights went off.

They returned in the early morning. He strolled by, carrying the tired child in his arms.

"When will you wake me up again?" I heard her ask in a sleepy voice.

"When the time comes," he replied.

"I like waking up," she murmured.

"And now you're tired and need to rest."

She said something more, but they had already left the room, and I didn't hear the rest of their conversation.

Of course, they returned, those snoopers. This time, Esty talked with the guard while Tzahi took photos. They disguised themselves. Esty wore a light wig, and Tzahi put on a fake mustache. They probably worried that the staff might recognize this couple that keeps arriving at the museum day after day. This time they were quick and efficient, didn't waste time on small talk.

I was a little sorry to see them leave the room so quickly. Their conversations in my presence broke up the routine a little, and their faces hid the painting of the boat that I've gotten sick and tired of by now. Maybe the next time the Curator chooses me, I'll ask him to turn me around a bit at the end of the night so that I can look at something else.

Night flooded the museum again, and the colored lights went on. The guards retreated to their corners, and the Curator strolled around the museum. He returned to my room, but instead of turning to one of the other statues, he picked me again.

"Wake up, my beauty," he said and touched my forehead.

The wave of sensation descended throughout my body. I took a deep breath and lowered my hands.

"You woke me up just three days ago," I said.

"I know," he said, extending his hand. "Let's dance."

I knew this wasn't fair to the others, but I couldn't refuse his extended hand. The desire to move my body took over. The waltz music came on, and we danced.

We went up, the music fading behind us. This time there were pancakes and strawberries with whipped cream, and fresh lemonade. I leaned back to savor the sensation of the food.

"Maybe we can just talk?" he asked.

He'd never brought me here before to talk. I looked at him, confused.

"I woke you up again because I wanted to talk to someone," he said. "You asked me what I'm doing. Showed some interest."

I wanted to tell him about the two snoopers. Maybe I'll mention them in the morning. I didn't want to waste my magic hour.

"What do you want to talk about?" I asked.

"I'm lonely. I haven't really spoken with anybody for months," he said.

"But every night, you wake up one of us."

"But I don't talk with any of you." He rose for the chair and stretched. "I used to talk with my wife," he said. "But it's been a long time since then. I hoped that maybe I could talk with you instead. You seemed interested."

If that means he'll choose me more often, I am certainly willing to talk. "I didn't know you were married," I said. "I've never seen her."

"I loved her very much," said the Curator as he sat on the bed. "I still love her." He looked at me directly and said, "It all began because of her, actually."

"What began?" I asked.

He gestured with his hand. "You. My statues."

I stared at him.

"Come, sit by me," he said and patted the blanket next to him. "I'll tell you."

I wanted to know, very much. He'd never explained why he did what he did to me. And he wanted to talk to someone, pour his heart out. And who listens better than a statue? At the end of the night, I'll return to my silence and won't be able to share my knowledge with anyone. But I'll know. I'll know the reason for my existence. I got up and sat next to him on the soft bed.

"Hanny and I were soulmates," he said. "She was the most important person in my life. We were so happy together. You have to understand, an artist's life isn't easy, but she was always by my side, good reviews and bad. And when people bought my art, she always supported me, helped me create. She was my muse. And I supported her, too, as she advanced her academic career."

He signed and leaned back on his hands. "And then she got cancer," he said in a tone that suddenly became very flat. "It was an aggressive disease. The doctors said there was nothing they could do. We discovered it too late, and she didn't respond to any treatment. She only had a few months left, and she wanted to live them peacefully."

"And then she died?" I asked.

"I couldn't lose her. I wasn't *willing* to lose her. I dropped everything and started to do research. I already knew that our salvation wouldn't come from the doctors. I had only one option left."

He looked at me, as if willing me to guess what he meant, and I remembered him standing above me, chanting words, waving his hand, and handing me a drink.

"A magic spell," I said.

His eyes shone.

"I was desperate," he said. "I went to all the shamans, witches, and fortune-tellers. I traveled all around the world. Hanny begged me to stay with her, but I just couldn't let her go. I had to examine every option. Most of them were charlatans, but a few were for real, and I learned from each one whatever I could. Gradually, I discovered that I have the talent, that I could perform magic."

I wondered when he'd get to the point. "And did you find a cure?" I asked.

He sighed. "No," he said. "But when I combined some things, I discovered the art of living stone."

Living stone? I froze in shock. That's what I am. He rubbed my cold hand to warm it.

"I discovered that I could prevent her from dying. Preserve her in this condition. She was already on her deathbed. I didn't have time to continue investigating and looking for cures. I had to use what I'd already found."

His wife? He did this to his wife? I felt my mouth gape.

"It was the only way to prevent her from dying. She, too, agreed that there was nothing to lose. The statue standing at the entrance to the museum, watching all the people coming and going, is her, my wife."

I saw that statue. I didn't know it was his wife.

"I wasn't planning to make more than one statue. I only wanted to save the life of my wife. And I succeeded – her condition stopped deteriorating. Occasionally I could wake her up, and she would be my wife. Alive. Forever. I thought we'd be happy," he lowered his head.

"She wasn't pleased?" I guessed.

He shrugged. "At first, she was very pleased," he said. "But there was one small detail we hadn't thought about. I preserved her in exactly the same condition, so I preserved her cancer as well. As long as she's a statue, she doesn't feel anything, but she's in agony when I wake her up. The pain is terrible, and the only drugs that take away the pain make her drowsy as well, so what's the point?"

He raised his head and looked into my eyes.

"The last time I woke her up, a few months ago, she asked me not to do it again. She said the pain was too much to bear. She enjoys standing and watching people, but she can't take the pain."

"And you respected her wish."

"I can't make my wife suffer."

And since then he is lonely, I thought, but I didn't say anything.

He let go of my hand. "That's the story," he said. "I wanted to tell someone. Thank you for listening."

That's it! But how did he move from one statue that he'd made to save a dying woman to filling an entire museum with people like me? I felt I had to know. I wasn't ill. I hadn't known him at all. He's probably waiting for me to ask.

"You said that you'd planned to make only one statue," I said. "How did you fill up an entire museum?"

His face lit up.

"The statues, yes…" he said, and I could see his enthusiasm building up. "I turned my wife into a statue to save her life, but no one knew it was my wife. Everyone thought that she had died and I'd made a statue in her memory." Now he was speaking faster, and he got up from the bed.

"I got rave reviews," he said. "Although I had made other statues just as great that I'd carved myself from real stone, the statue of the living stone did something to people. Something in the material, in the feeling that it gave the viewers. I didn't know what it was. But it was my creation. Albeit with magic rather than chisel and mallet, still, it was my creation."

He turned to look at me, spread his hands and said, "Art! The most divine cause, the pinnacle of the human spirit. An artist must continue to create, you understand? I *had* to create more statues."

I stared at him, trying to process what I've just heard.

"You didn't create me," I said.

"Of course I did," he said and smiled.

"No," I said. "You kidnapped me and made me drink this liquid and then…"

He sat down next to me again and held my hands.

"I turned you into what you are today," he said. "You're so beautiful. When I saw you, I knew I had to preserve this beauty of yours. I couldn't let you grow old, wither and rot. For my art, for the things that I can do, people are the raw material. In the hands of the right creator, they become divine art. I preserved you at the precise moment of your greatest beauty. It's been eight years since, and you haven't changed a bit. This is such a wonderful miracle." His eyes were shining when he looked at me, and I realized that he genuinely believed he did me a favor.

"I didn't ask for it," I said.

"Since when does one ask an art creation what is her wish?" He smoothed my hair and said, "No, my beautiful statue, I can't ask. You cannot stop art, and mortals cannot perceive eternity. I sacrificed your humanity and won an amazing creation that people come from all over the world to see. You are my creation. I made you. Eight years, and I still get a thrill every time I look at you."

I opened my mouth, but I couldn't find the words.

"Or the little girl I chose yesterday," he went on. "I brought her in twelve years ago. She looked so sweet when I saw her walking home from school with her small backpack and lunchbox. Nature's perfection. I couldn't let her grow up, grow ugly, grow fat. Just then, I had learned the secret of living metal, and she was my first metal sculpture."

"She has parents, maybe siblings…" I muttered.

"Her laughter each time I wake her up. And at night, we sit in the next room and play with Lego blocks or model trains. Twelve years and she still spends the whole night playing with blocks. Just as perfect as on the day I made her."

Nothing I can say will make him think of us as human beings, I realized, *or at least as the humans we used to be.* He's on another plane of thinking.

He lay back on the bed and held one of my hands. He stretched his other hand above his head and stared at the canopy above.

He can turn people into statues. I didn't know what else he could do.

"Can you turn me back into what I was before?" I asked.

"No," he said. "It's a one-way change. I took something away from you that cannot be restored."

"Please," I said.

He looked at me and grasped my hand.

"I really can't," he said. "Even if I wanted to. In any case, it is inconceivable that I would damage a perfect creation like you, turn you back into a living, aging creature. It's better this way. I see what happens to people. It is not good." A silence fell between us for a moment. He narrowed his eyes and asked, "Are you unhappy?"

"Yes."

"That's a shame. Many of the statues are happy, especially the children. They adapt so quickly. And most of the adults, too. One day you too will find your happiness and peace, I'm sure."

A knock on the door startled me. The Curator also sat up, looking alarmed. No one has ever interrupted us during our magic hour.

"What happened?" he shouted.

"Sorry for the interruption, sir," someone shouted from behind the door. "We caught an intruder."

The Curator got out of the bed and shouted, "Let him in."

I held my breath. The intruder will see me, and that will be the end of him.

"Should I hide?" I asked.

"No," said the Curator. "If he wants to know what's going on here, why should I hide it from him?"

I tried to cover myself with the blanket anyway, but by the time I pulled it out from underneath me, they already came in. Three guards pushed the man in. He nearly lost his balance.

"Tzahi," I said out loud, without thinking.

He stood up and stared at me, petrified. The Curator also turned to look at me with lifted eyebrows.

"He was walking around me these past few days," I said. "I heard his name."

"The statue," Tzahi muttered. "It really moved. I knew it."

"He snuck into the metals wing," said one of the guards. All the guards looked the same to me. Bald-headed, stocky. Even their heights were the same.

"What was he looking for there?" asked the Curator.

"He was photographing the statue of the little girl," said the guard. He handed the Curator a tiny camera.

The Curator took the camera and put it on the table without looking at it.

"What were you trying to find out, Tzahi?" His voice was low and dangerous.

Tzahi pointed at me and said, "I knew she had moved. I took pictures yesterday and the day before. And I saw in the pictures that the metal girl had moved too. Just a bit, but it was enough. I had to find out what's going on here at night."

The Curator smiled and said, "So you found out. My statues can move. What are you going to do now?"

Tzahi faced him. His gaze went back and forth between the Curator and me.

"I don't know what's going on here," he said. "But I intend to find out. I'll make sure that someone investigates and puts an end to this thing."

The Curator scratched his chin lightly. "Really?" he asked.

"Yes," Tzahi announced. "When the police come to arrest me for breaking in, I'll tell them everything. And I have the photos to prove it."

Poor, naive Tzahi. He hasn't realized yet that he'll never leave this building. The Curator will not let anyone expose his secrets. But what will happen to him? As far as I knew, the Curator made only one new statue each year. And the last one had been inaugurated not long ago. The Curator kept scratching his chin. His eyes scanned Tzahi.

"Undress him," he instructed the guards.

"What?" shrieked Tzahi.

Yes, he intends to do it.

Two guards held his arms while the third one cut off his clothes. Tzahi struggled and screamed, but he didn't have a chance. Soon he was standing naked in front of the Curator. He was sweating and shivering, probably imagining something other than the truth. I felt sorry for him. After all, he took this risk to help me.

"Please, don't do this to him," I begged.

The Curator came close to me and patted my head.

"Don't interrupt, my beauty," he said. "Or I'll put you back downstairs right now."

The Curator returned to Tzahi, scrutinized him and touched his face. Tzahi squirmed in the guards' hands, but to no avail.

"You're not my ideal choice," the Curator said. He was speaking to himself. "But I think I can use you."

"What do you mean?" shrieked Tzahi.

The Curator smiled again. He gestured to the black chair at the corner of the room. I remembered that chair. I, too, had sat on it years ago. The womb, the Curator called it. He left the room through a door I had never passed through while the guards dragged Tzahi to the chair, forced him to sit down, and strapped his hands and feet. I didn't want to look, but I couldn't look away from the tableau, see from the sidelines what had been done to me.

Tzahi attempted to persuade the guards that they were aiding and abetting criminal activity. They'll be sent to jail if they won't release him immediately. So naïve.

The Curator returned, holding a dark-colored glass.

"You must be thirsty," he said. "I brought you something to drink."

Tzahi struggled against the straps that bound him to the chair. "What's this?" he asked.

One of the guards grabbed Tzahi's head from behind. Tzahi must have realized they were going to force him to drink and cried out, "Okay, okay, I apologize! I promise not to say anything."

But his imploring went unanswered. They forced the liquid down his throat and blocked his nose until he had to swallow. Some drops dribbled down his chin.

The guards left Tzahi breathing heavily on the chair.

The Curator stood in front of him, his arms folded, as Tzahi started to lose consciousness. I knew that I won't be able to watch the entire process. It took several days, and I only had a little time left until morning. But maybe I could learn something important anyway.

Tzahi resumed struggling against the straps. Sweat beads ran down his forehead, and he started breathing rapidly. I remembered when I had been on that chair, with the disgusting taste of the liquid still in my mouth, not knowing what to expect. I was terrified. I looked at the Curator, and when I saw that he caught my glance, I gestured with my chin toward the chair. He nodded.

I approached the chair and knelt beside Tzahi. I held his left hand. At first, he shuddered at my cold touch.

"He'll turn you into something like me," I said softly.

"What?" He turned his head to look at me, his eyes agape with fear.

"So you won't be able to tell anyone what you discovered," I continued. "It's not so terrible; you'll get used to it."

"No," he murmured.

I kept stroking his hand until his eyes closed, and the Curator motioned me to move away. I went back to the bed. There was nothing I could do to stop what was happening. The Curator could turn me into stone with a touch of his finger. I did not want to lose minutes of sensation in a fruitless effort to save a stranger from his fate.

I sat and watched. The Curator chanted strange words and moved his hands in an intricate dance. Tzahi's body contorted and went limp. The Curator forced him to drink some more of the liquid and continued chanting his incantations. After a while, I turned away and tried to enjoy the sensation of the soft mattress under my back. I listened to the soothing voice of the Curator, the voice that took away my life.

The night hours passed, and in the morning the Curator fell silent. He approached the bed. "Time to sleep," he told me.

I looked at poor Tzahi. His breathing was shallow, his face pale and his eyes half-closed. I knew that soon he will start to feel sharp pains. I did not want to leave him alone.

"Perhaps…" I hesitated. "Perhaps you can let me stay today? I can help comfort him when he's in pain."

The Curator clicked his tongue and extended his hand, indicating it was time to go back.

We left the room and walked toward the stairs. "If I don't put you to sleep now, your body will start turning to stone on its own in two to three hours. The process will be slow and painful, and you won't have control over your posture. Eventually, you'll find yourself distorted, staring at a point on the wall. It's not worth it."

We went down the stairs.

"He was only trying to help me," I said softly.

"Of all the options I had, this was the least horrid," said the Curator.

We walked through the museum, silent statues all around us, the guards retreating to their corners as we passed by. Only I and the Curator, in a sea of silence. If I were braver, fiercer, perhaps I could have given Tzahi a chance to escape. We reached my place, and I climbed onto the pedestal. My gaze fell on the painting with the silly boat in the meadow.

"Can you put me at a slightly different angle?" I asked.

"Why?"

"I'm tired of looking at the same painting."

He turned his head around to look.

"You don't like the painting?"

He looked around the room and turned his head back to me.

"I'm sorry," he said. "I can't change your position now. But I'll try to think of a different arrangement of the exhibits soon. Raise your hands."

I raised my hands and clasped them together above my head. He touched me gently and rearranged my body to look the way I always did.

"I know this was an unpleasant magic hour," he said. "I'll make it up to you soon, I promise." He smiled at me. "We have an eternity together. Go to sleep, my beauty." He touched my forehead, and a wave of numbness passed through me.

He stroked my stony cheek with his finger and returned upstairs to resume working on his new statue. I remained alone, my gaze fixated on the red sail of the boat. What he'd said a minute ago hit me.

Forever? How old was he, anyway? He looked about thirty. But he's had me for eight years. The metal girl has been here for twelve years. The museum had been here when I was a child. I came to visit with my parents when I was in kindergarten. And before that, he'd been married to a woman who was rising in the academic world. He couldn't be thirty. And then I understood. He never grows old. He had said earlier that he takes away from us something that cannot be restored, and he takes care to create a new statue every year. He's not turning people into statues just for the sake of his art. Maybe that was the initial motive, but now – now he wants to stay young. Doesn't want to leave his wife. Doesn't want to leave us, his statues. He'll never stop. When the museum fills up, he'll build another wing. And another. And meanwhile, he'll keep accumulating knowledge and power. I imagined him thousands of years hence, master of the universe, living in a palace with thousands of statues. Will he ever wake me up again?

For several nights there was no magic hour. The museum remained dark and silent, and no statue was chosen to dance through the rooms. The Curator worked. And then, at dawn, he came down with Tzahi. They entered my room, with the Curator's arm wrapped around Tzahi's shoulder, propelling him gently forward. Tzahi was completely white, white like me. A guard followed them with a pedestal.

"Put it here," the Curator pointed to a spot right in front of me.

"We'll put the new statue here," he continued. "He'll block the view of the painting that my beauty doesn't like."

The guard placed the pedestal in front of the painting. The Curator instructed Tzahi to climb onto the pedestal. Tzahi obeyed. *He's in shock, doesn't understand what's going on, terror freezes his mind,* I thought. I was like that too, thinking that I'm dreaming and need to wake up. The Curator walked around him, totally focused on his creation, on the best way to arrange his body.

"Maybe I'll lower your head," he muttered to himself and pressed down gently to bend Tzahi's head down.

"Actually, I'm not that cruel," he said and pushed Tzahi's chin up. Now he was looking directly at me.

"It's better this way," the Curator muttered. He continued to rearrange until he was satisfied. Tzahi's eyes were turned in my direction, his back slightly bent, his hands folded behind his back.

"Now you can rest from what you've been through," said the Curator and touched Tzahi's forehead. His chest stopped moving, and he turned into stone. The Curator touched him again, tried to put pressure on his arm. The stone did not budge. The sculpting was completed. The Curator turned his back on him and left.

I looked at Tzahi, and he looked at me.

There was something I should have told the Curator. Tzahi had a girlfriend, and apparently, she didn't know that he went to the museum in the middle of the night. She waited for him, and when she couldn't find him anywhere else, she came to the museum looking for him.

When Esty entered my room, she walked right up to me. Her hair was disheveled, her clothes unkempt, and new wrinkles appeared around her eyes.

She put on her glasses and stooped to get a close look at me. "Tzahi was obsessive about you," she muttered, "maybe there's some clue."

Don't look back, I begged her in my mind.

She continued to scrutinize me. She was so close, I could almost imagine her scent.

"There has to be something here," she said and knocked on my head.

"Ma'am," yelled the guard. "Don't touch the exhibits."

Esty straightened up and turned around. She froze instantly.

"Tzahi," she cried out, and started running forward.

"How is it that you have a statue that looks exactly like Tzahi?" she yelled at the guard.

"Ma'am, please step away from the exhibit," said the guard, approaching her. He looked threatening with his bald head, buttoned-up uniform, and stocky build, but she didn't budge.

"This statue is new," she said. "It wasn't here last time. This means that you're holding Tzahi here; you used him as a model."

"It's only a statue, ma'am," said the guard. "We're not holding anyone here. Please leave."

Esty approached Tzahi.

"He is here," she said. I heard her voice rise to a shrill. "I feel it. I can really feel it. He's inside this – you glazed him with porcelain or something."

"Ma'am, move away," said the guard.

"Tzahi, I'm going to release you," screamed Esty. Her voice echoed throughout the museum. I heard voices from outside, people asking what's happening. Esty began to bang on the statue.

"Hold on," she screamed.

"Ma'am, stop," said the guard and tried to pull her away.

As the guard took hold of Esty's shoulders and pulled her back, she turned sideways, bent down and threw him against the wall. He hit it bodily and fell on his head. The painting wobbled. Other guards were already in the room, but Esty, crazed with fear and fury, took hold of a nearby bench and lifted it with desperate power.

No, I tried to scream. My lips wouldn't move. The guards were running toward her, but she slammed the bench onto the statue, which fell off the pedestal and smashed to pieces with a resounding clatter. The bench fell from Esty's hands, and she stared at the debris. The guards froze in their place. Esty scanned the floor and grasped her bag tightly.

"There's nothing in there," she stammered. "It's just stone."

"You broke a statue," said one of the guards.

"I'm sorry," said Esty. "I was sure Tzahi was in there."

"What's going on here?" I heard the Curator's voice.

"She broke a statue," said the guard. "We couldn't stop her."

"No!" I heard the Curator howl. I've never heard such a sound coming out of his mouth. He came running and knelt beside the broken pieces.

"I don't know what came over me," said Esty, rubbing her forehead. Her glasses had fallen off, and she didn't even notice. "I was sure my boyfriend was in there. That statue looked exactly like him. I tried to get him out."

I saw the Curator lay his hands on the broken stone. He went silent for a moment. His shoulders stooped.

"I'm really sorry," continued Esty. "I'll pay for the damage."

"You bet you'll pay," I heard him say.

"How much does a statue like that cost?"

The Curator rose, his face contorted, his cheeks hollow.

"Get rid of all the visitors and staff," he told two of the guards. "Tell the cashiers to give the visitors free tickets in compensation."

The guards left. I heard them shouting out instructions.

"You must have worked hard on this statue," Esty said. "I'm really, really sorry. I'm just stressed out because my boyfriend has been missing for several days. I must have been imagining that the statue looked just like him, and I suppose I went out of my mind momentarily. I really promise to pay for the damage. I can write you a check right now."

"You don't understand what you did," said the Curator.

People passed by us on their way out, lingering to look at the wreckage. The guards pushed them along. Esty's face was flushed in shame, and she was holding her head between her hands. The museum fell silent.

"Everyone's gone," said one of the guards.

"Let's finish this now, please," said Esty. "Just tell me how much." She opened her small bag and pulled out a checkbook.

"He's dead," said the Curator.

The checkbook fell from Esty's hands. "Who's dead?"

"Your boyfriend."

"Tzahi?"

"You killed him."

She gasped and took a step back.

"I broke a statue."

"He was supposed to live forever, but you killed him. I didn't have a chance to wake him up even once."

"I… I don't understand."

"You killed one of my statues," his voice was choked.

"Okay, I'm getting out of here…" said Esty and took another step back.

The Curator gestured to the guards.

"You're not going anywhere. You have to pay for what you did," he said.

They grabbed her arms. She fought and screamed but was eventually subdued.

"Take her upstairs; I'll be there in a minute," said the Curator.

"Leave me alone," screamed Esty. But they kept dragging her, kicking and screaming. I heard her screams getting further away.

The Curator bent down to touch the stone again and stroked the smashed head. He sat like a child on the floor and hugged his knees.

"I promise you," he told the broken stone, "she'll pay for what she did. She'll have to serve me – that will be her punishment."

He sat for a while, and then got up and left. He returned with two guards and a large steel plate. They gently loaded the broken stones onto the plate and cleared everything. And then they all left the room, and once again, I found myself staring at the boat in the meadow.

As PUNISHMENT, the Curator decided that Esty should spend the rest of her life as a guard. And so, after several quiet days and nights without magic, the Curator returned to the museum with Esty by his side. Large. Stocky. Wearing a hat that hid the baldness of her head. Wearing a guard's uniform, with a small handgun in her belt.

"This room has two doorways," I heard him explain. "And the visitors pass through it sometimes on their way out."

"Yes, sir," said Esty in a muted, dull voice.

"The visitors feel safer in rooms that have only one doorway. There you have to be very alert," he said. They passed me, and I didn't hear any more of their conversation.

And so the routine resumed. In the daytime, visitors would come and look, and Esty would scream, "Don't touch the exhibits." At night, she retreated to the corner with the other guards and watched the Curator dance with one of the statues. Every day I saw her passing by me, her expression threatening and her eyes vacant. Watching over the museum. Watching over me.

But deep in her heart, she struggled. In his sorrow and pain, the Curator made a big mistake. The spell he used on Esty was meant for men. Not for women – and certainly not for hurt and angry women. Not for grieving women. Not for independent women. But just as she'd lost her self-control, so had he. All of us, statues and guards, we all yielded to him. But Esty never did. The fire of rebellion burned deep inside her. She was strong, and something in her eluded the magic spell. Every day I saw her a little more alive, not as harsh. A little warmer to the visitors. A little more hesitant to obey orders.

I'd wanted to tell the Curator about it, but he didn't choose me. Nights went by, and he danced with others. It was hard for him to go into my room, where one of his statues had been murdered. And meanwhile, Esty was becoming less of a guard and more Esty. One day, I saw her stop and gaze at the spot where Tzahi once stood. On another day, she let a boy stick chewing gum under the bench. And once, she stood in front of me and gave me a poisonous look. I feared she'd heave the bench again, but another guard entered the room, and her gaze dimmed again.

THAT NIGHT HE CAME. Finally. He walked up to me and said, "Wake up, my beauty," and touched my forehead. The wave of sensation descended throughout my body.

"I'm sorry it's been so long," he said. "Because of what happened. I just couldn't." He gave me his hand. "Let's dance."

As usual, the joy of movement swept over me. We started dancing to the tune of the waltz. The music carried us from one room to another. I let the pleasure take hold of me. We entered a side room and were dancing in the middle of it, when suddenly something hit us from the side. I fell down, and the music stopped. I sat up and saw the Curator jump to his feet. Esty stood facing us, her eyes glittering in the colored light, her teeth bare.

"It's all because of her!" she growled, pointing at me.

She pulled out her gun and aimed it at him.

"Tzahi was obsessive about her," she growled. "He wanted to investigate, find out what's going on. If not for her, he would be alive today."

"It's not her fault," said the Curator.

"Of course it's not her fault," screamed Esty. "She's a victim, a victim just like all the rest of them. It's your fault. You did these horrible things to everyone."

"Put down the gun," said the Curator.

"No, sir," she mocked. I saw she was trying to pull the trigger, but the spell was still dominating her. She couldn't turn against him. A groan erupted from her mouth. The Curator moved closer to her and tried to take the gun away. They started to fight. I sat there stunned and watched them. Esty was strong, but the spell was holding her back. They struggled over the gun. I heard the other guards approaching. Esty kicked the Curator, who hit her back, and the weapon flew from their hands and slid across the floor until it stopped at my feet.

Everything stopped. Esty and the Curator stood up and stared at me. I moved a trembling hand and took the gun.

"Give it to me," said the Curator.

"Shoot him," said Esty. "It's loaded, all you have to do is pull the trigger, and that will be the end of this nightmare."

I lifted the gun.

"Sir?" The question came from the doorway. The Curator held up his hand to stop them.

I got up slowly, moving the gun between them.

"Come to me and give me the gun," said the Curator.

"Shoot him," said Esty. "He didn't cast the same spell on you that he did on me. You can do it."

I steadied my trembling hand. I couldn't miss at this distance. The same vision of the future came back to me. The Curator in control of the world, thousands of statues filling up his home. People continue to offer a sacrifice to him each year so he may preserve his youth. I can stop it. Now.

I tried to aim, and then another vision came to me. I shoot him. The guards are free of their slavery. Maybe I'll even have time to explain to someone from outside the whole business with the statues. And then the magic hour will be over, and I'll start to petrify and get stuck in some horrible posture. And no one will know what to do with us. Eventually, they'll throw us into some dark warehouse, and I'll spend eternity looking at orphaned spiderwebs.

Both the Curator and Esty stepped forward. In my heart, I begged forgiveness from all the people I could have saved, all the people he will turn into statues, and then I shot Esty. Briefly, she looked surprised. Her mouth gaped open, and then she fell back. The gun dropped from my hand, and I started shaking.

The Curator moved quickly and gathered me in his arms.

"You're OK," he said. "You did the right thing."

I saw Esty on the floor, moving slightly. She was only injured. The guards came in.

"Take her upstairs," said the Curator. "I'll see afterward what I can do for her."

Four of them grabbed her limbs and dragged her out. We were left alone, only the statues and us.

"Now I owe you a reward," said the Curator.

"I shot her," I mumbled.

"She didn't die," he said brightly. "I'll try to cure her later."

He looked at my face and smiled. The terrifying vision came to me again.

"In the future," I said, "when you'll have thousands of statues, will you still wake me up?"

"My beauty," he said and stroked my cheek. "I shall always wake you up."

"And what if you get tired of me?"

"Never, I promise." He kissed my hand and said, "Let's dance."

The music resumed, and the thrill of moving took over me again. I took his extended hand.

And we danced.

Askuni-Askuni

By Dafna Feldman
Translated by Emanuel Lottem

DAFNA FELDMAN, AN AUTHOR AND A POET, was born in Jerusalem in 1972 and raised in an Anglo-Saxon religious-Zionist home. After her military service, she studied cinematic and television arts at Hadassah College, obtaining a B.A. degree, and education at the David Yelin College. Her resumé includes teaching film and communication, and managing a Reform Jewish community. Among the programs she participated in were "Life Issues" – leading therapy groups using Talmudic bibliotherapy, and "Healing Hatred" – spiritual coaching for treating traumas resulting from the Arab-Israeli conflict" in the Arab town of Beit Jallah.

Feldman won the 2019 Almog Prize. Her stories and poems were published in a variety of magazines, as well as several printed anthologies. She is a member of the editorial board of the *Kol HeHamon* magazine. Her first novel, *Kurmiza*, is due to be published soon. These days she is completing a volume of poems and two movie scripts. She is married and has four children.

In Bedouin tradition, it is believed that when a person has been murdered, a strange bird called the Hāmah comes out of the dead person's head after the burial and shouts over the grave: "*Askuni-Askuni!*" – "Let me drink!" That is, "Avenge me!"

IN THE MORNING, hikers found Asmahān in a gorge at the bottom of the great cliff. A military helicopter was called in to rescue her. Toward noon, Mother realized that Asmahān had not returned from school, and it was only after midnight that Ṭāher, his father, and his uncle Fādi, set out to fetch her.

They drove fast because they had to get the minibus back to Ismāʿīl by 4 A.M. That's when he must pick up some people and drive them to work. Asmahān lay in a black bag between the benches. The bag bounced and rebounded each time the minibus took turns. This frightened Ṭāher, and he removed himself to the back seat. The policeman who'd met them at the Abu Kabir morgue informed them that given the forensics at the site, the deceased's cause of death was ruled a suicide and the case was closed. He handed Uncle Fādi a transparent plastic bag containing a ḥijāb and one pink flip-flop which had been found at the edge of the cliff. In Ṭāher's hands, he placed a white envelope, seeing as he was the only one among them who could read Hebrew. He then patted him on his shoulder after Ṭāher told him that he was an eleventh grader. "Stay in school," the policeman said. "Do something with yourself."

Ṭāher was too confused and sad to respond.

Uncle Fādi drove the minibus, and Father sat next to him, wiping his runny nose and his tears with the *keffiyeh* he wore, all the way back to Umm Butain. In the light of the small fixture above the back seat, Ṭāher opened the envelope. Under the letterhead of the Abu Kabir Department of Forensic Medicine, there was the following statement:

Expert opinion:

Based on the findings of the autopsy performed on the body of __________, I hereby state my opinion that her death was caused by severe damage to the central nervous system. The traumatic injuries to the brainstem indicate that she lost consciousness immediately. In addition, it was found that numerous bones were fractured, and severe trauma was caused to several internal organs, although there had been little internal hemorrhaging into internal cavities, from which it can be deduced that her death came very shortly after the trauma had been caused. The totality of trauma and fracturing findings concur with a blunt force trauma caused by a relatively great force and coincides with the circumstances as provided (fall from a high place).

There was another note, one that Ṭāher had to read several times before he understood its significance: "Lacerations were observed in the posterior fourchette at the lower junction of the labia. A sample of substance taken from the vaginal mucosa is believed to be sperm cells." He put the page in the envelope and shoved it into the inside pocket of his coat. Asmahān was only 11 years old.

Mother found no solace in the dozens of visitors to the women's mourning tent. She just sat there, detached and indifferent to the grieving wails of the hired mourner from the nearby village of Bir Haddāj. Aunt Intiṣṣār took matters into her hands and urged the younger siblings to hurry up and carry the trays of dates and the trays of *qahwa mura* [bitter coffee] to the men's tent. Most of the day, Ṭāher sat on a mattress between Father and Uncle Fādi. Only in the late afternoon, and only after the *Ṣalāh* [prayer], was he allowed to go out and stretch his body that was aching all over from this prolonged sitting.

Ever since he was little, he used to run away to the great cliff. He loved watching the last rays of the setting sun, how they moved among the crevices and folds of the mountains until they gave way to darkness. Sometimes Asmahān would manage to dodge her chores and join him. She would press against his slender body, sucking her right thumb, and with her left palm gather a handful of sand and scatter the grains to the wind in the fading sunlight. "You see?" She would smile, her eyes sparkling. "Gold powder!" Ṭāher knew how rare the moments were when she could just be a girl, and swore he would forever protect his kid sister. The one who came, *al-ḥamdu lillāh* [thank God], after four sons, and immediately captured his heart.

Ṭāher stood on the edge of the great cliff and started descending quickly, as if possessed by a demon, clinging to its cracked face with his hands and feet, displacing rocks, determined to find the other flip-flop. After a few meters, he found it stuck in the mouth of a hyrax den. There he collapsed, hugging the flip-flop. And for the first time since his trip to Abu Kabir, he dared to burst into tears over his beloved sister Asmahān.

At night she appeared to him in a dream. She lay, as was the custom of the place, on her right side, wrapped in five layers of *akfān* [shrouds]. Perching on her head, the *Hāmah* bird shouted *"Askuni-Askuni, Askuni-Askuni!"*

Ṭāher woke up, drenched in a cold sweat. He reached under the mattress, where he'd hidden the pink flip-flop and the Abu Kabir report. He opened it and read again: "Lacerations were observed in the posterior fourchette at the lower junction of the labia. A sample of substance taken from the vaginal mucosa is believed to be sperm cells." And then he read it again, and again, and again.

At the six-year ORT regional school in Bir Haddāj, the rumor mill was bustling with speculations over how sixth-grader Asmahān Abu Zakut found her death. Most of them revolved around a twelfth-grade student, Fatḥi al-'Azāzmah. As these rumors had it, Asmahān fancied him, but he did not care for her. Disappointed and heartbroken, she plunged to her death. At the end of the three days of mourning, Ṭāher had to return to class, despite his objections. In his mind, the vicious whispers mingled with the screams of the *Hāmah*. He sat in the classroom pretending to be listening. During class breaks, he remained in the classroom to avoid the slanderers, the sympathizers, and the indifferent. One day, 'Ayisha al-'Azāzmah ventured to approach him. She was Asmahān's classmate and friend, and Fatḥi's sister.

"*Allāh yeraḥmah. Salāmāt rāsak* [God have mercy on her – you be healthy]", she murmured.

Ṭāher raised his head, and for a moment, their eyes met. 'Ayisha hurried away. Her brother Fatḥi, who has never offered any condolences, continued to strut around school with a smug smile on his face, indifferent to the rumor mill that linked him to her death.

The rage known as *al-thār* [vengeance] permeates the body like the venom of a yellow scorpion. It originates in the nervous system, from which it seeps into the cardiovascular system. Its first symptoms are difficulty in breathing, suffocation, and restlessness. Then comes paralysis. The venom of *al-thār* was boiling in Ṭāher, rendering him helpless before the screams of the *Hāmah*. Sorely distressed, he decided to turn to Sheikh Abu Nihād, whom he had known since childhood as a regular guest at their home.

The Sheikh's home was an extension of the mosque that stood at the center of the village. It was, like most of the village houses, a shack with a roof of solar panels. On one side, it clung to the mosque wall, and on the other side there was an impressive vine arbor that sheltered a seating area full of mattresses. In it, the Sheikh received those who sought his blessing or advice.

Abu Nihād welcomed him with open arms and invited him to be seated. Ṭāher sat down, and the Sheikh took hold of his hands and said:

"*Innā lillahi wa'innā ilayhi Raji'una* [We are in God's hands and to Him we return]."

One of his wives approached with a tray of refreshments for the guest. Recognizing Ṭāher, she hastened to say, "*Allah yeraḥma. Salāmāt rāsak.*"

Ṭāher nodded his gratitude, and she hurried back into the house.

Abu Nihād took out a pack of Gauloises and offered Ṭāher a cigarette, which he politely declined. The Sheikh lit one for himself, and they both drank the bittersweet coffee in silence.

"So tell me, how can I help you?"

Ṭāher pulled the coroner's report out of his shirt. He handed it to the Sheikh and let him read it. When the Sheikh had finished reading, he took a long drag from his cigarette, looked up from the page, and stared gravely at Ṭāher.

"What are you asking for, *yā Ṭāher?*"

Ṭāher pointed to the last line, to make sure the Sheikh had read it. Abu Nihād nodded.

"So what are you asking for?"

"*Al-thār!*"

Abu Nihād got up immediately and shoved the report back into Ṭāher's hands. "*Al-maut walā al-dhul. Al-maut walā al-adhlal* [Death rather than humiliation. Death rather than disgrace]," he declared.

"Your sister chose to die rather than defile her family's honor. Do you understand? No *al-thar*, no nothing! Do you understand?"

Ṭāher was stunned by the Sheikh's angry reaction. He now realized that the rumors about some connection between her and Fatḥi had reached him too, and Asmahān's death was a worthy, sacred, and honorable one. Tears of pain and rage escaped his eyes. He tried as best as he could to stop weeping, to no avail.

"Every night the *Hāmah* appears to me in my dreams and shouts, *Askuni- Askuni*. It won't leave me," he said, crying. "I must avenge her death, please tell me it's okay."

Outraged, the Sheikh got up, knocking over the coffee pot on his way. Its boiling contents spilled on the carpet, which quickly absorbed the dark liquid.

"*Lā taïr walā Hāmah in Islām!* [There is no bird and no *Hāmah* in Islam]," he shouted, flailing his arms. "Thus spake our Prophet Muḥammad, peace upon him." Ṭāher looked into his eyes and recognized fear. The Sheikh was afraid of the ʿAzāzmah family. They were the dominant clan in Bir Haddāj. *Al-thār* between the Abu Zakut clan from Umm Butain and the ʿAzāzmah clan from Bir Haddāj would shatter the peace that the elders have carefully preserved for over 40 years. Except for a few incidents, the clans have managed to maintain a serene coexistence. Sheikh Abu Nihād would not allow the death of an 11-year-old girl to destroy this balance. Ṭāher's blood was boiling. He rose from his seat and stood in the middle of the dark stain on the carpet.

"I will not take anyone's life," he said decisively. Perhaps to reassure the Sheikh, perhaps to assure himself aloud that he would not kill anyone. Then he turned and walked out of the arbor.

"Asmahān preserved her family's honor!" Sheikh Abu Nihād shouted after him.

Ṭāher turned and stared at him with bloodshot eyes.

"*Al-'ain in al-'ain wal-sin in al-sin* [An eye for an eye and a tooth for a tooth]," he said.

IN THE DEAD OF NIGHT, Ṭāher crossed the hills that lay between Umm Butain to Bir Haddāj. He carried with him a bottle of water and the knife his father used to slaughter sheep. He knew where to find the home of the 'Azāzmah family. Fathi's mother was a pediatric nurse in the village, and more than once had he accompanied his mother to her clinic with a child who was suffering from diarrhea or suddenly got a fever in the middle of the night.

Ṭāher's shirt was drenched in sweat, and his rapid heartbeat was the only sound he heard in the darkness of the desert. When he got to the house, he quietly moved the shack's door and went straight into the children's bedroom. By the orange light of the oil stove that burned in the center of the room, he saw 'Ayisha lying in her bed near the far wall. There were also three cribs next to the other walls.

Ṭāher approached her. The pounding of his heart sounded so loud in his ears that he feared it would wake everybody in the house. The thought of having to do what he needed to do was frightening and exciting at once, and he felt his groin awakening in anticipation of the revenge he was going to take for his sister. He knew that he was obliged, as per tradition, to wake her up. He leaned over her, covered her mouth with the palm of his hand, and pressed the knife to her neck. Alarmed, 'Ayisha woke up and looked at him with terrified eyes.

"Shhh," he whispered, pressing the blade to her neck. "If you'll keep quiet, I'll let you say the *Shahāda*. But if you try to scream..." He added pressure to her neck. 'Ayisha nodded, and tears started flowing from her eyes. Ṭāher removed the blanket and revealed her body which was tucked into a yellow nightgown, several sizes too large for her slender body. 'Ayisha looked at him, her eyes horrified like a trapped animal, but kept quiet and did not try to resist. Ṭāher pulled up her nightgown to expose her thighs, then pulled off her panties and spread her legs. Her crotch lay before him, adorned with thin, dark pubic hair buds. For a moment, he wondered if that was what his sister's private parts looked like, but he immediately cleared that thought from his mind and unbuttoned his pants. His burning penis stood up like a pillar of fire.

"Start," he ordered her in a whisper.

'Ayisha began to recite the verses in a trembling voice.

"*Ashhadu an lā ilāha illa-llāhu, wa-ashhadu anna Muḥammadan Rasūlu-llāhi* [I bear witness that there is no god but God and I bear witness that Muḥammad is the messenger of God]," she uttered.

"Again. Say it again."

"*Ashhadu an lā ilāha...* please, *yā* Ṭaher," pleaded 'Ayisha.

"Continue." He felt how badly his hand holding the knife was trembling, and the fire burning in his organ began to die out.

"*...illā-llāhu, wa-ashhadu anna Muḥammadan Rasūlu-llāhi,*" she continued, staring at him unflinchingly.

"Again, say it again." he rebuked her more firmly, hoping that his masculinity would reawaken if only he could get angrier. But when she began to mumble the verses for the third time, he realized that nothing was further from the truth. The knife dropped out of his hand, and when she reached the words *Rasūlu-llāhi*, he felt how his organ contracted, and his body froze all over. Ṭaher got up and hurriedly covered her thighs with a blanket. He needed to puke. He put a hand to his mouth and ran out of the door through which he had entered. He left the 'Azāzmah family's home and ran away, far away from Bir Haddāj. Away to the darkness of the mountains. Ṭaher stopped there, bent over, and heaved his guts out. To his dismay, he noticed that he no longer had his father's knife. He burst into tears. That night, the howls of the jackals mingled with the moans and sobs of a boy who realized that his doom has come upon him.

Arab mythology speaks of the *'anqā'* bird, the phoenix, who lives in the desert and once in a thousand years prepares a nest made of myrrh and cinnamon branches and burns itself. From the ashes, it is resurrected, symbolizing immortality.

ṬĀHER FOUND HIMSELF SITTING on top of his and Asmahān's cliff, hugging his knees and watching the first rays of the sun as they climbed among the crevices and the dark folds of the mountains, giving way to the fresh soft light of dawn. The time has come for *al-Fajr* [the morning prayer], and Ṭāher followed the custom of purification and cleansing when there is no water. He dipped his hands into the deep sand, rubbed them, and knelt on his knees facing east.

A black plastic bag landed next to him, and Ṭāher rose in panic. 'Ayisha stood there at a safe distance, not daring to come closer. He opened the bag and saw his father's knife, the one he has used to slaughter sheep. Ṭāher nodded at her in gratitude, put the bag as far from him as he could, and gestured for her to come closer. 'Ayisha, wearing a ḥijāb, walked gingerly in her pink flip-flops. She sat down next to him and began to draw lines in the sand. They sat in silence for a few minutes, watching the rising sun. Ṭāher gathered a handful of sand in his hand and showed it to 'Ayisha.

"Do you know what this is?"

"No," 'Ayisha shook her head.

"This is golden dust," he smiled and threw up the grains of sand, which flew and fell down the cliff. 'Ayisha giggled shyly.

Wind blew from the east, bringing with it scents of myrrh and cinnamon that surrounded them, filling them both with excitement. They stared enchanted at the glowing orange and yellow ball that was approaching them.

"*'anqā'!*" cried Ṭāher fervently as they watched the giant bird that soared above them with a mighty flap of wings.

"*Ghalata* [mistake]," said 'Ayisha, her eyes shining. "Listen carefully."

From high above came the loud cries of the *Hāmah*.

"*Hādi-hādi, hādi-hādi* [It is over, it is over]."

Latte, To Go

By Rotem Baruchin

Translated by Rehavia Berman

Rotem baruchin grew up in Tel Aviv, Ramat Gan, Petach Tikva, and Giv'at Shmuel, all in Israel, and in Swiss suburbia. She began reading science fiction and fantasy at the tender age of eight, and started writing it at about the same age. For years she has combined fanzine writing with original fiction, published in both printed and online magazines, and then went on to study screenwriting at Tel Aviv University's School of Film and TV.

Rotem wrote plays for Israeli LGTB groups such as the Gay Ensemble, which were produced on commercial stages. She was a writer for a children's show, *The Dreamers*, broadcast by an Israeli TV channel. She directed several plays and musicals for several theaters, festivals, and conventions, including an interactive production involving audience choices. Her Internet series *The Grey Matter*, filmed in the US, can be watched online. For the Israeli youth magazine *Rosh 1*, she wrote two story series, published over a couple of years.

Rotem won six Geffen prizes for her short stories. Currently, she is working on her first full-scale novel in a planned series, *The Cities' Guardians*, which is based on the premise that every community has a "spirit of place" that manifests itself as a living entity – supernatural, eternal, and almost omnipotent. Rotem has a profile on Patreon, which allows readers to support her writing. Some of her stories have been translated into English.

Rotem Baruchin is a regular participant in Israeli SF/F conventions, in which she runs writing workshops, and is also a member of a volunteer group dedicated to the prevention of sexual harassment at conventions. She lives in Tel Aviv with her partner and their three cats. Her favorite genre is urban fantasy. She loves looking for magic in cafés and bars, in dazzling streetlights, in broken pavement stones, and in anyone alive in the city's boulevards after three a.m. who is still drinking coffee.

THE CITY SPIRIT OF JERUSALEM flies by my car as it climbs up from the sharp Motza curve. When I accelerate, she just flies faster, gently tapping on the window with her fingers, as long as pine boughs. She leans her head back and laughs with a voice as deep as a wadi, and I know she won't give up. She has thousands of years of patience.

I give up and push the button to open the window, but she tosses her head, and thick hair hides her face for a moment as she rises in the air. I wonder briefly if her only purpose was to get me to open the window, and if she'd never meant to get in the car, but then she drops, half-translucent, through the car roof and re-solidifies, seating beside me like a contented cat on a warm sidewalk. The vehicle immediately fills with the smell of pine and mountain air as clear as wine. She reaches back with a practiced hand and adjusts the seat.

"Do you always have to make an entrance?" I ask.

She laughs again with that wadi laugh of hers but doesn't respond.

"Put your seatbelt on," I almost hiss.

"Why, what do you think will happen to me if you have an accident?"

"I'm not worried about an accident, but I'm not getting a ticket for you."

She rolls her eyes. "What do you think I am? An amateur? Nobody's going to see me but you."

"I've already gotten a ticket with Modi'in."

She rolls her eyes again, but this time her lips purse into a thin line. "As I said, I'm not an amateur."

I don't respond. We're silent for a few moments. She stares out the window, drumming her fingers lightly on my GPS – it's covered with a thin layer of dust and hasn't been turned on even once since I bought the car. She's humming "From the Top of Mount Scopus" as I begin to merge into the traffic as we approach the city. We both avoid discussing the reason I came.

"Did you know that Ben-Gurion requested that they call this road Highway 1?" she asks me suddenly. "He specifically requested that number for the road leading to the capital."

I smile out of the corner of my mouth. "But he decided that it would be the road from Jerusalem to Tel Aviv. So, he crowned the real capital city without even knowing it."

She stops drumming, and I know I've hit a sore spot. She and Tel Aviv have never liked each other. The blow was well-aimed, of course. Jerusalem has never been my favorite. She doesn't have Eilat's youthful spirit, Kfar Saba's modesty and shyness, or even Hadera's quiet melancholy. She's vain, arrogant, religious, constantly wrapped in self-importance, and usually spouting mysterious pronouncements that supposedly arise out of wisdom and deep contemplation, which gets on my nerves.

But I feel no joy from hitting back at her. I glance at her sideways and frown. She stares silently out of the window, looking west, the hills reflected in her eyes. Maybe she's dreaming of a beach or rivers, of dunes and valleys. When was the last time she left the city for more than a few hours? When was the last time she managed to rest a little?

"It hasn't snowed in three winters," she notes – a strange statement for the middle of August.

"Maybe it won't, either, if they're right about this whole global warming thing."

"Not that it has anything to do with it, but they're right."

"How do you know?"

"I feel it. That's how it is when you've been here from the start. You remember. Ashkelon remembers too sometimes, and Safed and Caesaria.

I look at her, with her layers of clothes, her ancient crumbling skirts piled one on top of the other, a scarf that looks like cobwebs draped over her shoulders, a touristy T-shirt with "Welcome to Israel" emblazoned on it peeking from underneath. Hamsa pendants and leather necklaces from the Old City market hang around her neck, and her sneakers are fit for climbing.

"Where shall I drop you off?" she asks.

"Shouldn't I be asking you?"

She laughs for the third time, and my moment of sympathy passes. The others are delighted when I come to visit. They're happy to have company. So few people are aware of their existence or can talk to them, look at them, remember them. The little ones can at least leave for longer periods sometimes, visit one another. Jerusalem has no such luxury. She's always on guard, always tense and alert, always juggling between too many residents, conflicts, peoples, nationalities, religions. She tells the others that the last time she'd slept was before the War of Independence, and I don't think she's exaggerating.

"How long will you stay?"

"Not long at all. I've come to find Yad Hashmona."

She grunts derisively. "Is that a real place?"

Charade, of course. She knows it is. There is no city spirit who doesn't know all the places around her.

"She ran away."

"No, seriously? It's true?" She's amused. "Are there even enough people there for a Place Spirit?"

"Ninety-something. It's enough." We both know a lot less is enough. "Anyway, she hasn't come through here."

I look at her sideways. "Are you sure you're not hiding her?"

"That's all I need. I have enough religious wars as it is." She folds her arms on her chest. "Besides, you would have seen right through it. If she'd asked me where to hide, I would have sent her to Safed or something."

"If she'd asked you where to hide, I hope you would have told her to go back, since nothing good has ever come of a runaway Place Spirit."

She shrugs. I scowl. The little ones often run away while they can, before they grow and become bound to the place. Some want to see the world, experience a little more than the few square miles in which they are trapped for life, and some sometimes just get fed up. None of them asked for this job.

"A place whose Place Spirit has disappeared is in danger," I remind her, "and the larger it is and the longer the absence, the greater the danger."

"It's only Yad HaShmona," she rolls her eyes. "What can happen? A tiny dining hall will collapse on the heads of a few immigrants from Finland?"

"You have no appreciation for human life, have you?" I say through clenched teeth.

She doesn't bother to reply. I gesture at the endless traffic jam at the entrance to the city. "Would you do something about this?"

She's amused. "Like what? Another lane? We're on a mountain, you know. There's a limit to where you can pave."

"I meant something more immediate."

She waves her hand. Most of the traffic ahead of us diverts into various streets. I don't ask how she does it. Most likely, a combination of traffic lights further on opening up, traffic reports, smartphone alerts, clearer road signs, roads a little smoother, maybe even a police officer directing traffic ahead. She's pretty good at this, though not as good as

Tel Aviv – with *her* help, I can cross the city from one end to the other in three minutes, without even taking the Ayalon Highway.

The next time we get stuck is on Agrippas Street. A taxicab cap has grown on the top of my car, and I can see her wry smile. I take advantage of the stop, open a window, cock an ear and listen through the thundering bus engines to the sounds of the market floating in the air, the prayers rising from the old, narrow lanes of the Nachlaot district, even the curses. She shows a shred of curiosity for the first time.

"What? Can you smell or hear or feel her? Is that some City Guardian superpower or something?"

"Something like that. What do you care?"

She shrugs.

"Didn't you say she hasn't come through here?"

She shrugs again. The traffic light changes and I drive on.

"Interesting place, Yad HaShmona. Established by some crazy Scandinavians in the early seventies."

"Finns," she corrects me absentmindedly.

"They called the settlement 'Yad HaShmona,' after eight Jews in Finland who were betrayed to the Nazis during World War Two," I say. "They believed it was their mission to live in Israel and help build the land, but the Ministry of Immigration and Absorption couldn't understand why a bunch of crazy blond, devout Christians, would found a humble moshav in the middle of nowhere. They denied the settlers permanent citizenship. The Ministry of Housing was also suspicious. It took years before they received construction permits. And then came the Messianic Jews – the ones who believe in Jesus, you know – well, they did get construction permits, and now they're part of the moshav. So it's a story about two underdogs discovering that together they have power."

She falls silent, looks out the window. At the entrance to one of the alleys of the Mahane Yehuda Market, ultra-Orthodox Jews wearing long black coats argue in loud voices and waving hands with ultra-Orthodox

Jews from another sect, who are dressed in long black coats with thin stripes. Someone pushes someone else. A woman wearing a tank top who happens to be in the way stumbles and falls. She, too, joins in the shouting. A child with red sidelocks curses the woman, calling her a harlot. The Arab laborers quickly clear out of the market. I park the car on the sidewalk.

"My father knew Yad HaShmona. He saw her grow into a young adult, changing from a fair blonde with floral dresses to a brunette in a Sabbath dress who rides a bicycle. She was particularly addicted to the sauna."

She keeps looking out the window. A few police officers arrive from the marketplace to disperse the escalating mayhem. I didn't see her make any gestures, not so much as a blink. It's so mundane for her, so natural. Again I am filled with pity, and it doesn't disappear even when she says coldly, "And why exactly do a hundred people need a sauna?"

"They were used to it, from Finland. They wouldn't give up their sauna, never mind how hot it was outside; and the Jews got used to it and fell in love with it too."

"How wonderful for them. Just great, all this peace and camaraderie." She finally turns to me. "Why did I have to hear this story, exactly?"

The police officers disappear back into the market after calming down the fight. The group of black-clad men crosses the road in front of us and disappears into the alleyways of Nachlaot. I point at the way they've gone. A tall structure rises from the thicket of cramped stone buildings, European in style, dark, and built of solid wood. Two blond youths and a young woman with pigtails sit on the porch in bathrobes, chatting. "I don't think there's a sauna in the middle of Ohel Moshe."

She returns her glance to me, frozen. "How long have you known?"

"I've suspected from about the entrance to the city. Evangelist Christians and Messianic Jews have a very distinct look. You didn't have much chance of hiding her." I turn off the engine and open the door to get out. "Make sure I don't get a ticket, okay?"

She slams the door and runs after me. A strong yet fragile hand grabs my arm. "Let her stay."

"Why?" I turn to her coldly. "So that her place will die out? So that you'll have more religious wars? Don't you have enough?"

"No! So that..." for a moment, the mask of pride and arrogance fades. "I just wanted..." She casts her eyes at the wooden structure, the young brunette with the pigtails. The girl laughs, and her laughter fills the alleys. For a moment, the tense atmosphere between us seems to evaporate. I wait. She remains silent. We look at the sauna together.

I reach out to touch her shoulder, hesitating for a moment – you can never know when she's restricting physical contact with men as per religion, and when she isn't – and then I recall that she touched me herself a moment before. Still, the gesture already seems devoid of meaning.

"I didn't really think I could switch between us. I just thought how nice it would be if I could take a vacation. Not for a few hours – for a few days, even a week. Just to take a trip in the mountains, swim in the Lake of Galilee, visit Nahariya. Let someone else deal with all... this." She gestures around her, and I know that she doesn't mean just the market.

My jaw drops. "Are you serious? Does she know what you've gotten her into?"

She folds her arms over the hamsa pendants. "She agreed."

"Of course she agreed! She's half Evangelical Christian and half Messianic Jew. There's nowhere in the world she'd rather be!" I sigh. "That doesn't mean she can be you. Do you have any idea what you would have found when you got back? Chaos!" I shake my head. "Would you let little Kfar Azar replace Tel Aviv?"

"Would you stop talking about Tel Aviv already!" she growls, and I raise my hands, soothing her. You don't argue with long-standing hostility. Besides, she's right. I do talk too much about Tel Aviv. "Tel

Aviv has exactly half my population. Do you know what it's like to care for eight hundred thousand people?"

"No," I admit.

She brushes pine needles off her shoulder. I'm not sure where she managed to pick them up. "It's tough here."

"I know. I see that."

"But you don't live it." She looks at me with the unequaled gaze of an ancient city. She's tired, and for a moment, I drown in those eyes, drown in thousands of years of violence and sacredness and love.

"Nobody really lives it, except you. And nobody ever can."

She glances again at the wooden structure, so alien to the neighborhood. "No human was supposed to see it. I did a good job."

"I know. You're not an amateur. And I'm not just another human."

Her lips finally curl in a smile, and I suppress a sigh of relief. Had she decided to fight, I don't know what I would have done. "You've grown, City Guardian," she says, almost formally. "You have grown wise."

"I'm not so wise," I confess. "I looked first in El'ad, Kfar Etzion, and Efrat. I didn't think she'd come here. You've given me quite the runaround, both of you."

"Sorry," she says. And then, after another moment of silence, "You know, if you ever want to leave your ramshackle cabin there in the woods... I have a penthouse freeing up in the Holyland buildings. With a jacuzzi, swimming pool, the works."

"Yes, I know, thanks." They always invite me. I always say no. I've lived enough in cities. She nods. My answer was predictable, but she's sad, nonetheless. I sigh. "*Yalla*, come on. We'll take the kid home, and then you can make it up to me with hummus in the Old City."

It's NOT EVEN SIX in the morning when the knocking begins. If I didn't live in a secluded cabin in the middle of nowhere, I might have been able to delude myself that they're looking for the neighbors, or hope that they'd give up and leave. They don't mean to wake me up, but they don't have a human sense of time. When I lived in cities, the knocks on the door could have come ten or twenty times a day, at all hours.

At least now, when they make it all the way out to see me, I know it really is an emergency.

I peek out through the slat – peepholes are for homes with electricity and running water – and curse when I see the twins standing there. Ramat Gan and Giv'ataim. They're not really twins. I just call them that because their limits are intertwined to such a degree that some streets are split lengthways between them, with each one controlling one side. Sometimes, when they talk, it's not clear where one finishes and the other begins. And they're never easy to deal with. I don't want to open the door. I want to pretend that I'm not home. I want to go back to bed and sleep till it's too hot for a house with no air conditioning. I want a different job, dammit. The kind you can quit, for a start.

"Don't you know I have a phone?" I say as I finally open the door. "You could call. You could leave a message; you could send a text."

"It's an emergency," says Ramat Gan, pushing in by me. I knew it. Coming to a remote place, way out in the sticks, means being hours away from their limits. They don't do that lightly.

"Please, come in, feel free. It's not like I have basic human needs, such as sleep."

Ramat Gan rolls her eyes, but Giv'ataim blushes a bit.

"Don't you want to, um, get dressed?" she asks. I'm wearing boxers and nothing else, but I shrug. Even if Bnei Brak had appeared on my doorstep at six, with her floor-length skirts and her covered hair, she would have had to take me the same way. They woke me up. Let them deal with it.

Ramat Gan sinks into the threadbare couch and puts her feet up on the table. I haven't seen her for some months now. She now looks like a cross between an art student and a businesswoman in her button-down shirt with a starched collar, purple, star-print pants, rainbow highlights in her hair, and boots that are a tad too long and a tad too leopard-skin, which somehow remind me of the hookers that trawl the Diamond Exchange district at night. Her sunglasses have strawberries on them, meticulously hand-painted, as far as I can tell, with nail polish. The red fruit with the white dots and the green leaves soften the mature appearance of her overly made-up face. She smells of chocolate, even now, years after the factory shut down.

Giv'ataim, on the other hand, is tastefully dressed in a light blue dress with sleeves, which, oddly, could have belonged to both a little girl and an old lady. Her feet are in expensive heels, and her perfume smells like flowers, or maybe she herself does, I'm not sure. She has a regal look, but when she passes by me, I notice that the little silver medallion on her neck is in the shape of a pita with falafel, and dangling from her golden bracelet are tiny golden ice-cream cones and popsicles. She sits majestically in the chair, almost like an old British lady, but then ruins the image by swinging her feet back and forth, because they do not reach the floor. She wasn't as short when she passed by me a moment ago, and I wonder whether she shrunk or the chair grew larger.

For a few moments, I still consider throwing out both of them, but my sense of responsibility finally prevails over my reluctance. Instead, I go to the kitchen, which is just an oven with a stove-top at the other end of the cabin. "Coffee, ladies?" I strike a match and try to light the gas underneath the coffee pot, but it refuses to cooperate.

They shake their heads. Giv'ataim asks for tea, and Ramat Gan gives her a scornful look.

"Would you like a biscuit to go with that? Something soft for your dentures?"

Giv'ataim snarls at her: "Last time I checked, you have more old people than I do."

"I have more people. That includes old people, and young people, which you don't have at all. Which reminds me, you're going gray again. Need help with the dye job?"

"Yeah, droves of young people are streaming your way," Giv'ataim's voice drips venom. "I'm sure Tel Aviv feels neglected."

"Tel Aviv feels neglected because all her streets that border yours are filthy!"

"Maybe if someone would let my sanitation workers drive down the streets!"

"Maybe if someone would stop stealing my streets!" Ramat Gan screams.

"Those have been my streets since 1919!" Giv'ataim raises her voice accordingly.

"You didn't even exist in 1919!"

I feel a headache coming on, the likes of which will require much alcohol to chase away. I spare myself the rest of the argument by going out to replace the gas tank. There is no new tank. I forgot to order one. Maybe I should spend in this cabin more than an occasional night every once in a while. I go back inside.

"You want to talk about parking vouchers?" Giv'ataim yells, "Let's talk parking vouchers!"

"Girls!" I interrupt the escalating dispute, raising the coffee pot before their eyes. "What are the chances one of you can heat this? I'd really appreciate it."

They exchange a glance, look at me and shake their heads in perfect unison. Twins, like I said.

"Really? Nothing?" Tel Aviv would have had my pot boiling with a light, focused, and sun-filled flick of her hand.

"Outside our limits? In the middle of the forest? Are you serious?" Ramat Gan rolls her eyes. "Who do you think we are, Eilat?"

"I have a coupon for coffee at the nearby gas station," Giv'ataim suggests.

I sigh and go off to get dressed after all.

We must be the only ones who have ever sat at this gas station's dirty coffee tables, especially so early in the morning. Ramat Gan stirs her orange juice with her straw. Giv'ataim drinks her tea and munches a cookie, despite Ramat Gan's poison-laced chuckles. I sip the latte I ordered. It's horrible. I put it down. I miss a good latte – coffee with creamy-textured foam, warm but not boiling milk, and the precise amount of fine espresso. I think I haven't had a good latte in eight months.

The clerk blinks. His eyes try to focus on my companions but slide over them. He knows they're there, obviously – he just sold us drinks. But for some obscure reason, he can't really look at them, work out why they look familiar, or decide what he thinks about their odd appearances and mannerisms. And once we leave, he'll find that mine is the only face he could recall.

"Well?" I shoot into their silence. They fought in the car all the way here, like little girls. Now they seem embarrassed, self-conscious. They exchange glances, and I see the hesitation on their faces. Suddenly I feel a stab of guilt. My father would have treated them patiently and with empathy. He would never have fled to a secluded cabin in the woods. We always lived in inhabited places, and there wasn't a Place Spirit in the country we didn't regularly visit, from Neve Ativ in the north to Yotvata in the south.

I'm not him. He was more of a city shrink than a City Guardian. And yet, I can't help but wonder what it took for two large cities to come to ask for my help. The spirits of small places need me quite a lot. First, they run away all the time, and I have to find them and persuade them to come back. Second, some of them are young, inexperienced, and don't have enough contact with others like them. They have trouble understanding their inhabitants' wants and needs, and they often come to me for my guidance or opinion. I'm not a sociologist, a psychologist, or an architect, but I'm a human, and sometimes that's enough. And when it isn't, I have dozens of books and diaries by City Guardians that my father left me. They're always glad for a bit of advice.

The larger ones are a different story. Their problems are more complex. Sometimes they require diplomacy – not puny, everyday fights like Ramat Gan and Giv'ataim have, but an actual city conflict, like when Kiryat Ono invaded Giv'at Shmuel in 1998. Sometimes it's human wars – Katyusha rockets, Qassam rockets, Scud missiles, terror attacks. Sadly, we have no shortage of those, and most times, I can't really help; I just lend an ear and give moral support. Sometimes, nobody can solve the big cities' problems, not even they can, and certainly not their human, special-powers-devoid City Guardian. I'm often frustrated.

"What's up?" I start again, trying to sound supportive, calm, and sympathetic, but I have to settle for sounding a little less annoyed. I look at the twins. Ramat Gan looks back at me from under long, over-mascaraed lashes. Giv'ataim looks at her tea, which is swirling in the cup as though she's holding an invisible spoon.

They exchange a glance, and then Ramat Gan crushes her straw.

"It's Tel Aviv."

"What about Tel Aviv?" I force my voice to sound casual. I knew this day would come. I'm a City Guardian. I couldn't avoid that city forever.

"She's going through something."

"Something bad."

"Can you be a little more specific?"

They exchange glances again. It's growing old.

"Fine," Giv'ataim smooths her dress. "But it'll sound –"

"Really silly," Ramat Gan finishes. Now that they're not fighting anymore, they're completing each other's sentences. Like they're looking for ways to irritate me.

"Probably."

Giv'ataim goes on. "Tel Aviv has changed."

"You all change all the time."

"You know the Tel Aviv Marathon?"

I nod. The marathon takes place once a year, usually in March or April. They shut down half of Tel Aviv, and several tens of thousands of maniacs run anything from three to twenty-six miles.

I've never been much for sports.

"It's taking place twice a month now."

I nearly drop my miserable cup of imitation coffee. "Twice a month?!"

Ramat Gan nods. "The gridlock is impossible. All the streets are closed, and the two of us can't handle the increased load – nor can Holon, Bat Yam, Ramat HaSharon, and Herzliya. And each time there are –"

"– more runners," Giv'ataim finishes the sentence. "I've heard they're thinking of holding it once a week!"

"Once a week? In August?!" I sip too fast, and the "coffee" burns my tongue. I nearly drop it, but manage to save the cup at the cost of a large coffee stain on my shirt. It's an old rag anyway.

"That's not all," says Ramat Gan. "The Yarkon Park is packed all the time. Riding and canoe races."

"Well? What's so bad about a few canoes and some bicycles?"

"Horse-riding," Ramat Gan nearly hisses, "and you know very well that part of this park is mine. The whole other side of the Yehoshua Gardens looks like it's been gone over with a steamroller. I simply can't get the damage under control. And now they've begun to advertise hunting competitions."

"Hunting is illegal in Israel."

"So is the unauthorized cutting down of trees," says Giv'ataim, "but people are still cutting them down –"

"– to make bows," Ramat Gan purses her lips. She's always been so sensitive about trees, for such an… urban city. "She's gone bonkers, I'm telling you."

"And that's not all," Giv'ataim continues. "There are constant sailing competitions. Herzliya can't handle the congestion at the marina. And we haven't even mentioned the boxing matches, the military marches…"

"Long jump, javelin throwing…" Ramat Gan continues. "It's like she's decided to host the Olympics and didn't bother to ask anyone."

This is starting to sound less like the usual kind of trouble, and I reluctantly gulp down the rest of my coffee. I have a feeling I'll need it today. "How long has this been going on?"

"Months," says Giv'ataim. "At first, we tried to talk to her ourselves, you know, work it out. But she was evasive. She told Herzliya that she really does want to host the Olympics –"

"– Which is bullshit," Ramat Gan cuts in. "As if someone at the International Olympic Committee would ever agree to hold the games in Israel –"

"And us, you know what she told us?" Ramat Gan is almost shouting. "She said it wasn't her decision, that it came from City Hall! City Hall!"

I haven't seen her this furious in a long time, and I anxiously imagine how many ventilation machines at the Tel HaShomer hospital suddenly malfunctioning. I thought only young, small Place Spirits still use the excuse of "it's not me, it's City Hall." City Hall is meaningless for city spirits, an amorphous entity that mostly does the will of the city spirit anyway; a human justification when she doesn't want to do something or wants to do something and needs to justify it. Personally, I always thought that the distinction was stupid. The City Spirit is the essence of the city, the essence of life in it, the essence of the character of its inhabitants. It is affected by City Hall just as City Hall is affected by it. But the Spirits themselves view "City Hall" as something despicable.

"She's hiding something," Giv'ataim says at last. "At least, I hope she's hiding something, because if she believes all these things… something very strange is going on."

I rest my elbows on the dirty plastic table and look at them, trying to think of other questions to help me understand what's going on. But deep inside, I already know I'll have to go there. I knew this moment would come. I'm a City Guardian. I'd have to go back to Tel Aviv sometime. Maybe I should have done this long ago, instead of always making a detour around her, as I've been doing for the past eight months.

"Fine," I finally blurt out, the word nearly refusing to emerge from my lips.

"Really?" Ramat Gan asks, a slight doubt in her voice.

"Yes. I'll go talk to her."

They're both looking at me now, and the expression on their faces is almost identical. I can't decipher it. They remain silent, and it's getting on my nerves.

"What?!"

Ramat Gan peers at me over her strawberry glasses. "Do you, uh, maybe want –"

"– Us to come with you?" Giv'ataim completes, and the slight irritation I feel turns into anger. I narrow my eyes. How much do they know? The others may have heard rumors – surely not many of them, but these two are very close to Tel Aviv. Maybe they know more.

"No, I am fully capable of handling my duties as City Guardian without babysitters. Thank you."

Giv'ataim lowers her head in compliance, but Ramat Gan's strawberries are still looking at me.

"We just thought you might prefer –"

"I would prefer to be in my bed right now, sleeping," I cut her off, no longer able to keep the anger from my voice. "And since that is impossible, I prefer not to be told how to do my job and be allowed to work in peace." I know I sound angrier, crueler, and more hurt than I intended, and that this only reinforces whatever they know or believe, but I don't care. Eventually, Ramat Gan, too, lowers her eyes. I crush my paper cup and throw it in the garbage can.

I GET IN MY CAR and part with the twins on Highway 4. Giv'ataim sinks into the ground and fades. Ramat Gan prefers to recede in flight. They asked for a ride – not because they really needed it, just for the company, but I refused. There are things I want to do before I enter Tel Aviv again, and they're too nosy as it is.

I return home, change the clothes I'd thrown on before I knew what I was getting into, in favor of my nice blue jeans and an ironed, collared black shirt. I find a new barbershop at the limits of Giv'at Shmuel, right outside the city proper, and I shorten my hair that has been untouched by scissors for two or three months. I take the opportunity to lose the week-old stubble on my cheeks.

When I get off at the Aluf Sade interchange leading to HaShalom Road, my heart starts racing, and I can no longer lie to myself that all this effort was for no particular reason. My eyes are already seeking her on the sides of the road, where she used to pretend to be hitchhiking for me to pick her up. She thought it was funny when sometimes people noticed her and stopped. But she's not on the side of the road. It's almost a relief to me. They were right. There's a lot of traffic on the streets, but not vehicles. They're packed with people, not walking, but running. There are teenagers and young adults everywhere, practicing various sports. An enormous group of runners training for the marathon crosses the city, forcing me to stand for almost fifteen minutes at the light. I also notice some new fashion trends, rather odd, but these I dismiss with a shrug. She's always had strange ideas about such things. There are hordes of soldiers everywhere, not just around the IDF headquarters compound. I recognize the beret colors of combat units – light blue, brown, purple, red. Many of them are carrying weapons.

She still doesn't appear. I drive on to all her favorite spots. Rothschild Boulevard, The Culture Palace, the ice cream parlors on Ibn Gabirol

Street, the Cinematheque, Dizengoff Center and Square, Meir Garden, the second-hand clothing stores on Bograshov… the coffee shops in the Yemenite Quarter, the Nachlat Binyamin Street arts and crafts fair, Masarik Square, the Yarkon Park, the seaside boardwalk, the harbor. I drive around for hours, but she doesn't show up. I weigh my choices. I don't want to use the *call*. They hate it, and it's considered quite rude. But soon I will have no choice.

I find parking by the beach quite easily – which perhaps proves more than anything that something is wrong. There are very few cars on the roads, compared to bicycles. I go down to the beach. People are exercising here too, running, swimming, stretching like they're doing morning calisthenics in the late afternoon, sweating under the sweltering sun. What's come over this crazy city?

I kneel by the water and reach out, letting the waves lap at my fingers. It's a long shot, but she loves the sea. "I know you don't want to see me," I speak to the water, feeling rather foolish. But in any case, everyone's too busy working out to look at me, and if they did, I'd still be far from the strangest eccentric this place has to offer. I pick up wet sand and let it drip through my fingers. "I can't blame you. I wouldn't want to see me either if I were you. But we have to talk."

When I dip my hand in the water again, I feel something, a combination of surprise and anger followed by – attraction. I'm not sure whether I'm feeling mental attraction or if the waves pull me in, but the result is the same: I lose my balance and fall into the water.

When I rise, cursing and brushing sand off my best shirt, she's standing behind me. I feel her before I even turn around. She looks just like she did when I've last seen her, which I suspect is intentional, in her tiny orange beach skirt, a tank top with a ninja print, hipster glasses, and purple hair. The only things that are different are the sweatband holding her hair and the rollerblades. How did she get on this sand with them?

"Hi," I mumble.

"Hi," she says, and her voice is rich and quiet and soft, like I remember it.

"You look good."

"So do you."

I smile and feel relief as her lips curl as well. I'm full of sand and seawater. "I suppose I deserved that."

She laughs. Her laugh is like a sea breeze sweeping up popsicle sticks on the beaches. "Sorry. You surprised me. It wasn't intentional, although you did deserve it."

"Surprised you?" I raise an eyebrow. "Do you know how long I've been in town?"

"Ten minutes, if you took the Ayalon?"

"More like five hours," I say. She blinks rapidly, her gaze turning hazy for a moment, and I know she's scanning the city, connecting with her awareness.

A cold breeze, not typical for August, brushes my wet skin, making it prickle. She purses her lips. "Am I supposed to snap to attention the moment you enter, like Arad and the other tired ones? I have a few other things occupying me besides you, City Guardian."

My title sounds like an insult, coming out of her mouth. I raise my hands in a gesture that I hope is conciliatory. "I just meant that you used to know the second I entered your limits."

"Once, you used to toss a maple leaf in the air the second you entered my limits so that I'd know you'd arrived."

That's true. I'd forgotten. Or rather, I'd tried to forget. The open window, the outstretched hand, the red, five-fingered leaf tossed to the wind. It never fell to the road. A breeze would catch it, take it, play with it till it was gone. When I got home, it would already be there, hanging from a chain of leaves in the kitchen. They dried well. In the fourth month after we moved in together, the kitchen began to look like a maple tree. She refused to throw them away. Not even one. And she'd never let one drop to the road.

The weight of memories in her eyes is as heavy as mine, but hers carry real weight, of asphalt roads and shopping malls and hundred-year-old trees. "I could never figure out where you got them."

She would always try to find out, and I would always refuse to tell. She knew all my secrets – after all, she's watched me every moment I have been within her limits. That was the only thing she couldn't find out. Now the secret seems meaningless. "When I was a kid, I began to exchange letters with the son of a City Guardian in Canada, Matthew. After we grew up a little, we traveled the world together. We wanted to visit all the places we would never have the opportunity to see again. We didn't go to Israel or Canada. That seemed like a waste of time. But then his dad passed away, and, like any City Guardian in similar circumstances, he was permanently grounded. I went to visit him for a few weeks. He was sorry he hadn't found the time to visit me that he never will be able to. When I got back, I sent him dried chrysanthemums so he'd feel Israel a little. He sent me maple leaves, and we still add them to all our letters."

"And you would give me all the leaves he'd send you?" Her eyes soften slightly. She knows I have very few friends. It's hard for City Guardians to make human connections. It's hard for us to make any kind of connections that aren't with our cities. There just isn't enough time for it.

"It's no big deal," I mumble. Ironically, now that the silent warning is gone from her eyes, I feel less at ease, more awkward. I know how to deal with furious cities. I don't know how to deal with ex-lovers. "Anyway, I would have only lost them or accidentally destroyed them. And you loved them so much."

"Yes," her eyes grow hazy again. "I remember you showed them to me in pictures. I couldn't believe that there's a place where such trees grow, whose roots are buried under the snow and whose fallen leaves are so pink and red and orange. I'd think, *I wish I could see it for real. Just once.*"

"I imagine Toronto feels the same way about your amazing jacarandas." We sometimes walked hand in hand on Friday afternoons, under violet trees on sidewalks violet with fallen flowers. The jacaranda flowers would fall on my hair, and she would laugh as she'd reached up to pluck them out.

She smiles. "Jacarandas only flower once, in the early spring, all out. Then they fall."

I feel lost in the metaphor, and suddenly, I wonder how we even came to talk about flowers. The saltwater is sticky on my skin. I want to shower. "Do you know why I'm here?"

She laughs again, but this time her laughter is more like the cold roar of an airplane taking off from Sde Dov. "Who ratted me out? Bat Yam? Holon? Ramat Gan? Herzliya? Ramat HaSharon?"

"It doesn't really matter. What's going on?"

"You mean, aside from the paranoia of City Spirits so stuck in their conservatism, they can't accept that some places don't want to stay the same all their lives?"

I don't buy it for a second. "What's with the sudden interest in sports?"

"You'd rather the whole city develop an interest in vegging in front of the idiot box?"

"I didn't say that, but you have to calm down."

"I don't have to do anything. Look around you. Do you hear anyone complaining?"

"The Cities are complaining."

She shrugs and folds her arms on her chest. The bead bracelets on her wrists make soft, chime-like sounds. "Let them. The people are happy."

"If you keep this up, they might convene a Cities Council." That's a sort of intercity intervention, one they only do in extreme circumstances. I've been to very few of these in my lifetime. It was a decidedly unpleasant experience. "You know that any decision they reach will be binding on you."

"Let them convene a Council." She smiles again. There is no joy in her smile this time. "It'll take them too long to reach a decision anyway."

This statement reinforces my feeling that she's gotten herself mixed up in something big. Too long to reach a decision? Compared to what? For a City, time is measured in eons.

"Aviv." She stiffens as I use my pet name for her. I take two steps closer. Usually, she smells like the sea. Now she smells like a latte. Maybe because I've missed good coffee so much. I reach out to take her hand, but she pulls it back quickly. "Are you in trouble? Do you need help?"

For a moment, I see rebellion in her eyes, a challenge. Then she sighs, and suddenly looks very tired. "Go, Guardian," she says, almost officially, and turns away from me. "Leave me be." She doesn't fly away or disappear, just rolls back to the boardwalk. Her rollerblades glide easily on the sand as though it were a smooth road, but her posture is heavy, exhausted, and I suddenly think that she doesn't look athletic enough compared to all the sporty people around us. At the least, she should have been dressed like an Olympic sprinter. Another riddle. Too many riddles, and I realize that I can't leave it like that. I run after her, grab her arm. "Aviv –"

"Is this man bothering you, miss?"

The man standing on her other side is not one of those working out, but he's dressed in one of the new asymmetric tank-top fashions. I think he looks ridiculous. He's shorter than I am and has dark hair and pale, piercing eyes. I can't quite place his slight accent. I'm surprised that he could see her. And then, when I look again, I'm no longer surprised. There's something behind those piercing eyes. Power.

"No, I'm fine. Thank you." She shakes my arm off hers. "I am quite capable of dealing with harassment."

He doesn't look convinced. Looking at it from the side, I probably wouldn't have been convinced either, but I have no time for knights in shining armor right now.

"Do you mind? We're having a personal conversation here."

"I think our personal conversation is over," she snarls at me.

I want to object, but it's impossible with this strange man standing next to us and looking at me with his piercing eyes. That's the trouble with this town. People are too sensitive, bordering on nosy. When I realize he's not about to leave, I finally give up. I hadn't made any progress anyway. I have no idea what's going on.

"We're not done," I tell her.

She shrugs, indifferent, mechanical. I turn to leave. When I turn my head, half a minute later, not only has she disappeared, but he has too.

Despite her expressed wishes, I do not leave her be. I can't, not when I've been left with more questions than answers after our painful little encounter. I pace along the boardwalk, moving slowly, examining the people walking around me. What could it be? Some sort of mental disease? She sounded alright. A physical disease? What disease could have such an effect on such a powerful, immortal creature? I dig through my memories, trying to recall relevant pages from Dad's books, seeking more information, passing my hands over buildings, fences, trees, trying to find the answers she wouldn't give me, but I no longer feel the consciousness I felt in the water. She's gone, or rather, she doesn't want to communicate with me.

I go back to my car, and discover that it is covered in dust, as though it had been standing beneath a construction site. There is, of course, no construction site nearby. "Great. Very mature of you," I whisper into the air. No response. But when I open the car door, I feel eyes resting on me. On the other side of the road stands a young woman, blonde, also dressed in the strange new street fashion. Her face is noble, proud, and beautiful, her body athletic, her hair gathered on her pate in an old-fashioned hairdo. She holds a staff, maybe like they use in pole vaulting, I'm not sure. When I meet her gaze, I shiver. There is not a morsel of interest in that gaze. Only coldness, condescension, and hostility. Why is she looking at me like that? My fingers tingle. I decide to draw nearer, maybe talk to her, but as I'm about to cross the street, she suddenly speaks, and her sharp voice stops me. I don't understand the words – the language is foreign and sounds like no tongue I know. But the tone is clear. The shadow of a smile crosses her lips, and then I curse. I'm forced to stumble backward as I'm nearly trampled by what looks like a herd of wild horses. A race. The twins were right.

When the equine onslaught has passed, the noble-looking woman disappeared. More riddles.

Leaving the city, I stand at the Namir-Arlozorov intersection for another fifteen minutes, waiting for a long stream of girls to finish what looks like their light afternoon jog. No wonder there are so few cars on the streets. It's worse than gridlocks. Much worse, I think, quickly lowering my eyes, trying as best I can to ignore the bare limbs passing by me. Could some of them be naked? No, that doesn't make any sense. A trick of my incorrigible, touch-starved brain. It's been too long, and I haven't wanted anyone else since I'd been with her. I don't even know if I'll be able to be with a normal woman again. Memories float to the surface again, of soft, delicate skin like a cloud under my hands, wild hair caressing and tickling my skin like sea waves, hands with fingers as long as tree boughs, with sharp nails that would burrow into my skin when –

There's a honk from behind me – no, not a honk, a bicycle bell. I realize that the semi-nude procession of underage girls has passed, and I drive on, struggling to gather my thoughts, put the memories back in the closed, opaque box in which they were sealed. It's this damn city, these damn places. I can't be here without thinking about her.

When I finally turn down Jabotinsky Street, irate and gloomy as storm clouds, I am unsurprised to see the twins waiting for me before I even reach Ramat Gan's Abba Hillel Street. I am tempted for a moment to floor the gas pedal and be gone, but they'll just wait for me at the next light, more stubborn than before. Besides, I need them. Maybe they'll have a clue to what's going on here. But I just don't have the energy for it. I want to be alone. I want to think.

Then I notice that they're not alone. Ramat HaSharon is here, as are Bat Yam and Herzliya, and they're all pale and anxious. Something is wrong. Something happened while I was in the city.

I slow down and stop on the side of the road. Before I can even remove the key from the ignition, I am pulled out, and they swarm over me: Hands pass over my shoulders, my face, feeling me, searching for damage. I don't understand it, and I can't get a word in edgewise with the flood of questions that assails me.

"What happened?"

"Are you alright?"

"Did she do anything to you?"

"Why didn't you summon us? You know you can use the *call* when you're in danger!"

"I told you we should come with you!" Ramat Gan concludes, and before I realize what's happening, all the air is sucked out of my lungs as I am held in the terrifying grasp of a sobbing City Spirit. She has never hugged me before.

I pat Ramat Gan's back awkwardly. "Danger?" I finally manage to say.

Ramat Gan and Giv'ataim exchange glances. Herzliya doffs a wide-brimmed hat. "He doesn't know."

"Doesn't know what?"

"We couldn't get in," Ramat HaSharon looks at me with big, pretty eyes. "From the moment you entered, we couldn't follow you into the city. There was no communication. She blocked us."

"I was so worried," Ramat Gan whimpers. Giv'ataim takes a baby-blue handkerchief from her purse and hands it to Ramat Gan, who blows her nose loudly. "I couldn't stop thinking, what if something happened to you, and we sent you there…"

"I was worried that you haven't bothered to spawn a few children before that lunatic murders you and scatters your pieces to the pigeons in Dizengoff Square," says Bat Yam, and the smoke from her cigarette stings my eyes. I sense the hidden anxiety behind her casual cynicism.

"I'm fine, girls, really." Their concern is touching. I smile at them, a smile that I hope is soothing. "She didn't do anything to me. We just talked." But my thoughts are racing, searching, groping. She didn't let them in. Why? A Spirit needs to invest tremendous efforts into putting up such a barrier. Even her. Maybe that's why she looked tired? But why would she block them in the first place? She didn't even know I had entered the city until much later. And that, of course, is another mystery. The absence of a five-fingered maple leaf should change nothing. Cities always know it when I arrive. They are attuned to me. Their response time once I cross the city limits ranges from one minute to five. The last time it took a city spirit so long to acknowledge my presence was in Kiryat Shmona when she was under a Katyusha barrage. I came to see if I could help and found her only two and a half hours later, playing her guitar for a bunch of kids in one of the bomb shelters. War with Lebanon. That's what it took for her not to notice me for hours. But there's no war in Tel Aviv.

"Did you talk?" Ramat HaSharon blinks, long lashes touching pink cheeks. "For five hours?"

"What did you talk about?" Herzliya is curious.

"Was she prepared to listen?" Giv'ataim adds.

"What did she say about the trees in the park?" Ramat Gan plucks at my sleeve.

I stop them again with a raised hand. "Girls, I'll tell you everything, but right now I'm tired, hungry, thirsty, and sticky from the sea."

"She tried to drown you?" Bat Yam growls. "That's my job!"

"Let's go to my place," Giv'ataim suggests. "Holmes Place has a spa and a shower. And a coffee shop."

"You're kidding," Herzliya looks highly derisive. "We're going to the marina."

"The marina!" Ramat HaSharon pulls a perfect lock of blond hair around a manicured finger. "He wants food, not junk!"

"*Yalla-yalla*," Bat Yam makes a rude hand gesture. "Come on! He doesn't need your fancy-ass food. I have a gyro stall, the freshest —"

"Girls!" It's always like this when there's more than one of them. I don't like the attention, but I usually try to take it kindly. It's just that right now, I really am too tired, and I need time to think. I need quiet so that my head will stop hurting. They comply with my unstated request and fall silent, waiting for me to decide. But I can only think of one thing right now. I want a latte, the kind I can get only in the city I've left behind. I settle for the next best thing. "Can one of you get me instant coffee?"

Ramat Gan lifts a cup of coffee in hands that were empty until a second ago. It's a latte, in a clear, tall glass, a wonderful brown with creamy soft foam on top. I stare at her.

"I have cafes too, you know," she spits. "How many sugars?"

"Uh… two."

She passes a hand over the cup and then hands it to me. I sip and close my eyes for a moment. Perfect. At least, more perfect than any I've had in the past eight months. I've underestimated her.

"We're going to the place that serves this coffee," I finally decide. "Come on, let's go."

I WAKE UP ALONE ON CLEAN, soft, scented white sheets, in a bed I don't remember going to sleep in. I sit up and look around the luxurious room. A deluxe suite, no doubt, although it's hard to see much in the meager sunlight sneaking in through the elegant curtains. I try to understand what woke me, and I decide that it was my nose. The smells of pancakes, omelets, freshly squeezed orange juice, and coffee are coming from the door. I turn my head. Ramat Gan is standing at the doorway, holding a trayful of goodness. "Good morning!" she greets me, as cheerful as I've seen her in a long while. She's more of a businesswoman than an art student now, in her starched skirt, collared shirt, and pumps, her hair fashionably coiffured. However, the strawberry glasses are still resting on her head, and her lips are painted blue, as though she'd just licked a grape icicle. Around her neck, there is something that could be a scarf, but it looks more like a boy scout's tie.

She approaches with the tray. A low table moves on its own from the center of the room to my bed. She lays the tray on it and beams a sunny smile at me. "How did you sleep?"

I blink at her grouchily. "How did I end up here?"

"You were tired, and we wouldn't let you drive home, remember? Here was the closest."

A vague memory of last night begins to return to me. The conversation was long, heated, and exhausting. They came and went several times because of incidents requiring their attention within their own limits, so that I had to repeat the story of my meeting with Tel Aviv several times. The repetitions drained me and wore down my defenses until I became less and less successful at omitting the personal details. They argued a lot, raising theories, some of which were more far-fetched than the others. They passed on broken telephone messages to Cities that hadn't attended the meeting and debated whether to convene a Cities Council and what sanctions to lay against the rogue City that was disturbing all their lives. I didn't know what to tell them. I could only try to calm the Spirits, pun intended, which was more like trying to redirect a tornado with a vacuum cleaner. No wonder I was tired.

"Where is here?" I ask.

The curtain is pulled back by an invisible hand, and the sun burns my eyelids for a moment before I adjust to the light.

"Leonardo City Tower," she replies proudly. "Want a massage while you're here? Spa? Pedicure?"

"No, thanks," I grimace. They know I don't like to sleep over at any of them. Over-pampering is one of the reasons. Aviv didn't treat me like this. Maybe that's why I could live with her.

I lift the blanket and notice that I'm only wearing my boxers. My clothes lie on the chair beside me, dry-cleaned and ironed. I look at them, then at her.

"Good as new," she beams at me. "Drink your latte. It's getting cold."

Despite my grouching and bitching, I feel much better as I hit the road and head back east, in clean clothes, with a full stomach and not feeling tired, for a change. And now that I finally feel good physically, I begin to worry about her again. I shouldn't have left. I should have insisted. She would have told me eventually what happened. I want to go back, but the others made me promise I wouldn't return without backup, and anyway, there's no point in going back, not until I find out something that will help me. Whatever the problem is with Tel Aviv, it's evident that none of the Dan Region's younger Cities have a clue. I need someone more experienced.

I intend to go to Jerusalem, then to Jericho, and if that won't help – to Acre, or Safed, or Tiberias. But I am deep in thought, and I continue on Route 1 all the way and then turn right, passing by Jericho without stopping. When I look at the road again, I have no idea where I am, embarrassing for a City Guardian. I could turn on the GPS – it might even work. Instead, I examine the road closely. I didn't just happen to leave the main road. I know this place. I've been here before, on one of my endless road trips with my father. It's an old, forsaken side road. No one is on it but me, and there's something gloomy about it, foreboding even. I don't remember what awaits me at the end of it, but I've long since learned to trust my instincts, especially when I don't understand them.

Near Mount Sodom, I slow down. Yes, I've been here before. Long ago. I now remember this road, but I was much shorter and could hardly see it over the dashboard. I was maybe six or seven. I sat in the passenger's side, seat belt buckled up, looking at Dad with admiration as he drove the red car that the roads always opened for. He took me to play in a different city each day, on a different beach, in a different park, a different sea. Wherever we went, there was always tasty food and a warm bed awaiting us, and nice aunties who gave me strange gifts… pebbles, flowers, vials of fragrant water. I neither knew nor wanted any other life. Eventually, he did make me go to school, a year or two later, when he realized he couldn't teach me everything himself. But at that point, it was still just the two of us in the world, and I thought we were going on just another adventure. I didn't know. He stroked my head. "I'm sorry," he said. "Maybe the others were right. Maybe you're too young. But you have to meet her. You have to understand."

The mental pull comes without warning, powerful, blunt, invading my thoughts as though they were her own. I struggle, but I don't really have a chance, and within seconds my hands clench the steering wheel of their own volition, pulling the car sharply to the right. For one long moment of panic, I'm on a collision course with one of the salt hills. But then I regain control, and I pull back left and hit the brakes hard. The car stops. My hands shake on the wheel. The pull was invasive, rude even. I knew they could do such things – they do it to other people quite a lot. But most of the time, other people don't feel it, and in any case, they've never done it to me. I struggle to catch my breath. When I finally manage to trust my legs and get out of the car, I see where I was pulled, and almost lose my balance. The sinkhole is deep, over thirty feet, invisible from the road. The fall would have killed me.

On a salt hill, in the middle of the nowhere we're in, sits a bony old woman wrapped in black, a rope holding an antiquated dress around her hips. She smiles toothlessly at me, and although the memory is distant and hazy, I know it's her I've come to meet. "Welcome, O Watcher of Places," she says, and the Hebrew on her lips has an ancient, unidentifiable accent, extinct for thousands of years.

"Hello, Sodom," I mumble, a bit embarrassed. I prefer City Guardian. It sounds less bombastic, but I wouldn't dream of correcting her.

"Thou hast finally come back to visit my domains," she gestures around her, and I look around at the empty, dry, barren salt hills, thinking to myself, as I did at age six, that she's completely mad. I feel the need to say something more.

"Thanks for saving me."

She nods. "Those sinkholes hardly ever claim the lives of humans. Most of you find your demise in the big cities, by the venom of the asphalt snakes."

It sounds so ludicrous that I struggle not to laugh, although technically speaking, she's right. With the wave of a hand, she invites me to sit on the hill across from her. "Please, be seated and feast."

A clay bowl rises from the hill in front of me. It is full of coarse salt. I stare at it for a moment, but I don't want to be rude, so I simply sit on the hill, pick up a pinch of salt in my hand and place it on my tongue.

"Uh… thanks." I move uncomfortably on the salt hill, and it scratches me through my jeans. "Do you know what's happening?"

She nods. "Great portents. The mountains whisper of it. But methinks thou hast not come thus far to bear tidings of the coast cities."

"I wanted to talk with you," I clench my hand on the salt, and the coarse grains lacerate it, "about the guardian who left you."

Her amber eyes grow hard. A deep sound, like thunder emanating from the ground, rolls around us, and for a moment, I'm afraid that a sinkhole is about to open its maw right under the hill we're sitting on.

"Certain was I that when we had this talk, thou wouldst present thy son to me."

I blink. "I have no son."

"Then what other cause might there be for thy arrival?" She studies me from head to toe. "For that is how you caution your children not to forsake your duty, your Cities. Through me."

I feel the tips of my ears burning, but she's right. That was why Dad brought me here. And it had worked. At least, I thought it had worked. After the events of the past couple of days, I'm no longer so sure.

"Your Guardian," I try again. "Why did he leave you?"

And then she does something I didn't expect – she smiles. "We had carnal knowledge for a brief but joyous time." The smile disappears. "As the time passed, that touched upon his face and his hair and his eyes, yet left me unscathed, he found love hard to bear. For me, it had no meaning, but he began to begrudge me my immortality. One day, he simply ceased coming. A City cannot survive without its Watcher."

My heart is cold in my chest, like the knots of a maple tree's roots frozen under layers of ice. And yet, I knew. That's why I came here.

"And he didn't return when…"

"When the overthrow began?" She shook her head. "I tried to summon him, to call him onto me, but I failed. The others, likewise, tried in vain. We only knew that he had left for Assyria and meant never to return."

"Maybe something happened to him."

She shook her head. "Had he been gathered onto his forefathers, we would have known it. He wished not to come back."

Like me. I lower my head to my bent knees and bury my face in my hands. We were together for two years, and even before that, since Dad died, I would visit the City weekly. It had been almost eight months since we broke up, and until yesterday, I haven't entered her limits once. Even if I had to go from Holon on one side to Herzliya on the other, I would circumvent Tel Aviv by taking Highway 4. I'd do anything not to find myself inside, anything not to deal with my petty, ridiculous, human embarrassment. And without asking her even once how she's doing, without thinking that she might need me, need her City Guardian.

"It's all my fault," I'm surprised to hear how choked my voice sounds. Her laughter echoes off the hills, bony, rich, grating. "Watcher of Places, I doubt thou canst have such power over her."

"You don't understand," I whisper. "I deserted her."

"How so? Thou didst not forsake Canaan." She still refers to Israel as Canaan. It almost makes me laugh. "Thou didst not turn thy back upon her. She can still touch thee from afar. Is that not all that is needed of you to do thy duty as it should be?"

"But we… she and I…" I swallow. I know that many of them know, or at least have guessed, but I've never admitted it to any of them.

She laughs again. This time the laughter sounds ancient. The salt in the air constricts my throat further. "Thou art not the first, Watcher of Places."

"I know, that's why I'm saying –"

"Nor the second." I raise my eyes and look at her. Her eyes, still as sharp as ever behind the locks of hair falling over her face, glint at me. "Hast thou ever wondered, Watcher, why the Spirits are always women, whereas the Watchers of Places are always men?"

My mind refuses to understand what she's saying, and for a moment, I simply stare at her, my mouth agape.

"You, the Watchers of Places, are almost the only humans who can know us, remember us, speak with us. Your lives are devoted to counseling us, to caring for us. From the dawn of time, deeper relations were part of this cycle."

"Relations…?" I echo her words. "You mean to tell me that my family tree includes…"

"Spirits of Places," she completes. "As I said, thou wast not the first, nor the second."

I exhale, surprised to find that my hands are trembling. She is old. Ancient. Maybe she doesn't know what she's talking about. I force my skittering thoughts to focus on the problem for which I'd come here. I could investigate this matter more deeply later. "And why do you think whatever she's going through has nothing to do with me?"

She brushes away salt with the tip of her bare foot. "The coercion of one City upon another is not among the things thou hast the power to prevent, Watcher of Places."

"Coercion?" I echo.

"Of course. Certain was I that thou shalt know. For thou hast met her." Her eyes turn to me, and I feel her again in my head. It's nothing like the soft, intimate, almost imperceptible pull of Tel Aviv. The touch is coarse, almost burning on the edges of my awareness. It wasn't meant to hurt – it was more like an old woman hurting your ears when she yells because she can't hear well. My most recent memories are pulled out, one by one, like tissues from a box. She stops at the proud blonde woman with the straight nose and the upturned chin.

"Her? A City Spirit?" I almost fall over. "That's impossible. I would have felt it."

"Methinks that thou wouldst be hard-pressed to feel Cities that are not thine own."

"Not mine?" I whisper. I recall the strange language spoken by the woman – I mean, the Spirit. I'm supposed to understand them, no matter what language they speak. "Do you know who she is?"

She shakes her head. "She comes from foreign lands, not from our soil, and she is ancient. Close to mine own time, it would seem. Her power and constancy hint that there is another Watcher of Places with her."

A face flashes in my mind. The man on the beach. The one who spoke so freely with my Tel Aviv, who in turn wasn't surprised at his presence. The one who vanished when she did.

Sodom nods, still tapped into my memories. "Of him it is that thou must beware, Watcher of Places, and not of her."

"Why?"

"Spirits are not evil by nature. Humans may be."

Great. A foreign City Guardian with patently hostile intentions and a City Spirit strong enough to take over Tel Aviv, and who has shown clearly that she doesn't like me. And I can't even use the *call* to talk to her. I don't know what name to *call*. Who knows if she'll even understand me?

Sodom senses my despair. I hear the dry salt rustle, and then a wrinkled hand lies on my shoulder. "The Council of Cities may be able to stop her."

Unlikely. They don't know who they're dealing with. How can you go to war without knowing your enemy? "If only I had a name to give her…"

"Did Tel Aviv try to hint aught to you in your brief encounter?"

I think, scrolling through the conversation in my head. Tel Aviv didn't act as though she was in distress. She looked uncharacteristically tired, but no more. If she had feared for my safety, she would have quickly sent me away rather than talk about flowers and maple leaves. If she needed my help, she had twenty verbal and non-verbal ways to convey it, more than any other City. I knew every muscle, every nerve in her face and body. I knew the meaning of every twitch of her lips or raised eyebrow, of the slightest motion of her fingers. Was she too proud to ask for help, or was she protecting me?

"Let the others take care of her, Watcher of Places," Sodom is still gripping my shoulder, and I don't know if she's reading my thoughts or deducing them from my expression. "The coercion has been going on for many months. They need only to search for telltale signs that would reveal the name of that other City."

"Telltale signs?"

She nods. "Tel Aviv is a city of cultural life, letters, erudition, society, and art. The foreign City needed to replace these in her own ways. All that is needed to know of a City's identity can be learnt from its arts." Her face grows dour, and her eyes turn hazy once again, ancient stone structures reflected in them.

Her hand rests on my shoulder, wrinkled and fragile. I hold it in my own. Her eyes focus on me again.

She smiles, and the Dead Sea in its entirety present in her smile. "Do not make a promise thou canst not keep, Watcher."

"I made no promise."

"But thou wert about to do so."

I say nothing but swear to myself that I will come to revisit her, even before I have a son, and I don't care if the others think she's a crazy old hag. She, too, is a City of mine, even if she no longer has a city.

"Do not put thyself in harm's way, Watcher of Places," she asks of me again. Her thick brows shade her eyes. "They can cope with it without thy intervention. Cities' wars are dangerous to humans. We would all fain lose a sister-city than a Watcher." Had I not encountered this attitude from the others as well, I would have thought it ludicrous. But I can't stay out of this. The foreign City, whoever she is, won't let them in. Maybe together, they can break the barrier, but it would take immense efforts, which would mean an all-out bloody war. I can't let that happen. Sodom is wrong. The takeover may not be my fault, but had I been more attentive, more caring, less preoccupied with my own embarrassment and discomfort, perhaps I could have prevented this. Had I not avoided Tel Aviv like the plague over the past few months, I would have seen it earlier. I would have noticed. I could have helped.

But I intend to help now.

NONE OF THEM BOTHER to receive me as I enter the Dan Region, even though I sense the presence of many of them, crowded, overloaded, like a hum between the streets and the roads. I don't remember the last time so many of them left their limits. My conclusion is clear: I'm returning into a war council.

A Cities Council is a complicated matter. I'm invited to observe and advise, but I can't interfere in their decisions, be they as they may. They made sure to leave clear road signs for me, leading to the astronomical observatory in Giv'ataim, a place from which you can look out. Spy. When I enter the little chamber at the top of the tower, they are, of course, deep in a loud, tumultuous dispute. I sometimes suspect they enjoy fighting. I shouldn't have hurried back. Customary councils last between a week and a month and a half on average, in rotating shifts, so they can each get back to their various cities for at least a few hours a day.

A war council can last two, three months, or more. Time is meaningless to immortal Spirits. This will show in the war as well, if it comes. A city war can last for months, even years. I've never been present in such a war, but my father taught me about them. I'm not sure what shape the war would take. If we were in ancient times, they would have led an army to her gates, but we're not, and armies are a tiny part of modern city wars. Trade, industry, art, culture, traffic, construction, animals, maybe even weather – they could fight her in dozens of ways that would hurt all sides, particularly the residents.

I manage to halt the argument for long enough to tell them what Sodom had said. Bat Yam lets loose with a salty expletive. Ramat HaSharon rolls her eyes. "Oh, come on, do you believe that insane old bat?"

"Yes," I say as I glance from one to the next. They don't have to believe Sodom, but they still believe in me. "I believe another city is trying to take over Tel Aviv."

Raanana bites her lower lip. "Then we have an even better cause to go to war."

"Will you try to stop us?" Rishon LeZion asks. It seems like the T-Rex on her T-shirt is snapping its claws.

"No." I take a deep breath. "On the contrary. I'm going to help you."

It takes me a long time to convince them. They really don't want to let me enter the city without their protection, but they finally relent, muttering and complaining all the while. I suppose the only reason they don't keep arguing for weeks is that the more time goes by, the more Tel Aviv slips out of our reach. Some may not be mad about her, but they like her presumptive replacement even less, whoever she is. She has successfully blocked five strong cities from entering her limits and has done this with skill and talent, without provoking immediate war, without causing mass hysteria. She's a pro. She knows exactly who they are and how to prevent them from entering, and we don't know anything about her. She has an enormous advantage over us. Our only advantage over her, right now, is me. She doesn't know me, and I hope our brief encounter near the beach didn't leave enough of an impression for her to know when I enter the city. If I can discover who she is, maybe that information will help us understand her, communicate with her. And if she leaves us no choice, we could attack her in a more focused and less destructive way.

They all insist on waiting at the city limits to begin the attack with full force as soon as needed, so I can summon them if I find myself in trouble. I'm not sure I'll be able to make the *call* work through the foreign city's shield, but I keep my doubts to myself and agree.

Over the next few hours, they begin to arrive, one by one. Rehovot, in overalls, her hands dirty with soil, flowers threaded in her hair. Tiberias, with sleeves a tad longer than Bnei Brak and a skirt a tad shorter. Haifa, in jeans, flowers from the world-famous Baha'i Gardens in her hair, and a navy T-shirt. Nahariya, with her nose, lips, and eyebrows pierced, surrounded by a gang of kibbutz and moshav Spirits. Maccabim-Reut, true twins, not like Ramat Gan and Giv'ataim, in IDF officer uniforms, carrying assault rifles. Beersheba, tanned, sunburned hair under a military beret, her face constantly changing from young to very old and back. Netanya, a bit intimidating in her leather clothes and gold chains, despite the coquettish beret on her head. Mitzpe Ramon, with her fisherman pants, Source sandals, and sparkling eyes that reflect the stars even in broad daylight. Eilat, dressed as a hotel maid, with long, thick dreadlocks and skinny braids interspersed with corals and dolphin ankle bracelets.

I pass my gaze over them all while they get ready, exchanging hushed words, making final arrangements. When they're done with me, I'm wearing shorts, a running tank top, and a cap. I've never been the sporty type, and I'm glad I have no mirror to look at because I'm sure I look ridiculous. Ramat Gan and Ramat HaSharon giggle together like a pair of teenagers. I leave my car at the observatory and board a bus heading into the city. My body is tense, primed, expecting an assault at any moment, but the bus calmly passes by the bicycle riders and the horse riders, the runners and the athletes. I press against the window, trying not to miss a single detail along the way, anything to help me understand, decipher. There's a small gathering near Ichilov Hospital, where a tall, imposing nurse receives babies from a long line of couples and places them in an oversized playpen. The couples leave without their children. Before I have time to ponder the situation, the bus drives on, stopping in front of the Tel Aviv Museum of Art and the Beit Ariela Library. That's my cue to get off. Look for the arts, Sodom had said.

I barely recognize the enormous square, which is packed with people. The sculptures of birds and mechanical instruments, which I'd always found slightly disturbing, have been replaced by gorgeous stone and marble statues, some with their hands cut off, and I thread my way through the crowd to take a closer look. The last time I'd seen such sculptures was during my trip around the world with Matthew. I recognize the statues as figures from Greek mythology: Artemis, Heracles, Achilles. By my side, two young women in tank tops and short shorts are staring at the statues. When they touch one of them admiringly, I sense that what they truly want to do is get down on their knees and kowtow in front of it. And then I understand.

Like on the way to Sodom, I feel that here, too, I actually knew the answer. How could I not? The obsessive engagement in sports, the alarming number of soldiers everywhere, the babies abandoned at the hospital, the statues, even the naked girls running down Namir Road, now free of its usual intercity congestion. I only needed to look.

"Sparta."

I don't use the *call* as much as say the word, but it doesn't matter. A sharp shiver runs through me, and something cold and sharp presses against the back of my neck, forcing me to turn around. There she stands, proud, like an ancient marble sculpture that's come to life. She's wearing a traditional white Greek dress hanging off one shoulder. Her blond hair is now unbound, and it falls around her shoulders in waves. She's standing erect in a racing chariot harnessed to three white horses. I almost expect to see a gryphon or a hydra behind her. The drama is a little ludicrous – City Spirits of our time would never let themselves go that far, but I see no humor in the situation. I feel danger. Her proud, cold eyes focus on me. Her staff has sharpened edges, and one of them rests on my throat now. The slightest movement, and she'll draw blood. I raise my empty hands in a gesture of surrender. "Please," I say. "I just want to talk."

She says a few words in a language I can only guess is ancient Greek. I can't understand her, but I concentrate, trying to communicate on a higher, mental level. I'm not very good at it – I haven't had much reason to try communicating like that till today, and usually, the Spirits are the ones controlling the interaction, not me. I can only sense basic emotions floating behind her words, and she makes no effort to help me understand them or hide them from me. Behind her proud façade, I sense rage rising like a tidal wave as she looks at me as though the very fact of my presence within the limits of Tel Aviv is a terrible insult to her. Why? What is she so mad about?

"Wait, please," I repeat, but she has already dismounted the chariot and is walking toward me in slow, measured steps. She has no cause for hurry. I leap around one of the bronze statues and run across the street, dodging two buses and a horse, try to circle back, but she's quicker than me. She traps me against the wall of the IDF headquarters compound, looking at me through narrowed eyes as she approaches. The rage she radiates now has a strong scent of victory, and a slight taste of bloodlust. I suppress a shiver. "I'm a City Guardian," I try again, struggling to keep my voice from betraying the terror I feel. "You're a City Spirit. We have no reason to hurt each other." She shows no sign of comprehension and keeps moving forward, her pale eyes icy and merciless. A sword is drawn from a scabbard on her back. She lifts it –

And then I hear terrible Hasidic music in high volume, and a van full of Breslov Hasidim flies down the street, blocking her path. The Breslovers get out of the van and start to dance. I stare at them. For a moment, it seems like an exceedingly stupid choice, but she doesn't know how to deal with these strange creatures, and the music confuses her. She quickly refocuses, but then a refreshing breeze carrying a sea scent caresses my sweaty face, and Tel Aviv is standing on top of the van, looking at Sparta with narrowed eyes. She holds the scabbard of a toy sword in her hand. "Are you out of your mind??" she bares her teeth at the other City. "I told you he was off-limits!"

Sparta replies in a stream of words in ancient Greek, in an equally furious tone. Tel Aviv lifts her arms in despair. "Mago!" she yells, "Where are you? You promised to teach her to speak a normal language!"

Sparta says a few more words. Tel Aviv shakes her head and rolls her eyes. "No comprendo, stupido! You want this city? Learn Hebrew, Arabic, English, French, Russian, Spanish…"

"Aviv…" I try.

"And you, be quiet!" Her eyes burn as she turns to look at me. "I told you to leave and not come back! How big an idiot –"

"Watch out!" I scream.

She spins around just in time. Sparta's sharp sword crashes into the gleaming blade drawn from Tel Aviv's toy scabbard. Somehow, the plastic is strong enough to stop the blow, but some mechanism makes a scraping noise, and the gleaming blue light beneath the toy blade malfunctions and vanishes.

"A lightsaber? You're fighting her with a lightsaber?" I stare at her. She swings the toy in a way that makes sure we're both doomed.

"Fencing is not exactly my strong suit!" she shoots at me. "If you have better ideas, I'll be glad to hear them!" The plastic breaks with the next blow, and she leaps from the van and lands by my side. Sparta's blade strikes, nearly cutting the van in half. Tel Aviv pushes me behind her, toward Ibn Gabirol, and spurs me into a fast run. Sparta whistles for her horses, and I hear hoofbeats behind me.

"Will you get the hell out of here already?" Tel Aviv yells at me. "I have more important things to do with my time than protect you from this maniac!"

The revelation is so surprising that I stop, and she slams into me, still seething with anger. She's not fighting Sparta for herself. She's fighting her for me. And she's fighting well, as an equal, not as a City who has lost the ability to control her streets, her residents, her limits. "You agreed for her to take your place?"

"None of your business!" She kicks my feet, and I fall just as an immense stone ball whistles past where my head just was. Patrol cars speed around us, separating us from Sparta. The horses stop, confused by the red and blue flashing lights. Sparta smiles at us coldly from her chariot. The movement of troops around us increases. My city spirit's face is dark.

"The police are still mine," she says, "but the army is already hers."

As though by signal, the heads of all the soldiers turn to us, like thousands of marionettes moving in complete unison. I freeze. They're all wearing combat unit berets and carrying arms. They cock them in such perfect harmony that I hear only one clack. The policemen around us also respond by cocking their weapons, and someone rattles on a megaphone, warning the soldiers to stand back.

"All these people will die," I whisper.

"Not if I have anything to do with it," she replies. Her gaze locks on Sparta's, and her body slowly levitates. She moves her hands around. An enormous flock of pigeons passes by us, lands on the shoulders of those present, and covers them with droppings. Alley cats leap from the trees, scratching people's faces. Bats fly, despite the heat and the light, smashing into heads and arms and shoulders. Cries of disgust come from every direction. Sparta, the only one to somehow remain clean, advances upon us resolutely. More stone balls are shot, enormous in size, and I suddenly realize that catapults and trebuchets are looming over the walls of the IDF's headquarters. Tel Aviv reaches the same realization, and when the next ball is fired, engulfed in flames this time, she flies down to me, like the Phantom of the Opera, pale and beautiful. I reach out, and she snatches me off the ground. My weight doesn't shift her even slightly off course. She presses me to her, and for a moment, I feel safe and secure in her embrace, but then my breath gets choked as a few javelins, discuses, and shot-put balls are hurled at us. She looks down and grimaces. We've outdistanced the catapults, but the soldiers are running after us. Concentration creases form between her eyes. An absolute mayhem of people bursts from the streets, disrupting the orderly columns of soldiers. Hipsters in a headphone party dance on the pedestrian crossing. A bunch of freaky kids from Dizengoff Square arrives from the other end, playing blaring music. From the direction of Rabin Square, demonstrators stream in carrying signs, yelling social justice slogans. From the south end of Ibn Gabirol, a procession of people dressed as zombies – blood, torn clothing, the works – stumble along, pretending to attack the soldiers, who look uneasy and confused. Aviv takes advantage of the confusion below us to soar higher, her hair flapping around, whipping my face. Within seconds, I'm gaping at a view that's usually reserved for those traveling by aircraft. I regret all the times she offered to take me flying and I refused. The view is breathtaking.

She moves away from midtown and flies toward the Yarkon Park. She stalls for a moment, catching her breath, and I know she can't keep this up for long. The clouds are very close above us. The sun is hotter here, and I feel a sudden stillness in the air. "Why did you come back here?" she mumbles, looking at me. She's breathing heavily, her chest rising and falling rhythmically, her hair floating like a halo around her flushed cheeks. I think how beautiful she is. "Couldn't you just leave me alone?"

"I'm a City Guardian. It's my job." This is not how I wanted to have this conversation, hundreds of feet in the air, fleeing an insane ancient city. "I can't let you make such a mistake because of me."

"Because of you?" Her eyes widen and then narrow. I can see the anger in the slight motion of the brows, and for a split second, I think she's about to drop me. "You think I want to leave this place because of you? How arrogant, conceited, lacking any self-awa—"

"So you admit you want to leave," I cut her off.

More stone and fire projectiles pass by us before she can reply. We're not as high up as we were a moment ago. Where is Sparta attacking us from? City Hall? Aviv renews her flight, but I can still see the anger in her eyes. "What am I going to do with you?" she asks, of herself more than me, panting with the effort of keeping us both in the air, far from Sparta's artillery range. "How am I going to get you out of this mess?"

Conflicting emotions rise within me. Warmth in response to her efforts, anger at her behavior, and a touch of damaged ego. "You can drop me off at any of your limits. I'll manage."

"I can't," she sighs. "I can't fly with you to the limits."

I blink. Limits aren't meant to matter much. I mean, yes, they're stronger within their boundaries and grow weaker the further they move away, but that shouldn't have any impact on simple flying, even when carrying another person. She's growing weaker. I notice that now.

The shots get closer and closer. She shrieks in terror and shields me with her body as a few more pass a hair's breadth away from us. She grabs a javelin just before it pierces my heart, and we're both hyperventilating with fear now. The javelin seems alien in her hand. She looks at it for a moment, maybe considering hurling it back, but then passes. It falls from her hand and pierces a parasol on a residential roof below us.

How long can she hold out? Sparta is a trained warrior, from times when battles were routine and a source of pride. My Tel Aviv has taken some sniper fire in the War of Independence, and since then has practiced mainly in PlayStation battles. She has too many pacifists, desk jockey soldiers who haven't held a gun since basic training, and high-tech geeks. This is not a fair fight. It's a joke.

I notice that we're descending toward the park. "What are you doing?"

"I need to distract her, so you'll have enough time to escape," she says.

"And what about you? You need to come with me. Get out of the limits. The others can —"

"No." She raises her chin in defiant pride. "It's still my city, part of it anyway. I mean to take care of this. I just need to find Mago."

"Her Guardian?" I glare at her. "You really think he's not part of this?"

"I told you, I'll take care of this." She lands me on a pedestrian bridge and runs a hand through her hair, thinking feverishly. "Do you still ride a bicycle?"

"I haven't had much opportunity," I admit.

"You will now." She runs a hand across my forehead, a fleeting, almost caressing touch, and my consciousness is flooded with images. "You need to get lost. She may know about war, but she doesn't know about streets. She doesn't know the city like I do."

I try to concentrate on the rapidly incoming images. I see what she wants me to do. There's a municipal rent-a-bike stand at the park's edge, and a warren of alleys and little streets beyond it. If I go by the route she outlined, I'll be in Ramat Gan within minutes. But I still have to get to the stand itself. I suspect there will be an impressive Spartan contingent among the runners on the park lanes.

She nods, still mentally linked to me. "I didn't mean for you to run."

"So what did you mean? I can't fly without you," I remind her.

Her eyes flash to the Yarkon river below us.

"What? No, no!" I protest. "That's the filthiest, most repugnant, disgusting water —"

"Stop being a baby! For your information, the Mayor himself swam in it earlier this year."

"Before or after he got inoculated?"

"This is the best way. Do you trust me?" she asks.

I nod, albeit with some reluctance. I feel the need to tell her something else. "Aviv…" she waits. Catapult shots whistle in the distance, growing nearer. We have no time. "Be careful, okay?"

She removes her hand from my brow, and even after all this time, my heart skips a beat when she smiles at me. "Close your eyes and hold your nose."

I do so, and she drops me into the Yarkon.

Sickening green water surrounds me, and although my mouth is closed and my nose is held tight, it feels like it's filling every pore in my body. Whenever I'd complain about the pollution of the Yarkon, she'd take pride in it. She'd say that there were enough places for bathing on the beach, but the people themselves, with their waste disposal, chose for the Yarkon to support only the most resilient of aquatic life forms. They didn't want to bathe in it. They just wanted to look at it from afar, green and mysterious.

But now the water clears, and I can almost feel the change as I open my eyes. I don't think she cleaned the river – maybe just the spot where the water is carrying me. The river isn't deep at this spot. I dare to look up. Rocks, javelins, discuses, and iron balls roar over my head. Just as I realize that I'll have to surface soon to breathe, something large and round approaches me, closing over my head before I can flinch away.

It's an air bubble, three times larger than my head. Astounded, I take a large gulp of air. I didn't know she could do such things. Air under water, decontaminating spots in the river – which I'm pretty sure is carrying me right now against the currents. How much energy is she putting into letting me escape? I feel a stab of guilt. If Sparta manages to hurt her because of me…

I try not to move, let the water carry me to the bank near the Bavli neighborhood. I come to a halt for a moment, hunching over to catch my breath. And then I run for a few dozen yards until I see the rent-a-bike stand. One of the bicycles comes loose. I climb on it and start pedaling with all my strength. I'm wet, and my feet slip on the pedals a few times, but finally, I find my hold and maintain a rapid pace. I must look ridiculous, but that doesn't matter. I just need to get out, give the information to the others. Sparta is a well-known city. There's plenty of research about her. She has weaknesses. There are things she doesn't know. We just have to find them.

I fly through the maze of alleys. There's no chance I'd find my way here without her guidance. The streets around me are silent, but in midtown, fireworks suddenly burst in the sky in a myriad of shapes and colors. Smart lady. They are harmless, of course, but Sparta won't know that. I hear gunshots, screams and shouts, more catapult missiles whistling. How many people have already died in this conflict? How will the media explain it? I can already see the Halacha interchange, and beyond it, Ramat Gan's Diamond Exchange buildings. I'll be safe in a few minutes.

"Guardian!"

The voice makes me hit the brakes hard. I lower a foot to the ground to balance myself and turn around. He's standing there, the man, the Guardian – Mago, I remember she called him. He's dressed in the same odd way he was the last time we'd met – a classical-era fretworked tunic, I finally realize. And now I also recognize the power in the piercing pale eyes. Yes, he's a City Guardian. He has the same energy that Matthew did – and myself, I guess – but heavier, almost ancient. How long has he been Sparta's City Guardian? How did he even become the Guardian of a City that's been extinct for so long?

"We have to talk, urgently, before our Cities kill each other," he says, and despite the slight accent in his voice, I am surprised at how good his Hebrew is. It takes me a moment to comprehend the words he says, and then I'm even more surprised.

"I thought that's what you wanted," I say, and my hand tightens on the bicycle handlebar.

"A City war? No one wants that," his lips purse. "Especially with all your other Cities lying in ambush outside the city, waiting to destroy mine once she's not strong enough to maintain the barrier. How did you persuade them to intervene in this?"

I don't understand the question. Since when do Cities need persuasion to interfere in each other's affairs? Most of the time, I need to keep them from poking their noses in the others' business, not vice versa. And this time, they're all fully justified interfering. Sparta is causing havoc for them, too.

"They don't want to destroy her," I say. "They want to stop her, and rightly so."

"Why?" he asks, and I blink. "Your City wants to leave, Guardian. She's unhappy."

Again, guilt, looking at me with big, beautiful eyes whose color changes from sea-blue to Yarkon-green to asphalt-gray, and with simpler, brown eyes; my father's. He would never have neglected one of his places, ever. If the Spirit of a city, village, kibbutz, or ninety-soul hamlet wanted to leave, he'd know about it.

"My city is willing to take her place," Mago continues. "Sparta is a good City. A bit combative, perhaps, but with plenty of experience in managing large, complex cities. And she wants so badly to be responsible for a city again. She'll do an excellent job here."

"I'm sure," I say, although I'm not sure at all. "But this place belongs to Tel Aviv. Nothing good ever came from a Place Spirit who ran away."

"She doesn't want to run away," says Mago. In the distance, the last fireworks fade from the sky in a whirl of colors. For a moment, silence ensues. Then the catapults resume. "She wants to leave in a responsible, controlled manner. We've been in the process of transferring control for almost six months."

Six months. My stomach turns. Six months, and not a word. No hint of what she was planning to do. Where did she intend to go? Would she have even bothered to say goodbye? Would she have disappeared, and I'd never have seen her again? A lump of insult and pain coagulates in my throat. Why didn't she say anything?

"She didn't want to tell you anything," says Mago, guessing the significance of my expression. "She convinced me it would be the right thing for both of them."

"But…" my thoughts run in all directions, turning upside down. "If the process is agreeable to both sides, why did Sparta attack me?"

He sighs. "I've warned her about this before. She sees things differently than we do. In her time, a city was a city-state, a polis. Each of them had their own City Guardian, and they were at war all the time. One city's Guardian would never enter another's territory unless his city wanted to declare war." He stops for a moment. "I wanted your first meeting to be… in more relaxed circumstances. I meant to ask Tel Aviv to arrange a meeting between all four of us toward the end of the process, so that Sparta would get to know her new Guardian."

"What does that mean? Aren't you her City Guardian?" My eyes hang on his tunic.

He follows my gaze and smiles. "No, I adjust myself to whatever city I'm currently taking care of. My job is to find a home for abandoned City Spirits. After we complete the transfer, Sparta will be handed over to you, with all the duties and responsibilities that entails, and I'll move on."

A City Guardian whose job is to find a home for abandoned Spirits? My father never spoke of any such thing, nor did Matthew, nor did any of the Cities. I fight to arrange the thoughts in my head. I sense that something isn't right. I have to talk to one of the others, ask them about it. My hands tighten on the handlebar. Mago notices.

"Come with me," he says, and I sense the urgency in his voice. "We have to stop them before they cause more damage than they can fix."

He's right. We have to stop this. But…

"The situation is more dangerous than you think," I say. "The others have formed a war council. I asked them to wait until I return, but they're watching the city, and the longer the battle continues, the less patient they're going to be."

I don't recognize the words he says next, nor even the language – it doesn't sound like Sparta's language; it's something older. I'm pretty sure he's cursing. "You have to stop them," he finally says.

I nod. "I know. I must go. I'll be back in –"

"No!" he grabs my arm forcefully. The touch is almost electric. "You have no time. Summon one of them."

"They can't get past Sparta's barrier," I say and try to free my arm.

Mago frowns and doesn't let go. "If I help you, we can get one of them across. The power of my summons should be enough, even if it's not my City."

I've never heard of such a thing, but then again, I haven't been in touch with many City Guardians. Cries of pain come from midtown, and I can hear gunfire. Time's running out. I must decide.

"Fine," I say, and Mago's face clears, his piercing eyes finally softening. His hand moves to my shoulder, gripping me.

"Summon the spirit who'll find it easiest to enter, the closest one geographically. I'll help."

I concentrate and close my eyes. Mago's hand on my shoulder feels like it's running electric currents through me. The fatigue, the pain I'm feeling, the scratches I got on the way – all recede, and I'm feeling more refreshed than I have been in a long while. I peek at him again, resisting the temptation to shower him with the questions I long to ask. How does he know how to do this? Who taught him? How did he become an itinerant City Guardian?

"Ramat Gan!" I employ the full force of the *call*. For a moment, it hangs in the air, echoing, breaking against the buildings around us as though I'd yelled it using an underwater sonar. A moment later, the air in front of us shines, twinkles and crackles, and then Ramat Gan is standing there, panting. Judging by her expression, she's suffering from slight nausea, and she shakes herself for a moment like a wet dog. "I hate that. Yuck! If this wasn't wartime, I swear…" she starts, but then notices Mago and stops. "Who is this?"

"Meet Mago –"

"We have no time," he reminds me.

"He's Sparta's Guardian," I finish.

"Sparta?!" Ramat Gan seems impressed. She raises the strawberry shades to look at him, and I notice the military helmet on her head for the first time, with a General Adjutant Corps stamp. She looks fascinated. "Excellent. That will help. I'll get the others –"

"No, wait!" Mago, on the other hand, looks nervous. He looks at me. Ramat Gan raises an eyebrow.

"This whole thing is a misunderstanding caused by lack of communication," I explain. A very unsatisfactory description of the situation, but it'll have to do for now. "She doesn't speak our language. Mago and I are going to stop them now, but you must delay the others. Tell them they have to give me a chance to set it straight."

Her face darkens. "You're going to get in the middle of this battle?" she points toward midtown.

"I'll be fine. Mago can communicate with her."

Ramat Gan looks at Mago. She studies him from head to toe, and he seems to shrink under her gaze. Her eyes narrow behind the strawberry shades. "And why hasn't he already done so?"

A question that's been troubling me too, but now is not the time for interrogations. "It doesn't matter. Please, go to the others and give them my message. We'll sort it out once we get to them. An hour, tops," I promise, trying to show confidence I don't really feel.

"Fine, Guardian," she sighs. "I'll tell them, but I don't like it."

She disappears in a flash of light, leaving the smell of chocolate hanging in the air. I turn to Mago. "Okay, let's go –"

A fist meets my face. Mago's muscles are like stone. His hand, which he's removed from my shoulder, has taken away the energy I'd felt, and I stumble backward, stunned. "What –"

He hits me again. I try to defend myself, but he's fast and well-trained. I stumble sideways, trying to duck, to fight back. He fends off my pathetic efforts easily and drops me to the ground with a well-aimed knee.

"Ramat –"

He kicks my stomach again, this time with his shoe, hard. All the air is expelled from my lungs before I can complete the *call*. He kicks me again. The dancing spots become orange and black.

"I'm very sorry for that," he says, his voice almost soft. "But I really have no other way. Now that you've stupidly told them it's Sparta, it won't take them long to break the barrier."

"What…" I whisper, too weak and choked to speak.

He grabs my neck and lifts me up. His grip is like iron. "So many Cities. So much power at your disposal, and you don't use it. You don't even know how."

I want to scream, investigate, understand, shout, ask, fight, but I can no longer do anything. The black spots spread, filling my entire field of vision.

Of him it is that thou must beware, Sodom had said, not of her.

I'm securely buckled in when I come to, and my hands and feet are tied with ropes. Mago sits next to me in the driver's seat and navigates toward midtown, to the affluent Kikar HaMedina area, where the sounds of battle are coming from. Navigating isn't easy. The streets are filled with wars. The bloodshed isn't as bad as I'd feared, but the mayhem is horrific. The roads are cracked open like after an earthquake; trees are burning, people and animals flee past us, going the other way.

"I'm glad you woke up," says Mago without looking at me. "I'll need your help to stop this battle, and I'd rather it happens with your cooperation."

I try to speak but can only make a muffled sound. A gag is covering my mouth.

"I hope you can forgive me," he continues. "I don't think you can summon Ramat Gan or one of the others without my help, but I didn't want to risk it." He stops the car on the side of the street, although there's really no need. His car is the only vehicle on the road. "I will remove this gag from your mouth, but if you try to use the *call* to summon one of the others, I will make sure you could never make another sound, ever again. Since I mean to let you live, it will be a terrible shame if you have to communicate with the cities from now on using a whiteboard."

I let him remove the gag from my mouth and take a deep breath. Dozens of questions are on the tip of my tongue, but I can't say a word. I know I should fear for my fate, but I'm more concerned for Aviv.

"Nothing? Really?" He's amused. "The other City Guardians who had the misfortune of crossing my path usually curse me or yell at me at this stage. You might want to start there."

"What are you doing?" I finally find my voice. "I thought you wanted to stop this fight."

He nods. "I do. It's a waste of energy and resources, and it endangers both of them. But my priority is your City Spirit, and I'm pretty sure she doesn't intend to continue with the transfer now."

I didn't think of that, but I suppose it makes sense. Aviv may have wanted to leave, but if she'd really started to transfer her territory in a responsible, controlled, and measured way, this attack by Sparta is exactly what'll make her change her mind. The city looks like a war zone.

And all of this still does not explain why I'm tied up. "So you mean to force her to go on with it? With my help?" I glare at him. "I thought that was your job, to help Cities who want to leave." He smiles and says nothing. "Wouldn't it be easier to find another City who wants to leave, maybe closer to her original location?" I go on. "If you take her back to Greece, I'm sure that –"

"You don't get it, do you?" He cuts me off and shakes his head as he turns toward Arlozorov Street. "It's not about Sparta. It's about Tel Aviv. I didn't want to do it like this. I wanted a quiet, controlled transfer, like always. But because of you and the other Cities, I no longer have a choice."

He sighs and looks at me. "I've dealt with enough stubborn City Guardians, ready to protect one of their Cities at all costs. But I've never met a Guardian who united all the Cities around his City to help her. Why are they so close to one another? Why do they have enough individual identity to become separate Cities and not merge into her? And why the hell do they listen to you?"

Despite the catapults, the gunfire, and the screams around us, it seems as though nothing can penetrate the sealed car windows. I stare at Mago, and my thoughts race in all directions.

"Don't worry," says Mago, starting the car again. "I don't mean to harm you, City Guardian. You have a vital role here. I meant what I said. You're the one who will have to stay with Sparta when it's over."

"Why is it so important for you that they switch places?" I find my voice again. "What's in it for you?" He smiles again, and I recall what Sodom had said. "You're not really a City Guardian, are you?"

He smiles. "I am a City Guardian. Yes. Absolutely. For thousands of years now. I was there when the legions entered Caer-Lud and it became

Londinium, when the walls of Constantinople fell and it became Istanbul, when the revolutionaries turned Sankt Petersburg into Leningrad. I take my mission very seriously."

Thousands of years? "You're lying. City Guardians are mortal."

He laughs aloud. A stray cat runs in front of us, and he slows down to not run it over. "They didn't tell you. Don't feel bad. It's a secret most of them don't know, only the old ones. Haven't you ever wondered, Guardian, how you're supposed to protect the Cities when they, the Spirits, have so much power and you're just a mortal? Or what you're supposed to do when a City goes mad, loses control, becomes dangerous to the Cities around it?"

"That's what City Councils are for," I mutter through clenched teeth, but I know exactly what he's talking about. That hopeless feeling in dealing with creatures that are near goddesses, when you're limited to only what you can do with two hands; the frustrating knowledge that no matter what you do, you can't prevent your Cities from suffering from war or air pollution, or even an outbreak of swine flu.

He smiles. "Must be nice to live in a country where all the Cities are so close to one another and care so much about each other and about you, enough for you to unite them. In other places in the world, Guardians have to spend a whole day flying between their Cities, begging them to show an interest in each other, and City Councils are just an ancient custom nobody observes." His smile disappears. "The Cities here are too nosy. They jeopardize the whole process. If I'd known it would be like this, I wouldn't have brought her here."

Little pieces click into place in my mind, like dead-end streets that suddenly spill and lead to one another. "You don't mean to let Tel Aviv go."

He hears the fear in my voice and glances at me. "You love her," he says. "Of course, you love her. How can you not love them? They're amazing creatures, City Spirits. Beautiful, wise, fascinating, and so powerful." He clenches his hand into a fist and looks at it. The gesture seems odd to me. "I, too, once loved one of them. Perhaps you've heard of her. Her name was Carthage."

My jaw drops. He reaches to his neck. At the end of a silver necklace dangles something that looks like a piece of old brick. "This is all I have left of her."

"You killed her." My lips almost refuse to move. "You're the reason she was destroyed."

He narrows his eyes at me. "No. I loved her. I would never have hurt her. It was she who chose to give me this gift. After that, I had to keep taking it from others by force."

"What gift?" I ask, and he smiles and doesn't reply, but a horrible suspicion is already forming in my brain. I think of Aviv, and my fear-frozen maple heart rebels, breaks through the layers of ice, I struggle against the ropes that bind me, the seat belt, I even try to reach for the door. No. He can't. No matter what he means to do, I won't let him do it to Aviv.

Mago's hand, strong as steel, reaches out and almost casually grips my throat. I choke, my throat screams for air, and then he lets go. I struggle to breathe for a long moment. "Don't make trouble, Guardian," he says. "It will only hurt you more, and the child."

I cough and choke before I can breathe normally again. The pain subsides somewhat, but the deep breath reminds me of my head and body, which hurt from Mago's blows. He seems at ease as he slows the car down on one of the streets near Kikar HaMedina.

"She's not a child," I say.

"What?"

"Tel Aviv. She's not a child. She'll kick your Sparta's ass."

He parks the car and releases his seatbelt and mine. "I'm sorry for what I'm about to do. If I had another way to retain my immortality, I'd use it. I have no choice."

"You have no choice?" I almost spit at him. "You can grow old and die, like the rest of us!"

"No, I can't. When you taste the power of a City, you'll realize that you won't ever be able to give it up." He gets out and opens the passenger door. I stumble when he pulls me forcefully to my feet – the rope tying my ankles is only loose enough to let me take small steps. "Come on, let's go to them. You promised the other Cities we'll stop the battle."

I'm sure that stopping the battle isn't really what he cares about, but I can't resist when he drags me after him.

"Does Sparta know what you're doing?"

He shrugs. "Sparta only cares about having a city. Strange creatures, City Spirits. They try all their lives to leave their limits, and when they're finally free, they only want to have a place that belongs to them again. Lonesome Spirits will do anything to get a new place."

"I won't let you do this to Tel Aviv."

He smiles at me, a smile half condescending and half almost paternal love. "My dear Guardian, if you had the power to change anything, I would have told you nothing."

A biting retort sits on the tip of my tongue, but then we enter the vast plaza, and I stop. For a moment, every other thought is driven from my mind. I don't know if I should be glad that they chose a part of the city that always seemed to me one of the ugliest, or sad that they've managed to make it even uglier. Trees have been knocked over, massive craters have opened in the ground, the buildings are in ruins, the sidewalks and roads are broken and scarred. At least the people have fled the area long ago, and there are no dead and wounded around us. The two powerful City Spirits are in the air above the plaza's center, eyeing each other intently. Sparta has added a shining golden shield to her sword. Lightning bolts flash around her, even though there's not a cloud in the August sky. Tel Aviv holds a broken street lamp in one hand and a surfboard in the other – an odd combination, but better than a toy sword. She is surrounded by waves of water, which encircle her like hoops, floating around her body. Even in the empty plaza, even a war just between the two of them, is like a clash of the titans, encompassing earth, trees, electric posts, buildings. They both look awful.

I look at them for a few moments, or rather, I look at Mago looking at them. A fascinated expression on his face. "A waste," he mutters, "so much waste of so much power."

He continues to watch the battle for another moment and then sighs and looks at me. "Call her."

I find my voice, deep within my burning, bruised, and aching throat. "No."

"Fine. I'll call her." He raises his voice. "Tel Aviv!"

She stops. Both Cities turn to look at us. "At last," Tel Aviv sighs. The swirling waves around her body freeze and then drop to the ground, soaking into it. "Control your maniac, Mago!"

Sparta also blurts a few angry words, waving her free hand at Tel Aviv. I concentrate. Wrath still radiates from her, but there's something else as well – excitement, joy, pleasure. She's enjoying the battle, I realize, a bit stunned.

Mago answers her in fluent Greek, and then glances at my city. "You've attracted too much unwanted attention. We have to complete the transfer, quickly."

Tel Aviv laughs briefly. "What are you smoking, Mago? Look around you. She's like a walking tornado! She can't control this place. And even if I wanted to continue the process with her, we've agreed on a transfer period of six months –"

"Tel Aviv," Mago cuts off her verbal stream by pulling on the ropes that hold me, and I almost fall. His tone is cold, matter-of-fact, uncompromising. "Come here, or your human gets hurt."

She notices me for the first time. She reacts instantly. Her face, which is already lacking its usual tan, pales even more, and the streetlamp and surfboard drop from her hands. Her skirt, lying on her thighs in tatters, flaps slightly as her feet touch the ground beside us. Your human, he said. Not your City Guardian.

"What kind of game are you playing, Mago?" she demands.

Sparta is very quiet, looking from her to me and then to Mago again. I sense the bewilderment rising from her, almost as though someone has drawn a large question mark over her head. This wasn't part of her battle plan. Tel Aviv moves in until she is right in front of us. "What do you want from him?"

"From him? Nothing. Only from you." He looms over her, tall and threatening. "I'm sorry. I wanted to do it more gradually, but he and your friends have left me no choice."

He takes another step toward her and shoves his hand into her stomach.

She screams. I can't see what he's doing, but I imagine him ripping out internal organs, and I'm filled with terror. Then again, I'm thinking of her as a human. When I manage to look, I see that his hand isn't really touching her stomach. It has disappeared at the edge of her skin in a thin, glowing stripe of sickly green, and the glow is spreading, sending tendrils of gleaming brilliance that wrap around his arm, around his body. He's smiling. His face assumes a transcendent expression. A gasp of pain escapes her lips. She is pale, sickly. She tries to move away from him, but he grasps her shoulder forcefully. I've never seen someone hold a City Spirit in one place. Sparta yells something. I don't understand, but caution, anger, and a slight sense of fear emanate from her. Tel Aviv is swaying now, and I'm not sure what he's doing to her, but it's killing her, I'm sure of it. He's digging his fingers into her shoulder with his free hand, and I know that despite the ropes cutting into my flesh and stabbing me, I must do something, must –

But Sparta beats me to it. A surge of pure, unadulterated rage, accompanied by the full force of a City Spirit, hits Mago who's standing next to me, and he is thrown backward. Her staff, shaped like the letter T, has struck his chest hard. Sparta says something in a sharp tone. I sense fury again, and this time insult as well. He replies with an angry shout. She says something else, waving feverishly at me, at Tel Aviv, at him, at herself. She radiates offended pride, a sense of betrayal, and these are now colored with vengefulness. He does not reply. Her hand reaches for her sword. A grim smile touches his lips. He extends his hand for her fallen staff, and it flies to his grip. I don't know what's about to happen, but I'm sure I won't like it.

And I'm right. At that moment, the attack begins. I feel it before I hear or see anything, like a wave passing through my body, and I almost fall over from the force of it. Ramat Gan hasn't managed to convince them, then, and I don't know whether to curse or be happy about it. I feel the attack around me, in some City Guardian sense, even where I can't see it. Rocks fly through the air, shattering windows all over the city. Pipes deliver waste into the Ayalon Stream, which overflows and floods the highway next to it. A sandstorm carrying the smell of the desert rattles bicycles, people, cars. I hear sounds of collision. A cloud of filthy smoke comes from the north, unpleasantly moist and burning the skin. Hundreds of honking and fuming cars fill the streets that have been almost empty of motor traffic in recent weeks. Fuel spills from a tanker on Namir Road. People and vehicles slip and slide in the viscous fluid. Brakes squeal. More honks. People are crying, screaming. A heavy cloud of haze makes it hard to breathe. An explosion sounds from someplace nearby, gas containers, maybe. The attacks are hard, fast, paralyzing; can't fault them for lack of creativity. The only ones acting like bulls in a china shop are Ashdod and Haifa, whose submarines and battleships bombard the city. It will be very challenging to explain this away as an exercise later. On the other hand, I'm not sure we'll be able to explain any of this, even with the power of City Spirits. The city is in complete chaos, and we're right in the middle of it.

Somehow, during all this, my binds come loose, and my City Spirit pushes me down, shielding me with her body, even though she looks like she's about to collapse to the ground at any moment. When it's all over, a frozen silence descends, and Aviv collapses in my arms. She's not the only one. Sparta, too, looks pale and sickly, and her sword-wielding hand trembles slightly. Mago is affected the most. He gasps, sways for a moment, and then collapses. He may be able to steal a City Spirit's power, but I can't imagine he knows how to deal with her pain. In any event, I don't care about him right now. Carefully, I lay Aviv on the ground. Her hair has lost its color and turned almost gray. Her skin is greenish. Her eyes are closed, and she won't wake up. I put two fingers to her neck.

"Not much point in what you're doing," Jerusalem remarks casually. "Pulse is a matter of taste with City Spirits. If she were dead, she'd just disappear."

I raise my head to look at her. We're not alone. They're all there, standing around us. The attack collapsed Sparta's barrier, and they managed to enter the city. They form a circle around her, making sure she can't get away. She looks around for a moment, blond hair waving every which way as she seeks a hole in their defenses, not finding one. She still can't speak our language, but I feel the surrender even before she sighs and allows the sword to drop from her hand.

"Didn't I ask you to tell them to wait?" I ask Ramat Gan.

"You did," she answers, looking at me through the strawberry shades, "but that whole conversation was too weird. Something was wrong about this character." She points at the unconscious Mago. I can only be glad that her gut feeling was better than mine.

I slide one hand under Aviv's neck and shoulders, another under her knees, and try to lift her. She's as light as an autumn leaf and as heavy as the Azrieli Towers, and my mind struggles with the contradiction, but I can't move her even an inch. I've lifted her before, even to bed when she fell asleep in front of the TV, but she must have been conscious enough then to make sure that her weight was human. I let go of her, defeated, and instead, I straighten her body on the ground. Even such a simple thing is denied me. We are so different.

The City that caused all this mayhem is standing in the center of the circle of Cities. She's looking at us all coldly, her hands folded on her chest, still proud and regal even in defeat. The moment they knew her identity, she had no chance against their united force. "Ladies," I gesture at her, "meet Sparta."

A few whistles of wonder and appreciation. "Get out!" says Ramat HaSharon. "This is, like, really Sparta? I thought Ramat Gan was kidding."

"Isn't she extinct or something?" Holon asks.

"What is she even doing here?" Rehovot asks.

"What shall we do with her?" Giv'ataim asks.

"I have a few ideas," Netanya narrows her eyes, and Bat Yam chuckles unpleasantly.

Haifa turns her nose up. "I say we send her on the first ship to Greece, preferably in chains."

"Too much work. Let's drown her in the sea." Herzliya folds her arms over her chest. "Let her try to take over Atlantis."

"That's a continent, not a city," Acre corrects her.

"And it's not real, dummies."

"Hey!" I stop the discussion before it turns into an argument. "Before we decide what to do with her, does anyone here know ancient Greek?"

A few of them raise their hands. I motion for Jerusalem to come forward, but it seems that Sparta is more interested in Mago than in me. Netanya has picked up his unconscious body by the scruff of his neck, like a kitten, and is studying him carefully. "He doesn't feel like a City Guardian to me. Something's wrong," she remarks.

"I think he hasn't been a City Guardian," I say, "for a very long time."

Sparta steps forward, and I feel her power reaching ahead. The others move to block her, but I sense that she's focused only on Mago, and beyond the terrible anger she feels, she is driven by purpose. "Wait, hold on," I say. They step back, and she sends a strong mental push that wakes Mago up. He opens his eyes slowly and chokes, looking like he's about to hurl. He says a few words in Greek. She replies. Her tone sounds unpleasant.

"She's angry at him," Jerusalem translates. "He… betrayed her?" Her eyebrows rise.

I look from Sparta to Mago. He thought that all she cared about was to have a city again. But she saved Tel Aviv, even though she could have had this place. He didn't give her enough credit.

Spirits are not evil by nature, Sodom had said. Humans can be.

"He promised her the city," I explain. "But he didn't tell her that he wasn't going to let Tel Aviv leave. He wanted Tel Aviv for himself, to maintain his immortality."

The other cities look at Mago. Various expressions of nausea, disgust, and hate on their faces. "I didn't know City Guardians could do such things," says Kfar Saba.

"I knew," Jerusalem admits. Tiberias, Acre, Haifa, and a few others avoid my gaze. I want to be angry, but this isn't the time.

Sparta keeps talking to Mago. She doesn't raise her voice, but every word from her mouth is dripping with frost, blame, and hatred. Sparta glances at Tel Aviv, then looks back at Mago. "She's angry," Jerusalem needlessly translates. "She's accusing him of having no honor."

Mago stops answering. He just looks at her, a slight smile on his lips. He has what he wants. Maybe he hasn't taken everything he could have if she hadn't stopped him, but she can't take away what he stole. It's Tel Aviv's power, not hers. Sparta apparently reaches the same conclusion. She looks at Mago, at Tel Aviv sprawled on the ground, pale as snow, and then her gaze rests on me. I feel her resolve building up again, and with it, decision. She steps toward me. Five cities leap to stand in her way. "Stop," I say. "She doesn't want to harm me."

I can feel it.

They give way reluctantly, and Sparta takes my hand and pulls me toward Mago. We stop in front of him. She looks at me. When she holds my hand, the emotions coming from her are clearer. Right now, it's expectation. Jerusalem asks something, and Sparta replies with a burst of Greek, pointing at Mago, at me, at Tel Aviv, and at Mago again. Mago's eyes grow wide, and although I can't feel what he feels, his terror is palpable.

"She wants you to return what he took from Tel Aviv," says Jerusalem. "She says you can do it."

"What?" I protest. "I don't know how!"

Sparta grabs my hand again and places it on Mago's stomach. She transmits a rapid succession of images at me. It's still not a real language, but I think I understand what to do. I spread my hands and concentrate. Within less than a minute, my fingers begin to tingle, and I notice that they're shining. A green glow rises from his stomach and loops around my hand. Mago gasps. "No!" He looks at me, terror and begging for mercy alternating in his eyes. "Please, Guardian, you can't do that! It will kill me!"

I hesitate, but only for a moment. Dozens of eyes are watching us, and I cannot mistake their expression. Cities aren't evil, but when one of them is harmed, they can be merciless. I slowly become aware that I am filling up with energy and vitality. My wounds heal, any pain I feel subsides, even my skin looks healthier, shinier. I increase the pulling force. The green glow is now too bright to look at. He gasps. His eyes widen, and he tries to escape, to move back, but Netanya holds him tightly. None of us moves. The process is frightening to behold, like hyper-accelerated aging. Finally, he jerks, twists, and it's over. He withers in Netanya's grip. He's still alive, but barely. He's an old man now, almost ancient, whose vitality and life force have been taken from him. But they weren't his anyway.

I let go and breathe deeply. And then, for the first time in my life, I feel what it's like to be a City Spirit. I become aware of the breaths around me, not just of the others but also of the people, animals, and trees. I feel hundreds of thousands of people, millions of living creatures. I sense every breath in their bodies as though they were standing beside me, exhaling on my skin. I feel the waves of the sea undulating on the shore, the Yarkon flowing into the harbor, the cars and bicycles on the asphalt roads, the footsteps on the sidewalks, the birds in the air, the fear and concern of the people in the tall towers, sitting huddled, uncomprehending. The cries of the children, the firefighters and rescue crews coming from other cities, the sand and the wind, the soil and the trees, and the jacaranda flowers falling on the sidewalks. I feel the motion of the earth itself, its rotation around its xis and around the sun. The eternity of the soil upon which I stand. My awareness is so broad, so mighty, and my power is so great that if I so wished, I could wash the entire city with the waves of the sea and drown it forever. If I wanted, I could spread a canopy of darkness over it to blot out the sun forever. Even now, in my weakened condition, despite the nausea and the unpleasant sensation scraping at the edge of my awareness, indicating all the malfunctions in my territory, even now, I am as mighty as a god.

It seems to me that a long time has passed before I feel anything, and then much more time before I realize that the sensation is coming from my corporeal body, which I have almost completely forgotten. I force my consciousness to return to it. It is too small for me, too small for my immense size. I fight myself, fight the voices telling me to break free, to abandon it forever. When I finally manage to focus my gaze and force myself to look, not through the all-seeing eyes of the city but through my limited human eyes, I see faces looking at me, piercing, penetrating eyes. It takes me a moment to remember. Sparta. I look around, meeting the anxious gaze of the others. I am floating a few inches above the ground. I force myself to land and turn around to look at Tel Aviv, pale, lying on the ground, her breath shallow. For a moment, there's a struggle within me. Mago was right. Now that I've tasted the power of a City, I find it very hard to let go. Mago was a fool. Immortality was negligible compared to the wondrous things I can do. How can I give it up?

Sparta touches my hand again. She transmits a request to me, almost a plea. I open my consciousness for just an instant and dive into her memories. I see Mago for a moment, the promises he made to her a scant few months ago, the hope she had, to belong to somewhere again, to have land of her own, people of her own. She takes me further back, to thousands of years of sitting on ruins, sharpening her sword, gazing at the horizon. A new city named Sparti arose, and for a few years, she had hope. But she was too far removed from the new era, too different. She didn't fit the city, and the city didn't fit her. While she struggled to understand the automobile, and print, and industry, a new city spirit had already come into being, and she was left alone again. I am vaguely aware of tears rolling down my cheeks. It is only thanks to the power suffusing me that I am not overwhelmed by an unimaginable weight of pain and loneliness.

And then I dive further back as Sparta takes me to her. To the beautiful city, the pearl of the Peloponnesus in the glory that was Greece, to the wondrous, immense stone structures carved with magnificent artistry, built so solidly that some still stand. She could not believe that anyone could ever demolish such solid foundations. The city is full of people, majestic and beautiful as herself, waving banners, riding horses, children playing, laughing and running through the streets. Pretty women in short dresses walking down the streets, laughing, free. I look at it all from the side, from a high cliff upon which two white steeds stand, overlooking the city. Sparta's hand is in her Guardian's. He is a handsome man, fair-haired, with a straight nose and strong jaw, like one of those marble statues. He smiles at her, and her lips curl up in reply. She raises their hands which are clenched together. For a long moment, green light wraps around the holding hands. She waits, looking at him. He pulls his hand away. Her disappointment washes over me like a wave. A single tear rolls down her cheek. He reaches out to wipe it away and caresses her cheek, consoling her, and finally, he kisses her lips, but his answer does not change. No.

I gasp, almost collapsing under the weight of memories that threatens to devastate me. But the power of the city that I took from Mago upholds me. Sparta's eyes never leave mine. I understand. She is not fighting for Tel Aviv. She is fighting for me. She is fighting for me to be like him, and not like Mago.

Without another word, I turn to Tel Aviv, kneel by her side and hold her to me. I support her back with one hand – I have no difficulty at all lifting her now – and I place my other hand on her abdomen, hardly touching it. The tendrils of green light wrap around my hand again, and I concentrate on the inexhaustible energy within me, trying to let go of it. Sparta guides me, her hand gently holding my shoulder, and in an instant, the enormous awareness within me shrinks, dwindling into my waiting fingers. The waves and the cars, the asphalt and the trees, vanish. I release the power of Tel Aviv and remain once again alone in a human, fragile body, perishable as a withered leaf. I release a sigh, part loss and part relief.

The change is almost instantaneous. I didn't expect it to be so profound, but I didn't know how much Mago had managed to take from her in the past six months. Aviv's skin loses its pallor and looks tanned and healthy again. Her cheeks grow pink. Her hair, which had turned almost gray, is filled with color once again. Within moments, she already looks like herself. I manage to maintain some dignity and lower her to the ground without looking like a child who's trying to lift a grand piano. Sparta turns to me and says a few words.

"She'll be alright," Jerusalem translates and listens again. "She wishes to apologize to you. She hasn't had a City Guardian in thousands of years. She thought she could trust Mago. She didn't mean for you to be hurt, and she didn't mean for Tel Aviv to be hurt."

"Didn't mean for Tel Aviv to be hurt?" I repeat, disbelieving. I gesture around me.

Sparta sighs and speaks again. "In terms of values, she doesn't view war the same we do," Jerusalem translates. "To her, it's a sport, an inseparable part of her culture. Cities used to go to war all the time in her day."

"Charming," Ramat Gan grimaces. "I'm sure the residents loved it."

"In any case," Jerusalem continues, "she really didn't want to destroy Tel Aviv. She just wanted to be the Spirit of a real city again, not of ruins."

Despite myself, my anger dissipates quickly. The weight of Sparta's memories still lies somewhere in the back of my mind. I know how lonely she was. Just like Sodom.

"Yonatan?" I freeze. How long has it been since someone has used my name? Months, probably.

Tel Aviv sits up slowly and looks at me. She doesn't look good, despite having her powers back. Of course, her city has been badly damaged. Her eyes – usually sea-blue, or Yarkon-green, or asphalt-gray – are murky brown now.

"Yonatan," Ramat HaSharon mimics her, and a few giggles rise around us. None of the others use my name. She hasn't used it in a long time either. But I'm so glad to hear her voice that I'm not embarrassed. I don't care if they know.

"Are you alright?" Aviv mumbles weakly.

"I'm fine. You saved me."

The others giggle again. She blushes, and for a split second, crimson appears on her now pink cheeks. "Don't let it go to your head. I did it for them." She gasps and rubs her temples. "And I already regret it. What did you do, you herd of cows?"

The tension dissipates from the air around us. Finally. "We saved your ass, you idiot," Jerusalem replies, and laughs her wadi laughter. Sparta is the only one not smiling.

I help Aviv stand up, or at least pretend to, and she plays along. Sparta says a few words.

"She apologizes," Jerusalem translates. "She says it was a good battle and that she'll be glad to challenge you in a real ring, if you like."

In Aviv's expressive eyes, I read something between amusement and shock. "Uh… no. Thanks."

Sparta goes on. Her tone lower now, almost pleading.

"She asks," says Jerusalem, "if you still want to leave. Because she's still willing to replace you. At your own pace, on your own terms. She promises to learn everything she needs."

It seems very quiet around us suddenly. They are all waiting, looking at her. I feel eternity passing before she shakes her head from side to side. "Thank her for the offer," she says," but I've changed my mind. I'm staying."

I hope that the relief I feel doesn't show too clearly on my face. Sparta bows to Tel Aviv. A formal, graceful, regal bow. Tel Aviv replies with a bow that looks more like a move from a Pilates class. Sparta summons her chariot and horses and boards it – some of the others are trying very hard not to laugh, but she still looks impressive to my eyes. I lay a hand on the mane of one of the white horses, and she looks at me, a question in her eyes.

"Tell her I want to talk to her," I say to Jerusalem. "After things have calmed down a bit."

Jerusalem translates, and Sparta nods at me as the chariot rises in the air and flies into the distance.

In the silence left behind, my City looks around her, with her eyes and her senses, taking in the full force of the devastation around us. "Shit," she mutters.

"We'll help, Aviv," I promise her. I look at the others. "Right?"

They nod as one, their expressions grave, except for Bat Yam, who turns her nose up and declares that it's Friday night and she has pubs to be at.

I don't enter the city, just park nearby, at the ancient roadside caravanserai at Sha'ar HaGai, and wait by the side of the road. It takes her precisely three minutes to float in and land by my side on the sloping tree trunk I'm sitting on. I find the smell of pines comforting.

"To what do I owe this pleasure?" she smiles. "I thought you'd be in Tel Aviv all week." But the smile vanishes as soon as she notices my mood.

I dig in the ground with the tip of my shoe and don't look at her. "Was my mother a City Spirit?"

It appears all the air is sucked out of the mountains around us.

"Who told you such a thing?" she asks, her voice very soft. "Sodom?"

"Just answer the question."

"Yes, your mother was a City Spirit," she says at last.

A bitter taste sits in my throat. "Who is she? Can I meet her?"

She shakes her head. "Her city was destroyed, a little after you were born. Ever heard of the evacuation of Yamit?"

Yamit, a desert city on the seashore at the edge of the Sinai Desert. I know the story. It had been destroyed before the area was returned to Egypt under the peace agreement. "But that doesn't mean she's dead." I think of Sodom, of Sparta, of all the cities ever destroyed. "It just means she's wandering around somewhere, without a place to be in, right?"

She shakes her head. "It's not easy to survive when your place dies. You must realize it ahead of time and completely detach yourself from the land, from everything that's your responsibility and under your protection. You have to live as an independent Spirit, without a place… most of us can't do it, and that means we die with the city."

I exhale. For a moment, I had a mother. Then I was orphaned again.

"Would any of you have ever told me?"

"I don't think so." An honest answer, sharp, cutting, as always. That's why I came to her.

I sink my nails into the tree we're sitting on. "Is it always like that? Guardians and Spirits, I mean."

"No," she smiles, "There's no such rule. It just happens of its own accord from time to time."

"And you're okay with it."

"Why not? It strengthens the Guardian's powers."

"The powers you never mean to tell me anything about, you mean," I frown at her.

She sighs. "That knowledge is dangerous. Now that you know what it feels like to be a City Spirit, do you really think you could have released that power without outside help? Weren't you tempted even a little to keep it for yourself?"

I don't have to reply. She knows the answer. I lower my eyes.

"Once you take the power from us, only you can give it back. We have no way to force you. Surely you understand why we wanted to keep this information to ourselves." She passes her hand over the stump we're sitting on. It had fallen and died long ago, and yet, the dead wood assumes a deep brown color where her finger is touching it, and after a moment, a few new greenish leaves sprout out of it. "That knowledge is for emergencies, and in an emergency, none of us would have kept the information from you."

"Did Tel Aviv know?"

"No. She's too young."

My anger slowly subsides, but I remain with the annoying, troubling sensation of a lump forming in my throat. "But she knew there had been such relationships. She knew I need… I must have a son…"

I can't finish, and she stares at me for a long moment before she understands. "You're a real dumbass, anyone ever tell you that?"

"You want there to be heirs, don't you? That's the most important thing to you, to have a City Guardian."

"So you think we would manipulate and maneuver you just so that you'd get one of us pregnant?" Her eyes seem to be shooting pine needles. The entire forest around us whistles and rustles in protest.

"How should I know?" My tone rises too. "You're Cities! Your powers are enormous. The sights you see, the experiences you have, the number of people you feel inside you at any given moment… It's so different from the world I live in. I'm just a human being. Why would one of you actually love me?"

"You're not just a human being." She looks at my whitening hand around the tree stump. "And we're not really that different than you. Cities love a lot of people, more than you can imagine, but not many can love them back." She pauses for a moment. "Not many can deal with the force of a City's love."

I know exactly what she means. I had lived in cities even before Tel Aviv. It was terrible. Knowing that an entire City is attuned to you, that the trees, the houses, the very streets will move to make way for you if you only want them to. The life of a City Guardian was full of shortcuts. I never had to stand in line at the supermarket. Never had trouble finding a parking spot. Never had a problem getting a table at a fancy restaurant. Never got stuck in traffic. Never lacked a vacant bench when I wanted to sit. Hell, it never rained on me. With Aviv, it wasn't like that. Maybe that's why I fell in love with her. She never tried to please me and care for me and pamper me every single moment, like all of the others. Well, maybe just with parking spots. And yet, that power is always floating at the edge of your awareness. You're constantly aware that every minute, someone knows where you are, what you're doing, watching over you, worrying. "I'm not sure I can go back to that."

"Nobody's asking you to go back to that." Her voice is gentle. "Not even her. Start with being a friend, not a lover."

I sigh. That's how it started last time. Two friends, having a latte on Nachlat Binyamin Street. Then it turned into long walks through the park, and quiet nights on the beach, and her smile, and her eyes, and her hair, and her skin. It became inevitable. And in these last few days, while helping with the rebuilding, I felt it again. "I'm afraid it'll go horribly wrong."

"It won't go horribly wrong as long as you don't sulk and ignore each other like a couple of fourth-graders," she insists. "If things are broken, you fix them. Do you know how many City Guardians I've been with?"

"No, and I don't want to know," I say firmly.

"She didn't want to leave because of you," Jerusalem goes on, ignoring me. "She wanted to leave for the same reasons we all want to leave sometimes. But maybe if you'd spoken with her like you speak with all of us, you'd have helped her to understand that she has to stay, long before things got this far."

She's right, of course. I have nothing to say. My fears seem petty and foolish, but they still paralyze me. "Go to her, dummy," she says, stroking my hair with a motherly gesture.

When I sit back in my car, she knocks on the window. I roll it down, and she tosses a newspaper inside. "I almost forgot. Page fifteen, at the bottom."

I know what the item will be before I glance at the little text box. A new rural settlement is to be built in the Upper Galilee. The Regional Council Chairman gave an interview about a healthy mind in a healthy body and the wide variety of sports the new settlement will feature. In the little black and white photo to the left, he's wearing a toga. Brilliant advertising move, the reporter congratulates him.

"Ramat Saphra. Was that name your idea or hers?"

"I'm not sure," I admit. "She doesn't speak Hebrew very well yet, so we communicate with very basic telepathy, no words. It's a little confusing. Hard to remember which thoughts are mine and which are hers."

She smiles. "How'd you do it?"

"I pulled some strings at the regional council, that's all. There was talk of such a settlement for a long time. I just gave them a City Spirit."

"Just gave them a City Spirit! Sparta's!" Her wadi laughter is booming, rolling down the foothills. "Her new neighbors are going to give you a tough time."

"It's just a little settlement," I protest. "Three, four hundred families, something like that. How much trouble could she possibly make?"

Her eyes glint at me like candles in a tour of Hanukkah lamps in Nachlaot. "You want to bet how many years it'll take for the regional council to bid to host the Olympics? Or for the residents to decide to have a javelin competition to take out Hezbollah rockets?"

I groan in despair and throw the newspaper at her. Her wadi laughter follows me on my way west.

As I climb the exit ramp from the Ayalon highway, I open the glove compartment and take out a single, perfect, five-pointed red maple leaf. I throw it out of the window, and a gust of wind catches it, rolling and tossing it in the air until it disappears from my sight.

When I reach to close the glove compartment, I notice a purple flower inside. It wasn't there before.

It's a start.

My Life as an Israeli Science Fiction Fan

An essay by Ehud Maimon

IT STARTED WITH ASIMOV, as it often did with fans my age in Israel. I grew up in a home where everyone – my parents and my older brothers – read science fiction. When I was about nine years old, there was an argument in our family about the story "Profession" – is the future described in it optimistic or pessimistic? – and since I wanted to know what they were all talking about, I took *Nine Tomorrows* off the shelf and read it. And then I read the following story, and went on from there. And once I've gone through all the books we had at home, I headed for the library.

I was lucky because the '80s were a great time to become a science fiction fan in Israel. In the '70s and '80s, for the first time, genre fiction was being translated into Hebrew in bulk quantities. Before that, there had been just a few translated books here and there, but when I became a teenager, more and more publishers had what were, essentially, SF/F translation imprints. They were translating both the classics of the field and contemporary lit, and I read anything I could lay my hands on. Growing up in a somewhat out-of-the-way kibbutz, where we didn't have TV sets at home until the mid-'80s, books were much more accessible to me than movies and TV shows. I think I actually saw *The Return of the Jedi* before I saw *Star Wars*. To this day, I'm much more of a lit fan than a media person.

Another significant thing happened in the '80s – *Fantasia 2000*. A Hebrew science fiction and fantasy magazine! Only later I learned that there had been a few mags that preceded it, but they were didn't last for more than a few issues. Here was a journal that came out more or less regularly, and I could read each issue as it came out. Not only that, it had original stories, written by Israelis just like me. Sadly, I couldn't make a subscription, so my reading was sporadic, but I put that right once I got to university, by blowing off a few classes and reading what I'd missed in the library.

Fantasia 2000 also made me realize for the first time that there was an Israeli fandom. I knew of things like Worldcon from reading Asimov's blurbs to the stories in his Hugo winners' collections, but as far as I was concerned, this was something that happened in faraway, foreign lands – Israel couldn't have such things. It would be about a decade after *Fantasia 2000* closed down that the first Israeli con was held. But I suddenly became aware that there were other people who liked SF/F, outside of my family and a few friends in the kibbutz and at high school.

Not surprisingly, my actual induction into fandom was via the internet. A friend told me about the plan to hold a convention called ArmegaonCon in December of 2000 (a project that went down in ashes because of real-life politics). While looking this up, I discovered the forums, the Israeli Society for SF/F and *Bli Panika*, an online magazine that grew out of one of the forums. By that time, I was working on my masters' degree in the history of Islam and Middle East studies, and had a job as a TA in the university. This gave me the boost of confidence I needed to submit a few reviews and essays to a couple of sites. Thankfully, they were received rather well. The 2001 ICon (at the time, Israel's only con) was the first convention I attended, and a couple of years later, I gave a lecture at a con for the first time ever. I think there were about seven people in the audience for that particular lecture.

In 2005 Dotan Dimet, the editor of *The Tenth Dimension*, the ISSF&F's fanzine, decided to step down, and they approached me about replacing him. I was lucky because I had a great editorial staff that stayed on and helped me learn the ropes and gain some experience. *The Tenth Dimension* mainly published essays, reviews, and translated stories, but I also got to work on some original stories. A few years later, the Society decided that in order to advance the genre in Israel, it should start an annual anthology series of original stories, and I was asked to edit it. This was how *Once Upon a Future* was born.

The one thing I could not foresee was the thirst there would be for such a venue. In 2009, the first year *Once Upon a Future* cane out, a friend with some experience in publishing advised me to hold back some of the stories I'd received, in case I won't get enough submissions for the following year. Now, thirteen years later, I'm looking at a list of 56 submitted stories, and this number is actually down from what I'd had to the previous year. Looking back at original Israeli genre stories, I can distinguish three or four generations of writers, and that's only going back to *Fantasia 2000* and the late '70s. It has been, for me, an amazingly wild ride, one that I hope will continue for many years, and it all began for me with Isaac Asimov.

Afterword
By Marleen S. Barr

The Language of Israeli Science Fiction:
Or, The Cities Are Alive with the Sound of Hebrew

Dr. Marleen S. Barr is known for her pioneering work in feminist science fiction and teaches English at the City University of New York. She has won the Science Fiction Research Association Pilgrim Award for lifetime achievement in science fiction criticism. Barr is the author of *Alien to Femininity: Speculative Fiction and Feminist Theory, Lost in Space: Probing Feminist Science Fiction and Beyond, Feminist Fabulation: Space/ Postmodern Fiction,* and *Genre Fission: A New Discourse Practice for Cultural Studies.* Barr has edited many anthologies and co-edited the science fiction issue of *PMLA.* She is the author of the novels *Oy Pioneer!* and *Oy Feminist Planets: A Fake Memoir.* Her *When Trump Changed: The Feminist Science Fiction Justice League Quashes the Orange Outrage Pussy Grabber* is the first single-authored Trump short story collection.

[Although science fiction] uses many of the same words that mundane fiction uses, it uses them differently. To be able to understand science fiction, you must be able to crack its codes.
– Matthew Cheney, "Ethical Aesthetics: An Introduction to *The Jewel- Hinged Jaw*," xix

[Samuel R.] Delany writes that 'the conventions of poetry or drama or mundane fiction—or science fiction—are in themselves separate languages,' and . . . he called the process by which one approaches and reads those languages 'protocols.'— James Gunn, "Reading Science Fiction as Science Fiction," *Reading Science Fiction*, 160

ISRAEL IS SUFFUSED with science fiction tropes. The country sprang from the world-creating idea of establishing a Jewish homeland and engages in terraforming to make the desert bloom. Like Frankenstein's monster, Israel, the only Jewish state, is a one-of-a-kind entity. This unique otherworldly characteristic might cause non-Israeli readers to question what planet they are on in relation to encountering *More Zion's Fiction: Wondrous Tales from the Israeli ImagiNation*. Israeli science fiction functions as a different textual planet in relation to non-Israeli nationals who experience first contact with this subgenre.

I come away from reading *More* with this still well-known 1961 New York City-centered advertisement campaign for Levy's Jewish rye bread resonating in my mind: "You don't have to be Jewish to love Levy's." The phrase was emblazoned on photographs of conspicuously non-Jewish New Yorkers (such as a wizened male Native American) closely encountering rye bread slices. While all people can relish Levy's, the same cannot be said for fully engaging with Israeli science fiction. In order completely to comprehend *More*, you have to be Jewish – and Israeli.

My point about the importance of Jewish cultural literacy in relation to reading *More* is grounded in the reader response theory Norman N.

Holland described in *5 Readers Reading*. Holland argues that the reader makes sense of texts in accordance with her own characteristic style, life experience, and identity theme. I am one New York Jew reading *More*. Despite being steeped in Jewish culture and having traveled to Israel, I am an alien in relation to Israel and Israeli science fiction. Upon arrival in Israel, as someone who can neither speak nor read Hebrew to the extent that I am limited to the word "shalom," I felt like a stranger in a strange land. Ditto for my ability fully to engage with Israeli science fiction. While I am familiar with Yonkers-born Avram Davidson's "Help! I Am Dr. Morris Goldpepper" (which appears in this collection) to the extent that I have dated men who are Goldpepper's clones and I know Manhattan's "West End Avenue" like the back of my hand, I cannot relate to many of the cities and all of the street names mentioned in *More*. I cannot find many Israeli cities on a map. I am unfamiliar with the Israeli names of some *More* authors to the extent that I am unable to discern their gender. Oy, if this is my response, the mind boggles at how difficult it would be for gentile readers to make sense of Israeli science fiction.

Rotem Baruchin's companion stories about fantastic sentience in relation to cities, "Whiskey in the Jar" (which is not included in this collection, but is slated for publication in the third volume in the *Zion's Fiction* series) and "Latte, To Go" (which is this collection's last story), exemplify the confusion Israeli science fiction engenders in some readers. For example, to best appreciate "Whiskey in the Jar" it is necessary intuitively to be conversant with Jewish experience. It is important automatically to realize that the 9/11 attack routinely happens in Israel. Readers should recognize that the travel restrictions Baruchin's protagonist faces because he is an Israeli "City Guardian" – a fantastic entity who converses with its counterparts – stem from Israelis' real responsibility to be present to defend their country. Further, readers would be as at sea as Ashling – Baruchin's Irish uber-shiksa in "Whiskey" whose name connotes Jewish bodies turned to furnace ashes – when she makes first contact with a kosher salami: "I roll my eyes. Ashling looks a little strangely... at the well-packaged salami with a small stamp. 'What is... ko-sher?' she asks. I take the salami from her. It really does have a kosher seal. Not that I care about such things, but Ashling has never even heard of the term. There is no doubt this kind of salami has never before graced her trailer." When I read that "Ashling makes us an Irish stew for lunch on the stovetop in the trailer, chopping in the unfortunate kosher salami too, which surely never imagined it would meet its end alongside so many cheeses and milk," I automatically know why a sentient kosher salami meeting its end in the company of cheese and milk is experiencing an egregious gastronomical no-no. Many non-Jews would be positioned as readerly schlemiels in relation to Jewish religious imperatives. More simply stated, many goyim cannot grok (Heinlein) "kosher." They cannot be counted on to know the difference between "kibbitz" and "kibbutz." Baruchin's protagonist would roll his eyes in response to them.

The ideal reader of *More*, no New York Jew like me, is a born-and-bred Israeli. As for everyone else, well, they cannot rely on their familiarity with Jewish rye bread affinity alone. Reading *More*, comprehending the language of Israeli science fiction, involves embracing a new reading practice.

Reading Israeli science fiction is pertinent to adopting a subgeneric specificity relevant to what Samuel R. Delany calls "the language of science fiction." Delany emphasizes that science fiction language is a distinct communicative system, and in order to understand science fiction, science fiction readers must be fluent in this system. In this vein, James Gunn states that "the way we read science fiction differs from the way we read other genres or categories." He concurs with Delany's point and describes it: "Delany... said that he... had discovered that people who said they didn't read science fiction... actually *couldn't* read science fiction... Science fiction works differently from other written categories... [I]t has specific conventions, unique focuses, areas of interest and excellence, as well as its own particular ways of making sense out of language. To ignore any of these constitutes a major misreading – an obliviousness to the play of meanings that make up the SF text" (Gunn 160). I apply these insights to Israeli science fiction to point out that reading this subgenre involves engaging in a specific reading practice which necessitates learning particular language protocols.

Israeli science fiction uses words differently. Yael Furman's pervasive use of the word "guard" in "Set in Stone" (which is included in this collection) exemplifies this point. Her story about museum statues coming alive uses "guard" in a manner differing from how this word is understood in the film *Night at the Museum*. Unlike the film, Furman's story evokes concentration camp guards. Reading the Israeli story differs from viewing the American film. In a larger sense, in order fully to understand Israeli science fiction – in order to avoid misreading – it is necessary to be fluent in Israeli cultural conventions. This necessity is crucial to the extent that even though I am a Jewish science fiction scholar, because I lack Israeli cultural fluency, I am oblivious to some of the play of meanings which comprise Israeli science fiction texts. I am unable to crack all of the textual codes.

The language of Israeli science fiction relegates the language of science fiction to the mundane. Again, "guard" in *Night at the Museum* means garden-variety benign protective person; not so for Furman's story. Furman uses protocols which makes the same different in regard to language. In the separate language which constitutes Israeli science fiction, "sirens," no part of Kurt Vonnegut's *The Sirens of Titan*, is a danger signal which communicates the necessity to take cover. "Trains" evoke terrifying memories. A grandmother, no recipient of a visit by Little Red Riding Hood, may be the absent victim of genocide.

Below I provide examples of how *More* authors who I have not mentioned use the language of Israeli science fiction. I point out three characteristics: the disturbing implications of usually mundane words, content which is unfamiliar – or unintelligible – to non-Israeli readers, and concepts which Jewish readers immediately understand.

"Life in a Movie" by Yivsam Azgad

Azgad mentions a "street corner, Dizengoff and Yirmiyahu. A field of blooming anemones near Be'eri." Where are these street corner and fields? Are they real?

"Dress," by Gail Hareven

The "blazing furnace" evokes more than providing heat. The color "yellow" plays a starring role in the story.

"Five Four Three Two One" by Hila Benyovits-Hoffman

The word "wrists" pervades the story. Wrists are located near forearms, the place where Nazis inscribed genocide on Jewish bodies. "Shower" is not ordinary. In the description *"[h]e too is a kind of cow in this slaughterhouse,"* "slaughterhouse" differs from Vonnegut's use of the word in *Slaughterhouse-Five*.

"Composting" by Galit Dahan Carlibach

I was unaware of the following Israeli burial practice: "Coffins? They're only for Christians, not for Jews in Israel, unless they happen to be blown-up soldiers. The rest of us just get shrouds." The individualized dead body communicating from beyond the grave valorizes anonymous Jewish bodies in mass graves.

"The Thirteenth Fairy" by Nadav Almog

The princess "was most strictly forbidden to go anywhere near pins, needles, spindles or any other sewing notions that could cause her delicate skin to be pricked." No one worries that Sleeping Beauty is in danger of being tattooed. This royal family member "had skin and a body!"

Is the implication of this usually obvious information that the prince's attack involves turning her into a lampshade? When the princess seeks vengeance against the prince, she acts with the fervency of the Israeli Defense Force undertaking Operation Entebbe.

"Schrödinger's Gorgon" by Keren Landsman

The 9/11 imbued "siren sounds again." "SB 5977" could be a concentration camp tattoo. Israel is analogous to the story's space station in that it functions as a space of safety surrounded by a hostile environment. The disease in the story, as opposed to the Nazis metaphorically defining Jews as a disease, is a real biological pathogen.

"The Sea of Salt" by Elana Gomel

The yellow stars "are not sewed-on pieces of fabric but living organisms. They are parasites, feeding on the prisoners." The real yellow stars appropriately become science fiction protagonists. The guards are also science fictionalized: their "helmets were actually their real heads... She tried to figure out how they fed and came to the conclusion that they had mouths in the palms of their hands." In this Israeli version of Octavia E. Butler's *Kindred*, a descendant of the perpetrator who is not the perpetrator's victim time-travels to the historical past.

"CellShock" by Assaf Gavron

References to trains permeate this story. For example, "I wait for the locomotive and hear it a second later." The alienation the protagonist experiences reflects the dehumanization of Jews transported via cattle cars.

"The Word Farmers" by Lili Daie

This story, which links language to extraterrestrials, underscores that Hebrew is viewed as an alien language because only Israelis speak it. The dead protagonist is called "the Rewriter." When they established Israel in terms of world creation, the founders rewrote the definition of Jewish victim.

"Dragon Control" by Rami Shalheveth

The dragon offers welcome comic relief. The presence of fantastic creatures such as a mini-dragon and a troll at airline check-in satirizes stringent El-Al security procedures.

"The Assassination" by Guy Hasson

Because it is possible for a science fiction protagonist to turn his life story into attire, the story's first sentence – "[h]e wears the story of his life on his face" – coincides with Delany's notion of the language of science fiction. Reality and science fiction are juxtaposed via the presence of an audio time machine and direct references to Nazis. Focusing on individuality counters fascist dehumanization.

"Askuni-Askuni" by Dafna Feldman

The story begins by referencing Bedouin science fiction. No cultural appropriation, the use of Bedouin language is a gesture toward community-building. This is the first time I have ever seen Bedouin words.

"Above the clouds, above the mountains, above the sky..." by Pavel Amnuel

The phrase "getting to know new settlements" is politically fraught. "Why do I breathe? There is no air" alludes to gas chambers. A story which includes a protagonist called "the Traveler" underscores the fact that Israelis cannot peacefully travel across their country's borders.

"Me and Nana Go Shopping" by Hamutal Levin

Mentioning "the refugees" in reference to a fictitious historical event is historically resonant. The seemingly innocuous title suggests that some Israelis did not have the luxury of having grandmothers.

BECAUSE OF MY FAMILIARITY with "Whiskey in the Jar," I arrive at Baruchin's story "Latte, To Go" in terms of experiencing comfort analogous to the welcoming Law of Return. This erstwhile American stranger in a strange Israeli science fiction land is greeted by the now familiar to me Israeli City Guardian-like "City Spirits." My new-found lack of estrangement can be understood in terms of this Jewish colloquial phrase which refers to food routinely spread on rye bread: What do you think I am, chopped liver? "Chopped liver" connotes that the speaker is not someone ordinary, a mundane entity. Counter to the speaker's intention, becoming chopped liver is a good thing in relation to Israeli science fiction. In other words: try it, you'll like it. The more Israel science fiction you read, the more familiar and mundane Israeli science fiction will become. The subgenre can ultimately be analogous to sushi. Once upon a time, Americans freaked out at the thought of eating raw fish. Now sushi, no longer exotic, is ubiquitous to the extent that it is routinely stocked in supermarkets.

Baruchin's use of the language of science fiction proclaims that Israeli-personified cities themselves, not just the human inhabitants, are alive with the sound of Hebrew. I evoke the American Broadway depiction of Austria to assuage the alienation the language of Israeli science fiction poses for non-Israeli readers.

The Austrians are no fans of *The Sound of Music*. I attribute this lack of interest to the generically correct positioning of the musical as science fiction. It is science fictionally impossible to cross the alps near Salzburg and arrive in Switzerland. This refugee route involves traversing imaginative geography. It is a star trek in which walking in the Alps, not hills, makes mountains into mole hills. "The hills are alive with the sound of music" is the language of science fiction Americans authored about a Christian Austrian refugee family. Americans love their Austrian science fiction story with the universal fervor the Levy's commercial wishes to generate vis-a-vis rye bread. Perhaps some of the love and attention Americans devote to the sound of living Austrian hills they made up can be directed to the sound of living Israeli cities Israelis themselves author. Perhaps English speakers can love science fiction written in a different voice.

This focus on hills coupled with my reader-response-criticism personal voice leads me to be more specific about the fact that I am a New Yorker. I grew up in Forest Hills, Queens, in an apartment building filled with Holocaust survivors. The neighborhood – the home of Hugo Gernsback, Stan Lee, Donald A. Wollheim, and Spiderman – is a science fiction sodden locale. No Forest Hills resident – no New Yorker – ever articulated this observation about hills: "There's gold in them thar hills." This alien-to-me locution addresses cognitive estrangement to Israeli science fiction. Why? Because the willingness to embrace difference yields exposure to a literary treasure. When I read *More*, I don't think that I am in Forest Hills anymore. This is an expansive and good thing.

Fully engaging with *More* requires an openness to learning what Catharine R. Stimpson calls "where the meanings are." The effort to do so yields the love of understanding exactly why Israeli science fiction is wry.

More Zion's Fiction: Wondrous Tales from the Israeli ImagiNation functions as a portal leading to a new reading practice pleasure of the science fiction text. The anthology's last words, articulated in mundane language, speak to this science fiction reader response novum:

"It's a start."

Works Cited

Baruchin, Rotem. "Whiskey in the Jar." Manuscript.

Butler, Octavia E. *Kindred.* Boston: Beacon Press, 2003.

Cheney, Mathew. "Ethical Aesthetics: An Introduction to *The Jewel-Hinged Jaw.*" Middletown, CT: Wesleyan University Press, 2009.

Delany, Samuel R. *The Jewel-Hinged Jaw: Notes on the Language of Science Fiction.* Middletown, CT: Wesleyan University Press, 2009.

Gunn, James. "Reading Science Fiction as Science Fiction." *Reading Science Fiction.* Eds. James Gunn, Marleen S. Barr, and Matthew Candelaria. London: Palgrave Macmillan, 2009.

Heinlein, Robert A. *Stranger in a Strange Land*. New York: G. P. Putnam's Sons, 1961.

Holland, Norman N. *5 Readers Reading*. New Haven, CT: Yale University Press, 1975.

Night at the Museum. 2006. Twentieth Century Fox. Directed by Shawn Levy. Written by Robert Ben Garant and Thomas Lennon. With Ben Stiller, Carla Gugino, and Ricky Gervais.

Stimpson, Catharine R. *Where the Meanings Are: Feminism and Cultural Spaces*. New York: Routledge, 2014.

The Sound of Music. 1965. Robert Wise Productions. Directed by Robert Wise. Written by George Hurdalek and Howard Lindsay. With Julie Andrews, Christopher Plummer, and Eleanor Parker.

Vonnegut, Kurt. *The Sirens of Titan*. New York: Delacorte, 1959.

Vonnegut, Kurt. *Slaughterhouse-Five or the Children's Crusade, a Duty-Dance with Death*. New York: Delacorte, 1969.

The Editors

Emanuel Lottem

Born in Tel Aviv in 1944, Emanuel Lottem has been a central figure in the Israeli SF/F scene since the mid-1970s: Translator of some of the best SF/F books published in Hebrew and editor of others; advisor to beginning writers; a moving force in the creation of the Israeli Society for Science Fiction and Fantasy and its first Chairman; and the founder of its annual ICon convention and other activities.

Lottem's first SF translation was Frank Herbert's *Dune*, which has become a classic. According to Israeli literary historian Eli Eshed, "this translation is considered a masterpiece of SF translations". More SF/F translations followed, and Lottem's name became familiar to and respected by Hebrew-reading fans.

After a few career changes, Lottem became a freelance translator and editor. In addition to SF/F, he specializes in popular science and military history. In 1983, Lottem became chairman of the editorial board of the Israeli SF/F magazine *Fantasia 2000*. A few years later, in 1996, Lottem presided over the inaugural meeting of the ISSF&F, which he founded with a small group of devoted fans. Visiting author Brian Aldiss officially announced the ISSF&F open for business, and Lottem was unanimously elected its first Chairman.

To date, Lottem's SF/F translations include works by Douglas Adams, Poul Anderson, Isaac Asimov, Alfred Bester, Edgar Rice Burroughs, Lois

M. Bujold, Jack Chalker, C.J. Cherryh, Arthur C. Clarke, Hal Clement, Michael Crichton, Philip K. Dick, Robert L. Forward, William Gibson, Robert A. Heinlein, Frank Herbert, Ursula Le Guin, Ann Leckie, Anne McCaffrey, Larry Niven, Mervyn Peake, Frederick Pohl, Christopher Priest, Robert Shea and Robeert A. Wilson, Robert Silverberg, E.E. "Doc" Smith, James Tiptree, Jr., J.R.R. Tolkien, Jack Vance, and Connie Willis, among many others. In 1994 Lottem won one of Israel's highest translation awards, the Tchernichovsky Prize, for his translation of Richard Dawkins's *The Selfish Gene*. The ISSF&F gave him in 2016 a Life Achievement award on its 20th anniversary.

Sheldon (Sheli) Teitelbaum

BORN IN MONTREAL IN 1955, Teitelbaum attended Concordia University, where he earned an honors degree in history. Upon graduation in 1977, he came to Israel, where he joined the infantry and, later, the Education Corps, after which he was sent to Officer Training School and served as a staff officer for the Paratroopers Brigade for three years. During this time, he became a member of the editorial board of the Israeli magazine *Fantasia 2000*, and began writing the nation's first ever SF/F book review column to appear monthly in the daily newspaper, *The Jerusalem Post*. Upon completing his service, Teitelbaum began a journalism career working for the magazine *Newsview* as well as the *Jerusalem Post*, which put him to use as a night desk sub-editor and as a freelance writer on weekends. During the day he worked as a science writer for the Weizmann Institute of Science.

Teitelbaum moved with his family to Los Angeles in 1986, where he became Los Angeles Bureau Chief for the acclaimed film magazine *Cinefantastique*, a founding writer (and some years later, a senior writer) for the *Los Angeles Jewish Journal*, and a senior writer for the *Jerusalem Report*. Additionally, he held down a day job for three years at the

University of Southern California as a science writer and, later, for a subcontractor to the U.S. Department of Energy.

Teitelbaum has published on SF/F-related and other themes in *Al HaMishmar, The Los Angeles Times, The New York Times, The Forward, Time-Digital, Wired, The Montreal Gazette, SF Eye, Midnight Graffiti, Foundation: The Review of Science Fiction, Premiere Magazine, Entertainment Weekly,* the *Encyclopedia of Science Fiction* (2nd Ed. & Online Edition) and *The Encyclopedia Judaica* (2nd Ed.). He won Canada's first Northern Lights Award in 1998, and landed three Brandeis University/ Jewish Press Association awards for excellence in news and cultural reportage. He lives in Southern California.

Avi Katz

AVI KATZ IS A VETERAN AMERICAN-BORN Israeli illustrator, cartoonist and painter. His interest in SF/F illustration began early; while still a teenager in Philadelphia he sent a pack of his *Lord of the Rings* art to J.R.R. Tolkien, and received an enthusiastic response from the author, who told him he was the first illustrator to portray the dwarves as he had intended.

At age 20, while studying art at Berkeley, he was interviewed by John W. Campbell but decided to avoid the draft and Vietnam and complete his studies at the Bezalel Academy of Art in Jerusalem; he has made his home in Israel since then. He has been the staff illustrator of *The Jerusalem Report* magazine since its first issue in 1990 and is active in the international organization Cartooning for Peace, as well as the Association of Caricaturists in Israel. He has illustrated some 170 books in Israel and the USA, which have won the National Jewish Book Award, Hans Christian Andersen honors, the Ze'ev Prize and others; he was a nominee for the lifetime achievement Astrid Lindgren Award.

A founding member of the Israel Society for Science Fiction and Fantasy, Katz created many original book covers for SF/F published in

Israel; his illustrations graced the covers of Society posters and all the issues of *The Tenth Dimension* fanzine over the decade of its publication. He has exhibited at various sci-fi conventions including WorldCon 2003, and was Guest of Honor at ICon 2002. He is featured in the book *Masters of Science Fiction and Fantasy Art* (Rockport Press). In 2000, Katz created for the Israeli Postal Service a three-stamp series on Science Fiction in Israel.